THE BEAR HUNTERS

David Weaver

PublishAmerica
Baltimore

First printing

Softcover 9781630004439
PUBLISHED BY PUBLISHAMERICA, LLLP
www.publishamerica.com
Baltimore

Printed in the United States of America

PROLOGUE

For a millennium, the people of Golan had conveniently avoided the reality that soon extremely large and deadly plasma flares, produced by the expansion of its dying sun, would totally destroy their planet and solar system. When they realized the disaster could not be avoided, the entire population set aside their differences and started building five massive, self-contained spaceships named Golan, I through V out of respect for their planet and the millions of lives they knew would be lost by its destruction. They believed it would take twenty years and the combined resources of their planet to accomplish this huge project; material and labor had to be transported from the planet to the ships in orbit.

Twenty years later, after the last ship was completed all five were immediately positioned in permanent, elliptical orbits many miles above their dying planet. Due to their great distances from the sun, it was believed they would avoid most of its devastating influence, as it slowly expanded to the point of no return.

When the last ship was fully outfitted, the members of the regime voted to install a new form of government, with the assumption that they would survive the impending catastrophe. For the past fifty years, their quasi-government had not functioned as intended, and the present circumstances gave them an opportunity to adopt a pseudo-monarchy, instead of a newer version of their loose-knit system. The first order of the brand-new regime was to enact an amendment which would allow them to revert back to their old-style government, or install another should their newly installed monarchy fail. While they waited for the moment when they could safely escape from the sun's final death-throes, the government was activated and set into motion.

A King, a Parliament of Senators and a Lord from each nation was elected to oversee the government.

The five huge ships were divided into 25 countries, five for each ship, each one a small nation represented by one senator and one lord. The senators were accountable for the lords of their respective nations, and the lords to the Prime Minister who presided over the Parliament.

The massive project would have been virtually impossible, if not for the earlier discovery of anti-gravity and ion propulsion. Their scientists had worked many years on both concepts, but after the convergence of the sun's deadly rays had finally been confirmed beyond a doubt, the programs were accelerated and perfected.

The main function of the self-contained and fully-reliant ships was to transport the planet's total population to a new solar system and search for other habitable planets, before the sun's final convulsion. Their scientists had firmly believed there were other solar systems in their galaxy with planets supporting life, but after searching with long-range telescopes for many years they had found none.

Each year the gigantic plumes of plasma extended their deadly fingers hundreds of miles closer to the planet's surface. After many years monitoring their progress, it was established that the total destruction would come when the sun's magnetic field had caused the flairs to reach a critical and irreversible state—which could come at any time.

Scientists had known for many years their planet would soon become insufferably hot, to the point where it could no longer maintain life. They believed the first indication of its demise would be the melting of the polar ice caps, which would cause the ocean to rise and consume all properties along its vast shoreline. After that, small lakes in the interior would evaporate and larger ones produce deadly toxic fumes. Fruit and vegetation would rot on the vines and in the ground. Air conditioning would no longer exist; power plants would not be able to produce enough electricity to keep them running, due to heat and shortage of fuel. Commercial vehicles would no longer operate because of overheating and melting tar on the roads; consequently, all vehicular commerce would come to a halt.

After numerous calculations, they estimated there was only months, if not weeks, before the final convergence would take place, which would give them barely enough time to evacuate 80 percent of the population to bring on board the five mother-ships. The remaining 20 percent had elected to stay on the doomed planet, believing there would be no convergence and that a miracle would somehow happen. They would mainly depend on caves and subterranean facilities to keep them alive, but after a while even those were no longer adequate to sustain life.

By Earth standards, Golan was a relatively small planet with one massive continent covering 50 percent of the total area of the planet, which had a population of 40 million, and one gigantic ocean covering the remainder.

Prior to the onslaught of the sun's fingers-of-death, Golan was an extremely beautiful planet with massive forests, huge pristine lakes and snow-capped mountains. However, it wasn't long before it had changed dramatically. Consequently, the population became extremely angered over the realization their once beautiful planet would no longer exist, and mob-scenes broke out over the entire planet.

All 25 countries bordered the huge ocean; many with harbors accommodating vast numbers of sea-going vessels. However, due to the onslaught of the formidable heat, and the planet's impending doom, sea trade was not feasible; the harbors and anchoring facilities along the flooded shorelines could no longer maintain sea commerce.

When the scientific minds of all five ships were finally pooled, they discovered a way to create a vortex, or worm-hole, which they believed would allow them entry into another universe, a parallel universe, with the possibility of finding another planet similar to their own. They had worked many years on the concept, but the knowledge acquired by building the five huge ships made it all possible. For many years, they had believed they possessed the knowledge for such a feat, now they knew.

After many failed attempts, they managed to send a small observation craft through a newly formed vortex into another universe. When it arrived, it had discovered a medium-sized sun with nine planets. However, to their dismay, only one planet supported life.

After many failed attempts, they discovered that due to the mother-ships' massive sizes the vortexes were much too small, and they could not pass through them. Nonetheless, they continued sending smaller observation craft to the new planet to observe and take notes for when their mother-ships could enter, and they were confident they would. They believed they had the knowledge to overcome the vortex problem; all they had to do was find the right formula.

Scientists had known for a millennium the massive plasma flares would eventually engulf their planet and their entire six-planet solar system. Therefore, it left them no alternative but to work feverishly on the development of larger vortexes to accommodate their mother-ships. If that could not be accomplished, before their planets total destruction, they would be forced to travel throughout their galaxy to search for other solar systems with inhabitable planets. However, they realized that even at near-light speeds it would take many generations to reach the nearest solar system, and then pray it had habitable planets.

In the meantime, their newly established monarchy became fragile and on the verge of collapse—mainly due to their King's long-time illness. Each year his health had gotten progressively worse, until he could no longer reign effectively over his people. Although highly advanced in technology, they lacked the medical skills to cure him, or even diagnose his illness.

Because of the King's long internment, their newly established Parliament had required the Senate to vote for a prince-in-waiting to take his place should he die. To keep the crown in the royal family, the only person eligible was his twelve-year-old son, Meesha. Although his preliminary acceptance had been approved by most members of the Senate, there were those who objected, mainly due to their own egos, greed, and political ambitions.

Realizing there could be the danger to his son if he stayed on Golan One until the Parliament voted, the King ordered his brother, Kerac, to take him to Earth in one of the smaller observation crafts and stay with him until the vote was taken. However, if he did not return with the boy in time for the vote, Parliament would be obliged to vote for someone else, not of royal blood.

The King soon realized the only other person they might vote for would be Luchak, the son of his worst enemy, Senator Abron. If that were to happen, the senator would automatically be his son's counselor and adviser, and that would not be good for the people of Golan.

ONE

Charley Bertell was unquestionably the most stubborn, hotheaded, cantankerous eighty-year-old in the valley. How he had managed to make it to such a ripe old age, no one in the small township of Grande Ronde, Oregon, could imagine, except maybe Doc Halloway.

As he turned gray and lost most of his vision and teeth, even his grandchildren wouldn't come visit him, except on special occasions like Christmas, and then just to pick up the presents his wife, Gracie, so generously doled out. After that, they would only visit at the threat of being punished.

He didn't really care what the people in the small-town thought of him. They could all go to hell, as far as he was concerned. Where were <u>they</u> when he had needed them throughout his eighty plus years? Where were <u>they</u> when he and Gracie had tried to survive without a penny to their names? Where were <u>they</u> when he had fallen and broken his hip, several years back? Where were they then? Without a doubt, they could all go to hell. He had his Gracie, and that was all that mattered.

"Gracie?" he mumbled from his favorite horizontal position on the sofa.

"Yes, dear," she replied, looking up from her knitting.

"Would you get my medicine? I think it's about that time."

She got up from the Belcher rocker and walked slowly into the small bathroom. "Do you want both?" she yelled back.

"I think I had better. I haven't felt this bad in a coon's age."

After visually inspecting the labels, she took two bottles down from the medicine cabinet and put them in her apron pocket.

"You're in a lot of pain, are you?" she asked, concern in her voice.

"Like I said, I haven't felt this bad in a long time. I think it might be serious, this time."

She went to the sofa and unscrewed the caps. "Here, maybe these will help," she said softly. "Doc Halloway said they were strong enough to knock out a horse." Squinting her aging eyes, she again inspected the labels. Satisfied, she handed him two green pills from one bottle and a large, brown pill from the other. "You know sweetie, perhaps we should find you some place to go until you feel better, possibly a convalescent home."

He looked up with a deep frown. "You know we can't afford anything like that."

"Oh, I don't know about that. I've been saving a little from your retirement, each month, and from our Social Security. We could manage."

"You mean all these years you've been holdin' out on me?" A mock grin spread across his gaunt, unshaven face. "You mean you've been tappin' our retirement funds without me knowin' it?"

She looked at him apologetically, and with a slight blush said, "Honey, I wouldn't have done it, if I thought you'd mind." She sat on the sofa beside him and looked into his aging eyes lovingly. "I thought I was doin' the right thing, sweetie. Even so, I still think we should find one of those places, until you're feeling better. Maybe their therapy would help relieve some of your pain. It wouldn't hurt to try, you know."

"I was only joking," he replied. "I know you want to do what's best for me." He gave her a compassionate look, and added, "You've got the humor of a lead pipe. You know that?"

She got up from the sofa, swatted him gently on the shoulder and headed for the kitchen. "You're terrible!" she said, a veiled smile was visible on her pudgy face.

He watched her large, maternal body waddle leisurely across the room and disappeared into the kitchen. It was her domain. He knew that for a fact. Even before his illness she rarely invited him into its bowels, except to eat. That was all right with him, he had no reason to invade her inner sanctum. He was perfectly content with what came out of it. He saw no reason to risk losing his cornucopia.

"What do you feel like for supper, sweetie?" she called from the kitchen.

He thought for a moment. "What do you have in mind?"

"We don't have much. I haven't gone to the store in a week." The clatter of pots and pans broke the silence. After a few moments, she stuck her head through the kitchens swinging doors. "We have frozen macaroni and cheese, if that's all right. I could nuke it. It'd be ready in a few minutes. On the other hand, you could have some orange pop sticks." She smiled, knowing how he hated them.

"Ice cream," he yelled back. "I feel like ice cream. I hate orange pop sticks, and you know it." He was silent for a few moments, and then added, "Didn't we have some ice cream the other night, out on the patio?"

She stuck her head back through the doors, and with an impish grin replied, "Yes, we did, but you made a pig of yourself so now we don't have any."

"I hate orange pop sticks," he yelled back. "I'd rather eat macaroni and cheese than suck on pop sticks."

"Then I'll fix the macaroni."

"No! Wait!" he barked. "I don't feel like macaroni. Don't we have anything else, maybe somethin' in a can?"

"Not unless you want a can of sardines…or some cat food. How does that sound?" She closed the swinging doors, and giggles came from the kitchen.

"Oh, that's funny. You just graduated. You're no longer a lead pipe."

Several minutes later she came back into the living room with a shawl draped around her shoulders, and a 1920s vintage straw hat perched precariously on her head.

"Be right back, sweetie," she said and headed for the door.

"Where you goin' all dressed up?"

"I'm going to get my man some ice cream."

"Don't be silly," he grumbled. "I was just joking. Give me some macaroni and cheese. Maybe I'll turn into an Italian stud, or something. How'd you like that?" His face turned somber. "Besides, it's gettin' pretty damn nasty outside…rain, wind and all. You shouldn't be drivin' in that stuff."

She grabbed the car keys from the coffee table and headed for the door. Before leaving, she turned and said, "Behave yourself while I'm gone. Don't throw any wild parties or anything." With a mischievous grin, she walked out the door and into the cold, rainy night.

He leaned back on the sofa and closed his eyes and visions of his Gracie popped into his head. She had always been the strong one of the family. Ever since he had been laid up by his medical problems, she had taken over as man-of-the-house. Her fortitude, zeal, and passion for life were nothing less than endearing. She constantly put him up front in their relationship; always looking after him, showing him more love and affection than he could possibly return. Although she had gotten along in age, she never once complained. She was his Gracie, wrinkles and all, and he was her man. Nothing could change that, nor did he want it to.

The night became exceptionally dark. Heavy rain clouds had obscured the moon and stars, and a dense fog had settled in over the entire valley. The old Ford's headlights cut weak, yellow swaths through the fog, scarcely illuminating the winding road in front of her. By the time she got halfway to the convenience store, the visibility had dropped almost to zero. Even at 30 miles an hour, due to the glare of oncoming high beams, wind, and a slippery road, she could barely keep the vehicle on the highway.

After parking in front of the small country store, she darted inside. "Hi, George," she said to the slightly hunched-back man behind the counter, "got to get my man some ice cream." She walked down the aisle to the freezer, grabbed a quart of his favorite brand and hurried back to the counter. "This should hold him until I can get something healthier inside him." She set the ice cream on the counter and searched her large purse for her billfold. "He's actin' like a pregnant woman." She giggled. "Maybe I should get him a jar of pickles, too. What do you think, George?" They both laughed. "I really should pick up a few things while I'm here, but it's too wet and windy out there to be carryin' much. I'll let it go until mornin'."

He put the ice cream in an insulated bag and slid it across the counter. "How's the old geezer doin', Gracie? Somebody told me he wasn't feeling too well. Is it anything serious?"

"Don't know, George. Even Doc Halloway doesn't seem to know what's wrong with him. It might have something to do with his heart, at least that's what he implied…in a roundabout way. You know Halloway."

"Well, give him my regards. Hope he's feelin' better soon."

"I'll tell him, George. Thanks." She put the bag under her arm and headed for the door. "Gotta hurry, George. That road out there is gettin' mighty treacherous."

"You be careful, Gracie," he yelled, as he watched her almost fall on the slippery wooden steps. "Don't want the both of you flat on your backs."

The drive home had become even more treacherous, due to a sudden, intense rainfall and an increase in the thick summer fog, which by then had completely blanketed the entire road with an eerie glow.

A mile down the road her headlights picked up a shiny object lying beside the road. She slammed on the brakes. A few feet off the pavement appeared to be a small body. She sat behind the wheel motionless afraid to get out and look at what she believed would be an unpleasant sight. There were very few cars on the road and those that were had to swerve hard to keep from hitting her. She finally pulled off the road onto the muddy shoulder and left the car idling.

After a few anxious breaths, she gathered enough courage to open the door and slide from the seat. Cautiously, she approached the body, not knowing what to expect. When she got closer the body moaned and stirred, indicating it was still alive. Guardedly, she knelt down beside it and turned it over. It appeared to be a small boy, three or four feet tall, wearing a silver jump suit with a hood covering most of his face. He began to shiver, violently. She pulled her shawl from around her neck and wrapped it around his head and shoulders. She dragged him to the car, and with all her strength hefted him onto the passenger seat. She stood in the pouring rain for several moments to catch her breath, then rushed around to the driver's side and slid behind the wheel. After a few unsuccessful attempts, she managed to maneuver the car out of the thick mud of the shoulder onto the main road. Grinding gears, she sped down the highway as fast as the weather and the old Ford would allow.

Several minutes later she stopped under the old, dilapidated carport, opened the door and quickly slid the boy across the seat. Using all her strength, she managed to cradle him in her arms and carry him into the house.

Charley woke from his catnap in time to watch her lay the bundled object down on a love seat across the room.

"What do you have there, sweetie?" he asked groggily. "If it's ice cream it should be enough to last us a year. That's an awful lot." He laughed.

"Oh dear, it's in the car," she said, and rushed through the still open door. After retrieving it, she ran back into the house and shoved it into the freezer.

"Slow down there, kid," he scolded. "You'll have a heart attack."

Paying no attention, she sat beside the boy and un-wrapped the shawl from around his head and shoulders. He moved his head ever so slightly and moaned.

Charley looked over, when he heard the strange sound. "What the devil you got there, Gracie? Did you pick up another stray dog, like you did last year?"

"No, it's a little boy," she answered. "I found him lying beside the road on my way back from the store."

Charley's mouth dropped open, and his eyes widened. "You found a little boy, alongside the road? What the devil's a little boy doing out in this kind of weather? You don't suppose he fell out of a car, do you? On the other hand, maybe he fell off one of those open-bed trucks they use to transport them illegal aliens back and forth?"

"Don't think so," she said. "He doesn't appear to have any broken bones or bruises. He more than likely would have something physically wrong, if he fell off a truck. Wouldn't you think?" She got up from the love seat, went to the linen closet and pulled a wool comforter down from a shelf. "He's freezing. I've got to warm him."

Charley lifted his head to get a better view. "Does he have any identification? Who he is? Where the hell did he come from?"

"Don't see any. All he's wearin' is a thin jump suit with a hood, like those runners wear."

The boy's eyes were closed, and he appeared unconscious. As she scanned his small, delicate features a frown formed on her flushed face. His hairline formed a crescent, ending in a sharp peak slightly above the center of a single eyebrow running unbroken across his forehead. His breathing was erratic, continually gasping for air. He would open his mouth and suck in air, then close it and again struggle to breathe. She leaned over to rub his forehead, and he flinched.

"Wonder who he is and where he came from?" Charley said. "You know you can't keep him, don't you…like you did that stray dog last spring?" He snickered.

She gave him a sour look and shifted her eyes back to her charge. "I'm going to get a warm facecloth and wipe his face; he's still much too cold." She went into the bathroom, and a few moments later returned with a washbasin full of tepid water. As she wiped his face, he opened his eyes and looked up at her. When she returned his stare, she noticed his eyes were not normal; the pupils were vertical slits, like cats. She reared back in bewilderment, and then lowered her head for a closer look. "Gracious me!" she cried out. "What do we have here?"

The boy cringed, and then quickly crawled to the far end of the couch. His eyes filled with fear.

"What's the matter, hon?" Charley said, raising his head from the pillow. "Is something wrong?"

"You won't believe this, Charley."

"Try me."

"The boy has eyes like a cat. They're strange-looking…not normal."

"That's impossible," he said sitting upright. "People don't have eyes like a cat. You must be lookin' at 'em all wrong."

"No, I'm not!" she replied irritably. "See for yourself."

He got up from the sofa and hobble slowly across the room.

"I'll be danged. You're right!" he said. "They do look like cat's eyes. And would you look at that eyebrow and hairline? What the hell's goin' on here?"

At the far end of the couch, the boy had obtained an awkward sitting position…his knees bent up to his chest with his arms wrapped around them.

After the initial shock had worn off, she moved closer. She reached over to touch his arm, and he pulled away. She looked into his eyes and smiled. He opened his mouth as if to return the gesture, and then closed it and continued staring at her. She smiled again, that time exposing her teeth. He opened his mouth, baring his teeth as she had done. Noticing them, she looked up at Charley.

"Do you see that?" she said, pointing to his mouth. "He's definitely unusual. Look at those teeth. They all appear normal, except the front ones. There's one large one, where there should be two." The boy closed his mouth, as if he understood her comment.

Charley held out his hand in a gesture of friendship, but the boy remained motionless. "What do you think?" he said. "Who the hell is he? What the hell was he doing out there in that storm? Where does he come from? Why don't you ask him?"

"I don't know. I don't know," she answered irritably. "I haven't asked him anything. He doesn't appear to want to talk, anyway. Maybe we should call Doc Halloway. He might know where he came from or who he is. He's been around these parts a lot longer than we have. Besides, I believe the boy should be looked at."

Charley moved closer and again extended his hand. To his surprise, the boy reached out, took it and closed his eyes. With his other hand, he reached over and placed a finger on Charley's chest, then slid it up to a spot on his neck and held it there.

Charley jumped back. "What the devil is that supposed to mean?" He reached up and grabbed the boy's hand. "What's he doing that for?"

"I don't know, maybe he's trying to tell you something," she said. "Strange as it may seem, perhaps he's trying to tell you something about your heart problem."

"Hogwash!" he exploded. "The doc said I might have a heart problem. That's all. He didn't say it had anything to do with my neck. Besides, how could a little squirt like him know anything about that?"

"You really want to believe that, after what you've been witnessing... his face and all?"

Charley shuffled back to the sofa, resumed his horizontal position and crossed his arms defiantly. He shifted his body until it was comfortable, and then repeated, "Hogwash!"

As she sat beside the boy, looking into his eyes, like a mother to a child, he reached over and ever so cautiously put his finger on her forehead. Instantly, a host of images darted across her mind's eye. Not knowing what else to do, she leaned back in the love seat and closed her eyes. Visions of a beautiful but strange land suddenly appeared; grassy pastures with snow-capped mountains in the background, crystal clear lakes surrounded by tall verdant trees, and fluffy white clouds drifting lazily across a cobalt sky. However, there was something odd about the pictures. There appeared to be an extremely bright sun drifting lazily across the sky, but it was way too close to the images of the strange and beautiful world she had seen. She opened her eyes and stared at him. It had all appeared so vivid,.like she was standing there looking at it.

Again, he put his finger on her forehead. Within seconds, the beautiful images reappeared. However, as she took in their beauty and serenity, the green pastures suddenly turned brown, the mountains collapsed in gigantic plumes of dust, and the lakes disappeared in enormous clouds of steam. She looked at the sky, and the sun had expanded to an unimaginable brilliance. She gasped and opened her eyes. Had he planted those pictures in her mind, or was she dreaming them? She wasn't certain of anything. Had he shown her the devastation of another world, possibly his own? At that moment, she was convinced he was from some place other than Earth. But where was he from, and how did he get here? Were there others like him?

"Charley!" she called excitedly.

He squinted groggily at her. "Yes, Gracie, what is it?"

"You won't believe what just happened."

"What do you mean, what happened?"

"I mean with the boy."

"What are you talking about, girl? You said he was lying beside the road." As an afterthought, he added, "And you know perfectly well we're going to have to locate his folks in the morning. You can't keep him like you did that dog."

"Well, I'm going to keep him until we find his parents," she declared adamantly. "I'm not going to turn him over to some government agency. They would love to know what I know about him."

"And what would that be? You don't know any more about him than I do."

"Yes, I do. I believe he just showed me where he came from."

Charley pulled himself upright and frowned, "I think you're off your rocker. He hasn't spoken a word since you brought him here."

"He didn't speak to me. He touched my forehead and showed me pictures in my head."

"You've been watchin' too much late-night TV, Gracie. Nobody can do that."

"Well, he can." She looked into the boy's eyes, put her hand on her forehead, and then pointed to Charley.

The boy appeared to understand. He slid off the love seat and walked hesitantly across the room where Charley sat wide-eyed. He attempted to put his finger on his forehead, but it was slapped away.

"Charley!" she shouted. "Let him put his finger on your forehead, it doesn't hurt. Don't be stubborn."

"Oh, all right," he said reluctantly. "Go ahead boy, do your thing." He leaned back and closed his eyes. When the boy's finger touched his forehead, he flinched. Seconds later his somewhat perplexed expression changed to a deep frown. After a few moments, the boy removed his finger. Charley opened his eyes and stared vacantly across the room. "Well I'll be danged!" he said. "What do those pictures mean? Did you see what I saw?"

"I suppose so, the extremely bright sun, the mountains and the lakes—"

"Yep, those are the ones. How did he do that?"

She went to the sofa and sat beside Charley. The boy stood in front of them with a broad grin on his pixie face.

"I have a theory," she said, looking into the boy's eyes. "I don't believe he's from our world at all. I think he's from that place we just saw in our heads."

"If that's the case, how did he get here?" Charley replied. "And he seems to be all alone. Maybe he got lost from his folks." He looked up at the ceiling in thought. "But what was he doing beside the road on a night like this dressed like that? This is gettin' interesting. We'll see the doc in the mornin', maybe he can shed some light on it."

As if the boy had read their minds, he leaned over and put his fingers on both their foreheads. Instantly, images of a large metallic room with hundreds of flashing lights appeared in their minds. The boy sat at a console throwing switches and pushing buttons. Across the room stood a tall, muscular man, and at a keyboard sat a slender, blond-haired woman, both wearing silver jump suits, similar to his. The boy got up and walked into a smaller room. Suddenly, a man in a dark uniform burst into the room, put tape over his mouth, grabbed him under the arms and carried him quickly down a passageway into a larger room where there appeared to be a small space craft. He shoved the boy inside, and then pushed him into a metal cage with bars on it.

They looked through a small, round porthole, and the room was slowly moving from a much larger object. As it got farther away, they could see the huge object more clearly—a spaceship similar to what they had once seen on television. They felt a powerful jolt, and the smaller craft darted off at an incredible speed.

The boy dropped his fingers and closed his eyes, then started to collapse. She jumped up from the sofa, and he fell limply into her arms.

"Heavens to Betsy," she said, "I think he's fainted."

"We'd better call the doc," Charley said.

"No!" she insisted. "I don't believe we should bring him into this. He wouldn't understand, especially him." She thought for a moment. "You know yourself if he discovered the boy's abilities, he'd contact the government men, and they'd do all sorts of things to him. I saw that on TV, and I believe it, especially if they find out what he can do with your mind. They'd want to know where he came from, how he got here, and all sorts of things."

"I suppose you're right." He exhaled a long, raspy sigh. "But what in the world are we going to do with him, until we find his folks? We don't know anything about kids his age, assuming he's what I think he is…maybe twelve or thirteen."

"Let's play along with this situation, shall we?" she said, and carried the boy back to the love seat. "Land's sake alive, we have a little boy in our house. Something we haven't had in a long time. Not since Caroline's kids visited last Christmas. Let's take advantage of it."

"What are you suggesting, Gracie? I'll bet you want to keep him, don't you?"

"Pish posh," she mumbled. "It isn't anything like that. I just want to keep him away from those who might harm him…experiment on him. Like those government men do. I'll give him up, just as soon as we find his parents. Assuming he has some."

Charley cocked his head and gave her a hard look. "Like I said, you've been watching too much TV, Gracie."

Ignoring him, she took the afghan blanket from his sofa and wrapped it around the boy's shoulders. "What shall we call him? He looks like a Clarence to me."

"Oh, you're naming him already, are you? Sounds like you want to keep him. If you do, don't give him a sissy name like that. What about Tony or Michael, they're more masculine?"

"Okay," she said. "We'll call him Michael or Mike."

Charley clutched his chest and moaned. "Mother, I think you better call the doc, after all. I might have a little problem here." He stretched out on the sofa, his face pale.

She rushed across the room and sat beside him. "Oh, dear, is there anything I can do? Can I get you a glass of water?"

"I don't think water's a cure for what's ailin' me," he said. "You'd best call the doc."

She hurried into the kitchen and grabbed the phone off the wall cradle. After calling the doctor's office, she returned to his side. "His nurse said he was at a patient's house, but she would call him. He should be here, shortly."

The boy opened his eyes and noticed them sitting on the sofa. He jumped down from the comforter, rushed across the room and stood in front of Charley, a troubled look on his tiny face.

Taken back by the boy's sudden move, she threw her arms around Charley to protect him.

The boy held up his hands to reassure her that he wasn't going to harm him. Hesitantly, he reached over and put a finger on Charley's forehead, and then slid another to a spot on the side of his neck.

Instantly, Charley saw images of blood vessels running from his heart to his head. Halfway up his neck he noticed a vessel that had a small clot, which appeared to be blocking blood to his brain. As the boy held his finger on the spot, a red dot mysteriously appeared under it. He knew then the boy was trying to tell him something. But what?

"Get a felt marker, Gracie," he said. "I think he wants me to mark that spot he just showed me."

Not seeing the mental images, she questioned him, "What do you mean? Why does he want you to do that?"

"Don't ask questions, just do it! Please!"

She rummaged through a metal sewing box containing writing material and found a red felt marker. "Here it is," she said. "But I still don't understand what you want it for."

"I think the boy may have discovered my problem," he said. "When the doc gets here, I'll ask him to investigate what's under that mark."

"I can't believe that, Charley. You mean to tell me you think the boy may have found a cure for your illness?"

"I didn't say that," he snapped. "I only know what he showed me, by using his finger. The doc will have to do the rest."

A few minutes later the doorbell rang, and she looked through the French window. Doc Halloway stood on the porch looking through the stained-glass door.

"I have to hide the boy," she said quickly. "Michael, come with me! I don't want him to see you, he wouldn't understand." She took him by the arm, rushed him into the back bedroom, put him on the bed and covered him with a blanket. He didn't object and lay perfectly still. She went to the door and let Halloway into the foyer.

"Hi, Gracie," he said, walking into the living room. "It's been a long time. How's Charley been holding up?"

"See for yourself," she said scathingly. She never could hold back her negative feelings toward him. Most of the time she had tried to be civil, but occasionally it didn't work. It wasn't that easy. She truly believed he was the reincarnation of the infamous Doc Holliday. She hoped he couldn't sense her feelings, but most of the time they were pretty much out in the open. "It appears, he had an attack of some kind," she told him. "See what you think. Let me know what you find." With nothing more to say, she went into the bedroom.

Halloway went to the sofa and dropped his bag beside it. "Hi Charley, what's happening? So, you had a mild one, did you?" He pulled a stethoscope from his bag and put it against Charley's chest. "Hmmm," he repeated several times. "Sounds like your heart's the same as usual. That doesn't appear to be your problem, this time." He slid the instrument up and down his chest, and then moved it to the side of his neck. Several minutes later he looked up, and with a fake smile said, "You appear to be healthy as a horse, Charley."

"Doc, there's definitely something wrong, most of the time I can barely walk or get off this damn sofa. As long as you're here, would you do me a favor?"

"Of course, if I can."

"See this red mark on my neck?" He pointed.

"Yep, it looks like a felt marker. What's it there for?'

"I want you to x-ray that spot."

"What do you think is under it, Charley?" he asked condescendingly.

"Damned if I know, but I want it checked out. I have a suspicion it could be one of my problems." He gave him a defiant stare and added, "And don't patronize me, please."

"What makes you think there's a problem there?" Halloway asked. "It's just a red felt marker. That's all."

"Damn it, doc!" he exploded. "Will you appease me for once in your life? Every damn time you come you can't find anything wrong. It wouldn't hurt to check it out, would it?"

Halloway closed his bag and stared over his bifocals. "Okay, if that's what you want. However, I must warn you, if we find nothing wrong, the x-rays may not be covered by your insurance. Is that okay?"

"To hell with my insurance!" Charley erupted. "If there's something wrong, I want to know about it. If there ain't, that's fine too. I'll pay out of my own damn pocket, if I have to!"

"Okay, have it your way. I'll set it up. I'll send an ambulance for you. Don't want Gracie driving in this weather." He picked up his bag and headed for the door.

Hearing the squeaky front door, she came out of the bedroom. "Well, Doc, what do you think?"

"He wants an x-ray," he said with a scoff. "I'll appease the old goat, but only because he's been a patient of mine for so dang many years. I still can't believe there's anything under that stupid mark on his neck. He probably got it playin' with crayons, or somethin'." He chuckled on his way out the door.

An hour later the local ambulance arrived. After bickering with the driver over the price he would be charged, he was transported to the small outpatient clinic and ushered into the x ray room.

The small clinic had no horizontal machines like CT scanners or MRIs, only a vertical machine used primarily for mammograms. Charley twisted his neck to get it flush against the x-ray plate, and at the nurse's insistence held his breath.

The plates took over an hour to develop, and Charley sat in the waiting room fuming. Finally, the nurse came out and gave the plates to Halloway. He slid them into the lighted reader and made a quick study. When he turned around he bumped into Charley, who had slipped into the room undetected and was looking at the plates over his shoulder.

"I don't see anything abnormal here," he told Charley, pointing at the plates. "See, there's your heart." He slid his finger up the plate to an image of his lower neck where the red mark was located. "See, nothing there, either."

"Hold it, Doc," Charley interrupted. "There!" He pointed. "See it? It looks like a blocked vein, or artery, or whatever you call it. Directly under the red spot."

Halloway moved closer to the plate and adjusted his bifocals to get a better view. He detested being proven wrong, but there it was no question about it, a blockage in one of the smaller blood vessels going to his brain.

"I'll be danged," he said, turning to face Charley. "How did you know about this blockage? Did another doctor look at you? After all I've done for you over the years?"

"Don't get yourself in a huff, I didn't see another doctor," Charley replied. "There isn't any around for miles, anyway."

"Then how did you know about that blockage?"

"Trade secret. Can you fix it? That's what I want to know."

"It's a relatively simple operation," Holloway stated. "It wouldn't even hurt…too much. They'll just insert a small plastic tube called a catheter inside that blood vessel. That's it. You'll have a sore neck for a while, but on the bright side when the blood starts flowing again you should be able to walk normal and regain some of your energy."

"Can you do it now?" Charley asked. A faint smile spread across his gaunt face.

"Charley, I have other patients. You're not the only one. I'll try to get you an appointment tomorrow morning at the hospital in Salem, around ten o'clock."

"Come on, Doc," Charley pleaded. "You said it was a simple operation. Why can't you do it now? I got the time."

"Yes, I know you do, but I don't. Besides, I can't do that kind of work, I'm not a surgeon. I don't have the right equipment, anyway. I'll set it up for tomorrow morning." He turned and headed for the door.

"But doc, how the hell am I supposed to get to Salem? Gracie can't drive me in this kind of weather, it's twenty-five miles, or so."

"The storm will be over by morning," Holloway said, slightly irritated. "You can take our ambulance, if you'd rather. I might be able to get it covered by your insurance. I'll try." He left the room and slammed the door.

Charley called Grace to come and get him at the clinic. He told her he would rather have her drive him home in all the rotten weather than pay the outlandish price they wanted for the ambulance. She told him to take it, she had to stay with the boy. Begrudgingly, he took the ambulance.

When he arrived back at the house, he found the two of them in the kitchen polishing off a quart of his favorite ice cream. The boy's face beamed with contentment, as he shoveled spoonfuls of the unknown substance into his mouth.

"Did the doc find anything, sweetie?" she asked.

"He didn't want to admit it, but yes he did. He said I have a blockage in one of my arteries that affects the blood being pumped to my brain. That's why I've been dizzy, and have had trouble walking. I've got an appointment tomorrow in Salem, about ten o'clock, to have it taken care of. The kid was right." He slid a chair up to the table. "How are you two gettin' along?"

"Michael and I are doing just fine," she told him. "There's only one problem he doesn't say anything, not a word. Do you think he's a deaf mute?"

He eyed the remains of the ice cream container and gave her a disgusted look. He picked up her spoon and scraped the insides of the almost empty carton, smacking his lips with each sparse spoonful.

"You want to know what I think?" he said, as he inspected the inside of the empty container. "I think he came from the stars, a place where they don't speak our language. If you came here from another planet would you speak our language? I don't think so. It's lucky we can communicate at all. At least, he can show us pictures."

She thought for a moment. "You're probably right. Even so, I wish he could talk, instead of showing us pictures all the time." She looked at the boy across the table. "I would still like to know how he ended up beside the road."

The boy stared at her, as if he had read her mind. He got up, walked around the table and put his finger on her forehead. Once again, images raced through her head. Instantly, her mind was transported to the same small spaceship she had seen earlier. The man in the dark uniform sat at a console with hundreds of colorful, flickering lights surrounding him. Somehow, she knew the ship was in trouble, and that he had landed somewhere to make repairs. The boy was still in the cage, but the door had been left ajar. She could see a wooded area through a portal, presumably that of Earth. While the man in black was busy at a console, the boy pushed the door ajar and ran to the outer hatch. He pushed a button; the hatch slid open, and he rushed out into the wet, cold darkness.

The man chased after him, but he was too fast, and it was extremely dark. He went back inside, closed the hatch and the small craft lifted silently over the treetops and disappeared. The boy ran as fast as his short legs would carry him, until he had found a winding road. Exhausted, he stopped beside it. It was raining hard, and his only protection from the weather was his silver suit with the hood. He was soon overcome by the wetness and cold and collapsed beside the road.

She looked at Charley and smiled. "I know what happened," she said, "he showed me everything."

"So, what happened?" he asked, knowing she probably wouldn't tell him.

"I'll tell you later."

It was nearly ten o'clock, and the boy's eyes were drooping sleepily. She noticed them and escorted him into the second bedroom, where she helped him onto a large goose-down mattress. Within seconds, he was fast asleep.

"I guess he's more human than I thought," she mumbled.

TWO

Senator Kerac, a tall, slender figure in a silver uniform, stood at the helm of the 150-foot craft maneuvering it out of Earth's atmosphere and into the wraithlike vortex the ship had created. He had gone through that limitless emptiness many times before without mishap, but each time it had proven more frightening. He heard of ships going into the void between the two universes and never returning.

Their scientists had speculated that those ships had been caught up in strange eddy currents nobody could understand or explain. They believed the disturbances were somehow related to Earth's ongoing wars; frequently being bombarded by extremely high explosives. Therefore, when the detonations occurred, they believed the atomic structure between the two universes was fractured, causing a short-lived phenomenon making it virtually impossible to create a vortex.

Long before Golan's sun began its death-throes, the planet and Earth had coexisted side-by-side for billions of years, but in two different universes and two distinct dimensions of existence. When the two planets were created, nature had somehow decreed that both Golan and Earth would utilize the same atoms, molecules, particles and ions in their creations, but of opposite polarities. The atomic structure of both universes would remain essentially the same, but the atoms and sub-particles of one would be charged negative, while the other positive. Earth's universe would utilize the positive portion of the atomic structure and Golan the negative.

Many millenniums later, while experimenting with the possibility of vortexes, Golan's scientists discovered that the massive explosions in Earth's universe had somehow broken down the atomic structure between the two, making it possible to create vortexes. Although unstable at times, the vortexes allowed them to travel between the two universes in relative safety.

There was no question in Kerac's mind they wouldn't make it back to Golan safely; Earth's universe had been relatively stable for some time.

"Lulla," he called across the bridge. "We're almost there. One last barrier and we're home."

The slender, fair-haired woman looked up from her console. "It's about time," she replied with a sigh. "I don't think I could take much more of what we just went through."

"I know what you mean, it's been a long, difficult trip," he replied. He pushed several buttons, and then added, "When we get back we'll have to try to persuade Parliament to let us return for the boy." As they approached the landing area on the mother-ship, he put the craft in auto-land mode and joined her at the navigation console.

"Haven't you forgotten we were the ones responsible for losing the King's only son to Luchak?" she said. "We may not see him again. King Oltar may never forgive us." The corners of her eyes moistened. "I'll never forgive myself for letting that happen. I really didn't know Luchak was on board. He must have stowed away in the cargo bay and I never detected him."

"It wasn't your fault, Lulla," he said softly. "I'm sure Luchak was well hidden and just waiting for the right opportunity to abduct him. I should have realized something like that would happen. I'm sure Senator Abron was well aware that if he got the King's son out of the way Parliament would vote for <u>his</u> son to be prince."

"Even so, I blame myself for him even being on board," she said apologetically. "I still don't understand why we couldn't have found a secure spot on the mother-ship to hide him, until it was time for the senators vote." She rose from the console, put her arms around him and snuggled up against his chest. "Tell me Luchak won't harm him."

"I don't believe he has that in mind," he answered. "He knows if he harms that boy in any way all five mother-ships will do more than just reprimand him." He thought for a moment, and then added, "Maybe Luchak doesn't realize it, but he can't go home in that observation pod he swiped from us. I'm certain by now he's discovered he's truly Earth-bound."

"What can we do?" she said, shrugging her slender shoulders. "Do you think they will let us return for him?"

"First things first," he replied. "After we are called into Parliament, we'll explain what happened. They should give us the option of returning for him." He thought for a moment, then added, "One thing is certain, under the present circumstances even we would have a tough time finding him on Earth. I'm positive that by now Luchak has hidden him well. What's more, if we return too soon, the people of Earth might attempt to hunt us down, like they have in the past. They call us UFOs. Did you know that?" He laughed.

"Did you get a bearing on Luchak when he left with our pod in such a hurry?" she asked, ignoring his question. "If you did, and if we can get authorization to return, we can back-track to find him."

"Yes, I did," he answered, "assuming he didn't change course before landing. He was headed for a place on Earth called Oregon. My sensors told me he landed deep in a small forest. Unfortunately, we didn't have time to go after him. Wehad to return here to explain the situation to Parliament at their weekly meeting…which is right now. However, if they do allow us to return it shouldn't be too difficult to locate his brain waves, they're exceptionally strong, as you must know. Don't worry, we'll find him. He's the rightful heir to the throne, and no one can change that."

"Do you really think they will let us return for him?" she said anxiously. "Truthfully, I think they should, under the circumstances."

"We'll have to wait and see," he told her. "When we tell them the truth about what happened, I'm sure they'll take his abduction into consideration. In our favor, they know Senator Abron is the King's worst enemy." He looked at her with a frown. "However, in his favor, he's a big-shot and most senators are afraid to go against him."

After the hangar-deck controller landed their ship automatically on Golan One, they were instructed to go to the administration building and wait there until the senators had finished preparing for their weekly meeting.

Several hours had passed, before the senators took their respective places at the long table, and Kerac had become extremely agitated, his irritation grew by the minute.

Lulla attempted to calm him with a soft touch on the arm and a tender word, but to no avail. "Kerac, calm yourself," she scolded. "It will do no good to get angry it could make things even worse than they already are."

He shifted in his seat and stared down the long, statue-lined corridor, quietly fuming. "How could it get any worse?" he replied, giving her a defiant stare. "We've lost the King's only son, my nephew, who was to be voted Prince of Golan. Because of that we will probably lose their vote to return for him. They could very easily send someone else. And that wouldn't be good."

"Then you don't think they'll let us return for him?" she questioned. "You really believe that?"

He lowered his eyes and stared at the gleaming marble floor. A door swung open from the far end of the hall, and he jumped up and fixed his eyes on it.

The door closed, and Lulla continued her apologies. "We should have informed the King of Meesha's abduction, before we came to the chamber. The Parliament would then be aware of what's at stake here. If King Oltar dies, someone else would be crowned prince, and he and his sponsor would have power over everything. That wouldn't be good, especially since the King is on his death bed and slowly losing control."

"That's true," he replied. He heard another distant sound and again stared down the long hallway.

She frowned. "You know Golan would rather have Meesha as their prince, rather than someone like Luchak." She shook her head and continued. "I can't believe they would vote for someone else, since the King has made his displeasures known with everyone they have suggested…including Luchak."

"It should not be anyone but Meesha," he said. "However, long ago the King made a decree that if anything happened to his son, they could elect someone of their own choosing, not of royal blood."

A young intern walked casually down the hallway and stopped in front of them. "The senators will see you now," he said, an air of arrogance in his voice. "Follow me."

They were escorted down the statue-lined hallway, and into a large room where senators from each nation were assembled.

Tumac, the dully elected Prime Minister of Golan sat at the end of the gleaming table tapping a pencil impatiently. He looked at them coldly as they entered and were directed to a small table at the far end of the room. After the senators were all seated, he picked up a huge wooden mallet and pounded on the table.

He lowered his head and with dark, penetrating eyes stared at the two defendants "Senator Kerac," he said with a powerful, commanding voice. "I wish to know your response to the allegation set forth by Senator Abron of Keeti."

"And what is that allegation, Your Honor?" Kerac replied. "I know of no wrong we have done. At the King's request, we took Meesha to Earth to hide until Parliament was ready to vote. Before we could do anything, Luchak of Keeti abducted him and took him from our ship…in the pod he stole from us, I might add."

"It is quite obvious you did not bring either of the boys back for <u>this</u> meeting," Tumac said, using an authoritative voice. "They are still on Earth, and no one appears to know exactly where. You obviously do not." He looked down the long table, and his eyes locked on Senator Abron. "The senator has complained that you took his son, Luchak, to Earth against his will and left him there."

"Luchak stowed away on our ship, Your Honor," Kerac interrupted, his voice laced with cynicism. "He stole our pod and abducted Meesha. He is somewhere on Earth holding the boy hostage, which kept us from returning with him for this vote."

"How did this happen, Kerac?" Tumac demanded.

Lulla jumped to her feet and glared down the long table. "It was my fault, Your Honor," she said with a loud, piercing voice. "I did not know Luchak had stowed away in our launch bay. I didn't check it before we left Golan, like I should have." She was silent for several moments, and then added, "I had no idea he would stoop low enough to abduct Meesha from our ship and hide him until after the vote—unless his father told him to do so." She stared at Senator Abron, seated halfway down the long table. He lowered his head and started thumbing through a stack of papers in front of him.

"Could this be true Senator Abron?" Tumac asked, looking sternly at him. "Did you tell your son to stow away on Kerac's ship? Did he abduct Meesha at your request?"

Abron stood and shoved his chair back against the far wall. "Your Honor, I know nothing about this abduction Lulla speaks of. My son would never do such a thing. And I certainly didn't tell him to do it. You might ask why King Oltar would want Kerac to take his son to Earth, in the first place. If he were to be voted in as prince, as he surely would be, why would the King want him to be taken to Earth until after the vote?"

Kerac stood to face Tumac, his face flushed. "Your Honor, the King was concerned for his son's well-being. He knew all senators were aware of his proclamation that they could vote for someone else, if his son were not available. For that reason, he wanted to make certain he would be safe until time for the vote. The senators leaned across the table and whispered among themselves.

Tumac pounded the mallet on the table. "Kerac, are you telling us King Oltar believed someone might harm Meesha before the vote was taken? For what reason would anyone harm him? The title of Prince in itself has no authority, no power."

Kerac looked intently at each member, and turned his eyes back on Abron. He stared at him for a moment, and then looked up the long table at Tumac.

"Your Honor," he said. "Granted, the title of prince is merely a label, but what if the King should die? The prince would then be King and ruler of the empire. Is this not true?" Tumac nodded. "Furthermore," he added, "the King informed me of his displeasure with both Luchak and his father. He said he would not put it past them to do something sinister, just to keep Parliament from voting for his son."

Still standing, Abron expanded his medal-laden chest and glared at Kerac. "How dare you!" he yelled, his eyes on fire. "The King has never once doubted my loyalty or honesty. I demand an apology! Because you are the King's brother you think you can get away with making false accusations against me, a Senator of the Parl—"

"Gentlemen! Gentlemen!" Tumac roared, cutting him off. "Let us be civil about this." He looked down the long polished table at Kerac standing at the far end of the room. "Sir, would you care to explain your accusations? You must not accuse a senator of wrong doing without justification for your charges."

"As you must know, Sir," Kerac began, "the King is very ill and may not recover. It is a fact that if he does not recover the person elected prince will be the heir to the throne. My brother told me in confidence if he should die, he wanted only his son to be the rightful possessor of the throne, nobody else. However, he realized that he must abide by his own decree…if his son were not available, somebody of Parliament's choosing, not of royal blood, could be voted in as prince. His Majesty also told me he believed Abron's son would be the most likely person they would choose because of his influence over his son, and the majority of its members…and his ambitions."

A few members lowered their heads in righteous indignation, while others openly agreed with the accusations. A few members attempted to hide their own involvements with Abron—some were successful. Others were not.

Again, Tumac pounded the mallet on the table. Several minutes passed before the senators turned their attentions back to the Prime Minister.

"Gentlemen," he said, staring at each member. "We will have no more outbursts. We will conduct this meeting with decorum out of respect for the King, if nothing else." He held his intense glare for a few moments, and then continued. "Will the Senator of Keeti please stand and address the table?"

"What does Your Honor ask?" Abron replied, his face still flushed. "I have done nothing wrong. Kerac's words are not to be believed. Because he is the King's brother, he believes he can say anything, and we will accept it as a profound truth. His words are empty. I do not believe my son would kidnap or harm Meesha in any way. I believe it's the other way around; Kerac took both my son and Meesha to Earth and planned to keep my son there so he could not be voted on, while he returned with Meesha." He pulled on his lapel, took in a deep breath to expand his chest, and continued. "If my son took Kerac's observation pod and is now with Meesha, as Kerac has suggested, neither can return to Golan, the pod cannot make a vortex. Someone must go after them."

Kerac stood, almost knocking over his chair. "Sir, are you suggesting I left both boys there on purpose? Why would I do that? I told you the King wanted only his son to be prince. I was to bring him back for <u>this</u> meeting. However, thanks to your son, Luchak, I could not. Furthermore, what happened to my pod? Meesha could not have taken it; he's too young to handle it. The senator's son is eighteen and well versed in its operation." He stared at Tumac for a long moment. "Your Honor, what I have told you is the truth. Both Lulla and I were there when Luchak abducted Meesha and took him away in my pod. I'm sure he didn't do it as a prank. I believe his father believed if Meesha were kept out of the picture he could not return to be voted on." He thought for a moment, and then added, "However, Luchak must have known the pod couldn't make a vortex. It doesn't have the ability. And, if he couldn't return in the pod, someone would have to go after him, to take him back to be voted on…more than likely, his father."

Tumac gave him an icy stare. "Then both boys are in the other world with no means of returning to Golan? Is that what you're saying, Kerac?"

"Yes, Your Honor, that's precisely what I'm saying. Someone will have to return for both." He glanced down at Lulla, quietly fuming at his side. "Because we are being held responsible for both boys' absences, Lulla and I should be the ones to return for them. Unfortunately, we had to return prematurely to explain the situation to you gentlemen, before you voted." He scanned each member's face, and then added, "If you gentlemen will put off your votes until both boys can be returned, I'm sure this problem can be resolved. I realize if Meesha is not present you are obligated to vote for someone else. Nonetheless, let us go back to Earth and get them. Only then can we get to the bottom of this problem."

The Prime Minister looked down the long table expecting a response from the senators, but none came. "Gentlemen, what do you say? Do we authorize Kerac to return for the boys, and put off the vote for one week?" The members split into small discussion groups.

After a few minutes, Ekron, a Senator from Lechi, the second in command of the Parliament, stood. With a powerful voice, he said, "Your Honor, we have taken a vote and have agreed to let Kerac return for them. He must find and bring both boys back within one week. If he returns with them, and Luchak is found guilty of abduction, Kerac will be cleared of all blame, and we will take it from there. Nevertheless, if Meesha is not returned before the next meeting, we will be obligated to vote for someone else. However, at this time, there is no viable candidate other than Luchak, and he is not present."

Senator Abron glared down the long table at Kerac, and then turned his eyes on Tumac. "Your Honor," he called out. Tumac had been speaking to another senator and did not look up. "Your Honor!" he shouted again, louder.

Tumac glanced down the table, a deep frown on his long, stoic face. He was not accustomed to being interrupted. When he spotted the guilty party, he lowered his eyebrow and glared at him.

"Yes, Senator Abron," he said, annoyed by his verbal intrusion. "What is it? What is so important you interrupt me?"

"I'm sorry, Your Honor, but I must ask you and the senators to hear me out."

"Yes senator, what is it?" Tumac's patience clearly grew thin.

"Sir, my ship is capable of making a vortex. I ask for the Senators' permission to accompany Kerac on his mission. I believe two ships looking for the boys would be more productive than just one."

Tumac called for the assembly to return to their seats. "Do <u>you</u> have any idea where the boys might be?" he asked Abron. "Earth is a large planet. They could be anywhere. Kerac appears to know approximately where they are. If that is true, he would not need your assistance." He thought for a moment, and then added, "But we must honor your request. The senators will vote." He pounded the mallet on the table. "Gentlemen, you heard the request, what is your response? Raise your hands if you agree to Senator Abron's request to accompany Kerac." Eight members raised their hands, and 17 declined. Tumac slammed the wooden mallet down. "I'm sorry, Senator Abron. Your request has been denied."

Abron again slammed his chair back against the far wall and stormed out of the room.

THREE

Luchak had taken the stolen observation pod into the outer limits of Earth's atmosphere, where he believed Earth's long-range radars could not detect him. He sat behind the small helm and looked down at the beautiful blues and whites of Earth. He had been there many times, but never under such circumstances, only as an observer on one of the ships that Golan had sent to investigate life on the planet. There had been times when he dreamed of going down and blending in with the population, but he knew he couldn't. Even so, except for a few minor facial differences, he looked exactly like them. He believed he would be accepted as one of their own, but he was <u>not</u> one of them—not by any means. On the other hand, he could not go back to Golan in the pod. It couldn't make a vortex. If he tried, he and the pod would disintegrate. Such a dilemma, he thought.

What happened to Meesha? Where did he go? He wondered. Should he go down and look for him, or wait until his sensors found his brain waves? He had to find the boy; there was no doubt about that. He had to hide him from Kerac, until after the vote. If he remained on Earth, he couldn't be voted in as prince; he had to be present to accept the honor. However, he realized they couldn't vote for him either, as long as he remained on Earth. His father would have to come and get him.

Grace pushed the covers to the bottom of the bed and put her feet on the cold, varnished floor. She glanced over at Charley still asleep and quietly slipped out of the room. She filled the percolator hopper with coffee, then drew cold water from the low-pressure spigot and put the pot on the stove. While humming her favorite tune, she began stirring batter for a larger than normal batch of pancakes.

"I wonder if Michael likes pancakes?" she mumbled to herself. "Oh well, he'll just have to eat 'em." She stopped humming long enough to stare at the ceiling in thought. "Michael," she said softly. "I'd better check on him." She opened the door to the small bedroom and found he was gone. "Oh, my," she said softly. "I hope he didn't leave."

On her way back to the kitchen, she glanced into the living room. The boy sat perched on the French window ledge with his knees bent up to his chin and his arms wrapped around them, watching the school busses leave the yard. He looked over and smiled.

"Land sakes alive, child, you'll catch your death of cold sittin' by that drafty window wearin' almost nothing. Let me get you a blanket. It's cold in here and the window certainly doesn't help any." She took the afghan from the love seat and wrapped it around his shoulders. He looked up and smiled. "The children will be coming to school shortly, Michael. You can see them from the window. They always come by and wave." She went back into the kitchen and continued beating the batter until it turned into a thick paste.

"Is that coffee I smell?" Charley called from the bedroom door. "Boy, could I ever use some. It was a long night." As he moved his aging body slowly across the room, he noticed the boy sitting on the window ledge. "How's the little twerp doing?" he yelled to her. "He appears to be adjustin' okay."

She came through the swinging doors and helped him hobble into the kitchen. "I should get you some crutches. Maybe they'd help you walk a little better."

"Don't bother, sweetie. Doc Halloway said after I have this little operation, I'll be good as new. In a few days, I'll be runnin' a marathon."

"Did he now?" she said with a smile. "And don't call him twerp, his name is Michael. Call him that." She poured him a cup of coffee and set it on the table in front of him. He stirred several spoonfuls of sugar and a half-cup of cream into the large mug and took a loud sip. She looked over, scornfully. "And stop slurping your coffee. What will Michael think?"

"Yes, Mother," he said, and slurped it even louder.

"Michael," she called from the kitchen. "Come get some pancakes, dear. I made them just for you and Charley." He turned and saw her standing by the swinging doors, but didn't budge from the ledge. She went over, took him by the hand and led him into the kitchen. She pulled out a chair and slid it next to Charley's.

Charley eyed him up and down. "Hi there little buddy, how you doing this mornin'? You hungry? I sure am. I could eat the south end of a north bound polecat."

"Charley!" she complained, turning and glaring at him. "Watch your mouth."

"What difference does it make? He doesn't know what I'm sayin'."

"What if he can understand but can't talk?" she replied, plopping several steaming pancakes onto each plate. "It'd be rather embarrassing if we said the wrong thing, and he understood."

The boy looked down at the two, round objects, but made no effort to eat them. Charley reached over, cut the cakes into small squares and poured syrup over them. He stabbed one with his fork and put it in his mouth, then rubbed his stomach while making sounds of contentment.

"Charley, he's not a baby. I'm sure he can feed himself."

"What if he doesn't eat our kind of food, or even eat the way we do?"

"Well, he certainly helped me polish off that ice cream last night," she said with a shrill giggle.

The boy took his fork, stabbed a square and put it in his mouth. His eyes lit up and a smile spread across his pixie-face. He quickly devoured the pancakes, and looked up at Grace with a grin. She put two more on his plate, then stood back and watched him disposed of them.

"Land sakes, Michael, you're going to get fat eating like that," she said.

After he had finished the last pancake, he turned and pointed to her forehead.

"Charley, I think he wants to show me something, see his finger? I hope he wants to show me more pictures of where he came from."

She sat in the chair next to him, and he placed his finger in the middle of her brow. She closed her eyes and instantly a tall, fair-haired woman appeared swinging a small boy back and forth on a long rope with a seat attached. She kept pushing him higher and higher until he was about to fall, and then she screamed, "Meesha! Meesha!" He took his finger away, and the image disappeared.

She leaned back and looked at Charley. "I think his name is Meesha," she said. "I believe he just told me that. He showed me a picture of his mother. I think it was his mother. I believe she called out his name." She turned to the boy, and with raised eyebrows said, "Meesha? Is that your name? Meesha?"

He smiled and shook his head.

"Well I'll be danged!" Charley said. "I believe he can understand us. Not so much by words but by our actions and expressions. What do you think?"

The sound of children playing by the picket fence gave her cause to go to the window and look out. "Come, Meesha," she said, taking him by the hand and leading him back to the French window. "See the children? They're on their way to school."

"Gracie!" Charley shouted. "For cryin' out loud you know he can't understand you. Show him what you want by gestures, and I'll bet he'll mimic you like a little monkey."

"Don't call him a monkey," she said, scornfully. She looked at the boy, then pointed to the yard and waved to the children. "What about your appointment in Salem? You have to take the ambulance, you know. You better get ready. I'll drive you to the doctor's office to catch your ride to the big city."

"What are we going to do with little twerp, there?" he asked, pointing to the boy. "We can't leave him here alone. Maybe we should take him with us."

"I don't think that would be wise," she replied. "He should be all right for a few minutes. It's only a five-minute ride."

Fifteen minutes later Charley appeared at the door in his finest and only suit. "Okay, I'm ready, let's go. I want to get this over with soon as possible."

She went to the window and saw the boy watching the children go by. "Meesha, dear," she called out. "I'll be right back. You sit here and wave to the children. But please don't go outside. If they see you, they won't understand." He looked up and smiled.

Charley shook his head and rolled his eyes, as he walked through the door.

Doc Halloway met them at the front door of the clinic and escorted him to the ambulance. As soon as it pulled away, Grace hurried back to the cottage. When she arrived, she found the yard filled with twelve and thirteen-year-old girls. Meesha was standing among them smiling.

She rushed over and looked sternly at him. "Meesha!" she scolded. "What are you doing outside? You were supposed to stay in the house." She took him by the hand and led him inside. When she came back to close the door, she noticed none of the girls had left. "Children, please go to school," she called to them. "He is not from around here. He doesn't understand our ways."

A young girl walked through the gate and stood in front of the porch. "He's funny looking, Mrs. Bertell," she said. "Where's he from? He's nice though. He made us see things in our heads by using his finger. It was fun."

"He's not from around here, sweetie. What did he show you?"

"He showed us a new game that both boys and girls can play. We're going to play it at recess. It looks like fun."

"Please, sweetheart, don't tell your parents about him. Okay?"

"Why?"

She thought for a moment. "Because, sweetie, they wouldn't understand. Okay? Have fun with the new game, though."

"We'll play it at recess. Can he come out?"

"He can't, sweetie. He's leaving shortly. Nevertheless, I'm glad he showed you a game. I hope you enjoy it."

As they skipped out of the yard, heading for their classes, they turned and waved. He smiled and waved back.

Grace went to the window and took his arm. "Meesha," she scolded, "what did I tell you about going outside? For goodness sake, child, do you want everybody to know what you can do? If the government men found out about you, it'd be a circus around here."

He looked up with a smile.

FOUR

With Kerac at flight controls and Lulla navigating, they left Golan One. When they arrived at the correct coordinates, they began the process of making a vortex to Earth.

There were only a few known locations in both universes where vortexes could be activated and set into motion. For years, scientists tried to understand why, but with no success. They simply lived with the fact.

As they exited the vortex, thousands of miles above Earth, the ship materialized and quickly obtained orbit directly over the northwest territory of the United States. After setting all controls on automatic, he told Lulla to scan for Meesha's brain waves.

She pushed several buttons on a large console and watched the screen. "If I'm reading this correctly, I have a brain wave on the scanner, but it's not from the planet. It's somewhere nearby. And they're not Meesha's."

"Let me see," he said, and took over her console. Several seconds later he looked up. "You're right they are close by."

"It has to be Luchak," she told him, as she moved to another console and pushed several more buttons. "Yes, it is Luchak's waves. I just compared them to the ones stored in our archives—they're an exact match. What should we do?"

"Nothing, right now," he answered. We came here to find Meesha. He's obviously not with Luchak. Don't know what happened, but my sensors tell me he's not on that pod. He's not with Luchak. He has to be on Earth, and we'll have to locate him. We can get Luchak and our pod later."

"Our best chance of locating him is if he's mentally connected with someone," she answered. "That might take a while. But what if he doesn't communicate with anybody? What do we do, then?"

"Don't get discouraged," he replied. "If he's anywhere on Earth, he'll connect with somebody, knowing him like I do. He's a very outgoing boy. He'll connect."

"Kerac, I don't understand. I shouldn't be getting Luchak's waves, if he's not talking to someone or thinking hard about something. He's alone in that pod, isn't he?"

"Yes, I'm certain," he answered. It's possible for him to transmit brain waves by thinking extremely hard about something, or in a day-dream state…or in trouble."

"I can only imagine what he's thinking 'hard' about. He's probably trying to figure a way to get home in that pod he swiped."

"He's a clever boy, but not that clever," he replied. "There's no way that pod could make a vortex. It would disintegrate." He left the console and returned to the helm. "We'll deal with him later. Right now, we have to find Meesha. We can only hope he connects with somebody, soon."

Lulla leaned back in the chair and ran her fingers through her shoulder-length, flaxen hair. She closed her eyes and released a long sigh. Suddenly, a thought came to her. Why couldn't she communicate by using the ship's computer? She knew it was possible to send brain waves stored in the computer. Why not send them along with her own waves? She jumped up almost knocked her chair over getting to another console.

"What's going on?"

"I have an idea," she said, her face beaming. "Meesha's brain waves are stored in the computer archives, along with Luchak's and many others, including ours. If I transmitted his waves along with mine, do you he'd get them and respond? The computer is quite powerful."

Kerac thought for a moment. "He might. However, Luchak could pick them up and find him. He also has brain-wave equipment on that pod of ours, you know."

"It might be worth a try," she said. "But, more than likely Luchak already knows where Meesha is, assuming he communicated with somebody before we got here." It took only a few seconds for her to download his stored waves into the communications console. "Kerac," she yelled, "while I transmit the waves, monitor the sky for Luchak. See if you can get a fix on him and our pod."

"I've had him on the screen for some time."

FIVE

Charley returned from his operation in Salem and lay on the sofa grumbling about the soreness in his neck. It had been a minor operation, like Doc Halloway had said, and he was thankful for that. The hospital had wanted him to stay the night, but he insisted on going home. They told him if he left they wouldn't be responsible for anything that might happen if a problem developed. They lost the argument, and he went home.

Grace had spent the better part of the afternoon creating a beef stew for a late lunch, and Meesha sat on his favorite window ledge watching birds dart in and out of a birdbath, and small furry animals scampering about the yard.

"It's lunch time, gentlemen," she called. "Go wash your hands, Meesha." She realized he couldn't understand and went to the window, took him by the hand and led him into the bathroom. After demonstrating what he was supposed to do, he understood and complied with his usual smile.

Still grumbling about his neck, Charley rose slowly from the sofa, lumbered into the kitchen and sat at the head of the table.

"How about you, twerp are you hungry?" he asked, looking over at the boy. Meesha raised his eyebrow and smiled.

She carried the pot to the table and placed it on a hot pad. The boy leaned over, put his nose over the bowl and took in its beefy aroma. She drew a ladle of the thick brown mixture and poured it into his bowl. His eyes lit up. He picked up a fork, then noticed it was the wrong utensil and dropped it. Using a large soup-spoon he found beside his plate, he shoveled a huge portion of the extremely hot mixture into his mouth. It burned his tongue, and he fanned his hand in front of his mouth to help ease the pain. She giggled and poured him a glass of ice-cold milk. By making a drinking motion, he understood. Within seconds, the pain subsided, and he went back for more.

After he had finished his second bowl, and was about to leave the table, he suddenly threw his hands up to his forehead and cringed in pain. He closed his eyes, uttered strange sounds and ran from the kitchen into the living room. He stuck his head under the afghan and placed a pillow over it.

Lulla looked over at Kerac and shrugged. "I'm not sure if I made contact. I sent him my waves, but I didn't get an answer. I hope the waves weren't too strong. I haven't really used this machine much. If they're too strong, they could damage his mind. Assuming he got them at all."

"Try again," he said, "this time lower the power and sensitivity."

Frustrated, she turned several dials and pushed a big, red button. "I'll try it now," she said. "I have it as low as I can get it and still be effective."

"When you transmit this time, use your mind power along with the waves," he told her. "I'm certain he doesn't know it's coming from a transmitter. By now, he's probably totally confused."

After readjusting the transmitter, she closed her eyes and sent images of the mother-ship, and of his father. Several minutes later she leaned back and sighed. "If that doesn't do it, I don't know what else to do."

Meesha pulled his head out from under the afghan and a strange look spread across his face. He ran to the window ledge and jumped up onto it. He sat in his favorite position for several moments staring hypnotically out the window.

"Heavens to Betsy," Grace said, taken back by his strange behavior. "I wonder what's gotten into the little fellow."

As he sat in the window, his facial expression suddenly changed. He closed his eyes, swayed back and forth on the ledge, and produced the same eerie sounds as before. He opened his eyes, and a broad smile covered his face. He jumped off the ledge, rushed over to Grace and put his finger on her forehead.

"Land's sake, child, what's this?" she said with a start. "Are you going to show me more pictures?" Instantly, images of a blond woman sitting at a desk with hundreds of blinking lights ran through her mind.

He dropped his finger, sat beside her and closed his eyes. A voice echoed in his mind.

"Where are you, Meesha?" the voice said. "We will come for you, but we must know exactly where you are."

"Where are you, Lulla?" he threw his thoughts back.

"We're several thousand miles from you," her voice returned. "We've come for you and Luchak. Where are you, exactly?"

"I'm with some wonderful people in a little white house next to a school yard," he sent back. "But I don't know its exact location."

"Please, keep thinking of me, and I'll scan your waves to find you," she pleaded. "Don't worry, I will find you. What about Luchak? What happened down there?"

"I don't know, where he went," he sent back. "I ran from the pod when he was repairing it. He chased after me, but he couldn't catch me and flew away. I don't know where he went."

Several moments later her voice returned. "I have located you. Please, do not leave there, and we will come for you."

"Be careful, Lulla," he warned. "If you can find me so can Luchak."

"Don't be concerned about him," she replied. "He doesn't worry us. He will not bother you again. I promise."

She stopped sending, and his mind went blank. He looked at Grace, reached over and squeezed her hand.

She gazed into his eyes, like a mother to a child. "What was that all about, dear?" she asked. "Were you getting pictures, too?"

He smiled and ran back to his favorite window ledge.

SIX

Senator Abron rushed down the long, ornate hall of Golan One, stopping in front of a nondescript door. He glanced up and down the corridor, and then darted through it and into a small transporter, which had just arrived from Golan Two.

"Take me to our administration building, Gato," he told the driver. "Don't stop until we get there." The young man glanced in the rearview mirror and stepped down hard on the gravity accelerator. After receiving permission to leave Golan One, they headed for Golan Two. A few minutes later they arrived in front of the impressive gate of the small country of Keeti. He told Gato to stand by while he went inside. Several minutes later he returned. "Take me to the launch pad," he demanded. "Don't mention that I'm going on a trip to anyone, Gato. Nobody must know."

"Yes sir."

"After we arrive, take the vehicle back to my home. You can take time off until I return. I won't need you for a while."

"Yes sir."

On their way to the launch pad, Abron made several calls from the car. When he arrived at the docking station, two men were waiting in front of a gleaming 150-foot ship. A man in a military uniform escorted him up to the ramp and into the ship.

"Where are we going today, Sir?" the young officer asked.

"I'll tell you after we launch," Abron replied, sharpness in his tone. He looked at the man intently, and then added, "Does this ship have the latest ion drive? Is it equipped to make a vortex, and does it have up-to-date weaponry?"

"Yes sir, we have upgraded everything."

Abron eyed the man suspiciously. “The vortex drive has been tested, hasn’t it?”

“Yes sir, we went to Earth a few days ago. It worked fine. We’re here, aren’t we?”

“Good. I’d hate to go there and not get back.”

“Then we’re going to Earth?”

When Abron realized he had inadvertently compromised his destination, he said, “Where else? I don’t know of any other planet we’re familiar with.”

The man’s face blushed. “You know we can’t leave the mother-ship without permission from Golan One,” he informed him. “And we can’t make a vortex without the consent of Parliament.”

“Don’t worry about it,” Abron replied irritably. “I’ve made arrangements with the outer-door controller. There won’t be a problem leaving the ship.”

“What if we’re discovered making a vortex?”

“You worry too much, Lieutenant Nader. I have it all arranged.”

SEVEN

Kerac was in the process of storing Meesha's brain wave coordinates in the computer, when Lulla interrupted.

"Kerac," she shouted across the bridge. "Shouldn't we go after Luchak? I'm sure he's trying his best to find Meesha. He's a very persistent young man, and possibly a dangerous one. I believe he will use any means available to find the boy, before we do." She was silent for a few moments, and then added, "More than likely he picked up our mental conversation and knows exactly where he is."

"Can you pinpoint his exact location?" he asked. "If we find him before he gets to Meesha, we can bring him and the pod back by force, if necessary. I had him on the scanner before, but he disappeared."

"He has to be thinking about something extremely hard, before I can locate him again. He's probably aware of that and has turned off his thoughts, and the pod's signature, so we can't find him."

"Keep trying," he demanded. "In the meantime, we'll wait until it's dark down there, then go get the boy."

It was early afternoon in the small town of Grande Ronde. The children had been let out of school for the day and were waiting in the schoolyard for the busses. The boys had assembled in the grass field to play field hockey, and the girls had gathered on the short sidewalk in front of the Bertell's to skip rope and play hopscotch on the only concrete sidewalk available. Meesha sat at his favorite spot on the windowsill watching them play.

Several girls walked by the window on their way to the buses and waved. He waved back with a broad grin. A small, curly-haired girl remained at the gate and motioned for him to come out. He glanced toward the kitchen to see if Grace had been watching through the window, but she was busy preparing dinner.

He jumped down from the ledge, slowly opened the squeaky front door and joined her. The other girls saw him come out and joined them. The curly-haired girl pointed to her forehead and smiled. He put his finger on her brow, and instantly images of a gigantic spaceship appeared.

She looked at him skeptically, and said, "That's not where you live, is it?" He appeared to understand and shook his head. "Why don't you talk?" she asked. "You never say anything." He looked at her blankly, and then shrugged.

"What did he show you?" a small, red-headed girl asked. "Let me see, too." Anticipating her request, he put his finger on her brow. Startled by the images, she backed off. "He's joking with us! He doesn't live on a spaceship! He's messin' with our minds!"

The curly-haired girl walked closer and stared into his eyes. "My name is Caroline," she said. "What's yours?" Seeing his confused look, she repeated, "What's your name? My name is Caroline." She pointed her finger at her chest.

He appeared to understand and again put his finger on her brow. Instantly, the same picture he had shown Grace, when she had wanted to know his name, invaded her mind. She heard the woman call out, "Meesha! Meesha!" She turned to the others and said, "His name if Meesha, I think. That's what I just heard." She gave him a strange look, then turned and said to the others, "He's funny looking. Look at his eyes and his hair. But he's cute. I like him, even if he is odd looking."

Grace walked by the kitchen window and glanced through it. When she saw him standing with the children, she rushed out, took him by the hand and led him back into the house. Before closing the door, she turned to the startled children.

"Sorry, kids," she said, "he doesn't understand you or your ways. Like I told you before, he's not from around here. Please, don't tell anybody about him, or what he made you see. Okay?" The girls turned and skipped lightheartedly toward the school busses, which had just pulled into the yard.

Fifteen minutes later, Caroline jumped down from the bus and ran into a small, wood-framed house. She tossed her homework on an entrance table and rushed into the living room where her mother sat watching TV.

"Mom," she said excitedly. "You'll never guess what happened today."

"What is it, dear? Something nice, I hope."

"Mom, there's this new kid staying at Mrs. Bertell's house. He's from a spaceship. He showed it to us."

"A spaceship?" her mother mocked, as she switched channels. "How did he show you a spaceship? Did he take you there?" She giggled.

"No, silly," she replied with a smirk, "he didn't take us there he showed us pictures of it in our heads. He can do all sorts of things with our minds. He showed us his mother, too. At least, I think it was his mother. He's strange-looking…and really tiny. Even so, I like him."

"That's nice, dear. Now go wash your hands and start on your homework, before dinner. Okay? We'll talk about it when your father gets home."

Caroline hop-scotched into the bathroom and slammed the door.

Several hours later the loud, guttural sound of a diesel engine disrupted the quiet of the afternoon. An empty logging truck with a piggy-backed trailer perched on top pulled into the yard and stopped. After the engine made a few indecisive revolutions, it backfired and died. A tall, slender man in a red-checkered shirt with paisley suspenders jumped down from the high cab and trudged wearily onto the back porch. He sat on an empty apple crate and laboriously unstrung the long laces on his spiked boots.

"Hi, Eddie," the woman said, walking onto the porch. "How was your day? Did you make a bid for that timber on Henderson's south-forty? I know you really wanted it."

He stood up, planted a kiss on her cheek and walked into the kitchen to wash his hands in the cluttered sink. "I think he might take my bid," he yelled back. "I outbid Fred and George. It looks pretty good."

"That's great," she said, carrying a New England boiled dinner to the table. "I hear there's some good second-growth up there."

"Yep. It'll make us rich…more or less," he said, sitting down at the table. "Mmm, looks and smell yummy, and I'm famished."

"Don't wait for Caroline, she's in her room getting homework ready for after dinner."

Hearing her father's voice, Caroline rushed into the room, planted a kiss on his cheek and sat next to him. She looked at her mother sheepishly, and said, "Mom, can I tell him now, about the new boy?"

"If it's that important, dear, but I doubt if he'll believe you," she said, and scooped several large servings onto their plates.

Caroline overloaded her mouth with a hot potato and fanned it with both hands to ease the pain. She took a drink of cold milk, and then looked at her mother and giggled.

"Daddy," she said, after washing the potato down. "There's this new kid staying at the Bertell's house. Well, anyway, he's strange looking. He has eyes like a cat, and his hairline goes down his forehead to his eyebrow, which is only one long one." She paused, to blow on another bite. "And that's not all; his teeth are funny, too. He has one big one in front, where we have two or so. Isn't that odd?"

"Sounds weird, honey," he said. "Where's he from another planet?" He laughed, almost choking on a chunk of hot cabbage.

"That's not all, Daddy. He puts his finger on our foreheads, and he showed us pictures in our minds. He showed us pictures of his mother. She called out his name, Meesha. That's why I know his name. He showed me pictures of his spaceship. And he showed it to the rest of the girls, too. The strangest thing though he doesn't talk at all. He just shows us pictures in our heads. Weird, huh?"

He gave her a sideways glance. "You're joking, of course. You know what you just said is impossible, don't you? Nobody can do that. It's a trick, or something."

She held up two fingers, suggesting a Girl Scout oath. "Daddy, I swear I'm telling the truth. It really happened. Ask any of the girls, they were there. He showed them the same things."

"Sweetheart, I think you've been watching too much TV."

She dropped her fork, slid her chair back noisily, and headed for her room. Before going through the door, she turned and yelled, "Why won't you guys ever believe me? You never believe anything I tell you! Why don't you go see for yourself, if you don't believe me?" She rushed into her room and slammed the door.

He looked at his wife and raised his eyebrows. "What's gotten into her? Was it something I said?"

"Sweetheart, she's only twelve and easily influenced. P she did see this boy. Then again, maybe she didn't."

"She does have a vivid imagination," he replied. The phone rang, and he looked at her. "You want to get that, Jan? I'm kind of busy feedin' my face."

She picked up the receiver. "Hi. Who's this?"

"Hi, Jan," a soft feminine voice came over the earpiece. "This is Maggie."

"Oh, hi Maggie. What's up?"

"Has Caroline told you anything since she's been home that might seem a little strange to you?"

"She said something about a weird little boy," Jan answered with a snicker. "Other than that, nothing of any importance. Why do you ask?"

"Well," Maggie continued, "I went to pick Carla up at school, and she was standing in front of the Bertell house with a bunch of girls."

"Yes? And then what?"

"When I stopped the car, I saw a little boy sitting in their French window. I was curious about Gracie having a boy in her house, so I looked at him real close. The strangest thing, he looked more like a cat than a little boy. He had strange cat-like eyes and a weird haircut."

"You saw all of that from across the playground?"

Maggie giggled. "Well, I just happened to have my binoculars with me. That's not all though, on our way home, she told me the strangest things—"

"That he could put pictures in their heads by putting his finger on their foreheads?" Jan interrupted. "Stuff like that?"

"Yes," Maggie answered, surprised by her response. "Then Caroline did tell you?"

"Yes, but we didn't believe her. We just scoffed it off."

"Well, I wouldn't have believed it either," Maggie replied, "if I hadn't seen him with my own eyes."

Jan was silent for a moment. "That's weird. What do you think we should do? I hate to get involved in something really none of our business. Nonetheless, if it's true maybe we should go see Gracie and find out what's going on. What do you think?"

"I'm with you, Jan. Like you said, it's really none of our business. However, if something strange is going on there, I want to know about it." She hesitated for a moment. "Besides, I'm curious as all get out."

"Okay," Jan agreed. "If I can get any sleep tonight, we'll go over first thing in the morning."

Eddie finished his second helping, and looked up with a scowl. "What was that all about?"

"Carla told Maggie the same story Caroline told us…about the strange little boy at the Bertell house."

"You're kidding."

"No, I'm not. As a matter of fact, Maggie and I are going over first thing in the morning, after she drops Carla off at school."

"Do you think you should get involved?" he asked. "It's really not your business who Charley has in his house."

"I know, Eddie, but I want to make sure there's nothing strange going on we should know about. Gracie's too nice a lady to have anything weird going on in her house. Don't you agree?"

"Suit yourself. But don't look to me for sympathy, when you find out it's only a misunderstanding…or something like that."

She went to Caroline's bedroom and knocked on the door. "Dear, you can come out now. You've been exonerated. We believe you. Come on out and finish your meal. We'll talk about it, later. Okay, dear?"

EIGHT

"Lulla," Kerac called out. "I believe it's dark enough to go after Meesha. Put the ship on silent run and take it to a secluded spot close to where you detected his last waves. Just hope the Earthlings don't spot us."

After finding a clearing, she maneuvered the ship through a tall stand of second-growth timber, less than half a mile from the Bertell house, and set it down. She turned off the anti-gravity drive, cut all the interior lights and opened the outer hatch.

When they were about to leave, he stopped at a cabinet and retrieved a small stun gun from a drawer.

"Put it back, Kerac!" she said, glaring at him.

Reluctantly, he put it back and followed her to the outer door. "What if we run into trouble?" he said, opening the hatch. "A weapon might come in handy."

"What kind of trouble?" she replied. "We're deep in the woods, nobody here but us, and all the inhabitants probably sound asleep by now. You men are all alike; you think everything is going to hurt you and yours."

The sky was laden with extremely bright stars, and a full moon appeared to be stationary above the treetops on the eastern horizon. By its light, they forced their way through the thick, damp underbrush toward Meesha's last known coordinates. The earlier rain had made it extremely difficult to make headway, but they continued on toward their goal.

Lulla had brought a hand-held brain-wave scanner, and when they finally left the thick underbrush, she pointed it in all directions. When they arrived at the location indicated by the instrument, she saw the white house Meesha had told her about. The lights were out, and everything appeared calm and quiet. A single security lamp on the outside of the schoolhouse, 100-yards away, was the only light in the area.

"He must be asleep," he whispered. "If he is, you should be able to communicate with his subconscious. I've seen you do that before."

"It's difficult, but I'll try," she replied. "I hope he doesn't wake the people inside, when he realizes we're out here." She turned and glared at him. "If they wake up, don't hurt them. He seemed to like them."

"Why do you always think I'm going to hurt somebody?" he asked. "I wouldn't do that to an Earthling…certain Golans maybe, but not Earthlings. Get on with your communicating; we only have a few hours before sunrise. We certainly don't want to be around here when that happens."

She held the portable scanner against her head, to verify it was indeed Meesha's waves, then closed her eyes and adjusted her waves to match his. Several minutes later she opened her eyes.

"I've done everything I can," she told him. "I told him we were outside, and for him to come to us. I think I got through, but there's no way of knowing. He appeared to be asleep. We'll just have to wait here and see."

Luchak had noticed his brain wave instrument fluctuating wildly, and his eyes opened wide. He smiled mischievously. After a few strokes on a keyboard, he leaned back and watched the two green waves on the screen rise and fall in synchronization, and then form a resonant pattern. "Aha," he mumbled. "I've got you now, Lulla. Keep communicating." The waves suddenly disappeared. "What the—" He pounded his fist on the console. He knew if she had quit sending, it would be difficult to locate them.

As he leaned back in his chair, pondering the situation, a bright light appeared a few hundred yards from his pod and remained motionless. He scanned his instruments, and then realized it was a ship from Golan that had materialized beside him.

"Luchak!" a commanding voice rang out. "This is your father! What is your present situation?"

"Father, what are you doing here?" he replied nervously. "You weren't supposed to arrive today."

"Never mind what I'm doing here," an irate voice thundered over the speaker. "Tell me you found the boy, and that you have him."

Luchak thought for a moment. What could he say that would satisfy his father? He didn't dare tell him where he thought the boy was. He was known to be ruthless, and he didn't want the boy harmed in any way. As much as he hated to admit it, he was beginning to sympathize with the boy's plight. Regardless of what his father wanted for him, he knew he didn't have what it would take to be prince, let alone a future King.

"Well, Luchak?" the voice bellowed. "Have you found the boy, or not? What do you think I sent you to Earth for? You were supposed to keep him hidden until I arrived. We do not want Kerac to take him back to Golan."

Luchak hesitated for a few moments, before answering. "No, Father," he said, sheepishly. "I do not have him. He is somewhere on Earth, but I don't know where." He had never lied to his father, but this seemed an opportune time.

"Bring your pod alongside and come into my bay," his father ordered. "We'll look for him together. We have to locate him or all is lost. If we don't, Kerac will find him and return him to Golan. Do you understand? We can't have that. We have to make certain he stays on Earth. At least for the time being."

Meesha opened his eyes. Had he been dreaming? Could Lulla really be here? He slid off the bed, went to the bedroom door and peeked into the living room. He saw nothing out of the ordinary. Where was the gray-haired lady? Was she still asleep? He went to the French window and looked out. Two figures stood beside the gate, silhouetted by the school's security light.

"Come to me, Meesha," Lulla threw her thoughts. "We're here to take you home."

He rushed to the front door, opened it and looked out.

Hearing a slight sound in the living room, Grace walked out of the bedroom and discovered him standing next to the door. "Meesha!" she cried out. "What are you doing up? It's past midnight."

Startled, he turned and looked at her. Realizing she had no way of knowing what was happening, he pointed out the door.

She turned on a night-light and went to the door. When she looked out, she could see the two dark figures standing by the gate.

"Heavens to Betsy," she cried out. "Who are they? Are they friends of yours?"

A smile spread across his face, as if he understood.

"Well for heaven's sake, invite them in. Any friend of yours—"

Before she could finish her sentence, he had opened the front door wider and motioned to the figures.

Lulla saw his gestures. "What do you think?" she asked Kerac. "When we were communicating, he told me the people were friendly, and that he liked them very much."

"I knew I should have brought a weapon," he replied with a grin, "that is the worst kind."

"Don't be ridiculous," she whispered. "At least we can find out what they're like. I'm sure they're elderly people and won't attack us, if that's what you're worried about."

Hearing Grace's voice, and noticing the night-light in the living room through the bottom of the bedroom door, Charley got up and put on his robe.

"What's going on out here, Gracie?" he said, opening the bedroom door.

She went over and put her arm around his waist to help him to the sofa. "We have company," she said with a smile. "They're Meesha's friends…I think. Now don't make an ass of yourself."

"I wouldn't think of it," he replied. "Who are they, more aliens? You know it's dang near morning, don't you?"

Without answering she went to the door and motioned for the two figures to come inside. "Hi," she said, as they approached the porch. "Have you come for Meesha?" She put her hand to her mouth, realizing they probably couldn't understand.

Lulla extended her hand. "Yes, we have come for Meesha," she said in perfect English.

Grace's eyes lit up. "Oh, you speak our language?"

"Yes," she answered. "Meesha has not been here long enough to speak your tongue." She accepted the invitation to sit on the love seat, and Grace sat beside her. Kerac stayed at the open door staring into the darkness. "We have traveled from our parallel universe to yours many times and have learned your language. However, this is Meesha's first trip. It will take him a while to master it, but he is a fast learner."

Grace stared into her cat-eyes. "Can I offer you some coffee?" she said, not knowing what else to say.

Sitting in his favorite sofa, Charley folded his arms and leaned back. After a few moments, he held up his hand, like a schoolboy asking to go to the bathroom.

"Whoa," he said with a deep frown. "What's this parallel universe stuff?"

Lulla smiled. "It is difficult to explain so you will understand, but we, you and I, live in two different universes. Can you understand that?"

"I'm not stupid, lady. I know what a universe is," he said sharply. "But it's hard to accept that bit about you and me living in two different ones."

"We believe there could be many universes," Lulla replied. "We have only visited yours, but with our technology, I am certain we will find others in the future." She thought for a moment, and added, "When you hear of flying objects appearing and disappearing in your skies, that would more than likely be us arriving in your universe, and then leaving and returning to ours. Do you understand that?"

"No, I don't understand," he said. "How do you do that?" He thought for a moment, and then added, "And how does that little twerp show us pictures in our heads?"

"In your world, you might call it an advanced form of tactile communications," she answered with a smile. "It is the ability to communicate pictures and information to others by touch, and mind waves."

Kerac called to her in their native tongue, "Lulla, I think it's time to leave. We did not come here for a social call." He stared at her fixedly. "Now that we have found Meesha, we should be going after Luchak to get our pod back."

"Yes, I'm sorry," she answered in English, "you are right, it is time to go."

"But you haven't had your coffee," Grace complained.

Lulla rose from the love seat and walked to the door. "Possibly another time," she said with a smile. She glanced at Kerac, halfway out the door. "We have many things to do, before returning to our world." She took Meesha by the hand and led him outside. As they approached the gate she turned, and with a smile said, "I would like very much to come back some day for that coffee."

Before Kerac could close the gate, Meesha ran back to Grace standing on the porch. He looked up at her lovingly, wrapped his arms around her waist and hugged her.

Luchak had serious reservations about boarding his father's ship. However, at that moment he had very few options. He knew if he went on board his father would force him to help him hunt for Meesha. If they found him, he would hide the boy somewhere on Earth, until after the vote, then return and insist that his son be brought before Parliament to be voted on, since Meesha would not be present.

He had no hatred for Meesha; they had been casual friends on the mother-ships. Nonetheless, his father was quite adamant about him, instead of Meesha, being prince. He didn't know why his father wanted that so badly, he could only guess. Perhaps for the power a prince in the family would bring. He knew his father better than anyone, and he didn't like the idea of him having such power. It could very easily be the downfall of all the mother-ships of Golan. He already had control over most members of Parliament, at least enough to pressure them into doing his biddings. With the addition of a controllable prince, he would have all the power needed to fulfill his aspirations of becoming the most influential and powerful man on all five ships.

He picked up his communicator, and after a long, nervous sigh keyed it. “Father, I will stay on the pod for the time being. I’ll come aboard later, after we have located Meesha.” He realized his father wouldn’t go along with that, but by staying in the pod he could not be forced into bowing to his demands.

Abron’s angry voice filled the pod. “What do you mean you’ll stay in the pod? I gave you a direct order to dock with my ship! Do not play games with me, Luchak, there is too much at stake for you to disobey me now. Come aboard, at once!”

Luchak had previously pulled the pod alongside the ship and was ready to board, but when the bay door opened he veered off.

“Luchak!” an angry voice thundered through the speaker. “What are you doing? You will regret this, I promise! I will not stand for your impudence! Do you understand?”

Not knowing what else to do, Luchak activated the ion drive and took the pod into the upper limits of Earth’s ionosphere, as far as he could get from his father’s ship without leaving the gravitational influence of Earth. After he had put the pod in a high elliptical orbit around Earth, he cut the drive to make it harder to detect. Even so, he realized it would be futile to even attempt to hide from his father. With his sensitive equipment he could very easily locate him, if he wanted him badly enough. But he didn’t know what else to do; he had no other plans or places to go. On the other hand, there was one thing in his favor…he knew approximately where Meesha was, and his father did not.

Kerac had beaten a path through the thick foliage back to the ship with Lulla close behind. Meesha had been plodding along a few yards behind them.

“Meesha, come on,” she called in Golanese, “we don’t have much time left before the sun comes up. And, I’m sure by now Luchak knows where we are.”

Meesha stopped short of the ship and sat down on a moss-covered log. He glanced up the path at Lulla, who had been waiting for Kerac to open the hatch.

As the hatch opened she looked back down the path. "Come on, Meesha," she shouted, "we don't have time for this. We have to find Luchak and get our pod back." He didn't move. She walked back and sat beside him. "What's the matter? You seem tentative about coming with us."

"I don't want to leave," he said. "I would rather stay here with my friends. They are nice people. I like them."

"But Meesha, you can't stay. You must come with us to hunt for Luchak. We all have to go back to Golan together."

"I don't want to go back to Golan," he cried out. "I don't want to be prince. I want to stay here where I have friends."

She put her arm around his shoulder. "Meesha, I can understand your feelings, but you must go back your father demands that you to be prince. He has decreed it. You must not go against his authority."

"I know nothing about being a prince, or a King."

"You would be taught," she said, squeezing his shoulder. "Your father is very ill. I'm afraid he won't be with us much longer. He has chosen you to take his place. But first you must be voted in as prince. Do you not wish to honor your father?"

"I do not want to go back to Golan," he said stubbornly. "I want to stay here on Earth. Why can't I stay with my new friends? I have no friends on Golan. Because I'm the King's son, they all talk about me. It hurts when they say bad things about me."

"But Meesha, there is nothing you can do about being the King's son. It is something you have no control over." She glanced through the boughs of the tall fir trees at the fading stars in the night sky. "Your uncle made your father a promise. He said he would keep you on Earth until the vote was ready to be taken, and then bring you back to Golan. Do you want to get your uncle in trouble with your father?"

"Lulla! Meesha! Come on!" a voice thundered through the open hatch. "We have to go. Luchak is certain to find us if we stay here much longer. We have to take off immediately!"

She took Meesha by the hand, pulled him off the log and gently pushed him toward the ship. When they reached the outer hatch, he pulled free and quickly ran into the underbrush. Stunned by his swift, defiant move she could only watch as he disappeared into the darkness.

"Meesha! Meesha!" she shouted.

Kerac heard her calls and looked around the corner of the hatch. "What's the matter, Lulla?" he demanded. "Where's Meesha?"

"He ran away," she yelled. "He wanted to stay with the gray-haired lady. I couldn't stop him." Kerac shook his head and started to go after him, but she grabbed his arm as he went by. "It's too late! You would never find him in this darkness. We have to leave."

"You're right," he said. "I guess if he stays with those people he'll be safe from Luchak…at least for the time being. We're the only ones who know where he is."

"We think we're the only ones," she replied cynically.

Luchak leaned back in the chair and closed his eyes. He didn't want anything bad to happen to Meesha, but he knew if his father found him he would do everything in his power to keep him from returning to Golan. He was ruthless. He had known of his pressuring the senators to do his biddings, on many occasions. He would do anything to meet his agenda.

A musical tone interrupted his thoughts. He opened his eyes and looked down at the console. Green LEDs blinked rapidly on the program he had installed to monitor Meesha's brainwaves. He checked the coordinates, and with deft fingers flipped a few switches and pushed several lighted buttons. Instantly, the pod turned and headed for Earth. He had him now, he thought. Meesha and Lulla had been communicating a few minutes ago, and his sensors had locked onto their waves and stored them.

Before Kerac could bring his ship up to full power to lift off, Luchak's pod had stopped a few feet above him and hovered over him like an umbrella. The sheer force of his anti-gravity engine had pinned Kerac's powered-down ship to the ground.

Luchak's voice boomed over a speaker, "Kerac!" he shouted. "I want to help you find Meesha. I have to speak to you! Secure your ship and I'll come aboard."

"Luchak!" Kerac shouted back angrily. "What's the meaning of this? I have nothing to say to you, except that you have my pod and I want it back."

"I will return it when you totally secure your engines," Luchak replied. "I must warn you, my father is here on Earth and he's also looking for the boy. Right now he's probably listening in on our conversation. Please, do as I ask, before he comes after the both of us. I've made him extremely angry, by telling him I didn't want to go with him to hunt for Meesha."

Kerac looked at Lulla and sighed. "What do we have to lose? He can't harm us. If he's telling the truth about wanting to help, we could certainly use him on our side."

"I suppose you're right," she said with a deep sigh. "But I can't say I trust him. Not after the sneaky way he kidnapped Meesha and stole our pod. But at least we'll get it back."

"I don't trust him either, but what's the alternative?" he asked. "If he found us so can his father. And I'm certain he'll be coming after us, thinking we have the boy." He pushed the mike button. "All right, Luchak. But I'll be watching every move you make."

Luchak cut the ion drive and his ship settled gently to the ground. After being certain Kerac's ship was powerless, he opened the hatch and saw him standing beside the pod with a stern look. Cautiously, he walked toward him.

"Now, what's going on?" Kerac demanded. "You said your father was here? Where is he? And what's he here for, Meesha, you, or both?"

"Yes, he's here and I knew where a few minutes ago," Luchak replied. "The last I saw of him he was in Earth's ionosphere waiting for darkness so he could go down and try to locate Meesha's brain waves. He will stop at nothing to find him. We'll have to make certain he doesn't."

"Then there's no time to lose," Kerac said, excited by the thought of a battle of wits with the senator. "Pull the pod into the bay and we'll go after him, before he finds us."

"I don't think we'll have to worry about him finding us, I believe he already knows where we are," Luchak answered. "I'm sure he's been monitoring my moves, ever since I defied him. I'm almost certain he knows where we are."

"Then we'll have to take off, before he gets here," Kerac stated. "I know his ship is fully loaded with weapons, but so is mine. Let's hope neither of us has to use them."

He rushed to the helm and prepared for take off. After the engine had come up to full power, Lulla threaded the ship through the large boughs of second-growth timber, and then hovered a few moments above the tree line, while she set in the coordinates.

Luchak looked at Kerac with a frown. "The sensors in the pod told me Meesha was with you after you landed on Earth," he said. "What happened? Where is he now?"

"It's a long story," Kerac replied, "one I don't have time to go into right now. He's in a safe place on earth, where I don't believe your father will find him. He will have to rely on us, if he wants him. And, we'll do everything in our power to make certain he doesn't get him."

Luchak leaned back in the seat and stared at the massive array of pipes and tubing running across the silver-lined overhead. He closed his eyes in thought. What was Kerac up to? He couldn't go back to Golan without Meesha. If he did, Parliament would be forced to vote for someone else…probably him…if he ever got back himself. That would make his father happy, but not him. Before, his sensors had told him that Meesha was somewhere in the area where Kerac had landed before, but with the pods limited technology he couldn't pinpoint the exact location. However, he figured Kerac knew what he was doing, so he'd play along with him, at least for now. He opened his eyes, when he heard the ion drive engage, and felt the slight jolt of the ship as it darted into the night sky.

After they obtained orbit, Lulla noticed a fast moving blip on her screen. "Kerac!" she yelled. "Do you see that blip in the scanner? I believe it's the senator."

"Yes, I see it!" he yelled back. "We have to take evasive actions, immediately!"

Kerac applied full power to the ion thruster and the ship darted into the outer limits of space. On its way up, it sailed past Abron's ship as if it were standing still. He headed for the location where he could make a vortex, but when he arrived at the coordinates, Abron's ship had fallen in behind him and closing on him fast. He made a 360-degree turn and pointed his bow directly at Abron's fast approaching ship. A blazing shaft of plasma shot from Abron's ship, barely missing them as he sped by.

Kerac turned his ship quickly, to avoid being fired on again so close to the vortex coordinates; a blast from an ion gun could very easily damage the wormhole to the point where it would be temporarily out of order. As he turned the ship away, another searing shaft shot by his ship, narrowly missing.

"Kerac, that shot was intended for our ion grid," she shouted. "He's trying to disable us. I guess he thought we were going to make a vortex and leave Earth."

He shook his head "Yes, I know. But two can play that game!" He went back into outer space, stopped a few thousand miles above Earth and waited for the senator to catch up. He had been told Abron's ship was outfitted with a retro-drive, in addition to an up-to-date ion engine, which made it a much faster ship than his, at least in Earth's atmosphere. Even so, he had something up his sleeve. When Abron's ship was within firing range, he shot off at a right angle and headed for Earth. Obligingly, Abron followed, but out of range of Kerac's aft weapons. When Abron's ship was positioned directly behind him and ready to fire an ion salvo, Kerac applied full reverse power to his bow thrusters and the senator darted by him at an incredible speed. Abron suddenly found himself in danger of Kerac's forward guns. Kerac took advantage of his successful maneuver and made ready to fire.

It didn't take Abron long to realize what had happened, and the dangerous situation he had put himself in. Instantly, he veered away and headed deep into outer space. Kerac chased after him, his weapons fully charged and ready for any error in judgment the senator might make.

Both ships raced across the night sky, each waiting for the other to make a fatal miscalculation. After several futile attempts to dominate the other, the confrontation ended in a stalemate. Both ships came to rest several hundred miles apart, slightly out of ion firing ranges.

"Kerac!" the senator's voice sounded over a speaker. "Don't play games with me. I want my son back, immediately! If you let me come aboard, we can discuss it."

"I think not," Kerac shot back.

There was a long pause, and then Abron's voice returned. "I will only talk to you in person," he said. "Let me come aboard and we can resolve this little matter."

"Little matter?" Kerac yelled back. "This is not a 'little matter', this is one that could very easily determine the future of the ships of Golan."

"Don't be so naïve, Kerac, you know very well Meesha is not prepared to be prince, let alone King. He is hardly old enough to play with toys, let alone govern us."

"And I'm supposed to believe Luchak is?"

There was a lengthy pause before Abron replied. "Yes! With my help, he could very easily govern. If you have not forgotten, I am the senior Member of Parliament. The others would follow me."

"That's what I'm afraid of, Senator."

"Have no misgivings, Kerac," Abron bellowed, "it's only a matter of time, before I have complete control over Parliament. The Prime Minister is weak and can easily be controlled…or replaced."

"I may consider your request, Senator," Kerac said. "But give me some time to think it over."

"Make it quick," Abron demanded. "I'm sure Golan will be sending someone after me, as soon as they figure out where I have gone, if they haven't already. As you must have figured out by now, I defied the Prime Minister and Parliament by coming here."

"I would never have guessed!" Kerac replied sarcastically.

NINE

It had been a long, cold night and Meesha had left Grace's house early that morning with nothing on but bib-coveralls, tennis shoes, a baseball cap and a red plaid shirt, all donated by Grace's grandchildren, from one of their rare visits.

After running away from Lulla, he had hunkered down in a hollowed out log to wait for the warmth of the morning sun. He had no idea where he was, or even how to get back to the house. The thought of backtracking from where Kerac's ship had taken off had crossed his mind, but even if he could find the landing site he wouldn't have the slightest idea which way to go to get back to the house.

He left the hollow log and wandered aimlessly through the darkness, fighting for footing in the midst of fallen tree limbs and overgrown brush. While searching for another place to rest, he spotted a small fire faintly visible through the tangled underbrush. Cautiously, he approached it.

Peeking through the branches of a hazelnut bush, he noticed an old man sitting beside a fire stirring a large black pot with a stick. Curled up beside him was what he believed to be a small, male dog with one eye closed; he had only seen pictures of dogs, they had none on Golan. As he leaned into the bushes to get a better look, he accidentally broke a branch and it made a loud snapping sound.

The dog's other eye popped open and he jumped to his feet. He stared into the darkness, growled several times, and then barked. The old man quit stirring for a moment and sat motionless, eying the darkness. After several moments he appeared satisfied that it was nothing important and went back to stirring.

"Hush, Corky!" he snapped at the dog. "Ain't nothin' out there worth worryin' about. You're gonna wake the whole dang neighborhood, you keep barkin' like that."

The dog stopped barking and stood motionless, the hair on his back standing up straight. He stared in Meesha's direction for several moments, eyed the darkness once more, and then moved closer to the old man.

The man reached down and rubbed his neck. "Here, dog, have some of this fine stew I concocted. I got the recipe from my dear old grandmother rest her soul." He reached into his duffle bag and pulled out a large spoon and two bowls. After filling the bowls half full of the thick, dark mixture, he set one in front of the dog. "Careful, Corky, it's hot as hell, you'll get pizza mouth."

Meesha could smell the stew and his mouth salivated. He hadn't realized how hungry he really was, until the scent wafted in his direction. His stomach growled and churned, as he envisioned a steaming bowl of whatever it was in front of the old man. If only he had the courage to approach and ask him for food. However, he could not speak his language, and the dog appeared to be guarding both the old man and the food.

Half hidden in the bushes, he peeked through the branches to make a quick study of the old man. By the light of the campfire he looked ancient. He had two deep creases in the sides of his face that ran from the corners of his eyes down his cheeks and ending at the corners of his mouth. A short, white beard with patches of dark stain around his mouth covered most of his face. He didn't look dangerous, he thought. Nonetheless, he was hesitant about approaching to ask for food. What about the dog was it dangerous?

His foot slipped on the damp soil and he let go of the branch he had been holding onto for support, and it rustled up against the others, making a loud swishing sound in the quietness. The dog stopped eating, stared at the bush for a moment, and then started barking.

"What's gotten into you, dog?" the old man yelled. He reached into his pocket, pulled out a plug of chewing tobacco and bit off a small chunk. "Ain't nothin' to fret about, it's just some kid hidin' in the bushes over there." He pointed in Meesha's direction. "That's right. I know he's out there. Go get him, Corky. Bring him over here by the fire, it's cold as hell out there."

As if the dog understood, he crept slowly toward Meesha. When he was within a few feet of the bush, he looked directly at him and growled.

Meesha stared into the animal's eyes, not knowing what to do or what to expect. He moved his hand toward the dog and let it sniff his fingers.

"Hey, boy," the old man yelled out, and motioned with his hand. "Come on over and get warm. I don't bite."

Meesha could not understand his words, but he had recognized the friendly gesture and moved hesitantly toward him. He stopped for a moment in front of the fire pit to feel its warmth, and then shifted his eyes to the old man sitting on the log next to it.

"Well, don't just stand there boy," the old man said. "Sit down and get yourself warm." He pointed to a log next to the fire, and then spit a long stream of tobacco juice into the flames.

He looked at the old man tentatively, and then slowly sat down on the log. He stared at him for a few moments, and then shifted his eyes to the empty bowl in front of the dog.

The man noticed his inspection of the bowl and said, "Corky, bring your bowl over here." Wagging its tail, it grabbed the edge of the bowl with its teeth, carried it over and dropped it in front of him. Meesha looked on with eagerness, as the old man wiped the inside of the bowl with a cloth and poured several steaming ladles into it. He reached into his backpack, pulled out a spoon and handed it to him.

Meesha devoured the stew, as if he hadn't eaten forever, which he felt was almost the truth. He looked up and smiled, then continued eating

The old man was taken back by the boy's eating gusto, and watched in amusement as he quickly devoured the contents of the bowl. He had noticed his facial peculiarities, but said nothing. He reached into his backpack, pulled out a handful of cookies and handed them to him.

"Them there's corn doggies," he said. "Best you'll ever eat." He leaned toward the fire pit, spit the remains of the tobacco into its flames and put one in his mouth.

Meesha bit into the round object and the sweetness of molasses made his face glow. His thoughts flashed back to Grace and the pancakes she had made for him and Charley.

The old man cocked his head and fixed his eyes on him. "So, young fellow, what brings you way out here in the woods? Don't get many visitors you know, especially at this hour of mornin'. Most of 'em come here lookin' for ferns to cut and sell, or camp meat to shoot." He continued to stare at the boy. "You're not very talkative are you, boy? Cat got your tongue?" He snickered, seeing the resemblance.

Meesha realized he was being asked questions, but he had no way to understand or answer. If only he had learned their language before leaving Golan, he thought. His father's quick decision to hide him on earth had not allowed the time to have the mental procedure done, necessary to learn it. He had picked up a few words by listening to Charley and Grace, but not enough to hold on a conversation.

As he sat watching the red and yellow flames devouring the wood, his mind wandered back to Lulla and Kerac. Where were they? Had they gone back to Golan? He didn't think so his father would be very displeased if they returned without him. Lulla had tried to take him back, but because of his obstinacy he had fled into the forest. He only hoped his actions wouldn't get his uncle in trouble with his father, the King.

"What's your name, boy?" the old man's voice interrupted his thoughts. "I can't call you boy all night. Mine's Daniel, but everybody calls me Digger. Don't know exactly why, but they do." He thought for a moment, swished a twig through the dying embers, and then added, "Maybe it's 'cause I been pannin' gold up here in my little creek for so many years. That must be it. You see I got this little stream by my shack that's loaded with gold nuggets the size of golf balls. Everybody tries to find out where they are, but I ain't tellin' a soul. Not a soul." He looked over and smiled. "'Ceptin' maybe you, but you won't tell anybody, will you?"

Corky got up, walked over to Meesha, sniffed his legs and lay down beside him. He looked up, stuck his tongue out and panted. Meesha reached down and rubbed his neck.

"I can see Corky's taken a hankerin' to you," Digger said, as he threw another small log onto the dying embers. "He ain't friendly toward many people. He growls at 'em a lot. Of course he's too dang small to do much else." He chuckled. "He ain't much of a watchdog, you know."

Meesha could tell by his body language he had asked for his name. He pointed his finger at him, and said, "Digger?"

"That's right, my name's Digger, and that's Corky," he answered, pointing a long, arthritic finger at the small dog. "What's yours?" He moved his finger back and forth between them.

Meesha got to his feet, walked over and guardedly laid his finger on the man's forehead. Surprisingly, he didn't pull away. As soon as it touched his brow, images of a middle-aged woman flashed into the old man's mind. Startled, he pulled back and looked at the boy in disbelief. After a few moments, he allowed him to continue. He saw a woman pushing a swing, and she called out, "Meesha! Meesha!"

"Meesha? That's your name?" he asked, turning to look at the boy. "How did you do that?"

Meesha nodded and smiled. "Digger…Meesha…Corky," he said, pointing at each of them and repeating, "Digger…Corky…Meesha."

Digger pointed his finger at his head, as if wanting to see more pictures.

Meesha understood and put his finger back on his brow. Suddenly, vivid images of a strange world overwhelmed the old man's mind. Then, the scene changed to him running from the spaceship.

"Well I'll be danged!" Digger said. "So, you're from somewhere out there, huh?" He pointed to the sky. "And you're hiding from somebody?" He got up from the log, kicked at the ashes in the campfire and doused them with the remains of the coffee pot. "Well if that's the case you better come with me. We'll go to my shack. Ain't nobody'll come up there. I got a twelve-gauge shotgun and I ain't afraid to use it." He picked up his backpack and cooking utensils and headed up the well-beaten path. He looked back at the boy still sitting on the log. "Come on boy…Meesha, let's go. They won't get you where we're goin'." Halfway up the slope, he pulled out his plug of tobacco and bit off another chunk.

As the sun slowly crept over the tree line on the distant mountain, the small town of Grande Ronde began to bustle with activity. Morning breakfasts had been devoured, and children were standing alongside the country roads waiting for school busses.

Grace had put the finishing touches on Charley's breakfast, and about to join him, when a knock came at the door. She looked through the kitchen window and saw two women standing on the porch peeking through the glass door.

"Maggie, Jan, how nice to see you," she said, opening the door. "Please, come in. Won't you join Charley and me in a cup of coffee? We're just sitting down to breakfast." She escorted them into the kitchen and pulled two chairs out from under the table. "What brings you here? I'll bet it has something to do with what your girls must have told you about the boy. Right?" The women stared down at empty cups, outwardly embarrassed.

After their cups had been filled, Maggie looked up and said, "Gracie, there's a few things we don't understand about what the girls told us. Maybe you could fill us in, if you don't mind."

Grace took a long sip of coffee and stared across the table. "What's on your minds, ladies? If there's anything I can tell you that will satisfy your curiosities, feel free to ask."

Jan lifted the cup to her lips, and without drinking set it down on the table. "Gracie, our daughters told us you have a strange young boy staying with you." She ran a nervous finger around the rim of her cup. "I know it's none of our business, but what they told us about him was slightly disturbing. Anyway, it sounded strange to us. Maybe you could shed some light on it, if you don't mind. What they told us seemed impossible."

"And what did they tell you?" Grace said, putting her elbows on the table and leaning forward.

Maggie fidgeted with her spoon, and then looked over. "They told us the boy had extraordinary powers. That he could make them see strange things in their minds. And, that he was from a spaceship of all things." She giggled and took a small sip to hide her uneasiness.

Grace looked over at Charley. "Do you want to fill them in?"

"No!" he said obstinately. He wolfed down the remains of his breakfast, picked up his coffee cup, limped into the living room and plunked his aging body down on his favorite sofa. He turned on the TV, switched to his favorite channel and leaned back to enjoy a rerun of "I Love Lucy". After a few seconds he yelled from the sofa, "That's your problem, Gracie, leave me out of it."

"Yes, girls, he was here," she agreed. "But he's gone now. They came and got him."

"Who?" Maggie asked. "Who came and got him?"

"I don't rightly know who they were…some relatives, I guess."

Maggie continued her inquiry. "Was he really from where he said he was from…a spaceship, or were the girls having fun at our expense?"

"I don't rightly know," Grace said with a shrug. "But he showed us the same things he probably showed your girls. Charley and I saw things that seemed impossible."

"What do you mean?" Maggie asked, raising her eyebrows. "What did he show you?"

"Well, for one thing, he showed us where he came from, and yes it was a spaceship. At least that's what he showed us, and that's what it appeared to be."

"That's impossible," Jan said. "There are no spaceships. At least I don't think so."

Grace got up from the table, brought the coffee pot back and refreshed their cups. "Well, draw your own conclusions, ladies. But he definitely showed me and Charley a spaceship. He also showed us how he ended up here in Grande Ronde."

"What do you mean?" Jan said with a frown.

Grace leaned across the table, looked into their eyes and explained everything that had happened; how she had found him beside the road, and how he had discovered Charley's medical problem

"Where is he now?" Maggie asked.

"I don't rightly know. I suppose he's with his folks. At least some people came and got him this morning, about two o'clock."

"Did you see them?" Jan asked.

"Yes, of course," Grace answered. "Somehow, they contacted him. They stood by the gate and I invited them in for coffee. Lulla, that's the woman's name, wanted some but they didn't have time. Although she did say someday she would come back and take me up on the offer." She blew steam from her cup and took another sip.

"This all seems so utterly impossible," Maggie cut in. "Especially when you consider it happened here in little old Grande Ronde. Why here, of all places? We're such an insignificant little town. I could understand it more if it happened in another place, but not here in Grande Ronde, Oregon."

"Well, that's it ladies," Grace concluded. "I've told you everything. It's up to you to believe or not to believe."

"Is he coming back?" Jan asked.

"I don't rightly know. But I doubt it."

The girls got up and Grace walked them to the door.

"Gracie," Maggie said, "we believe you, but what you told us would be hard for anybody else to swallow, especially if it came from us." She giggled.

"You don't have to tell anybody else," Grace informed her. "Why don't we keep this our little secret, at least for now? I'll definitely let you know if anything of interest happens in the future." She opened the door and they left.

Charley yelled over the din of the TV, "Did you tell them everything?"

"Yes. But I don't think they believed half of it."

"Good! Then maybe they won't be spreadin' it all over town. Especially if they think it might embarrass them." He turned back to the antics of Lucy.

“Kerac!” Abron’s voice thundered over a speaker on the bridge. “I’ve given you more than enough time to make up your mind. What’s your decision? Can I come aboard? We have to talk.”

“Very well,” Kerac replied, “but come alone. Leave your men on the ship. Bring your pod to the hangar bay and I’ll open it. But no weapons! Agreed?”

“Agreed! I’ll be there in a few minutes. Open your bay door.”

“So, little fellow, you’re bein’ chased by bad guys, huh?” Digger said, opening the door to the shack. “Well, they won’t find you here, that’s for sure. Nobody comes up here ‘less they’re tryin’ to get my gold. And they know I guard it well…me and my shotgun. Ain’t nobody comin’ up here it wouldn’t be healthy for ‘em. Know what I mean?”

Meesha walked into the shack and looked around. The first thing he noticed was a mounted deer head on the wall. He stood in front of it, a strange look on his face. He reached up and touched the soft hair on its neck, then looked back at Digger.

Digger watched him stroked the deer’s head. Noticing his bewilderment, he cleared his throat and said, “That there’s a deer, son. Don’t suppose you have ‘em where you come from. We got lots of ‘em here in Oregon. Good to eat. Matter of fact I’ll go to the smokehouse and get us some venison. I’m sure you’re still hungry, after only havin’ that little bowl of stew.” He knew the boy couldn’t understand him, but at least it was somebody to talk to. “Come here and sit down at the table while I light a fire in the woodstove.” He slid an old, slightly broken rattan chair up to the table and pointed at it. “After I get this dang thing draftin’, I’ll get us some grub.” He blew on the tinder in the combustion chamber until it had ignited, then threw several sticks of kindling on top of it and closed the cast-iron door. “I got chickens too, how about some nice scrambled eggs to go with that venison?”

He rushed through the door and up the steep incline to a dilapidated smokehouse next to a chicken-wire coop where a dozen hens were pecking at their breakfasts, and another dozen lying in small straw beds.

Corky nudged the door open. He looked around, then trotted over and curled up at the boy's feet.

Meesha reached down and rubbed his neck, and he rolled over on his back. He figured the dog wanted to play and tickled his stomach. His hind legs flailed wildly in the air, as if he were chasing something. He had often wondered why they didn't have pets on the mother-ships, then he remembered they only had room for people the pets had to be left behind they would have taken up too much valuable space. Even his pet, Rodo, quite similar to Earth's squirrel, had to be left behind. Only animals used for food were taken on board.

Digger returned with a small slab of smoked venison and a dozen eggs. He put them in the sink and went to the stove to check on the fire. Not satisfied with its progress, he swung the cast iron door open and blew on the kindling. When it finally caught, he shoved several small logs onto the raging inferno.

"Fire's gettin' hot now," he said. "We'll be eatin' 'fore you can say Jack Frost."

Meesha looked at him curiously. "Jack Frost?" he mouthed the words.

"Yeah, Jack Frost, that's an old sayin', here on Earth. It means when the frost comes…I guess. See, you <u>can</u> speak our language." He took the venison from the sink, put it on the waxed tablecloth and hacked off several pieces with a large cleaver.

Suddenly, Meesha put his hands to his head, moaned loudly and rocked back and forth on the chair.

Digger stopped cutting long enough to stare at him. "What's the matter, boy, you got ants in your pants? What's goin' on?"

Meesha leaned back and closed his eyes.

"I hear you, Lulla," he threw his thoughts back. "I understand and I will stay here. I am with a nice old man. He will not let the senator get me. He has a shotgun and a dog." Her thoughts faded away. He looked over at Digger and said, "Lulla…friend."

"You were just talking to somebody, were you?"

"Lulla…friend."

TEN

After Abron entered Kerac's hangar bay, he secured his pod and stormed onto the bridge. "Where is my son?" he demanded. "And where is Meesha? Where are they?"

"Your son is in my quarters," Kerac replied coldly. "I don't know where Meesha is."

"Don't give me that!" Abron bellowed. "I know Meesha is here. You got him when you landed on Earth. My sensors told me you landed in the northwest corner of the United States. Why else would you land, if not to pick him up? Where is he?"

"I only have your son," Kerac stated flatly. "I don't have Meesha. I don't know where he is. He's somewhere down there. Even if I knew, I wouldn't tell you."

"Then if you don't have him, or know where he is," Abron shouted, "I'll take my son back to Golan and let Parliament vote for him."

"I think not!" Lulla yelled across the bridge. "He doesn't want to go back with you."

"Don't be stupid, Lulla, I'm a Senator!" he shouted, glaring at her. "I will not put up with your insolence and disrespect. Do you understand? Besides, you have no say in this matter, it's between Kerac and me."

"Stupid or not, I won't let you take either of them back!" she yelled. "Neither of them wants to be prince." She pulled a stun gun from a drawer and pointed it at him. "Do you hear me, Senator? Your son does not want to be prince, and neither does Meesha. You should honor their wishes."

"Honor their wishes?" he exploded. "I don't have to honor their wishes!"

She glared at him. "I don't think you have much choice in the matter."

"My son will not defy me again he will do as I say!" Abron screamed at her.

"I believe your son has finally realized you're only interested in being the most powerful man on Golan, and you'll stop at nothing to achieve that." She glared at him and lowered the weapon.

"If you don't have Meesha, then bring Luchak to the bridge!" he demanded. "I will take him back and <u>make</u> Parliament vote for him. I still have the power."

"I think not!" Kerac growled. "He doesn't want to go back with you!"

"He's my son!" Abron shouted in his face. "You can't keep him here. I forbid it!"

Kerac stared at him defiantly. "Luchak is eighteen years old and quite capable of making up his own mind," he said. "He does not want to return with you, and that's final!" He walked over, snatched the weapon out of Lulla's hand and pointed it at him. "You can leave now, Senator. There are still a few days left, before the deadline to bring the boys back. If you returned now with only Luchak, what would you tell them about Meesha? I'm sure you would say you couldn't find him and put the blame on us."

Abron stared at the weapon. Realizing his demand was not working, he turned and walked toward the hangar bay.

"I will remember this, Kerac!" he shouted, halfway down the passageway. "You can count on that!" He got into his pod and went back to his ship.

When he returned, his two-man crew glanced at him, but said nothing. They knew better than to question him. They had been with him long enough to know that if they made any derogatory comments, he would make them pay for it.

"First Officer Nader!" he shouted, as he walked across the bridge and slumped down in the Captain's Chair.

The tall man at the helm looked over. "Yes sir."

"Did you get Kerac's coordinates, when he landed in Oregon?"

"Yes sir, but it's only approximate...within a mile or so."

"Record it carefully," Abron replied. "When it gets dark enough we'll go down and look for the boy. If I find him, I can exchange him for my son."

"Kerac has your son on board his ship?" the First Mate asked cautiously.

"Yes, and he will not give him up."

Nader turned his head to hide a smug grin, and said, "We could disable his ship...so he couldn't return to Golan. We have the ability."

"I know that," Abron snorted, "but I don't want to make Tumac any angrier than he already is. He and Parliament would come down hard on me, if I took such actions. Kerac is still the King's brother, you know. Parliament might not vote for my son, if I were to return with only him. Especially if they found out we disabled his ship." He glared at his First Mate. "I'm sure you're aware that if Meesha is not available Parliament can vote for my son."

"Yes sir, I'm quite aware of it," Nader replied." Nonetheless, if you made an exchange, Kerac could still return with Meesha in time for the vote. And, if he did Parliament would vote for him." He paused for a moment, and then said, "Do you really believe we can find the boy? We don't have the best long-range brain wave equipment on board. We might have to try to get close to his location, then rely on a manual search."

"I'm positive he's not too far from where Kerac landed before," Abron declared. "His ship must have left a footprint in that forest. At least, we have the equipment to detect that. We'll find him." He sneered. "To answer your question, I do not intend to let Kerac return to Golan ahead of us with Meesha. Period!"

"Then do you want us to stay out of Earth's radar range until it's dark down there?"

"That would be the most logical thing, don't you think?" Abron replied callously. He slid from the Captain's Chair and stormed off the bridge.

ELEVEN

It was early afternoon, and school had been let out for the day. While the children waited in the yard for busses, the boys played soccer in the small field, and the girls congregated in front of the Bertell house to skip rope on the only concrete sidewalk available. Occasionally, the girls would glance up at the French window, hoping to see Meesha, but he never showed.

Grace had noticed the girls looking at the window and went to the door. "Girls," she yelled. "Meesha is gone. He left early this morning."

"Where did he go?" a dark-haired girl asked. "Did he go back to his spaceship?"

Grace chuckled. "I guess so, sweetie."

"Is he coming back?"

"I don't rightly know, maybe someday."

The girls huddled together for a moment, and then one of them turned and said, "Mrs. Bertell, if he returns will you let us know? We liked him."

"Oh course, dear. Now go to your busses they just arrived."

Charley was sitting in his favorite sofa watching television, when Grace came into the living room. "What was that all about?" he asked.

She lowered her aging body into her Belcher, picked up the Oregonian newspaper and briefly scanned the pages.

"Guess the girls liked the little guy," she said. "They wanted to know where he was, and if he was coming back."

"And what did you tell them that he went back to his spaceship?" He laughed.

"I didn't know what else to tell them."

He picked up the remote and switched channels.

As the sun descended behind the highest mountains on the western horizon, the late afternoon quickly turned into evening, and semi-darkness invaded the little town of Grande Ronde.

Night foraging owls sat on their perches in the highest branches, searching the forest floor for small game, and high-flying buzzards scanned the meadows for dead carcasses. The little town had settled in for the evening.

"Kerac," Lulla called, turning to look at him. "I think it's dark enough down there to go after Meesha?"

"Not yet," he replied. "Besides, you know very well if we go down we'll lead Abron to him. I don't want that to happen."

"Of course not, you're right," she answered. "However, now that we have Luchak, we shouldn't wait too much longer. If we returned with both boys, Parliament would be very pleased. Don't you think?"

"Yes, they would. However, I don't trust the senator," he said. "If we picked up Meesha, he would go to great lengths to keep us from returning home. I wouldn't put it past him to try to disable us, so we couldn't return."

"For what purpose?" she asked. "He wants Luchak to be there for the vote. As long as we have him, he would have to let us return."

"Lulla, think for a moment, if he were to disable us, he could very easily make us give Luchak up for the repair of our ship, and the return home. He could then take him back for the vote. If I know him, like I believe I do, he would take his time asking Parliament to send a ship for us. But the damage would have already been done they would have voted for Luchak, and he would be prince-in-waiting. If that were to happen, Abron would most likely be in command of the mother-ships. That wouldn't be good. By the time we returned, he would have had Parliament swayed in his favor."

"Then what do you suggest?"

He thought for a moment. "When you communicated with Meesha, didn't he tell you he was with somebody he trusted?"

"Yes. It was a man with a shotgun and a dog, deep in the forest in an old shack. Why?"

"Try to communicate with him, again," he suggested. "Tell him to go where we landed before. Hopefully, he will remember how to get back there. We could make a quick landing, pick him up and be on our way before the senator found us."

"You really think he would go back to that spot to be picked up?" she asked. "If he didn't want to come with us before, I don't believe he would now."

Giving her a disgusted look, he said, "Try again, we have nothing to lose."

Each night Digger and Corky would go to their favorite campsite for their evening meal, and that night was no exception, regardless of the circumstances. With Meesha trailing behind, they headed for the site. When they arrived, Corky curled up beside the fire with one eye open, and Digger sat on his favorite log next to the fire peeling potatoes.

Meesha went into the forest to gather firewood. When he returned he dropped a few limbs on the fire and sat on a log next to it to warm his hands. Suddenly, he started to moan and rock back and forth on the log.

Digger stopped peeling and looked over. "Are you talking to somebody again, boy?" he asked. "If you are, tell 'em to come on down and get some grub, there's plenty to go around." He chuckled, as he filled the huge frying pan with venison, onions and potatoes.

Meesha closed his eyes and images of Lulla at her computer, and Kerac standing behind her invaded his mind's eye.

"Meesha!" he heard her call. "Can you hear me? I have something important to tell you."

He threw his thoughts back. "Yes, Lulla, I can hear you."

"Kerac wants you to go back to where we landed before. We'll pick you up there. But we have to make it quick or the senator will know where we are."

"Please don't come for me," he sent back, "I am happy here. I have made many friends and do not wish to leave. Go back without me. Take Luchak and let him be prince. My father would understand."

"We can't do that," she replied, "Parliament insisted we bring you both back. Your uncle would be in a lot of trouble, if you didn't return with us. Do you understand?"

"I understand and I am sorry," he answered, "but I do not wish to return to the mother-ship." He cleared Lulla's thoughts from his mind, opened his eyes and looked over at Digger, then down at Corky lying at his feet. They were his friends and he knew he could make many more, if they didn't force him to go back to the ship.

Digger filled a metal plate with a helping and handed it to him. "Were you talking to your friend again?" he asked, setting a small bowl down in front of Corky.

Meesha pointed at his head. "Lulla…friend."

"We have a problem," Lulla said, looking at Kerac with a scowl. "He won't go to the landing area. He still doesn't want to go back to Golan. What can we do?"

Kerac went to the helm and stood there motionless, staring through a porthole at the blues and whites of Earth. He turned and said, "I believe it's dark enough now. Let's go where we landed before. We'll wait in the ship, until you locate his waves. Then, if you find him, I'll bring him back forcibly, if necessary."

"Do you really think you can make him come with you?" she asked. "He said the old man had a shotgun and a dog."

"Do you think an old relic like a shotgun is going to stop me?" he answered.

"I don't want you to harm that old man in any way," she said firmly. "Do you understand?" She stared at him angrily for a few moments, then turned to her console and plotted a course for Oregon.

After they had finished eating, Meesha walked to the edge of the clearing to relieve himself. While standing behind a tree, he heard a faint sound a few feet away. Frightened, he hurried back to the campfire and pointed into the darkness. Corky had heard the sound and started barking.

Unmoved by the commotion, Digger picked up a long stick and swished it back and forth through the hot coals. "Hush, dog," he yelled and threw the stick at him. "Ain't nothin' out there that can hurt us, it's just that old half-breed Injun tryin' to sneak up on us. He ain't as good as he used to be, you know. He used to get within a foot or so, before you even knew he was there. He's some Injun, that Quasi." He looked up, and with aging eyes scanned the bushes. "Come on in here, Injun, get somethin' to eat. I got somebody I want you to meet."

The bushes parted at the edge of the clearing and a huge figure with a slightly hunched back emerged, dressed in bib-style buckskins and carrying a rifle. Not saying a word, he moved up close to the fire and stuck his large, callused hands nearly into the flames to warm them. He looked at Digger and nodded, then glanced over at the boy and winked.

"That's Quasi," Digger said, looking at Meesha and pointing at the big man. "I think he was named after that hunch-back, Quasimodo, in the book about Notre Dame. At least, that's what they tell me. 'Cause of his hunched back, I guess." He hesitated for a moment, and then continued. "I read it when I was a mere tyke, but I don't remember much about it. He's the best danged tracker you'll ever find in these parts, though. Ex when he's had a few drinks." He looked at the boy and chuckled. "That venison you ate was shot by him…skinned and dressed, too." He looked at the big man and pointed to Meesha. "That's my new friend over there, Injun." He picked up a fairly clean plate, filled it with the leftovers of the meal and handed it to him.

Quasi took the food and sat on the log next to the boy. He turned, fixed his dark, almost black eyes on him and held out his hand. Meesha looked at the large, rough hand, and glanced over at Digger. He held his hand there for several seconds then dropped it, shrugged and continued to eat.

Meesha stared up at the big man. He had never seen anyone so large. As he scanned his long, golden face, his eyes stopped briefly at his nose, which looked like the picture of a hawk he had once seen in his mind. His jaws looked as if they had been carved out of a block of granite. From what he could see in the semi-darkness, his eyes were jet-black.

"What's your name, boy," Quasi mumbled through a mouthful.

"He don't talk much, Injun," Digger volunteered. "He's not from around these parts. He don't know our language. His name is Meesha, though."

"Meesha?" the Indian mouthed the word. "That's a strange name, ain't it?"

"No stranger than yours…Quasi," Digger replied with a chortle. He handed him a slice of bread to soak up the thick gravy.

"You say he can't talk?" Quasi asked, looking down at the boy. "Then how do you two communicate, if he can't talk?"

"It's not that he can't talk. He doesn't know our language," Digger explained. "He can't speak much English."

"Something like you, huh?" Quasi replied with a grin. He finished most of the bowl and set the rest on the ground, and Corky quickly lapped it up. "Where's he from, if he can't speak English? Mexico? Does he have a green card?" He leaned back and filled the darkness with throaty laughter.

"He's from a spaceship," Digger said, a twinkle in his eye. He knew the big Indian wouldn't believe him, but he continued. "He's from another world…another universe…or somethin' like that."

"Yeah, okay," Quasi said, eying him. "Then how do you two communicate? How'd you find out his name and such, if he can't speak our language?"

"He doesn't talk. He shows me pictures. He lets me know things by sendin' pictures into my head."

Quasi cocked his head and gave him a skeptical smirk. "Yeah, all right, you got me there," he replied. "What kind of pictures does he send you, any good lookin' women?"

"They ain't those kind of pictures, you half-breed. He showed me pictures of where he came from, and of some people who want to take him back to a place where he don't want to go."

"And where might that be? Where's he from?"

"I told you, a spaceship."

"Come on, Digger, you know there ain't no such things as spaceships. He's pullin' your leg."

"Well, I believe what I saw. And that's final!"

"Will he show me pictures? Maybe I'll believe it, if I see it for myself."

Digger looked over at the boy, pointed to his forehead and then at the big Indian.

Meesha stared nervously at the huge man's copper-toned face.

"It's all right, boy. He don't bite," Digger told him. "Show him the pictures you showed me." He knew the boy didn't know what he had said, but he figured somehow he understood.

Meesha stood up and put his finger cautiously on Quasi's forehead. Undaunted by his actions, the big man leaned back and closed his eyes. Instantly, pictures of five huge spaceships raced through his mind, then pictures of his doomed planet. Finally, images of men in silver uniforms chasing the boy appeared. After a few moments, he dropped his finger and sat back down on the log.

"I'll be danged," Quasi said wide-eyed. "How did he do that? I saw things I wouldn't have believed possible." He hesitated for a moment, and then added, "I saw the spaceships you were talking about, too."

"Well, now do you believe me?"

Ignoring him, Quasi said, "I also saw pictures of those men chasin' after him. Some appeared to be friendly…but the others—"

"Yeah, they're the ones I'm talkin' about," Digger interrupted. "They're after him, and for some reason, want to take him back to his planet. Don't know why, but he doesn't appear to want to go back. I believe he's quite serious about that." He stared at the big Indian for several moments. "What do you think we should do about it, Injun? Maybe we should protect the little guy from those men? What do you think?"

Quasi grabbed his rifle leaning up against a nearby tree, and stood up, his 6' 7" frame towering over them.

"If you think we should stop 'em from takin' him, let's do it!" he said. He lifted the Model 94 Winchester to his shoulder and sighted down its barrel. "When do you think they'll be here? I didn't get a picture of that."

"Don't know," Digger answered, "but I think we should be ready for 'em when they do come. Let's pack up the gear and go back to the shack. We'll have more protection there than out here in the open…in case they want to start somethin'. Okay, Injun?"

Instead of hovering above the forest floor, Kerac decided to land where he had earlier. The moon was full, but it was not bright enough to hinder his plans. Luchak came onto the bridge and watched as Lulla manipulated the controls for the delicate landing.

"I'm going to try to communicate with him, once more," she said. "I know he's still somewhere in the area, but I can't pinpoint his exact location. I was too busy before, trying to convince him to return with us, and I didn't get a positive fix on him." She left the navigation console, moved to another position and switched on the brain-wave equipment. "I should be able to come close enough to his location that you can go after him on foot. You'll have to make it fast though, I'm certain the senator will be here as soon as he discovers the brain-waves. If he does come, there's no telling what he'll do."

"Never mind the small-talk," he said, "just find the boy's waves! Cut the anti-gravity engine and go into a stealth mode. He'll have a much more difficult time finding us, if he can't locate our signature."

After securing the ship, Kerac rushed to the hangar deck and headed for a surveillance pod. He sat down at the controls and turned on the anti-gravity drive. As he was about to leave Lulla's voice blasted over the pod's speaker.

"Kerac!" she shrieked. "What are you doing? You can't take the pod. The senator will detect it. Besides, it's less than half a mile to where I believe the boy is. Go on foot!"

"Lulla," Luchak said, walking up behind her. "Why don't I go with him? I believe Meesha will respond to me better. I think I can talk him into coming back with us."

"Do you think that's wise?" she said. "What if your father arrives and goes after you, too? He could very easily force you into going back with him. He has the power and several men on his ship to help him."

"I'm past the point of being afraid of him," he replied. "Respect, yes, but I do not fear him. I will not go back with him, under any circumstance."

"Are you sure you want to do this?" She turned and looked into his eyes.

"Yes, I'm certain."

After securing the pod, Kerac returned to the bridge. "Sorry," he said. "I wasn't thinking. Of course, I should go on foot. Assuming you know his exact location. I don't want to be wandering around out there without know exactly where he is."

"I'm working on it. Give me a minute."

He murmured something under his breath, and then went to the helm and sat in the Captain's Chair. "Let me know when you've found him," he said tersely.

She gave him a cold look and turned back to her instruments. "If you'll let me concentrate for a moment," she replied curtly. Several minutes later she located the boy's waves and yelled, "Got him! He must be concentrating on something. I'll tell him you're coming."

Kerac jumped out of the chair and stared down at her screen. After being certain that it was the right coordinates, he walked across the bridge and reached into a cabinet for a small stun gun. Knowing she would object, he hid it under his utility belt, and then started to leave the bridge.

"I have the coordinates," he said, as he got to the door. "I'm leaving now before we're discovered." Then he added, "Don't tell the boy I'm coming. If he knows, he might turn off his thoughts, and you won't be able to find his waves again."

"Wait for a minute, Kerac," she said, turning to look at him. "Luchak wants to go with you. He believes he stands a better chance at talking him into coming back."

Kerac stopped at the door, turned and snarled, "He what?"

"Calm down," she replied. "If he's with other people they might object to you coming. You could use a strong boy like him. It might not be as easy as you think, to bring him back. Luchak's a big boy.

You might need him." She frowned and added, "And leave the weapon here!"

"Not this time, I'm taking it with me," he insisted. "How did you know I had it?"

"Because I know you."

He gave Luchak a side-glance and nodded his head toward the door. "All right, kid, let's go. But don't do anything stupid, I'll be watching every move you make."

It took only a few minutes to return to the shack. When they arrived, Digger started the process of building a fire in the old earth-stone fireplace, to ward off the nightly chill soon to arrive. However, the kindling wouldn't ignite. Quasi ejected a bullet from his rifle, put the lead end between his teeth, pried it free from the casing and dumped its contents into the fireplace. When the powder landed, the nearly dead-embers, turned into brilliant red and yellow flames. Digger took several small logs from the wood box and threw them onto the crackling fire. Within minutes, the one-room shack was warm and comfortable.

Quasi found a sizeable, unbroken chair, sat at the table and laid his gun across it for easy access. Corky curled up beside Meesha, slumped down in the weather-beaten sofa, and Digger went to the sink to pump water from the old, shallow well. Except for a night-foraging bird clucking outside, and the occasional howl of a timber wolf, the only other sound was the antique clock on the wall chirping out several monotonous notes.

Suddenly, there came a loud whacking sound. Startled, Quasi jerked his head up and looked around.

Digger stood over the sink brandishing an over-sized cleaver, chopping off slices of smoked venison.

"Thought you guys might be gettin' hungry," he told them. "We didn't have much to eat down at the camp, and it could be a while before our next meal. If there's any trouble, we might as well handle it on a full stomach."

Quasi went to the sink and looked at the smoked shoulder. "Digger, that's a fawn," he said. "You ain't supposed to shoot baby deer."

"I didn't hunt it, it got tangled up in the underbrush and broke its leg. I had to shoot it, to put it out of its misery." Then he added, "Will you go up to the henhouse and get us some eggs? The boy and I polished off the last of 'em, earlier. Maybe you want me to open a can of beans to go with the venison? How about that?"

Quasi grabbed his rifle and headed for the hen house. Halfway up the slope, he heard rustling sounds in the bushes. Believing it could be timber wolves, he pumped a round into the chamber, and continued on up the path. When he got to the hen-house, he lifted several cackling Rhode Island Reds off their nests, gathered the eggs and put them in a small bucket he found beside the coop. After gathering a dozen eggs, he closed the chicken-wire door and left.

Halfway down the slope, two men in silver uniforms had thrashed their way out of the underbrush and stood in front of him. One appeared to be holding a small weapon. The three of them stood staring at each other.

In the semi-darkness Quasi could barely make out their faces, but he saw the gleaming weapon in the man's hand.

"What do we have here?" he said. "What do you fellows want? If you came for Digger's gold forget it. And if you came for the boy forget that, too."

The man with the weapon took a calculated step forward. Quasi pointed the rifle at his stomach, and he backed off.

"We did not come for your gold," the man said. "But we did come for the boy. He must return with us. He has an obligation to be fulfilled. He is not from around here…as you must already know."

Quasi lowered his rifle and narrowed his eyes. "He doesn't want to go back with you guys," he said. "He wants to stay here. You better leave while you can."

"We do not wish to harm anyone," the taller of the two said. He raised the small weapon and pointed it at Quasi's stomach. "Nevertheless, if forced to do so—" He moved a step closer. "The boy is very important to my people. However, he is too young to understand that."

"Kerac! Why are we wasting time with this man?" Luchak asked in Golanese "We know the boy is nearby, probably in that little house down there. Let's go get him."

"Patience Luchak," Kerac replied, also in Golanese. "We don't want any problems with these people. I'm sure they would give him up, if they knew what was at stake."

Quasi moved a step closer, towering over the man by a foot. He looked down, and their eyes met. "The boy showed me pictures of you and your friend there." He pointed to Luchak. "And he showed me everything about your world."

"Then if you saw everything," Kerac replied, "you must know why the boy has to return to his people." After a brief pause, he added, "I assume he is in that small house down there." He pointed to the shack. He shoved the stun gun into Quasi's stomach. "Please, take us to the boy. I don't want to hurt you."

Quasi looked down at the miniature weapon and put the barrel of his rifle between the man's legs. "I don't think so," he said, cocking the hammer. "The boy told us he didn't want to go with you. He must have had a good reason for sayin' that." Again, he looked at the small weapon pushed against his stomach. "You're going to force me down to the shack with that little toy of yours, when I got a fully loaded rifle pointed at your gonads?"

Slowly, and carefully, the man moved his other hand to the stun gun and clicked a switch on its side, taking it from stun to fully-charged. He looked into the big Indian's eyes, pointed the weapon at a nearby stump and pulled the trigger. A tremendous explosion shattered the silence, and the stump sailed a hundred feet into the air landing a few feet behind the chicken coop.

Quasi's eyes widened, and his jaw dropped. He lowered the rifle and the bucket of eggs to the ground and stared at the spot where the stump had been. When the shock wore off, he looked down at the man.

"Damn, fellow!" he mumbled under his breath. "What the hell you got there?"

"I was merely trying to make a point," Kerac replied with a grin. "Now, will you take us to the boy?"

Without saying another word, Quasi headed down the slope toward the shack. He remembered his rifle and the eggs he had left on the path and turned to go back for them.

Kerac grabbed his arm. "My friend will get your gun and those little brown things. Please, take us to that small house."

As they approached the shack, Digger stood in the doorway pointing his shotgun at them. "What the hell's goin' on, Injun?" he shouted. "What was that loud noise I heard?" When they got closer, he said, "Who the hell are these guys? Are they the ones after the boy?"

"You could say that," Quasi replied. "And don't try anything foolish with that gun old man, they got a weapon you wouldn't believe. That was what you heard."

"Well, I've got this shotgun, and I ain't afraid to use it," Digger came back, trying to look menacing. "What's that man doin' with your rifle? Did he take it away from you?" Quasi didn't answer, he went inside followed closely by Kerac.

"Where is the boy?" Kerac asked. "I don't see him." He looked at Digger. "Please, put your weapon down, your friend will attest to mine." He pointed the small gun at the old man.

"Do as he says," Quasi ordered, "you're definitely out-gunned."

Digger laid the gun on the table, backed off a few steps and said, "What boy? There isn't any boy here."

"I ain't afraid of 'em, whoever they are," Digger said defiantly.

"Where is the boy?" Kerac repeated his face flushed. "I do not have the patience or time for small talk. I must have the boy immediately. My people need him."

"Yes, we know," Quasi interrupted, "he showed us pictures. But he doesn't want to go back with you. He's happy here."

Kerac glared at him. "If the boy has told you everything you should know he is to become prince of my people, and possibly King. His desires do not matter; he is a subject of Golan. He must return."

Digger went to the fireplace and added a log, then turned to face him. "The boy is not here. He left about half an hour ago. I don't know where he went. He couldn't tell me he doesn't speak our language, as you know."

"He could not have left a half-hour ago," Kerac replied impatiently. "Our sensors detected him at this location a few minutes ago."

"Well, so much for your sensors," Digger replied sarcastically. He sat down at the table, drummed his gnarled fingernails on the tattered oilcloth, and then pointed to his head. "My sensors tell me he left a half-hour ago."

When Kerac realized he was not going to tell him anything, he pulled a communicator from his belt.

"Lulla," he said softly. "Do you still have the boy's waves?"

"No," a tinny voice came back. "I've not had them for some time now. What's going on? Didn't you find him at that location?"

"No, he isn't here, and these people say they don't know where he is." There was a short pause, and then he added, "Have you detected the senator's ship?"

"No, not yet," the voice replied. "He's probably waiting for us to find the boy. I'm sure we'll see him very soon."

"Keep the ship quiet and in stealth mode," he commanded. "I'll let you know when we find the boy. Tell me as soon as you locate the senator's ship. I don't want him to find us before we've located the boy." He switched off the device.

"From what I just heard, I guess you're the good guys," Quasi said.

Kerac smirked. "Yes, we are. I am the brother of the King of Golan. The person I mentioned on the communicator is a man named Abron. A senator from one of our countries called Keeti. He is the King's worst enemy. That young man standing by the door is his son." He pointed to Luchak. "Fortunately, he is on our side. He doesn't want his father to find the boy, either. His father wants only him to be prince of Golan, and possibly King. If that were to happen, he would be his advisor, which would give him absolute power over Golan. We cannot let that happen. We must find the boy. If he captures him, he will want to make a trade for his son." Again, he pointed to Luchak.

"What can we do?" Digger asked with a sigh. "I don't want anything bad to happen to that boy. I kinda like the little guy."

"Then you can tell me where he is," Kerac said.

"I told you I don't know," Digger insisted. "He left a few minutes ago with Corky, my dog. As soon as he heard that explosion he jumped off the sofa and high-tailed it out the door, my dog hot on his tail."

"Did you see which direction he went?"

"I think he went south, toward my campsite."

Kerac stared into his eyes, examining them for the truth. "I believe I can trust you. I sense it," he said. "Get your weapons and we'll go after him."

"Good," Digger said. "Let's get him before the bad guys do."

As they raced down the heat-hardened path, a voice exploded from Kerac's belt.

"Kerac!" the voice screamed. "The senator's ship just arrived, and he parked next to me. What should I do?"

"Don't do anything!" he shouted back "Above all, don't tell him where we are, he probably doesn't know, exactly. That guy just won't give up!"

When Meesha left the shack, he raced toward the campsite as fast as his legs would take him. When he arrived, he heard rustling and loud grunting in the bushes alongside the path. A large, male brown bear lumbered out of the thicket and headed for the fireplace, apparently attracted by leftover food. Meesha slid to a stop, stumbled and fell headlong in front of him. Startled, the bear stopped and stared at him.

At first, Corky eyed the huge creature from a distance, and then all of a sudden ran up close to him and started barking, irritating the animal. He rushed in and nipped at the huge creature's feet, and then darted back out of reach. Annoyed, the bear took several swipes at him, but he was too quick and easily avoided his paws. Then, unexpectedly, he raced in circles around the bear making it pirouette and almost fall.

The bear made one final swipe at the dog, caught him on his hind-quarter and sent him sailing into the bushes. With a loud roar, the huge creature looked back down at the boy, stood on his hind legs and extended his front paws out in front of his massive chest. He took several steps forward, then stopped and again stared at the boy, as if confused. Several moments later he dropped to the ground, let out a savage snarl and lumbered toward him.

Meesha's eyes bulged, and his face flushed. Panic-stricken, he attempted to get to his feet, but when he stood he slipped and fell on his back. Using his arms like an oarsman in a half-shell, he crabbed his way to the edge of the bushes.

A shot rang out. The bear jerked its head around and saw men with flashlights rushing down the path toward him. Immediately, he turned and headed for the underbrush at the tree line. Before he could get there a beam of light had illuminated his huge body, and another shot rang out.

Quasi kept the smoking rifle to his shoulder, waiting for the bear to fall. When he could no longer see him in the beam, he lowered the weapon and looked up the path at Digger and the others hurrying toward him.

"Think that last shot got him," he yelled to them. "I'll go check it out. You guys stay here there ain't nothin' more dangerous than a wounded bear."

"Wait!" Digger shouted with a grin. "Don't go after him. I don't like bear meat it's too dang greasy and tough."

Ignoring him, Quasi pumped another round into the chamber and fought his way through the thick brush to the edge of the forest. Before he was out of sight, he turned and yelled, "I know you don't like bear, but my people do."

Digger finally arrived at the fire pit, followed by Kerac and Luchak and stopped where Meesha had been half-hidden in the bushes.

As Kerac bent over to catch his breath, he caught sight of the boy wide-eyed and frightened. Between gasps, he said in Golanese, "Meesha, are you all right?"

The boy nodded. In his native tongue, he said, "Yes, I am all right. What was that thing? I have never seen an animal like that!"

"They call it a bear," he told him. "They say it's very dangerous." He grabbed the boy's arm and pulled him out of the bushes. After brushing leaves and dirt from the boy's clothing, he said, "We were worried we wouldn't find you. Senator Abron is also looking for you. We have to hurry back to the ship, before he arrives."

Meesha pulled his arm free. "I told you, I did not wish to go back to Golan. I have found a new home here. I like it very much. Please, do not force me to go back."

Luchak had been standing off to one side. "Meesha," he said, "your father wants only you to be prince. You must take his place if he dies."

"He also said someone else could be voted in, if I wasn't available," Meesha snapped back. "Do you not remember that?"

"Meesha, we must take you back to Golan," Kerac interrupted. "It was my brother's wish that you take his place when the time comes."

"Why doesn't Luchak be the prince?" Meesha said, pointing at him. "He's much older and wiser than me. My father would understand. Take him back and tell them you couldn't find me. Because of his father's influence, they would surely vote for him."

"It's not that simple, Meesha," Kerac said. "If Luchak were to be prince, and then on to be King, his father would have all the power he would need to have full control over Golan. I'm not ready for that, and I don't believe you are either."

"Kerac!" a frantic voice shouted over his communicator. "The senator is demanding I open the hatch and let him in. What should I do?"

Kerac wrenched the device from his belt. "Do nothing, Lulla! We have Meesha, but we will not bring him to the ship until Abron is gone." He thought for a moment, and then added, "Tell him to wait for us at the vortex. I'll bring his son there."

"Are you really going to give him up?" she asked.

"No, but he may think I will."

"I'll tell him." After several moments, her voice returned, "I have spoken to him, but he will not leave. He believes you will not honor your word."

"Try again!" he yelled loudly, and turned the device off.

"I don't want to go back with my father, either," Luchak said. He lowered his head and looked at the ground. "He will take me back to Golan and force Parliament to vote for me. I don't want that. I don't want to be prince, any more than Meesha does." He looked at Kerac pleadingly. "You know very well if you let him take me back he will do everything in his power to keep you stranded here. I'm sure he will make it so you can't return with Meesha."

"Yes, I realize that," Kerac replied. "However, I have a few tricks of my own."

His communicator sounded. "Kerac!" Lulla screamed. "The senator has been monitoring our conversations and knows exactly where you are. He's on his way there now. What are you going to do? What do you want me to do?"

"I told you before, do nothing!" Kerac yelled back. "I'll handle this!" He thought for a moment, and then added, "Do you have him on your scanner?"

"Yes, he's about halfway to your location. He'll be there in a few minutes. Be careful, he's armed and has one of his men with him. He is not happy."

Kerac turned to Digger. "Is there a place close by where we can hide? Somewhere he couldn't find us?"

Digger thought for a moment. "Yes, follow me. There's a cave a few hundred yards from here. We should be safe in there it's at the top of a steep slope. It's an old mica mine and it's lined with the stuff. I doubt if radio waves, or anything else, could penetrate it"

"What about your big friend in the forest?"

"Don't worry about him. He'll know where we are."

Kerac grabbed Meesha's arm and rushed him down the path. Halfway to the cave he looked back and saw Digger darting into the bushes.

"What are you doing?" he yelled. "We have to go!"

"I ain't leavin' my dog behind," Digger yelled back. A few seconds later, he came out of the bushes with Corky in his arms. The dog had not been seriously injured, but he was in a mild state of shock. "Okay," he said, rubbing the dog's neck. "Let's go!"

Before they could get to the cave, they heard the sound of feet running toward them. Suddenly, a searing shaft of plasma shot by them and hit a large fir tree. The tree exploded, sending limbs and splinters deep into the forest.

"Kerac!" a shout came down the path. "Stop where you are! Don't do anything foolish. Give my son to me and nobody will get hurt. Defy me and I'll be more accurate with my next shot."

"You fool!" Kerac shouted back. "This is no way to get your son. Parliament will have your head for this."

"To hell with them!" he bellowed as he approached. "I want my son! And don't worry about Parliament, they're under my thumb…as you know." He stopped in front of Kerac, holding his weapon on him.

"Senator, I thought you'd never get here," Kerac said with a sneer.

"Don't play games, Kerac," Abron roared. "I came for my son, and I intend to take him back with me." He glared at Kerac, and then turned and looked at Luchak. "Well, defiant son, I think it's about time you and I had a little father-to-son talk. Don't you?" He grabbed his arm and squeezed. Luchak pulled free, and with a sudden move knocked the weapon from his hand. Nader swung his gun around and pointed it at Luchak.

The bushes at the edge of the clearing parted and Quasi came out dragging a bear by its hind legs. When he saw the weapon pointed at Luchak, he let go of the bear and raised his rifle.

"Drop your weapon, ass-hole!" he shouted to Nader. When the man saw the huge Indian, he looked at Abron for guidance. "I said drop it, and I meant it!" He fired a warning shot over his head, quickly pumped another round into the chamber and put his sights on him. Nader put the weapon back in his belt. "I said drop it, buddy, that means to the ground!" Considering the size of the man, and the rifle in his hand, Nader pulled the gun from his belt and dropped it to the ground. "Get their weapons, Digger. I'll keep 'em covered."

"Hi there, Injun," Digger said with a grin, "nice to see you!"

Quasi ignored him and stared at the two intruders. "What's going on here? Did I hear an explosion? Was that another one of those weird guns?"

Abron turned and glared at his son. "You will regret your action. I promise."

"Well," Kerac said. "What do we do now? Should we tie 'em up like criminals, or let 'em go back to their ship?" He walked up to Abron and stared at him menacingly. "The boy is not going back with you. As a matter of fact, both boys want to stay on Earth." He moved closer to him, forcing him backwards. "When the time comes to return to Golan, I'll let the Parliament know what happened here."

"I think we should hog-tie 'em and let 'em rot out here in the woods," Quasi said, and moved toward them threateningly. "That's what they deserve, tryin' to take the boys back where they don't want to go."

"You won't get away with this, Kerac," Abron said in a low, controlled voice. "I have other men on the ship, and they'll come for me. You'll be in more trouble than you can handle."

"Oh, you mean your engineer?" Kerac said. "I know how many men you have, just the three of you. And, right now two of you are… shall we say, in trouble?"

Abron's face flushed in anger.

"Tie their hands behind their backs," Digger ordered. "We'll take 'em up to the shack and keep 'em there until we can figure out what to do with 'em. Let 'em think things over for a while. Maybe I'll feed 'em some bear meat. That should punish 'em."

Kerac removed the communicators and stuffed them in his utility belt. He took both weapons from Digger and slid them under his belt.

"That should do it," he said. "But I don't think binding them is necessary, as long as your friend is here." He pointed to Quasi, still holding his gun on them. "Besides, we have a VIP in our midst." He looked at the senator with revulsion. "Tying him would be inappropriate, humiliating."

They marched up the path toward the shack, Abron and Nader in the lead with Quasi behind them prodding them along with the barrel of his rifle.

TWELVE

"What do you mean?" Tumac asked the intern, who had rushed into the chamber and whispered in his ear. "Repeat what you just told me. I don't believe I heard you correctly."

The intern repeated, "Senator Abron of Keeti took his ship to Earth. He left with two of his men."

"When did you find this out, Daka?"

"This morning, Sir. I was not going to tell you, but I didn't want to get him in trouble. However, after I found out why he went, I thought you should know."

Tumac leaned back in his chair and frowned.

"Then he has defied Parliament's orders? Is that what you're saying? He has gone after Meesha and his son in defiance of our orders?"

"Yes, Sir, I guess so." The young man sat down beside him to catch his breath. He knew he could be in a lot of trouble, if Senator Abron found out what he had just told the Prime Minister. "Do you think he's going to Earth only to bring his son back?"

"I would imagine," Tumac replied. He turned and looked at the boy. "He has a mind of his own, and he's desperate. He wants his son to be prince." He exhaled a deep sigh, then tilted his head and stared at the ornate ceiling. "He believes if his son were to be voted in as prince, and later King, he would have all the power needed to control Golan. That would not be good for any of us." He looked into the boy's eyes and added, "Don't mention this to anyone. All right, son?"

"Yes, Sir, I mean no, Sir, I won't."

"After you leave here, go to the province of Keeti and see what you can find out about his trip to Earth…what he really intends to do there." He gave the young man a tired look and continued. "In addition to bringing his son back, I believe he's bent on causing trouble on Earth, before we've even made official contact with them. You're dismissed. Don't tell anybody at Keeti why you're there."

The intern headed for the door, but before leaving, he turned and said, "Your Honor, do you believe our mother-ships will ever make vortexes big enough to get us to Earth?"

"Our scientists are working on the problem, son," Tumac replied. "They should have the bugs worked out very soon. If they do succeed, which I believe they will, we can make official contact with Earth." He hesitated for a moment, and added, "A friendly one, of course."

"Do you believe Earth will accept us?"

"I don't know. However, I do know one thing—our scientists had better work out the bugs quickly. Our planet is on the verge of annihilation. When that happens, we must either be headed into outer space to find a new home, or have large enough vortexes to get our ships to Earth."

The intern's face turned pale, as he walked through the door and disappeared down the long, polished hallway.

Tumac stared vacantly into the emptiness of the Parliament chamber. After a few moments, he went to a control panel at the far end of the room and pushed a button.

"Senator Ekron," he called into his communicator. There was a slight delay, before a voice at the other end acknowledged. "Would you please come to the chamber? I believe we may have a little problem. Maybe you can help us with it."

Thirty minutes later, due to a 20-minute shuttle ride, Senator Ekron of Lechi walked through the door.

"Good morning, Your Honor, what's the problem?" he asked.

Without answering, Tumac walked behind his chair and stared through a porthole at the other four ships in the armada. Several moments passed, before he turned and looked at Ekron.

"Are you a friend of Senator Abron of Keeti?"

Ekron was taken back by his question. "Why do you ask, Sir?"

"I want to know if I can trust you enough to ask for your help."

"You know you can trust me. To answer your question, he is no friend of mine." He looked at Tumac with a deep frown. "What's on your mind, Sir?"

"I wanted to find someone I could trust, someone I could rely on to bring Senator Abron back from Earth. I thought of you."

"He's on Earth?"

"Yes, he defied me and Parliament by going there to get his son. I believe his intentions are to find Meesha and hide him on Earth until after the vote at the end of this week, and bring only his son back for the vote."

"From what I know of him, I wouldn't put it past him," Ekron replied. "Your Honor, you know I would do anything you asked of me in the interest of Golan. It would be my privilege to go after him. I believe he's after your position anyway. What's more, if his son were to be voted in as prince, it would be a step up in acquiring the power needed to sway the remaining members of Parliament over to his side. If that were to happen, he would also have enough power to vote you out and him in as Prime Minister."

"I thought you might feel that way," Tumac replied. "That's why I'm asking you to go after him, instead of somebody else. From what I gathered at the last meeting, most of the members are already under his control."

"When do you want me to go? I can have a ship ready to launch at a moment's notice."

"Go after him immediately," Tumac said. "Try to talk some sense into him. However, don't attempt to bring him back by force. His ship is well equipped for combat and could easily neutralize any weapons you may have."

"What if he refuses to listen?"

"Try to disable his ship, and then get out of there as fast as you can!" Tumac said with a cynical grin. "If you could damage his ship so it couldn't return to Golan under its own power, we could send a ship back for it later."

Ekron nodded his approval and headed for the door. "I'm on my way, Sir. I'll pick up the necessary items and leave immediately."

Tumac called to him, as he got to the door, "If you happen to run into Meesha, bring him back. I'm worried about him, since Abron is probably looking for him."

"I'll do my best, Sir," Ekron replied. He walked out of the conference room and disappeared down the long hallway.

When he arrived back at his country of Lechi, he called for his best crew; the ones who had made many trips to Earth with him, and whom he considered extremely capable of handling any situation that might arise. With that in mind, he didn't expect too many problems from the senator. However, he wanted to be prepared for the unexpected.

By late afternoon his ship was fully outfitted and the crew indoctrinated on their mission. After many attempts to explain his trip to the control tower, by saying he had permission from the Prime Minister to go on a training trip, he was finally given the okay to move his ship to the hangar-bay door and wait. The 150-foot vessel slowly approached the door, and then stopped and waited for it to open.

As the huge door began to open, a man in a military uniform rushed into the hangar control room and stood behind the operator, flailing about his arms and shouting orders at him. When he was finished with his animated conversation, the controller hailed Ekron.

"Senator Ekron!" an anxious voice came over the speaker. "You are directed to discontinue your flight, immediately! Return to the hangar bay!"

Ekron picked up his mike and shouted into it, "What's going on? What do you mean return to the bay? We have permission to go on this training flight."

"It will be explained, when you return to the bay."

A tall man in a lieutenant's uniform, wearing a long, leathery face, looked at Ekron with a cynical grin and shrugged.

"Well, Sir, what do we do now?" he asked.

Ekron thought for a moment, and then said, "Let's go, Keral! Give me all she's got, while the door is still open enough to get through!"

Lieutenant Keral looked at him skeptically, mumbled something unintelligible, and applied full power to the ion drive.

The huge door stopped opening and was in the process of closing. Ekron saw his only chance. He turned the ship sideways and shot vertically through the door, making it by inches. As soon as it had cleared the door, he took it into outer space, and headed for the coordinates to make a vortex. A few minutes later, and several thousand miles above the planet, he stopped.

"I wonder why they tried to stop us?" he asked his First Mate, as he flipped several switches on a control panel. "Another couple seconds and we would have been dead meat. I'd rather not go through that again. I can't imagine what the problem could have been. Nevertheless, I'm glad we didn't stick around to find out." He sat down at the navigation console and added as an afterthought, "The Prime Minister gave me permission to go on this little jaunt. In fact, he almost insisted on it." He glanced at his First Mate. "I imagine somehow one of Abron's henchmen found out about this little trip and wanted to stop it…for the senator's sake, of course."

"You're probably right," Keral agreed. "But how could they have gotten permission to stop our flight? It would have to come directly from Parliament."

"Let's not speak of Parliament, you don't know them as I do," Ekron replied. "Abron has most of them under his thumb, already. They'll do anything he asks, just to make a few points."

"You're not telling me anything I don't know," Keral replied. "His underhanded ways are common knowledge throughout the fleet."

"You're kidding," Ekron replied, surprised by his condemnation.

"No, I'm not," Keral answered. "Now, can you make a vortex and get us through it safely? You have the helm; I'm only an interested bystander." He chuckled. "You'd better make it quick though, we'll probably have company soon."

It only took the ship a few minutes to create a vortex that would take them into the eerie emptiness between the two universes. They hated the procedure, although they had gone through it many times. They had always dreaded its abnormal effects—the transformation of the atoms and particles in their bodies; the visual effects of watching others appear to stretch and float around in the cabin; the eerie sounds encountered when the ship's hull was altering its structure; and their diminished mental acuities when their bodies seemingly torn apart at the sub-atomic level and then reassembled. They knew it would only last a few minutes, but the anguish they had always encountered lasted a lifetime.

A few minutes later, like a phantom, the ship left the worm-hole and materialized high up in Earth's outer limits.

"Sit down, Abron!" Kerac demanded. "I don't want any problems out of you or your friend there. You're going to be here for a while so make yourselves comfortable."

"I'll rustle up some grub," Digger said and headed for the door. "I've got to get some more meat out of the smokehouse."

As soon as he left the cabin, Nader caught Abron's eye and nodded in the direction of Quasi, who had been busy lighting the stove. Confused, Abron turned and looked at the big Indian, then back at his First Mate. Nader pointed at a log on the floor next to the stove, and made a slight chopping motion with his fist. The senator understood. He got up from his chair and slowly moved closer to Quasi.

Kerac had been standing by the door watching Digger go up the path to the smokehouse and didn't notice Abron's movement toward the big Indian. The boys were slumped down in the couch discussing the deer-head and not paying any attention to the men.

When Kerac heard a whack, and felt the cabin shake, he turned and saw Quasi lying on the floor. He rushed over, but before he could do anything he was knocked to the floor by the log still in Abron's hand.

Nader grabbed one of his communicators from Kerac's belt and headed for the door. Abron ran to the couch, grabbed Luchak by his arm and attempted to pull him toward the door. The boy yanked free and picked up the log. He made a quick swipe at his father's head but missed. Abron realized it was futile to attempt to get his son and rushed out the door. When he caught up with Nader, they ran down the path toward the fire pit, then through the brush toward their ship, a quarter-mile away.

When Digger returned from the smokehouse, his arms full of venison and eggs, he saw the two men lying on the floor. Luchak was standing over them with the log still in his hand. Meesha sat on the couch at the far end of the room trembling.

Digger wrenched the log out of the boy's hand and raised it over his head to strike him, but hesitated. Luchak threw his arms up to ward off a potential blow, but Digger dropped the log and knelt down beside Quasi. He felt his pulse, and then looked up at Luchak.

"What the hell happened here, boy?" he demanded. "What the hell's going on? Where are those men?"

Luchak stared into his fiery eyes. "Abron hit them with that log, and they ran off. They went down the hill."

"Where's the boy? Did they get him?"

"No. He's over there." Luchak pointed to Meesha sitting with his knees bent up to his chin, and his arms wrapped around them. "I believe they got one of the communicators. They'll probably call their ship for help."

Digger went to the sink, got a glass of water and splashed it in their faces. Both men moaned and slowly opened their eyes.

"God damn!" Quasi shouted, as the water hit his face. "That's cold, you old fart."

"Had to do somethin' you were lyin' down on the job. You were supposed to be watchin' 'em."

"I was tryin' to light that damn fire, when they snuck up behind me," Quasi said, rubbing the back of his head. "Damn, that hurt!"

Kerac got up slowly and attempted to stand. After a few moments, he sat down in one of the rickety chairs and put his head between his legs.

"What happened?" he asked, looking around the room. "I suppose they got away?"

"Yep," Digger replied. "Some watchdogs you guys are. Now, we'll have to go after 'em."

Kerac felt his utility belt. "They didn't get the weapons, but they did get one of the communicators." His eyes rolled back and with a loud moan slumped to the floor.

Digger went to the sink, got a wet towel and put it on the back of his neck. "He'll be okay," he told Quasi. "He got a pretty good whack. It probably didn't hurt you much, you got a thick head!" He looked up at the big Indian with a guarded grin. "Why don't you take the boys? You know where to go. Keep 'em there until I come after you. Okay?"

"Yep, I know exactly where to take 'em," Quasi replied, still groggy. Are you goin' to be okay when that guy comes around?"

"Don't worry about me. I got my gun and my dog. I'll be okay. Besides, he's on our side."

Quasi walked over to Meesha and held out his hand. The boy hesitated for a moment, and then took it. He looked at Luchak and motioned for him to follow. After grabbing his rifle off the table, they rushed out the door.

A few minutes later they arrived at the camp site and Quasi stopped to listen for any sounds. Hearing none, he continued on down the path with the boys in tow.

Luchak walked up behind the big Indian and tugged on his shirt. "What happened to that bear you shot?" he asked.

"It's still in the woods," Quasi replied. "Digger didn't want it, so I'll take it to my people."

"You mean you eat animals like that?"

"Sure. They're kind of greasy, like Digger said, but it's meat and my people know how to fix 'em so they taste pretty good."

"Oh."

Several hundred yards from the fire pit they arrived at a steep incline and Quasi started up the slope. Halfway to the top he turned and noticed the boys had lagged behind, and he motioned for them to hurry. They glanced at each other tentatively, and then started up the rocky slope.

Quasi stopped beside a huge granite boulder, which had a vertical opening in one side. He reached into his pocket, pulled out a flashlight and entered the cave through the small slit. The boys hesitated for a moment, looked at each other hesitantly, and then followed.

"Come on, guys, we gotta light a fire so we can see in here," he yelled at them.

Back at the shack, Digger was still nursing Kerac. He had been hit on the back of his head hard enough where he was fading in and out of consciousness. He finally managed to get him to the couch, but it took a toll on his aging body and he had to stop and rest every few seconds.

Kerac finally opened his eyes and looked around. He saw Digger at the sink and said, "Where is everybody?"

"The Injun took the boys to a place where they'll be safe," Digger replied, turning to look at him. "They went to an old cave a quarter mile from here. That guy sure gave you one helluva wallop. You've only been coherent half the time. The other half you've been in la-la-land, or someplace."

Kerac attempted to get up from the couch but fell backwards. "Will they be safe, if Abron comes looking for them?"

Digger opened his 1970 vintage refrigerator and pulled out a few ice cubes. He wrapped them in a towel and returned to the couch.

"Here, this should help. To answer your question, the boys will be safe where they are. If those guys come back, we have a score to settle. Know what I mean?"

Kerac held the towel against the back of his neck and again attempted to stand, but he was still too wobbly and fell back onto the couch. "Guess I'm not ready to travel."

Digger went to the sink to make coffee.

"Okay, boys," Quasi said, his voice echoing in the large chamber. "Go get some dry firewood, but stay close to the cave. Don't know if those guys are comin' back, but I don't want 'em to see you, if they do."

Luchak relayed the message to Meesha.

As soon as the boys left the cave, Quasi took a small amount of dry fodder from his backpack and laid it under small twigs in a rock-lined fireplace in the center of the cave. He lit the fodder with an old Zippo lighter and blew on it until it ignited. Minutes later, the boys returned with several armloads of semi-dry limbs.

"Do you think it's wise to have a fire?" Luchak asked. "If they come back, couldn't they see the smoke?"

"No, we're far enough inside," Quasi said. "The vent is on the other side of the hill where they wouldn't be able to see the smoke anyway. Besides, they don't know we're in here."

"You think they don't?" Luchak said with a grin.

"Relax kid, we did 'em in before and we can do it again," Quasi replied.

Luchak smiled. "I hardly think being hit over the head is 'doin' 'em in.'"

"Well, it won't happen again, now that I know how sneaky they are. I'll be on my guard in the future. Just sit and relax, until we get word from Digger. Okay, fellas?"

A powerful vibration suddenly rattled the shack and Digger rushed to the door. He looked up and saw a large, black object hovering directly over the cabin. Kerac sensed the danger and yelled for him to get out. They ran outside and headed up the slope toward the chicken coop, Kerac swaying unsteadily as he ran. Before they got to the top of the hill, a brilliant shaft of light had surrounded the cabin. It intensified for a brief moment, and then with a blinding flash the cabin imploded. They had barely made it to the henhouse, when the ship turned and slowly headed in their direction.

"That's Abron," Kerac shouted, as he watched it approach. "He must have wanted to make a statement."

"A statement?" Digger cried out. "Look at my cabin!"

"I'm sure he believed if he could terrorize us, we would tell him where the boys are," Kerac replied. He reached for his communicator. "Lulla," he shouted. "Lulla!" he yelled again.

A few seconds later, a voice replied, "Kerac? Where are you? I can't find you on my scanner. Something's interfering with it."

"Never mind where I am," he shouted. "What can you do about the senator's ship? He's after us and he's mad!"

"You got that right," Digger mumbled.

"He's almost directly over us!" Kerac yelled. "I believe he's going to fire at us! Isn't there anything you can do?"

"Just a second!" she yelled back. "Kerac, I see another ship on my scanner. Who could that be?"

Frustrated, he yelled back, "Lulla, never mind the other ship, we're about to be cremated! Do something, quick!"

At that moment a searing shaft of plasma shot down from the sky and struck Abron's ship on its stern. The impact sent the ship sailing over the henhouse and into the night sky. The donor of the shaft slowly emerged through the early morning haze and hovered directly over them.

Kerac stared up at the ship. "That looks like Ekron's ship," he said. "I wonder what he's doing here."

"Who the hell is Ekron?" Digger asked. "Is he friend or foe?"

"He's a friend," Kerac replied. "He's a senator from one of our mother-ships."

The ship found a spot close by, descended to within a few feet of the ground and lowered its landing pads. A side hatch opened and a ramp slid down. A stout, full-bodied man in a purple uniform walked slowly down the ramp and approached them, a broad smile on his face.

"Kerac, it's nice to see you," he said in Golanese. "I noticed you were having a little problem here, so I figured I'd do something about it."

"Ekron, what are you doing here?" Kerac asked, extending his hand. "Did Parliament send you?"

"Not Parliament…Tumac," he replied. "He told me to find Abron and bring him back. He defied Parliament by coming here."

"You can't take him back by shooting him out of the sky," Kerac said in jest. "But I appreciate what you did. We could have been killed by that idiot."

"I didn't hurt his ship too much," Ekron confessed. "Just a flesh wound, more of less." Another broad smile spread across his ruddy face. "I targeted his gravity grid. He'll have to exert a great deal of ion power, just to stay afloat, or he'll fall out of the sky. It's not badly damaged, but he'll have to go into outer space and obtain orbit to make the repairs. He can't hover or land, because of what I did. He'll be back looking for us when he gets it fixed. I'm sure of it." He glanced at the remnants of the shack. “He certainly made a mess of that building. Was anyone inside? Anybody hurt?”

“We got out just in time,” Kerac told him. “If we had stayed a few seconds longer, we’d still be in there.”

“Where is everybody?” Ekron asked. “Did you find the boys?”

“Yes, we found them. But I don’t know where they are now,” Kerac answered. “However, this man does.” He pointed to Digger.

After an introduction, Digger said, “They’re with a very large native man. He’s taking good care of them.”

“Prime Minister Tumac asked me to bring the boys back, along with Abron,” Ekron stated. “That is if I could find Abron, which I guess I did.”

“Mister Digger,” Kerac said. “You do know where the boys are, don’t you?”

“Got a good idea.”

“Will you take us to them? My friend said he has to take them back to Golan, by orders of Parliament.”

“To hell with their orders!” Digger barked. “The boys said they didn’t want to go back, and that’s good enough for me.”

Kerac glared at the old man, and his jaws tightened. “Mister Digger, you do not seem to fully understand what I told you before, about Meesha’s importance to us. He is to be crowned prince when he returns to Golan. It is vital we find him right away.”

“Doesn’t he have anything to say about it?” Digger replied adamantly.

Kerac looked at him coldly. “Mister Digger, the King wants his son to be prince of Golan, and nobody else. Our King, my brother, gave me specific orders to find and return with him. I must obey his orders.”

“What about <u>that</u> fellow?” Digger pointed to Ekron. “He’s here to get the boy too, ain’t he?”

“Mister Digger,” Kerac replied irritably, “our situation is long and detailed. I do not have time to go into it. Please, trust me.” He thought for a moment, and then added, “If you allow us to take the boy back, I will personally speak to our King and see if he will let me return with him, after this is all over. He is a very understanding King and father.

If he permits it, I will personally return with the boy. How does that sound? It will be between the boy and his father."

Digger thought for a long moment. "Sounds reasonable to me," he said. "But it will still be up to the boy, whether he wants to go back with you, or not. Nevertheless, we'll have to find him first. Then, we'll see if he wants to go back, under those conditions."

"Then you don't know where he is?" Kerac asked with a frown.

"Well, I got a good idea."

Ekron said in Golanese, "Kerac, why are we wasting time with this old man? If I return to my ship, I believe I can locate the boy's waves. We don't really need him."

"Patience, Ekron," Kerac replied. "We must be civil to these people, if we want to cohabit with them in the future."

"Possibly cohabit!" Ekron emphasized. "The scientists still haven't found a way to get our mother-ships to Earth."

"It's only a matter of time, Ekron. Only a matter of time."

"Then what do you suggest we do in the mean time?" Ekron asked. "I have to return as soon as I have the boys, and possibly the senator." He thought for a moment, and then added, "The way things are going, I may be here for a while."

"Why don't you have your men take your ship someplace where it can't be found by Abron, or Earth's radars?" Kerac said. "We'll go get the boys, and then you can join us for dinner on my ship. There, we can discuss the matter in more detail."

Ekron could hardly believe what he had just heard. Here they were in another universe, no idea where the boys are, Abron on the rampage, and Kerac inviting him to a casual dinner. All the same, after thinking it over, it did sound reasonable. What else could he do, under the circumstances? He unsnapped his communicator.

"Keral," he called.

"Yes sir," a metallic voice returned.

"Take the ship and hide it where it can't be found. There's a spot on the other side of Earth you must be familiar with where you can hide and nobody can detect you, not even their military radars. Wait for my call, before you return. Try not to leave a signature, when you leave here."

"Is everything all right?" Keral asked.

"Yes. Everything is fine, just hide the ship. I'll call you when I'm ready to be brought back aboard." The speaker went dead.

Smoke from the fire had filled the damp, moldy cave, making their eyes water and nostrils burn. To avoid inhaling the dense smoke, the boys made excuses to go after more wood.

Quasi blew on the base of the fire to get it blazing so the smoke would be minimal and draft out through the vent hole at the rear of the cave. When he was satisfied it had made it on its own, he turned and looked at the boys.

"You guys hungry?" he asked.

Luchak interpreted for Meesha. His eyes lit up and he nodded.

Quasi reached into his backpack and pulled out several cans of baked beans, along with a few strips of venison jerky. He handed the smoked meat to the boys, and then cut the lids off the cans with his hunting knife and placed them at the edge of the blazing fire. He pulled out two spoons and handed them to the boys.

"Beans will be ready in a few minutes, boys," he told them. "Meanwhile, you can chow down on that jerky. I smoked it a couple days ago, it's nice and fresh."

The aft portion of Abron's ship had been severely damaged and was about to burst into flames. Ekron's shot had made a hole the size of a man's waist behind the anti-gravity grid and forward of the ion propulsion vent. The damage was allowing Earth's atmosphere to seep into the ion generator chamber and mix with small amounts of the highly unstable Element 115, which could cause the ion generator to over-heat and possibly explode. The outside anti-gravity grid had also received severe damage and was about to shut-down.

Abron shouted angrily to Nader, "Get somebody back aft to see what they can do about that leak. If it's not plugged, we'll explode!

My instruments tell me the anti-gravity drive is highly unstable, along with the outside grid!"

"We don't have anybody to send back aft!" Nader shouted back. "There's only the three of us, and I'm kind of busy trying to keep this ship afloat."

"Then call Kersey down in engineering!" Abron screamed, his face flushed. "If we make it into orbit at all, we'll have to get that anti-gravity back on line or we'll be forced to stay up there forever. Do you understand?"

"I'm sure he's already working on the problem," Nader replied. He picked up his mike and spoke into it, "Kersey, what's going on down there? How bad is the anti?"

There was a long pause before the engineer answered. "I can't fix this thing in orbit!" he shouted. "We've got to land to make repairs. That's the only way. We've lost most, if not all, of our hovering abilities. We'll definitely crash, if we don't land this thing before the grid goes out completely!"

"How the hell are we going to land without anti-gravity?" Nader asked.

"We have just enough grid left to make a 'rough' landing…I think!" Kersey replied.

Abron looked at Nader and sighed. "Well, I guess we'd better find someplace to set her down. Look for a place deep in the mountains; I don't want the Earthlings to find us."

"Come on," Digger said, looking at Kerac, "let's go find the boys and that Injun before you guys chow down." They left the shack and headed for the campsite. When they arrived at the fire pit there was no sign of them.

"I thought you knew where they were, Mr. Digger?" Kerac said. "We don't have time to look for them."

"Patience, my friend," Digger replied. "I know exactly where they are. The Injun likes it there. It's nice and secluded."

They remained on the path until they arrived at the steep slope leading up to the cave. Digger climbed the rocky incline with Kerac and Ekron close behind, both panting heavily from the physical exertion.

Quasi stood behind the large boulder at the entrance to the cave, squinting to make certain it was Digger. Satisfied, he moved out from behind it.

"Hi Digger," he said. "What was that loud noise I heard a while back?"

"Oh, nothin', just my shack bein' blown up. That's all."

Quasi gave him a confused look, and then motioned for them to come inside. When they entered he pointed to the boys. "I guess you're looking for them."

Kerac saw Meesha at the far end of the cave and walked toward him. Before he got there the thick smoke had engulfed him and Ekron completely. They both bent over in coughing jags and rushed for the fresh air of the entrance.

Meesha followed them outside. "Uncle, are you all right?" he asked in Golanese. "It takes time to get used to the smoke in there. Please, go back inside. We are well hidden in there."

When they came back into the cave, Digger handed them a cloth to put over their faces. "That should help a bit, until the smoke ventilates," he told them.

Finding a large stone in front of the fire pit Kerac sat down, and then looked over at Meesha. He said in Golanese, "We have a little problem, son. The Senator from Keeti just blew up Mr. Digger's house. I believe it was because we wouldn't tell him where you boys were. However, my friend here came to our rescue and chased him off, but he did damage his ship." He pointed to Ekron. "The situation is getting quite complicated. At this moment, I'm not sure what we should do."

Quasi climbed down from his perch on a large boulder and squatted beside the fire. He fashioned a "Y" from a split limb and lifted a can of beans from the ashes. Taking two small bowls from his backpack, he filled them half-full and handed them to the boys. He looked at the others and pointed to the cans. They shook their heads.

When they had finished eating, Kerac moved closer to Meesha. "I know you would rather stay here than return with me," he said in

Golanese, "but I made a promise to Mr. Digger. I told him if you come back with me now, if your father agrees to it I will make certain you are returned to Earth."

Meesha dropped his head and stared into the smoldering fire. After a few moments he said, "Uncle, I have thought about what you said, but I do not believe my father would allow me to return. His mind is set on me becoming prince, and I do not believe he will change it. I understand about your promise, but if you told him you could not find me, wouldn't that be good enough?"

"That would be a lie. I would not lie to my brother, under any circumstances."

"Then tell him the truth that I would not come back with you."

"How do you think the senators would like that? They were the ones who gave me permission to return for you."

"I don't know what to tell you, Uncle," Meesha replied. "But I do not wish to return to Golan." He looked deep into his eyes and continued. "Of course you could force me to go back, I realize that. But think of my happiness. I was not happy on Golan. I never was. Everybody avoided me, because I was the King's son. But here on Earth I have made friends, and they do not care who I am."

Kerac got up, took a few steps toward the entrance of the cave and glanced back. "I can sympathize with your dilemma, and I understand. But right now I must return to the ship to figure out what to do about Abron. If you'll stay with Mr. Quasi until I return, we'll talk about it later."

Meesha didn't answer he lowered his head and stared at the crackling fire. He picked up a stick and began drawing unrecognizable pictures in the sand.

Kerac watched him for several moments, and then looked over at Luchak.

"Do you still want to help us find your father?" he said. "If so, let's go. We'll go back to my ship and make plans."

"Yes, I will help you," Luchak told him. "If I'm with you, my father cannot take me back to Golan." He hesitated for a moment, and then added, "As you know, I do not want to go back, either. I will do anything I can to help contain my father, but I will not go back to Golan with him." He headed for the entrance, but before leaving he turned and called back in Golanese, "Meesha, when I think it's safe, I will come for you." He joined Kerac outside the cave and the four men rushed down the slope and onto the path that led back to what was left of Digger's shack.

When they arrived, they stopped to survey the damage. Digger walked through what was left of the front door and into the collapsed living room. He sat down at the dilapidated table and eyed the remains of his shack.

"It ain't so bad, fellows," he said with a sigh. "I can fix it up. You men go on back to your ship. I'll stay here and fix this place up a little. I'll be okay." Then, he added with a smile, "At least it ain't rainin'."

"You're perfectly welcome to join us," Kerac said.

"No, you guys go ahead. You've got some serious thinkin' to do."

Kerac thanked him for his help, shook his hand and left.

What was left of the door swung open and Corky trotted inside. He jumped onto Digger's lap and licked his face.

"Well, hi there little buddy," he said. "Glad to see you're no worse for wear." He stood up and the dog dropped to the floor. "Come on boy, we've got work to do."

When Abron found a secluded spot deep in the forest, where he could make an emergency landing with only half an anti-gravity grid, he brought the ship in for an extremely rough landing. He looked at Nader and said, "Go see how that engineer is doing down there?"

"Now that we've landed, if you want to call that a landing," Nader replied, "I'll go down and see."

"Good. Get to it. We can't stay here long or we'll be discovered."

Nader left the bridge and headed for engineering. When he arrived, he found the engineer lying on his back beneath the anti-gravity drive.

"Kersey!" he called out.

Startled by the voice the engineer jerked his head up, bumping it on a sharp protrusion. He grabbed his head, shouted a few profanities and wiggled out from under the drive.

"What do you want?" he shouted, glaring at him.

"The senator wants to know how long it'll take to repair the ship."

Kersey wiped his bloody forehead on a dirty work cloth and shot back, "I don't know how much longer it'll take! Tell him it'll be fixed when it's fixed! No sooner! Now get out of here and let me get back to work!"

Nader returned to the bridge but didn't tell Abron what the engineer had said, only that it would be fixed soon. As he sat down at the navigation console, he heard a muffled bang, followed by a loud twang, on the hull of the ship.

"What the—" He jerked his head up, startled.

Abron had heard the sound and jumped down from the Captain's Chair. He ran to an observation porthole and looked out. In the semi-darkness of the forest he saw shadowy figures at the edge of the dense foliage. When they got closer he noticed they had rifles with laser sights.

"We have company," he said, as he returned to the helm. "It looks like they have weapons."

Nader went to the porthole and looked out. "That must have been what hit the hull. They're shooting at us. What do you want to do?"

"Don't worry about it they can't hurt us with those puny little rifles."

"That's not what I meant. They found our ship," Nader replied. "They'll probably get in touch with their military and we'll have more trouble than we can handle."

"How much longer did Kersey say it would take to fix that drive?" Abron asked.

"He wasn't sure. I guess the drive was more heavily damaged by Ekron's shot than he first thought."

"How do you know it was Ekron who made that shot?" Abron questioned.

"I saw his ship on the screen, just before he fired," Nader replied. "It had his signature written all over it. However, I didn't have time to move our ship out of the way before the blast hit us—so much for our defensive capabilities!"

Abron went to the helm and adjusted several knobs, then glanced down at his screen. He pushed a button and a powerful, rapidly pulsating strobe-light flooded the outside area. He pushed another button and an extremely loud, piercing tone penetrated the forest. The men had been hiding behind trees, but they were still blinded by the flashing strobe and deafened by the trenchant sound. They rushed blindly out of the area, screaming and holding their hands over their ears.

"That should hold them off, at least for now," Abron said with a cynical smirk.

"You didn't hurt any of them did you?" Nader asked.

"No. I just gave them something to think about…a headache. I had the power low enough where it wouldn't do too much harm. A few busted eardrums, at the most."

"I hope so," Nader replied, "we don't want to be hunted down by their military, given our present situation."

Abron turned and looked at him. "Don't worry about it. We'll be out of here soon."

"You hope so," Nader mumbled sarcastically

Quasi glanced across the smoke-filled cave at Meesha still scribbling in the sand.

"Meesha!" he called out. He put his finger to his forehead indicating he wanted to talk.

He understood. He got up from the boulder, went over to the big Indian and had him put his finger on his brow. Immediately, he saw a path leading to a beautiful pasture next to a rippling creek. He saw strange buildings set close together next to a small stream. He opened his eyes and smiled.

Quasi knew the boy would be safer in his village than in the cave. With the aliens' brainwave technology, he figured it wouldn't be long before they were discovered, even if the cave was lined with mica. He kicked sand onto the fire, took the boy by the hand and led him through the darkness to the mouth of the cave. They walked across the sharp rocks on the side of the slope, and then through thick foliage until they had reached the path he had seen in his mind.

It was early morning but the sun had not yet climbed over the horizon. It had taken them only a few minutes to reach the path beside the creek, and at the end stood the strange buildings his mind had shown him. He noticed something even stranger…wooden racks on long poles joined together and standing beside the cabins, laden with fish. As they approached the encampment a few copper-skinned children dressed in buckskins ran out to meet them.

"These are my people," he told the boy. "They are good people, they will not harm you." Knowing he couldn't understand, he folded his arms across his chest, put his hand over his heart and pointed to the village.

Meesha understood and nodded.

After they entered the encampment they walked up to a small, wood-frame cabin and stopped. A boy wearing nothing but a leather flap over his groin was busy chopping wood into small strips, with an axe half his size. He stopped chopping long enough to look up, and then continued cutting the kindling.

"White Feather," Quasi yelled to him. "We have a guest. Come and meet him. This is Meesha."

The boy laid the axe down, walked over and halfheartedly extended his hand. Meesha looked down at the outstretched hand but made no effort to take it. The boy held it there for several seconds, then dropped it and went back to the chopping block.

Quasi shook his head, and then went into the cabin. Several minutes later he came to the door and motioned for Meesha to come inside.

"Nakomi," he called out.

A petite, bronze-faced woman, dressed in a decorative leather dress, walked into the room. When she saw Meesha, her eyes lit up.

"What do we have here?" she asked. "Is this a new friend for White Feather? He certainly needs one there are very few children here his age."

"He's not from around here," Quasi explained. "He doesn't speak our language so I don't know how the two of them will get along."

"If he can't speak our language, where is he from, Mexico?" Then she added with a whisper, "He's strange looking, and where is he from?"

"It's a long story; I'll explain it all later. Right now I have to go back and get the bear I shot. Digger didn't want it so I'm bringing it to the village."

"You shot a bear?" She frowned. "You know it's not hunting season. You'll be in trouble if the warden catches you."

"I shot it to protect the kid," he said. "There could be another problem though; the boy is being hunted by some very bad people. I brought him here for his safety."

"He's being hunted? Why is he being hunted? Did he do something bad?"

"No, he did nothing wrong. Like I said, I will explain it all later."

"It had better be good," she said. "We don't need any more trouble around here; we have enough with the people in town."

"Yes, I know, but I couldn't let those men get him. They are not nice people. I've seen them in action. That's why I brought him here."

"Are you and the boy hungry?" she asked, walking into the kitchen.

"We'll eat when we return," he told her. "I have to get that bear before the wolves do." He went to the door and looked out. "White Feather," he shouted. "Come, we have to go get a bear I shot. You and the boy can help me skin it, and then bring it back."

The boy's eyes lit up. He dropped the axe, raced into the house and put on his walking shoes. Within seconds he returned and stood in front of his father, his face beaming.

"It's been a long time since you took me into the forest, Father," he said. "How far is the bear from here? Is he a big one? Did you get him with one shot?"

"Slow down and I'll tell you," Quasi answered with a chuckle. "He's about two hundred pounds. I left him about a half-mile from here. That's why I need you boys to help. We'll have to skin him there, cut him up and cart the good meat back to the village. The wolves can have the rest. By the way, it took two shots to down him. Does that answer your questions, Son?"

"Is he coming with us?" White Feather asked, pointing to Meesha.

"Of course, we'll need him to help carry the meat," he replied. Then he added, "You were not very friendly with him. Don't you think you'll like him?"

The boy thought for a moment. "I don't know if I'll like him, I don't know him. But he looks kinda frail to be carryin' meat, or even walkin' a half mile. What's with that funny haircut, and those eyes?"

Ignoring him, Quasi walked behind the cabin. A few minutes later he returned dragging a travois behind him—a crude sled made from two long poles, with a leather hide stretched across them, which is attached to a horse's harness and used for hauling heavy objects. He walked back behind the cabin and whistled. A pinto quarter-horse, leisurely grazing in the field, perked up its ears. It sprinted over and stopped in front of him. He threw a heavy blanket over its back and attached a make-shift horse-collar around its neck, then attached the travois.

Suddenly, he realized Meesha didn't know what they were about to do. He pulled him aside and pointed to his forehead.

Meesha put his finger on his brow and images of their journey sprung into his mind. He understood and shook his head.

Soon after they left the village they found a path that led deep into the forest. Quasi walked alongside the horse to keep it in the middle of the overgrown path, and White Feather ran a short distance ahead, a pre-strung bow stretched across his chest and a quiver of arrows slung over his shoulder. Without warning, he raced ahead, let out a war cry, and then rushed back down the tangled path toward them.

After a quarter mile, Meesha was exhausted. He walked up to the big Indian and tugged on his arm.

Quasi stopped the pony and looked down at him with a puzzled expression on his long, weathered face.

Meesha pointed to the travois and smiled. Quasi understood and lifted him onto the sled. They continued on down the trail, but after a few minutes bouncing up and down and almost falling off, he decided he would rather walk. He jumped off and reclaimed his position behind the sled.

A half hour later they found the bear's slightly torn and partially eaten carcass. The wolves had eaten only a portion and Quasi decided there was enough left to make it worthwhile, since the animals had only eaten where they could easily tear through the tough hide. From all appearances they had been interrupted; the bite marks were fresh and still oozing blood. Before they skinned the huge animal, Quasi scanned the area to make certain the wolves had not returned. He didn't see or hear them so he proceeded.

Halfway through the skinning, the pinto began to get restless. Quasi stopped for a moment and looked around the underbrush for signs of wolves. All of a sudden, a loud snarl, followed by a ferocious growl, came from the bushes. The pony reared up, bolted and charged up the path, the travois still attached. Quasi ran after it, but lost it in the underbrush. He yelled at White Feather to be on the lookout for another bear.

The boy pulled the bow from around his chest and attached an arrow. "Don't worry, Father, I will protect us," he yelled, scanning the area.

Moments later, the bushes at the edge of the tree line parted, and then exploded with activity. A huge, male black bear lumbered into the clearing. As soon as he saw Quasi standing over the carcass he charged. Before Quasi could react, the bear had knocked him to the ground and started mauling him. Desperately, he looked for his gun, but it was leaned up against a nearby tree and out of reach. He was being crushed by the weight of the bear. Barely conscious he feigned death, hoping the animal would back off.

White Feather pulled back on the bowstring and let the arrow fly, but it missed.

Meesha stood at a distance panic-stricken, watching the episode unfold. He spotted the gun leaning up against the tree and ran over to it. Although he knew nothing about guns, he had to do something. He grabbed it, pointed it at the massive body and pulled the trigger, but nothing happened.

"The safety is on! The safety is on!" White Feather yelled panic in his voice. He ran over, flipped the safety lever, and attempted to wrench the gun from the boy's hand. In the scuffle the gun went off and a loud explosion filled the air.

The recoil sent Meesha flying backwards into the shrubbery. Still holding the gun, he regained his footing and quickly re-cocked it with the lever he had seen Quasi use before. He aimed the gun and pulled the trigger. The .30 caliber hit the bear squarely in its chest and sent it reeling backwards. It let out a roar, took several steps forward falling off of Quasi.

White Feather rushed to his father's motionless body. "Father! Father!" he screamed. He crouched beside him and cradled his head in his arms. "Don't die, Father! Please, don't die!"

Meesha dropped the gun and ran over.

The big Indian lay in a pool of blood, mostly that of the bear's. He opened his eyes and looked at them.

"Damn!" he said, softly. "What happened? Who shot the bear?"

"It was the boy, Father." He pointed to Meesha.

"Meesha? He shot the bear? How—"

"I'll tell you all about it later, Father," he replied. "Right now we have to get you back to the village. You look terrible."

"I think my leg's broken…among other things. That damn bear sat on it while he tried to eat me."

"I'll go get the pony, he can't be far," White Feather mouthed with authority. "The boy can stay with you. I'll be right back." He turned and headed up the path.

"Wait!" Quasi yelled at him. "Hand me the gun, in case we have more visitors."

After White Feather disappeared up the path, Meesha put his finger on Quasi's brow and instantly images of White Feather running over and flipping the safety off appeared, and then him aiming the rifle and firing.

"I'll be damned!" Quasi said. "Then it <u>was</u> you who shot that critter."

Meesha smiled and took his finger away. He looked down at Quasi's leg. By its awkward position it appeared to be broken. He put his finger on his leg and moved it slowly up and down. He made a gesture of breaking a stick, and then shook his head negatively.

"Are you telling me it's not broken? How did you do that?"

The boy smiled.

"Sure feels like it," Quasi said. "Damn bears! Now we got two of 'em to skin." He sat upright, felt his chest and mumbled, "I think I got a busted rib, too."

The pounding of hooves on the hard-packed trail told them White Feather had returned with the pony. After tying it to a tree the boy ran down the hill and joined them.

"Can you stand, Father?" he asked.

With their help, he slowly stood. When his weight was put on the leg, he discovered he could walk without too much pain.

"Well, like the boy said, it ain't broken," he mumbled.

"I thought he couldn't talk?" White Feather said, pointing to Meesha.

"He can't speak our language, but he has other ways of communicating." He looked at him and smiled. "I'll tell you all about it later. Right now I think you better get me back to the village and let Doc Brave Wolf check these ribs out and take care of some of these nasty claw marks before they get infected."

After checking the travois for damage and finding none, Quasi struggled to the sled and they strapped him onto the rawhide seat. White Feather grabbed the reins and headed down the trail. Meesha stood in the middle of the path watching them leave.

"Wait," Quasi shouted, before they got out of sight, "we can't leave the boy here. He'll have to come with us."

"I'll only be gone a short time, Father. He'll be all right, until I return for the bear meat. I'll leave the rifle with him."

"I don't know about that. What if wolves come? He can't use the rifle on them, they always come in packs."

"Didn't he kill the bear that was goin' to eat you?"

Quasi thought for a moment. "Nevertheless, I think he should come with us."

Meesha approached the travois and put his finger on Quasi's forehead. He closed his eyes and a picture of him standing beside the dead bear holding the rifle appeared. Quasi sent him back an image of him sitting on the branch of a nearby tree.

After they left, Meesha picked up the rifle, swung the sling over his shoulder, and with much effort shinnied up the tree to a large branch.

Ekron wasted no time devouring the meal Kerac had so generously laid out for them. After they had all finished eating, he took Kerac aside and told him they didn't have much time, they had to put their heads together and go after Abron. The senator's ship would not be inactive long; he told him, he had not done that much damage.

"Kerac," he said, fondling his glass. "As you know, Tumac asked me to find Abron and try to bring him back to face charges. He also told me to bring the boys back, if I found them. What am I supposed to do? I don't have the boys, and undoubtedly Abron is going to be a serious problem in the future. What would you do, if you were me?"

Kerac thought for a moment, and with a broad grin said, "If I were you, I'd go back to Golan and forget all about trying to take Abron or the boys back."

"How can you say that? Tumac gave me an order, not a request."

"You would have a lot of problems, if you tried to take the senator back," Kerac stated. "You know that, don't you? And as far as the boys are concerned, they don't want to go back. I've tried to talk sense into them, but they won't listen. They definitely don't want to go back. Even I don't know what to do about that…Meesha being my nephew, and all, and the King's son."

"Meesha has to go back," Ekron said. "Both Tumac and the King were firm about that."

Kerac took a long sip of wine and eyed him. "Trust me, Ekron, he will not go back, as stubborn as he is. And, you cannot force him, like I said he is the King's son."

Ekron gulped down the last of his drink and stood. He walked to the other side of the cabin, then turned and looked back. "I think I know approximately where Abron landed to make repairs, maybe we could keep him pinned down there. It's worth a try."

"Then what?" Kerac asked. "Would you shoot him out of the sky, again?"

"I don't believe that'd be necessary. All we'd have to do is make certain he couldn't get airborne. Then, he couldn't go after the boys, or us."

"He'd put up a fight," Kerac stated flatly. "I know I would."

"He doesn't have many alternatives," Ekron told him. "The Parliament never gave him permission to come to Earth, in the first place." He thought for a moment, and then added, "If someone doesn't return with Meesha by the end of the week, Tumac might very well be out of a job…at least as Prime Minister."

"Okay, let's go after him," Kerac said. "First, get your ship out of hiding and we'll play it by ear." He gave Ekron a sly grin. "By the way, didn't I hear you say you also had some trouble coming on this trip?"

"We ran into a little trouble leaving the mother-ship. One of Abron's henchmen tried to stop us from leaving." He headed for the hangar bay. "I'll contact my men and have them pick me up. You can follow me where I believe Abron is making his repairs."

Ten feet off the ground, clinging to the bough of a fir tree, Meesha found himself alone, with only his thoughts to keep him company. He didn't have the faintest idea what he would do if wolves came. He wondered if his decision to stay on Earth was the right one. If he stayed, would he be confronted by other situations like this one? He knew that if he could only find his way back to Grace's house everything would be all right. He liked her very much. She had meant more to him than his mother ever had. Charlie wouldn't be so bad either, if he could get to know and understand him. Even the girls in the school yard had become his friends. He didn't know if he would like the boys, he hadn't met any of them. Even so, he believed he would like them. Back on Golan the kids his age were never his friends; his quasi-nobility had seemed to intimidate them.

The sound of thrashing bushes at the far edge of the clearing interrupted his daydream. The unexpected commotion forced him to relax his grip on the limb and he almost fell. He scanned the bushes but could see nothing. He cocked his head and listened for more sounds, but the forest was quiet.

Suddenly, a pack of six gray wolves charged out of the underbrush, yelping and howling, heading for the remains of the bears. After checking for signs of trouble, they crept toward the two carcasses. Several large males stayed close to the tree-line, checking the bushes for territorial signs. Finding none, they raised their heads, sniffed the air and woofed at the pack. Seeing no danger, they all trotted to the fresh meat and started feeding, gnashing their teeth at each other for dominance.

Wide-eyed and frightened, Meesha watched as they fought over the fresh kills. Those were Quasi's bears, he thought. There had to be something he could do. Maybe the rifle would scare them away. At least it was worth a try. He repositioned his body on the limb to keep from falling and put the gun to his shoulder. Before firing he remembered the kick he had received earlier. He put the butt of the gun up against the tree trunk and pulled the trigger. A thunderous explosion shattered the silence. The wolves jumped into the air, spun around several times in confusion and made a beeline for the forest.

Suddenly, he heard a rapid clumping sound in the distance.

"Meesha! Meesha!" a voice called out.

With the rifle slung over his shoulder, he climbed down from the tree. He hit the ground hard, raced across the clearing and waited for White Feather and the pony to come down the path.

Several moments later White Feather charged into the clearing with the pony in tow. "What was that sound?" he shouted. "I heard a shot." He looked at Meesha. "Did you shoot something?"

Meesha lowered the rifle and held it out in front of him. "Doggies," he said, and pointed to the tree line.

"Doggies?" White Feather questioned. "What do you mean doggies?"

Meesha made an attempt to howl like a wolf.

"Oh, you mean wolves?"

The boy howled again and pointed to the tree line.

"You mean wolves were here?"

He howled again.

White Feather tied the reins to a branch and scurried down the small hill to the carcasses. After inspecting them for damage he returned to the wide-eyed boy.

"I wish I could talk to you," he said. "Where did you come from? Why can't you speak our language?"

Meesha looked at him vacantly and shrugged.

"Man, this is going to be one helluva relationship," White Feather said, shaking his head in disgust, "we can't even talk to each other."

Meesha appeared to understand. He reached over and attempted to put his finger on the boy's forehead.

White Feather jerked his head back. "What are you doing?" he yelled.

Meesha moved closer and pointed at his forehead. Realizing he wasn't making any headway he took his finger and put it on his own brow, then pointed at the boy's head.

White Feather frowned, totally confused by his actions.

Meesha kept moving his finger back and forth between their foreheads.

After several more attempts, White Feather gave in to the boy's persistence and let him put his finger on his brow. Instantly, images of the wolves attacking the carcasses appeared in his mind's eye. Startled, he jumped back.

"What was that?" he asked. "How did you do that?"

He put his finger back on the boy's forehead, and scenes of him sitting on the limb scaring the wolves away with a shot from the rifle jumped into the boy's head.

White Feather didn't know what to make of the boy, or his actions. He had a strange power, but he couldn't talk. The only word he had uttered since he knew him was doggies. Where was he from? His father had not explained his strange powers or inability to talk; he had been too busy worrying about the bear meat.

After inspecting the bears for damage, White Feather spent the next several hours skinning them. He attempted to show Meesha how to skin them and cut the meat into large chunks, but he soon discovered it was a hopeless endeavor. He took the knife away from him and finished cutting the meat himself. After the usable meat had been cut into large chunks they hoisted them onto the travois and headed back to the village.

THIRTEEN

Tumac had arrived at the chamber early that morning to go over paperwork he needed for a special meeting of Parliament. The door flew open and the intern he had sent to Keeti to check on Senator Abron's trip entered the chamber, a solemn look on his face.

"Yes, what is it?" he said. "Don't tell me you have some bad news."

"Yes sir," the young man said, "I have what you would call disturbing news!"

Tumac looked up from his paperwork and stared at him. "Yes, what is it?"

"Sir, Senator Abron took his warship to Earth."

"Yes, yes, I know that. I have already been told of his illegal departure."

"Sir, a man at the docking station told me he was going after Kerac. Also that he was going to try to get the boys and bring only his son back." He paused, and then added, "I don't know if you were aware of it, but his warship left Keeti fully armed."

"Who told you that?'

"A lieutenant at their docking station told me, Sir." He hesitated for a moment, and then added, "I got the impression he wasn't too happy with the senator, anyway. I don't believe he would have told me, otherwise."

"Did he tell you anything more?"

"Only that his ship was outfitted with the latest weaponry, and that he was possibly going to use it on Kerac, and maybe Earth."

Tumac leaned back in his chair and put his palms against his forehead to soothe a tension headache, and then looked up at the young man.

"What was your name again, son?" he asked apologetically. "I'm sorry, I forgot your name. Too many things going on around here, I guess."

"That's all right, Sir, nobody else remembers it either." He smiled and relaxed his posture. "Daka, Sir, that's my name."

"Well, Daka, you did well. You found out what I wanted to know, and what I was afraid of."

"Sir?"

"I have believed all along Abron would eventually do something foolish, but I didn't think he would go that far…to take a fully armed warship to Earth." He closed his eyes and leaned back in his chair. "What would happen if the Earthlings captured his ship? We are not ready for that kind of encounter. I wonder if he has enough sense not to start something with them. That would negate everything we've worked so hard for. When we get to the point where we can send our mother-ships through, which I believe will be in the not too distant future, our efforts could be in vain. Earth would have lost all respect for us, and what we're trying to do—survive and possibly coexist with them."

"Yes, I understand. But what can we do?"

"I don't know, Daka. For the moment I have done everything I can, by sending Ekron after that idiot. But I'm not the least bit confident he will succeed, after what you just told me about his ship." He stared at the ceiling for several moments, and then continued. "Thank you, Daka. I appreciate what you've done. You may go."

"Sir!" Daka replied quickly.

"Yes, is there something else?"

"Sir, didn't you give Senator Ekron authorization to go to Earth?"

"Yes, why do you ask?"

I guess you haven't heard, they tried to stop him from leaving Golan Two."

"Who tried to stop him?"

"I don't know, Sir. But it's rumored Senator Abron and his henchmen may have had something to do with it."

"Thank you for the information, Daka. Just one more nail in my coffin."

"Sorry, Sir, I guess I shouldn't have told you."

"It's all right, Daka, you did well. I needed that information. You may go."

FOURTEEN

"Nader!" Abron shouted over the intercom. "Nader!" he repeated louder. "When is that idiot going to have this thing repaired? We have to get out of here! By now everybody must know where we are, even the Earthlings. Get him moving!"

Nader entered the engineering compartment and was immediately overcome by a room full of acrid smoke from a laser torch. He began coughing violently. He thought of answering the intercom, but instead he dropped the mike and pulled out a handkerchief to cover his face.

"Kersey!" he yelled over the hiss of the torch.

Startled the man jump up and hit his head on the same protrusion as before. He rubbed his head, gave Nader an angry glare, and then returned to his laser.

"What do you want?" he shouted over the noise of the cutter

"The senator wants a report on your progress."

"Tell him to—"

"Watch it! He's listening!" Nader cut him off.

The engineer stuck his head out from under the drive. "I don't really care. Tell him it'll be ready when it's ready. That's all I can tell him." He stuck his head back under the drive and mumbled, "It would get done a lot faster, if I didn't have so many damn interruptions."

Hearing another sharp ping on the ship's hull, Nader jerked his head around. He rushed to the bridge and looked through a porthole. The laser-lights had returned and their beams darted up and down the entire length of the ship.

"Are those idiots back?" he shouted to Abron. "I thought that little demonstration you gave them earlier would scare them off. But I guess not."

Abron had also heard the sound and looked through the helm porthole. “We’ve got to get out of here,” he bellowed. “Everybody on Earth must know we’re here.” He went to the intercom and yelled, “Kersey, what’s going on down there? We have to leave, immediately! What’s the prognosis?”

The engineer slid out from under the drive and rushed to an intercom on the far bulkhead. “Okay, you can activate the drive. I think it’ll hold until we can find a more secluded spot to land so I can fix this thing properly.”

Abron activated the power to the drive and waited anxiously for its familiar whirring sound. When it reached maximum speed and stabilized, he slowly eased the anti-gravity control forward. The ship hesitated for a moment, and then lifted a few feet off the ground. When he was confident in the drive’s ability, he shoved the control farther forward and the ship lifted halfway up the tree line. While the ship was still stationary, the men on the ground took several more pot-shots at it. Then, like a missile, it darted into the sky and disappeared.

“Those were not military men,” Nader said. “They were a bunch of hunters trying to make us mad.”

“Well, they made me mad,” Abron mumbled. “I’ll take care of them later. Right now let’s go after Ekron, he’s the one who shot us out of the sky!”

As the boys approached the village, a number of partially clad children ran out to meet them. A dozen men in buckskins and plaid shirts came out of the village and walked alongside the travois, until it had stopped in front of Quasi’s cabin.

White Feather tied the pony to a fish-drying rack and headed for the cabin.

“Mother,” he yelled.

Nakomi looked through the kitchen window. “White Feather,” she called. “Come in here, your father wants to talk to you.”

Brave Wolf, a self-appointed doctor and shaman had just finished tending to Quasi’s wounds, when White Feather walked into the cabin.

“Yes, Father?”

He motioned for the boy to sit on the side of the bed. “Son,” he said, “I have to tell you something about that boy.”

“I don’t believe you have to, Father, I know what he can do.”

“Then you know about him? How did you find out?”

“He showed me pictures in my head.”

“Son, I want you to promise me something. I want you to protect him. He’s a very important person on his planet. I promised Digger I would keep him safe.” He squeezed the boy’s arm gently. “Do you understand? You can do that for me, can’t you?”

“Yes, Father,” he answered with a puzzled expression. “There’s only one problem, he only talks to me with pictures. It’s kinda hard to communicate, you know.”

Quasi smiled. “Yes, I know. But he’s quick to learn. Teach him some of our language, he’ll pick it up quickly.”

“How long will he be with us, Father?”

“I don’t know. That might depend on you. If you see anything strange going on, something you don’t understand, take him into the forest…or to the cave by Digger’s shack. Okay?”

“Yes, Father.” He thought for a moment, then added, “I think he’s tired or sleepy or something. He keeps closing his eyes and nodding.”

“He probably is tired. I don’t think he’s slept for some time. Take him into your bedroom and let him lie down.”

“Yes, Father, I will. But first, I have something to show him.”

Meesha had been standing by the door watching the men take the bear meat from the sled and carry it into the center of the village.

White Feather left the room and walked by him. When he was a few feet away he turned and motioned for him to follow.

They stopped in front of a group of men cutting the meat into smaller portions for distribution to the village. Meesha watched them for a few minutes, and then turned his head away. On Golan the meat had always been frozen. All they had to do was go to a communal outlet and pick it up, along with the other food they needed. When they were in the forest he had watched White Feather skin the animals and cut them into large chunks, and was disgusted by what he saw. But now he was even more disturbed and turned away.

White Feather noticed his discomfort and giggled. After a few minutes he took the boy by the arm and led him back into the cabin. He pointed to the bed, cocked his head, closed his eyes and made a snoring sound, indicating sleep. Meesha understood and jumped up onto the feather mattress. Within seconds he was sound asleep.

"Charlie!" Grace shouted above the din of the TV. Not getting a response, she yelled again, louder, "Charlie!"

He turned the volume down and looked over. "Yes, Gracie, what is it?" he said, annoyed by the interruption.

"I think someone's at the door. Wonder who that could be at this time of day?" She got up from her Belcher, walked to the window and looked out. Two men dressed in dark suits wearing sunglasses stood on the porch. She opened the door, hesitantly.

"Ma'am," the taller of the two said. "Are you Mrs. Bertell?"

"Yes, I am."

"Ma'am, do you have a young boy staying with you?"

"Is that some sort of crime?" she asked.

"No, Ma'am, but we were sent to investigate an incident. We were told you have a young boy staying with you who looks…shall we say different." He took off the sunglasses and stared at her.

"Who told you a story like that?" she asked. "I'll bet it was Maggie Johnson, wasn't it? She's always tryin' to get people in trouble."

The man didn't appear overly impressed with her response, and said, "Ma'am, do you have a strange little boy living with you, or not?" he repeated irritably.

"Just what do you mean by strange?" she asked staring back at him. She could tell had become annoyed with her. "No," she said bluntly, "not now. We did have a little fellow staying with us for a spell, but he belonged to some friends. They came and got him last night. I guess he was lost, or something. I found him beside the road and brought him here. They came and picked him up last night."

"You say he belonged to some of your friends?" he asked. He put his glasses back on and slid them halfway down his nose. "That isn't exactly how we heard it, ma'am. Would you care to fill us in?"

"Exactly what are you trying to say," she said irritably, "that I was harboring a criminal or something?"

"Mrs. Bertell, I'm only doing my job. I was told to find the small, strange looking boy everybody's talking about. We believe he's…shall we say from another place."

"Gracie," a voice shouted over the TV. "What the hell's goin' on out there? Who's that at the door?"

"Never mind, Charlie, it's just somebody looking for a little boy."

Charley got up from the sofa and hobbled to the door. After scanning them, he said to the taller of the two, "Take your damn glasses off so I can see your face!"

The man stared at him for an uneasy moment, and then removed his sunglasses. "Is that better, Sir?" he said derisively.

"What the hell do you want?" Charley asked an edge to his voice.

"Sir, we're from the Defense Department. We're looking for a young boy. We were told he may have been staying with you." He put his sunglasses back on and stared at him blankly.

"Oh, you're from the government and you're here to help. Is that it?" Charlie said with a scoff. "Where's your ID? How do I know you're who you say you are?"

The tall man became even more aggravated. He reached into his coat pocket, pulled out a black billfold and flipped it open and displayed his credentials.

"Satisfied, Sir?" he said with a sneer.

Charlie took a long, deliberate look at the picture ID. "Didn't Gracie just tell you the boy ain't here? He left last night. His folks came and got him."

The man turned back to Grace. "Ma'am, did the boy seem different to you?"

"What do you mean different? He was just a little boy."

"I mean, was there anything peculiar about him…his looks?"

"He was very small."

"That isn't exactly what I meant," he said, shaking his head with disgust. "Was there anything strange about his facial features…

different?" He hesitated for a moment, and then added, "About his eyes, did they look like a cat's? And could he talk?"

Grace stared at him as if he were out of his mind. "You've got to be kidding!

Eyes like a cat's?"

"Yes, madam, like a cat's."

"I never really noticed," she said. "He looked like any other little boy to me." She glanced at the other man standing off to one side. "What's this all about? Did the boy you're looking for do something bad, something against the government?"

The man thought for a moment. "Ma'am, several people told us you had a strange looking little boy living with you. We were sent to investigate. That's all."

"We don't know anything about a 'strange' little boy," Charley said. "The boy we had belonged to some friends and they came and got him last night. That's it! End of story!"

"Where do your friends live, Ma'am? We would like to talk to them."

"I don't know," Grace answered. "I never asked them."

The man frowned. "They're friends of yours and you don't know where they live? That sounds rather odd to me, Ma'am."

Charlie interrupted angrily, "Just what are you trying to say, mister, that we're not telling you the truth?"

"No," said the tall man, "but the government is quite interested in the boy we're looking for. They think he might be a security risk."

Grace laughed. "A security risk? How in heaven's name could a little twelve year old boy be a security risk?"

"I'm afraid I can't go into details, Ma'am, the government has put a lid on it."

"A lid on it?" she mimicked, shaking her head.

"Yes Ma'am, a lid."

"Well, you tell whoever you work for I put a lid on it, too!" Charlie said, as he turned and grabbed the door knob. "You tell 'em they ought to be ashamed of themselves goin' after a little defenseless boy that ain't done nothin' wrong." He started to close the door, then turned and added, "You tell 'em he ain't no security risk, he's just a nice little fella' tryin' to get along in this world of ours."

The tall man grabbed the door before it closed. "Then you do know something about him, don't you?"

"I ain't sayin' nothin' more! Get off my porch!" Charley shouted. He ushered Grace back into the living room, returned to his favorite sofa and changed channels.

Not knowing how far their authority went, the men left.

"Do you have anything for me, Nader?" Abron yelled across the bridge. "Do you have a fix on Ekron's ship?"

"No. I'm working on it. It might take a while the scanner isn't working very well. Must be from that hit we took."

"Well, keep on it, I want to find him," Abron yelled back. "He's going to pay for what he did to my ship!"

"Right!" Nader said with a hidden smirk. "Hopefully, I'll have a lock on him in a few minutes."

Abron walked across the bridge and slumped down in the Captain's Chair. He drummed his fingers on the console, and then raised his eyes and stared at the overhead. He realized it would be sheer suicide to attempt anything when his ship was not up to full power…especially his weaponry. He also knew if Nader discovered what he had planned for Ekron he might not go along with it, at least not willingly. Although he was the captain he still needed his First Mate. He was considered an excellent pilot, but he would need Nader, if things got rough. However, for the moment he would keep him in the dark.

"I believe I have him on the scanner!" Nader cried out.

"You've located Ekron's ship?"

"Yes. I think so. I'm certain the Earthlings don't have anything like this."

Abron rushed over to examine the image on the screen. "It has his signature, all right. I'll take us into outer space, now that we've located him. I'm sure he's seen us, too. We'll wait for him to make a move. If he attempts to draw first blood, we'll move in for the kill! We have him out-gunned."

Nader took his hands off the controls and stared at him. "The kill?"

"You know what I meant," Abron replied. "We'll do what he did to us. You understand? We'll just inflict enough damage so he can't return to Golan, at least not right away." He paused for a moment, and then added, "If you get a good clean shot, hit his anti-gravity grid. That'll keep him in outer space for quite awhile. He can't land without it…as we almost found out. You can do that, can't you?"

"Yes sir," Nader replied. He sat down at the scanner and pushed a few buttons. Several minutes later he looked over and said, "I don't believe I fully understand, Sir. If we disable him, he'll be stranded here for a long time, at least until they can send a ship for him. By then the Earthlings will have given him a lot of grief. Are you sure you want to do that?"

"Are you questioning my decision, my authority?" Abron exploded.

"No sir, I wouldn't think of it," he mumbled under his breath.

Abron shoved the ion thruster forward and the ship darted thousands of miles above Earth, out of their missile range.

"Sir!" Lieutenant Chuck Beaver, sitting at a console in the war room at NORAD, called out. "I saw something strange on my screen, a minute ago."

A tall man in a colonel's uniform, chomping on an unlit cigar, turned and looked at him.

"Yes, what is it?" he asked, as he walked across the polished floor.

"Sir, I had a bogey on my screen going like a bat out of hell! It was only there for a split second, and then it disappeared."

"What do you think it was?"

"I don't know, it wasn't there long enough to get a fix on it. It went from the bottom of my screen to the top in no more than a couple seconds. Then, it just disappeared."

"Maybe it was a glitch. We've had a couple in the past several days. Keep your eyes open. Let me know if it happens again."

"Yes sir."

Colonel Steel walked back to his desk and sat down at his monitor. After shuffling through some paperwork, he glanced at his screen. A message from DOD caught his eye. He read it several times, and then rushed back across the room.

"Chuck," he said. "When did that happen, that glitch on your screen? A few minutes ago? Do you have a record of when it happened, down to the second?"

The lieutenant punched several keys and an archive menu popped up. "Yes, here it is…five minutes ago…exactly."

"Is there any way to find out how fast that thing was really going?"

"I might have a way," Beaver answered. "Our computer keeps a record of every blip it's received in the past month. Give me a few minutes, I'll bring it back up and let the computer analyze it in slo-mo. That should tell us exactly how fast it was." He glanced up at the colonel. "What's the problem, Sir, you think we might have a UFO on our hands?"

"Don't know, Chuck," Steel said. "I'm only following up on something I received from DOD. They said half a dozen radar sites around the country picked up the same blip. They all calculated it to be traveling about fifty thousand miles an hour. Do we have anything in our arsenal that can go that fast? Don't think so." He released a nervous grunt.

"Wow!" the lieutenant replied, as he watched the computer analyze the blip and come up with the same figure. "They were right, fifty-thousand."

Steel sat down at his keyboard and sent a message back to DOD, confirming their findings. He leaned back in his chair, folded his arms across his chest and puffed vigorously on his unlit cigar.

FIFTEEN

King Oltar's long, weather-beaten face clearly portrayed his pain, as he lay under a mountain of covers on the huge canopied bed with barely enough energy to move. His eyes were colorless orbs pushed deep into the dark, fleshy sockets on his pale face. His once robust body had become frail and nearly useless, over his long months of internment. However, Carlina, his handmaiden was constantly at his side tending to his needs.

From all appearances, the mother-ships were about to lose their King-for-life. Although his physicians had done everything in their power to keep him alive, he appeared to be on his final coil of life. And he knew it.

He raised his hand and motioned to the young girl. "Carlina!" he said softly. "Would you please come here?"

The slender, dark-haired girl walked nimbly across the room and knelt beside him. "Yes, Your Majesty. What is it your desire?"

He looked into her eyes caringly, and with a nod of his head said, "I want you to get in touch with my wife. I want her at my side." He coughed several times, and then continued. "Where is Meesha? I want him here, also."

She raised her head, and without looking directly at him, said, "Your Majesty, Meesha is on Earth, at your request. And your wife is on Golan Two with her friends. I don't know how long she will be there."

"Meesha is on Earth at my request?" He reached over and placed his hand under her chin. "Look at me, Carlina. What do you mean at my request?"

"Your Majesty, he went to Earth with your brother, Kerac." She thought for a moment, and then added, "Your Majesty, you asked your brother to take your son to Earth until the Parliament was ready to vote."

He put his hand up to his forehead and took a deep breath. "Oh, yes. Now I remember." Again, he placed his hand under her chin, raised her head and looked into her light blue eyes. "And is he still there?"

"Yes, Your Majesty, as far as I know. Your brother and Lulla returned briefly to meet with the Prime Minister, but I don't know what happened after that. I heard they were instructed to go back after him. But I'm not certain."

"Tell the Prime Minister I want to see him, right away."

"Yes, Your Majesty. I will send word to him." She rose from her kneeling position, bowed her head, took a few steps backwards and then left the room.

An hour later Tumac entered the King's huge, garish bedroom and approached the canopied bed. Oltar extended his hand. Tumac bowed and took his outstretched hand. When he was about to kiss it, a sign of affection, the King jerked his hand away.

"This is no time or place for reverence, Tumac!" he said sternly, but with a faint smile. "Raise your head and look at me. It's way too late in life for you to be submissive."

"Yes, Your Majesty." Tumac said, raising his head with a slight smile. "You wished to see me, Your Majesty?"

Oltar attempted to raise his head higher on the huge pillow. Tumac reached over, lifted his head and plumped the pillow.

"Thanks you. Now, tell me about my son. Is he still on Earth?"

"Yes, Your Majesty. I guess he must like it there. He ran away from your brother so he could stay there. I guess he's made many friends, there."

"What are you saying that he will not come back to be heir to the throne?"

"I have sent Kerac and Lulla back to Earth to try and persuade him to come back."

"And?"

"They have not yet returned with him, Your Majesty. But I will keep you informed."

"Please do, I don't believe I have much time left, before I succumb to my illness. When the time comes, I want him at my side." He turned his head and raised his eyes to the ceiling. "And, how is our planet doing? Is it any closer to its destruction?" He lowered his eyes and fixed them on Tumac.

"Your Majesty, I will do everything in my power to get Meesha back, before the next meeting of Parliament. And, I don't know what is taking place on our planet. The scientists themselves are not certain. However, it doesn't look good." He looked at him dolefully. "But to answer your question, in my opinion it will not be long before everything is lost. The lakes have all dried up, the ocean is nothing but hot water and the fish are all dead. If that weren't enough, fires are raging across the entire planet. There is no possible way the ones who stayed behind could survive. They may have a week or two, but that's about all."

"What about the larger vortexes, have they made any progress getting our mother-ships to Earth?"

"No, Your Majesty, not to my knowledge. The ships are much too large, and they cannot find a way to make the vortexes large enough for them to pass through."

"Then what are we to do?"

"If they cannot come up with a solution within a week or two," Tumac replied, "I'm afraid our mother-ships will be forced to leave our solar system. We will have to travel to the stars and search for planets that support life. As of yet, our long-range telescopes and sensors have located none that can sustain life."

"Then all is lost? Is that what you're saying?"

"No, Your Majesty, we still have the ability to send smaller craft to Earth. We could try to make contact with their leadership and pray that those who wanted to go to Earth would be allowed to assimilate. We could offer them technology, as a bargaining tool. The remaining population would have to remain on the mother-ships, until we found a suitable planet. If none were found, we would be forced to live the remainder of our lives on the ships."

Oltar stared up at the ornate ceiling, then turned and looked at him with a deep frown. "But there are many million on our five ships. We could not ask Earth to take all who wanted to stay."

"I realize that, Sir. However, we could have a lottery."

"A lottery?"

"Yes, it's a term used on Earth. All names from the five ships would be entered in a drawing, and those who were randomly selected would go to Earth. The others would have to remain on the ships."

Again, the King stared at the ceiling in thought. "What about the senators? Would their names be entered, also?" As an afterthought, he added with a weak smile, "I believe they should remain on our ships, the Earth would be much better off without those idiots." He laughed, and then grabbed his sides in pain. "From what I've been told about Earth, they have enough of their own."

"Whatever you think is best, Your Majesty. But we shouldn't be too hasty we still have a little time left to come up with a solution to our vortex problem. If they can't find the trouble by the time we are forced to leave, we can then think more seriously about a lottery, or whatever Your Majesty suggests. The lottery was merely my idea."

"Let me think it over," Oltar replied. "I will inform you of my decision, later. Now, please leave me. I want to lie here and wallow in my pain and frustration." He turned on his side and closed his eyes. "Oh, by the way," he added in a muffled voice. "I heard my old friend Senator Abron is also on Earth. What could he possibly want there? Maybe to make enemies, like he has here?"

"I believe he's after your son, Your Majesty. He believes if he can find him before Kerac does, he can keep him hidden until after the vote, and bring only his son back to be voted on. If Meesha were not available his son, Luchak, could be voted in as prince and successor to your crown."

Oltar frowned. "Are you saying he would hold my son hostage?"

"Not exactly hostage, he would only hold him long enough so your brother couldn't return with him for the vote."

"Is anything being done about this?"

"I have sent someone I trust to Earth to bring Abron back, along with Meesha and Luchak, if at all possible."

"Who did you send?" Oltar asked. "Not another one of my enemies, I hope."

"I have asked Senator Ekron of Lechi to go to Earth and bring all of them back. At least help Kerac find Meesha and bring him back."

"Ekron is a good man and a friend," the King replied. "I have confidence in him. He is one of only a few senators I sincerely trust. Keep me informed."

"By the way, Your Majesty, what is the prognosis of your illness? Do you think our doctors will ever find a cure, or at least discover what ails you?"

"No, they have not found a cure, and probably never will," Oltar replied. "To answer your other question, they're not even certain what my illness is. As you must know, our mother-ships only have a few slightly competent doctors left on board. The others, the good ones, stayed on the planet to help those who remained, even though they knew they would be caught up in its ultimate destruction."

Tumac moved closer to the bed. "Your Majesty, I have heard of Earth's medical expertise, from pilots who have been there many times. Medically speaking they are years ahead of us. I would like to suggest we make contact with them. If everything went well, we could take you to Earth and ask if they could find your problem, and possibly cure it."

Oltar turned back around and looked at him. "How can they be that far advanced in medicine?" he said skeptically. "They don't have the technologies we possess…anti-gravity, traveling at almost the speed of light, and the ability to travel between universes. How can they be so advanced in medicine?"

"Sir, we became more advanced in technology out of necessity. Because of our past lengthy war, and the knowledge that our world was doomed, we were forced to find a way to survive only by developing technology. Our whole existence depended on finding a solution to those problems. We did not have time to acquire advanced medical skills or knowledge. The war was the reason our planet's population went from several billion down to only a few million. That lengthy war definitely took care of our over-population problem." He scoffed, and then continued. "Apparently, Earth had the fortitude, the intelligence and desire to take care of its people, instead of sending them off to lengthy wars, and its population flourished, almost too much." He looked at the King benevolently, and then continued. "Sir, I am certain the Earthlings could find a solution to your problem, if we made contact with them. From what I've been told, by those who have made many trips, they could find your problem in no time and cure it."

Again, Oltar stared at the ceiling in thought. "Assuming they could do that, how would we bring it about? For one thing, as of yet we have not made official contact. I don't know if they would even talk to us, let alone take in an old weather-beaten reprobate like me." He smiled weakly.

"Sir, I would be honored to go to Earth and attempt to make contact with their leadership," Tumac stated. "I am almost certain that once they discovered we were not a war-like people they would open their arms to us, especially if we offered them technology in return. You do want to live, don't you, Sir? Wouldn't you like to get your health back, and the continued admiration of your people?"

Oltar lowered his eyes, and with a weak smile said, "Yes, I would. But only long enough to deal with Senator Abron." He scoffed. "I've wanted to kick him out of Parliament on many occasions, but I was unable due to my health."

"Then do I have your permission to make contact Earth?" Tumac asked. "I could make official contact on your behalf and explain your situation. I'm certain they would listen, assuming the right people were contacted. I believe Earth's country of the United States is the most advanced in medicine. Therefore, that would be the most logical country to contact. They are a democratic and capitalistic society, quite similar to what we were many years ago, long before the war."

"Are you saying the people in their government are idiots, like ours once were?"

Tumac smiled. "From what I've heard, it's quite possible. However, their democracy survived and ours did not. Maybe our new government will survive this time under the new political format we have just installed."

"Draw up the necessary papers and I will put my seal on them," Oltar replied. "Whoever you take, make certain they are the right ones for the job. I don't want any senators going, unless I approve of them. Most are under Abron's control anyway."

"Yes, I'm aware of that," Tumac replied. "I will try to make official contact on your behalf, and explain your medical problem. After that I will look for your son, and try to bring him back. Hopefully, I will return with good news." As he turned to leave, he added, "Your Majesty, I believe it prudent to go with only a small, trustworthy crew. The Earthlings might get the wrong impression, if I did otherwise. Too many could hinder my efforts, anyway."

"Whatever you wish, Prime Minister. Have a fruitful journey."

SIXTEEN

It was early morning in Grande Ronde, but the sun had barely crept halfway up the tall firs standing guard like silent sentinels on the partially bald higher mountains.

Although it was mid-September, the red-tailed squirrels were already scurrying about the forest floor in search of acorns or anything edible that would hold them over through the upcoming winter, their huge, fluffy tails signifying that the approaching winter would be a long and cold one. Birds had not yet found suitable places to nest, and flitted about the forest in search of woodpecker holes or underbrush that would protect them from the bitter winds to come. Black bears had already dug their secret caves for hibernation and a place to delivery their cubs during the long sleep soon to come.

From all appearances, it would be a bright and beautiful day.

“Meesha!” White Feather shouted, shaking the hand-made quilt. “Meesha!” he shouted again. “Wake up! It’s time for breakfast and chores. Get up, we have to go see if there’s anything left of the bear meat, and get the hides.” He knew the boy didn’t know what he had said, but he believed he understood.

Meesha opened his eyes and White Feather was standing over him fluttering his fingers in front of his mouth in a chewing motion. If nothing else, he understood what that meant. He slid off the high mattress onto the rough, cold floor. He looked out the window and noticed the sun had already climbed over the tree line on the mountain. Had he really been sleeping that long, he wondered? The last thing he remembered was them returning to the village with the bear meat, and then watching the men cutting it up and the women distributing it. White Feather made the gesture again. He followed him into the kitchen where Nakomi was busy frying thin pieces of meat and scrambling eggs.

"White Feather," Nakomi said. "Go get more eggs from the hen house."

White Feather motioned for Meesha to follow him. Behind the cabin stood a wire-mesh cage, filled with cackling white hens. He pried the flimsy door open, walked into the coop and motioned for Meesha to watch as he lifted a hen from her nest and retrieved her eggs.

Meesha grabbed a hen by the neck and lifted her high over his head. She squawked loudly, flapped her wings violently and scratched him with her feet. He dropped her and she scampered to the other side of the coop. With a triumphant shriek and a broad smile he grabbed three eggs from the nest and held them up for White Feather's inspection. White Feather shook his head and grunted. He locked the coop and they took the eggs into the cabin.

Quasi walked slowly and painfully out of the bedroom and sat at the table. White Feather looked at Meesha and pointed to a chair at the other end of the table. Meesha was famished and the smell of breakfast made him even hungrier. Nakomi slid several scoops of scrambled eggs and four strips of fried meat onto their plates.

"Son, take the boy and go get the hides and the rest of the meat, if there's any left worth bringing back," Quasi told him.

"Yes, Father, right after I feed the chickens slop the pigs and milk the cow."

Quasi shook his head. "Never mind the chores, I'll take care of them," he said with a sigh. "I'm a little banged up, but I can manage. You and the kid go right after you eat. We need all the meat and hides we can get for the winter. We'll rock-salt the meat and cure the hides." He looked at Meesha and pointed to his own forehead.

Meesha understood and put his finger on the big Indian's brow. A picture of him and White Feather riding on a horse with the travois trailing behind came into view. The scene changed to them cutting up the remainder of the meat and collecting the hides. A wide smile spread across his face. He finished his plate in record time and jumped up from the table. He loved it in the forest.

"Wait, Meesha!" Quasi shouted. The boy stopped and looked back. "White Feather, take the rifle. You probably won't need it, it's daylight, but take it in case more wolves are out there. I know you can handle it."

"So can he," White Feather replied with a grin, and pointed to Meesha.

"Don't shoot at anything unless it's absolutely necessary. They can hear that gun in Grande Ronde. And we don't have a license to hunt bear…or anything else."

White Feather thought for a moment. "But it's deer hunting season, Father. If they heard it they would think somebody was hunting deer. Don't you think?"

"Probably, but we have enough trouble with the sheriff, as it is. We don't need any more. Besides, we don't have a deer license, either." He snickered.

"Okay. I'll take it, just in case," the boy replied. He got up from the table, took the rifle down from the fireplace and joined Meesha at the door. "Come on, kid, let's go get some bear hides."

Abron's rapid ascent from Earth on his damaged ship had barely allowed him the ability to limp into outer space and secure an orbit out of Earth's radar range. Although his ship was far from being in perfect condition, he believed it would function well enough to avoid any offensive moves Ekron might make. He remained quite confident his ship, although not up to full power, could still outdo and outrun any ship in Golan's fleet. But he would wait to attack Ekron, after his first mate told him the ship was fully operational.

"Nader!" he shouted from the bridge "Why haven't you found Ekron's ship? And how is that idiot doing down there in engineering? I've got to get fully operational!"

Nader looked at him with a sneer. "I'm trying to locate him, but I believe he's somewhere on the other side of the planet. He doesn't show up on my long-range scanner. Maybe he's hiding on Earth with everything turned off and I can't detect him. And that idiot, as you call him, is doing the best he can in engineering. He told me the damage was worse than he first thought. He said the original problem was exacerbated by that speedy retreat you made from Earth, without the ion generator being up to par."

"Well, keep trying to find Ekron. He's got to be somewhere. I want his head for what he did to my ship!"

"Yes sir. I'll let you know when I've made contact."

Kerac had stopped his ship in Earth's outer limits, many miles above Russian territory and obtained orbit. He believed Abron could not locate him, if the bulk of Earth was between them. However, if Abron did locate him, he would make the first move against him, when he got within firing range.

Ekron walked onto the bridge and stood behind him. "What do you think we should do?" he asked. "Are we going to stay in orbit until he finds us? I thought we were going after him."

"We won't have to," Kerac replied. "I'm sure he'll come after us, especially after what you did to his ship."

Ekron looked at him and grinned. "You'd have done the same, if it had been me in trouble. Wouldn't you?"

Ignoring the question, Kerac looked over at Lulla. "Are we too far out to get Meesha's waves?"

"Way too far!"

"Keep trying," he said, "if the senator doesn't find us soon we'll go back to Meesha's last location. For now, I want to stay far enough away where he can't locate the boy, or us."

SEVENTEEN

Tumac entered the combat room of Golan One and approached a colonel sitting at a large desk going over paperwork. He eyed the man for several moments, but he didn't acknowledge him. He coughed.

The colonel looked up. "Can I help you?" he said with a forced smile.

Tumac laid the document with the King's seal on the desk. "I would like a medium sized ship with vortex capabilities."

The colonel picked up the document and examined it. Noticing the seal at the top, he squinted and said, "The King gave you this?"

"Yes, don't you see his seal?"

"Why do you want to go to Earth, Sir?"

"It is no concern of yours, Colonel," Tumac replied, looking at him coldly. "Our King wants me to go. I think that is reason enough."

The colonel stared at him for several seconds, then shoved the papers aside and pushed a button on his console. A long list of ship numbers scrolled down the screen. He scanned the list and made several notations on a pad.

"I only have one craft available with vortex capabilities," he stated. "However, it's only moderately armed. Does that matter?"

"I'm not going there to start a war!"

The colonel looked at him with a forced smile. "I see. How long will you be on Earth?"

"Not long, several days I suppose. Why do you ask?"

"This ship has provisions for four days. Will that be sufficient?"

"I would hope so."

"Then it's in hangar bay three," the colonel replied, leaning back in his chair. "I'll fill out the necessary paperwork."

"One thing more, how many men will be going with me?"

"You will have a crew of three; a pilot, a first mate, who will double as navigator, and an engineer."

"I have a pilot," Tumac informed him. "Include two armed military men."

"Two soldiers?" the colonel questioned.

"Yes, two soldiers. I don't know what I'll encounter on this trip. I want to be prepared, in case I run into trouble."

"Two soldiers it is." The man thought for a moment, and then asked, "What should these soldiers take in the line of weaponry?"

"The usual, I guess, whatever that is."

"All right," the colonel said with a sigh. "It'll take a couple hours to set up the military end of it." He glanced at Tumac suspiciously. "Are you sure this is what the King wants you to do, Sir? It's a dangerous mission, for a man of your…importance. I thought the King was on his deathbed, why would he want you to go to Earth?"

"Are you questioning his orders, Colonel?"

The man's face reddened. "No, but I have to be careful who I let go to Earth. I have orders."

"Orders? From whom?"

"The Parliament."

"Do you <u>really</u> know who I am? I am the Prime Minister, and head of the Parliament."

"Yes, I know who you are. But I was given direct orders to question any documents coming through here. I'm only doing my job, Sir."

"And who gave you those orders, Colonel?"

The young colonel hesitated before answering. "Sir, I'm not at liberty to say. I could get into a lot of trouble."

"You could very easily get into a lot of trouble, if you <u>don't</u> tell me," Tumac replied. "Then again," he added as an afterthought, "you don't have to tell me, I believe I know where they came from. Senator Abron, right?"

Appearing not to hear, the colonel slumped down in his chair and continued sifting through the paperwork in front of him.

Tumac watched in amusement, as the man's fingers nervously flipped through the pages. "When the ship is ready, please give me a call," he said. "I'll be in the Chamber." As he turned to leave, he added, "If I were you, Colonel, I wouldn't tell anyone where we're going or when we're leaving. Do you understand?"

"Yes Sir."

EIGHTEEN

The boys bounced painfully up and down on Red Wing's unsaddled back until they had reached the path that led to the carcasses. The pony stopped abruptly, reared-up in front of a thick barrier of bushes a few yards from the remains, and the boys lost their balance and slid off its back onto the hard-packed ground.

White Feather took the rifle from the travois and slung it over his shoulder. He fought his way through a thick cluster of blackberry bushes, and then leaned the rifle up against a young sapling. He scanned the area for signs of wolves that may have found the kill, but when he discovered there had been no activity he motioned for Meesha to join him.

Meesha stood off to one side and watched him delicately stripped off their hides, and then cut up the remainder of the meat. The pungent smell of intestines and belly contents drifted into his nostrils, which made him sick at his stomach. He could not believe anyone would kill, let alone butcher, such beautiful animals. On Golan, he had never witnessed death of any kind. By his father's orders, he had been sheltered from such things. His people were not savages, like some Earthlings Lulla had told him about. His mind drifted back to Grace and Charley. Why couldn't everybody be like them, he wondered? They were not savages.

"Meesha!" a shout rang out. "Come here, I need you to start loading the travois." He motioned with a bloody hand what he wanted him to do.

By the time they had finished loading the travois the sun had dropped behind the mountains on the western skyline, making the forest appear more ominous than usual. The finger-like rays from the sun, which had once given them safe footing, no longer filtered through the branches of the Douglas fir.

As they carried the last of the blood-saturated meat and hides to the sled, they heard a familiar howl at the edge of the tree line. White Feather threw the last armload onto the travois and grabbed the reins. Suddenly, he stopped the pony, let go of the reins and darted down the hill. He had left the gun leaning up against a small sapling. Meesha watched in terror, as a pack of wolves moved furtively toward him.

"I forgot the rifle!" White Feather shouted. He grabbed the gun and started back up the hill. Before he could get halfway up, six large male wolves had blocked his way. The smell of blood from the freshly cut meat had brought them out of the forest, and they were hungry.

Meesha knew they were about to attack, but there was nothing he could do about it. Panic-stricken, he hid behind the pinto. As he peeked around Red Wing, he saw White Feather lying on the ground halfway up the hill, terror on his face. The animals had crouched in front of him, the hair on their necks standing up like quills on a porcupine, and their red, beady eyes staring menacingly at him.

"Meesha!" White Feather called out. "Take Red Wing and go! I have the rifle, I'll scare them off!" He made a frantic gesture, and pointed to the path

Meesha understood and grabbed the reins. However, before he could get control of the pony it turned and bolted into the underbrush, the travois in tow. Instead of going after it, he froze in his tracks. He didn't know what to do. Should he go after the horse or stay with his friend? His mind suddenly went blank.

"Kerac!" Lulla cried out. "I have a reading on Meesha." She lowered her head to study the scanner readings closer. "Yes, I do! He must be in a lot of trouble; he's sending brain waves I haven't seen before."

"Are you sure they're his?" Kerac asked.

"Positive! Only he has waves like these, nobody else!"

"Can you get a fix on him?"

"I'm trying." She twisted a knob and pushed several buttons. "Yes!" she answered her voice filled with anxiety. "I have his location. He has to be in a lot of trouble to make waves like these! I've never seen anything like them!"

"Give me the coordinates, we'll go after him."

"What about Abron?"

"Forget him for now! If he wants to follow, let him. If he does, I'll have a little surprise waiting for him."

"Senator!" Nader yelled across the bridge. "I have Kerac's ship on the scanner. What do you want to do?"

"Is he moving? If he is, where's he headed?"

"It's too early to tell where he's going, but I'll stay on him and let you know."

"Don't lose him!"

"I won't," Nader replied. "His signature is extremely strong, like he's using his atmospheric pulse generator to get more speed out of that thing. It looks like he's going down to Earth." He arched his body over the scanner, like a snake ready to strike. "Yes, he is headed for Earth."

"Keep your sensors on him. Let me know where he lands…if he lands."

"It's rather stupid of him to land in daylight, don't you think?" Nader said.

"He must have a good reason, I'm sure he wouldn't take such actions, if he didn't."

"Colonel," a shout rang out, above the noise of the control room. "There it is again, it just darted across my screen…top to bottom. Looks like the same blip we had before. It's definitely headed for Earth."

Colonel Steel rushed across the room and stood behind him. "Is it still there?"

"Yes. It just landed, somewhere in Oregon."

"Landed, in broad daylight?"

The lieutenant pointed at a green dot on the screen. "Yes sir, it looks like it. See, it's still on the screen and it's not moving."

"I'll be damned!" Steel said. He rushed across the room and sat down at his console. After a few strokes on a keypad, he pushed the send button. Several moments later a short message appeared on the screen. "Yes, Colonel," it said, "we have it on our screen, too. Don't do anything. We're on top of it." The message ended and the NORAD icon reappeared.

Meesha's thoughts raced through his mind. He was terrified. He darted from his hiding place to a spot where he could see the wolves, and White Feather's dilemma, more clearly.

Lulla's voice suddenly boomed into his head, interrupting his thoughts. "Meesha! What's wrong? Are you in trouble?"

"Lulla!" his mind screamed back. "My friend is about to be eaten by a pack of wolves! Can you do anything to help him?"

"A pack of wolves?" she questioned. "What do you mean a pack of wolves?"

"Never mind what I mean, can you help him? They are about to attack him!"

"I'll see what I can do." She located his exact coordinates and hovered over them. "Tell your friend to stay on the ground, close his eyes and cover his ears."

"White Feather!" Meesha screamed. He looked at the boy, dropped to the ground, closed his eyes and covered his ears, hoping he would understand.

White Feather looked up, puzzled by his behavior. He stood there motionless as the wolves moved in closer.

"Lulla!" he sent his thoughts back. "He does not understand, and I cannot talk to him. What should I do?"

"Do nothing, Meesha. I just hope what I'm about to do will not harm you or the boy. Close your eyes cover your ears and stay on the ground," she demanded. "In a moment your friend will do the same, you can be certain of that!"

A few seconds later an extremely bright, rapidly pulsing light flooded the forest floor and a powerful, piercing high frequency sound surrounded them. White Feather automatically closed his eyes and covered his ears.

The wolves jumped up and down wildly, yelped in pain and ran around in circles as the intense sound partially ruptured their eardrums, and the flashing light momentarily blinded them. Unable to avoid the sound or light, they ran blindly into trees and thick, thorny bushes on their way back to the forest. Suddenly, the sound stopped and the light went out. Although their vision had been slightly restored, and the pain in their ears somewhat diminished, the wolves continued into the deep forest, yelping and howling all the way.

"Meesha!" Lulla's voice called out. "Are you and your friend all right? Is the danger over?"

"Yes, Lulla, we are fine," he sent back. "The wolves left in a hurry. Thank you."

"We cannot stay," she replied. "Senator Abron is after us. Remain with your friend and we will return for you later."

Meesha looked up and saw a thin beam of light shoot into the sky and disappear

"Senator!" Nader shouted. "I briefly had a fix on Kerac, but now he's gone. I believe he went back into hiding on the other side of Earth. Shall we go after him? I know approximately where he went."

"No, leave him alone for now, it's the boy I'm after."

"But I thought you said you wanted to get even with him?"

"That'll come later. You must have an accurate fix on the boy down there."

"I have a fix on the spot Kerac hovered over," Nader replied. "But what makes you think the boy is there?"

"Why else would he go down to Earth, especially in daylight? He didn't have time to get the boy though, I'm sure he's still there. Take the ship to those coordinates and hover. It's daylight down there so use the stealth generator and go in low and quiet. We don't want any more of those idiots shooting at us."

Nader maneuvered the ship to the coordinates and hovered. After he had stabilized the ship to keep it from drifting, he reduced the power to all systems except weapons and environment.

"All secure," he called out. "I've put us about a hundred feet directly over two boys. According to his waves one is Meesha, but I don't know about the other."

"Good! Bring up the brain wave communicator and set it for his waves. I want to speak to him."

"I figured that out all by myself," Nader said mockingly. "It's already set."

Abron slid the brain-wave headset over his partially bald head and looked down at the two boys. "Meesha!" he threw his thoughts. "This is Senator Abron. Can you hear me?"

Meesha had been walking behind the travois, when the voice boomed into his head. He cringed and put both hands up to cover his ears.

Again, the voice rang out, "Meesha, I am not here to harm you. I only want to talk. Please listen."

White Feather was unaware of what was happening and continued on down the path, the reins held tight in his hands.

"How did you find me?" Meesha threw his thoughts back. "I do not want to talk to you without Kerac or Lulla being here."

"That's understandable," Abron's voice came back, almost fatherly, "but they are not. Even so, please hear me out."

"I will listen," Meesha said, "but I will not tell you anything unless Kerac is here. Do you understand?"

"Of course. But I only want to know what your plans are. Do you want to stay here on Earth, or go back to Golan?"

Meesha thought for a moment. "In other words, if I tell you I want to stay, you will take your son back to be voted on. And, if I tell you I want to go back, you will try to keep me from returning. Is that not true?"

The brain waves were silent for several moments, then Abron replied, "You are a clever boy, Meesha," he sent back, his mind chuckling deviously.

"What if Luchak doesn't want to go back either?" Meesha asked. "What would you do then?"

"He is my son! He will do as I say!"

"Sir, you do not seem to know where your son is," Meesha sent back. "How can you force him to go back, if you don't know where he is?"

"Don't take me for a fool, I know exactly where he is, he is on Kerac's ship. I can get him any time. You must know by now it will only be my son who returns to Golan. If you attempt to go back, I will do everything in my power to stop you. Do you understand?" The brain waves were silent for a few moments, and then his voice returned. "Do not get too familiar with your new friends, Meesha. Just to let you know how serious I am about you not returning to Golan, I have made plans for them!" The waves stopped, and the ship darted into a clearing in the nearby forest.

As the boys entered the village, Nakomi stood beside the cabin watching them approach.

"White Feather," she called out. "You are late. Did something happen? Are you boys all right?"

"Yes, Mother, we are fine. But the wolves are not." He chuckled, as he pulled back on the reins.

"Wolves? What do you mean? Did you see wolves?"

"Yes, Mother, many. I will explain later. Right now we have to get this meat packed in salt and the hides put away for curing before the wolves smell them and come into the village."

The door to the cabin opened and Quasi hobbled outside, a white linen cloth wound tight around his chest. He looked at the meat, and then at the boys.

"Good job fellows," he told them. "The village will be happy. Did you have trouble getting it? Did I hear you say something about wolves?"

"Yes, Father, there were many wolves, but the boy has friends in high places." He looked at Meesha and chuckled. "I will tell you a story you won't believe, after we finish unloading the meat."

Quasi gave him a perplexed look, on his way to the travois to inspect the meat. "There's more here than I thought. We can surely use it. It will be a long, cold winter."

Several men noticed the boys arrive and made their way to the travois. As they unloaded the meat, someone shouted, "Look! Up in the sky! What is it?"

A huge, dark object had drifted silently out of the forest and hovered a few feet off the ground several hundred yards away. The men stopped to stare at it.

Meesha looked up and his face grew pale. He knew it was Abron. Everyone in the village would be in danger, unless he could warn them. He ran over and tried to put his finger on Quasi's forehead, but it was pushed aside. Frustrated, he yanked on his shirt and Quasi finally looked at him.

"What is it? What do you want?" he said, irritated by his persistence. He looked at the dark object, and then realized he must have something to tell him about it. He bent down and Meesha touched his brow. Instantly, visions of Digger's shack being blown up flashed across his mind's eye. "Of course!" he said, staring at him. "That's the same guy, isn't it?" Meesha shook his head. "Everyone!" he shouted as loud as he could. "Don't go back into your houses run into the forest and take cover!"

Before anyone could react, a bright shaft of light had lit up Quasi's cabin. The beam intensified for a brief moment and the cabin imploded. When the villagers saw what had happened, they rushed for the safety of the nearby forest.

"Senator!" Nader screamed. "What are you doing? You can't do that! These people didn't do anything to you! That's a good way to start a war with Earth. When they find out what you just did to that cabin, they'll be coming after us."

Ignoring his plea, Abron locked the beam on another cottage. When Nader saw what he was about to do he rushed across the bridge and yanked his hand off the firing mechanism.

Abron pulled out his stun gun and held it on him. "Don't do anything stupid, Nader," he yelled. "I've waited a long time for something like this. And I can thank Meesha for the opportunity." His eyes bulged like a madman's, and his voice snarled insanely. "I'm going to put fear into these people," he screamed. "You know very well their government would never allow us to assimilate, even if we did get our ships through. We might as well show them right now we are the superior ones. We could easily dominate these stupid, backward people and take over this puny little planet, without assimilation."

Nader backed off and sat down at his console. From past experiences he knew the senator was not bluffing. He realized if he had made another move toward him he would have fired. He leaned back in his chair and stared at him angrily.

Before the villagers could make it to the forest, a bright beam had focused on still another cabin, and within seconds it also collapsed inwardly. The villagers watched in horror and disbelief, as another two cabins were partially destroyed by the beam. After the fourth building, the dark object moved slowly and silently next to the tree line and hovered.

Meesha could hardly believe the senator's actions. On Golan, he had heard of his ruthlessness and savagery, but this was far beyond his comprehension. What were these people to do, now that they had no place to live, no shelter for the winter? These people were his friends, but he could do nothing to help them. He suddenly felt sick at his stomach. The expression on their faces, as they watched their homes being destroyed, was more than he could bear, he sat down on a nearby chopping block and dropped his head into his hands.

"This is your fault, boy!" Nakomi shouted, glaring at him. "This would not have happened if it weren't for you and your friends!" She picked up a freshly cut stick of firewood, raised it over her head and moved toward him

Quasi saw what was about to happen and wrenched the stick out of her hand. "Nakomi, control yourself!" he shouted. "The boy didn't do this it was those men who are after him. The bad ones I told you about. They are not his friends. It would do no good to take your anger out on him, he's not responsible."

"Then who the hell is?" she shrieked, blood rushing to her face. "If you hadn't brought him here we would still have our homes!" She put her hands to her face and wept.

"I know how you feel," he said, pulling her close, "but don't blame the boy. As you can see, he feels as bad as you do." He looked at Meesha, his head still buried in his hands.

She pulled away and glared at him. "How can he feel bad?" she shouted. "It is us who have nothing left. He can always go back to his kingdom, or whatever it is."

"We will all survive, Nakomi," he told her. "We have tents stowed away…the ones used for hunting. I'm sure the government will help us rebuild, when they find out what happened here…and who did it." His eyes scanned the partially destroyed houses, then back at Nakomi. "We didn't have much before so we didn't have much to lose." He walked over and put his hand on Meesha's shoulder. "It's all right, it wasn't your fault."

A tall, slender man clad in buckskins ran past them. "Why? Why did they do this? Why?" he kept shouting. "Why did they kill my little Velma? Why? Why? We did nothing to them!"

As he went by, Quasi caught his arm. "Walking Bear!" he shouted. "What happened? What happened to Velma?"

"Our house fell down on my little Velma," he shouted. "Why did they do that to my little Velma? Why? Why?"

Quasi walked back to Nakomi, put his arms around her and kissed her sobbing face.

"Ranger!" a tinny voice came over a speaker on General Elmendorf's desk. "This is. Colonel Wells of Ranger Two. What's the situation, Sir? We just got a scramble order. Over."

Elmendorf placed his unlit cigar in an ashtray and picked up the mike. "Ranger Two, this is Ranger. I want you to check out some unknown activity around Grande Ronde, Oregon. We've just been informed an incident just occurred in that area. Something we should check out. It looks like it might be UFO activity. We were informed by the Grande Ronde police that something happened at the Indian Reservation, a couple miles east of them. Check it out with a fly-over. Over"

"Roger, will do. We're over the Oregon coastline now. It'll only take a few minutes to get there. Out"

Ten minutes later, two F16s made a low-level pass over the reservation. After several more passes they shot into the sky and leveled off at 10,000 feet.

"What the hell was that?" Colonel Wells shouted into his intercom. "It looked like some of those houses had been severely damaged! What the hell's going on down there?"

"We'd better call Ranger," Captain Ed Cook in the second F16 replied. "Looks like a few of them are in pretty bad shape."

"Roger," Wells replied. "Elmendorf should know about this!"

"Ranger," a voice blasted over Elmendorf's speaker. "This is Captain Cook. I believe we have a problem here, Sir. A portion of that Indian village looks like it's been almost wiped out. We saw people wandering about looking like they were in shock. What do you want us to do?"

"Ranger Two, this is Ranger. It's starting to get dark down there, so turn on your FLIR and check out the area again. Look for any heat signatures. All of this happened less than half an hour ago. Whatever or whoever is responsible might still be in the area. If you get any contacts, call me before you do anything drastic. You damn sure better get authorization, before you shoot whatever it is out of the sky! Understood?"

"Roger, will do," Cook replied.

Colonel Wells keyed his intercom. "Captain, I don't know about you, but I don't think I'll be calling headquarters if we find out who did this."

"Roger, Colonel. I'm with you."

Several moments later the squelch broke on Cook's receiver. "I believe we're in luck, Ed," the colonel shouted. "Look out your starboard window. I just got a hit on something big and solid on my FLIR, over by the tree line. However, my FLIR isn't working very well. Point yours about forty-five degrees to starboard. See what you come up with."

"Holy Christ!" was Cook's excited response. "Would you look at that? It's about half the size of a football field, just hovering there. It's big and black. What do you want to do, Colonel?"

"The question is what do you want to do?" Wells came back. "You always said you were a top-gun, so show me. By the way, my radio contact with headquarters just wet the bed." He chuckled. "Unfortunately, I won't be able to contact HQ about this situation. Understood?"

"That thing's gotta be the culprit," Cook replied. "At least let's give it a headache!"

"Roger! You go right ahead, Cook, I'm just a bystander. Let's see if you can qualify for that top gun."

"Oh, you're funny, Colonel" Cook replied. "I'm going to spray the surrounding area with 50s, first. If that don't scare the hell out of whatever it is and make it run, you can load a missile and give it an over-the-bow shot. That ought to show it we mean business!"

"Try not to hit it, just scare the hell out of it," Wells yelled into his mike. "I don't believe Elmendorf would appreciate you doing anything more."

Cook flipped his F16 into a tight turn and headed for the object. He fired .50 calibers above and in front of the object, but before they landed the object had darted to one side, as if anticipating his move. He made another pass, but that time he aimed at its leading edge. The .50 calibers created sparks as they hit the object, and then ricocheted into space like pebbles on a pond.

"What the hell!" he shouted. "That's impossible. Those rounds should have done something."

"What's the matter, Ed, can't you hit that thing?" Wells replied.

"Colonel, I sent over twenty rounds at that thing and when they hit they didn't make a dent. Do you want to try one of your ATGs, and see what happens?"

"I'd rather not," Well replied. "We only want to scare the hell out of it. We don't want to damage it too much. We don't want to do anything too extreme, until we find out what the hell it is. Come on up and join me, we'll call Elmendorf and see what he wants to do about it."

"Senator!" Nader shouted. "That plane just shot at us! Why are we still here? We should have left a long time ago!"

"Relax, Nader, I'm testing their capabilities. See what they've got for firepower."

"You've got to be kidding," Nader shot back. "I know they have more than simple bullets on those things. If they launched one of their missiles—"

"I said relax! Even if they sent a missile, we could outrun it."

"How could we outrun it if we're parked here below the tree tops?"

"You worry too much, Nader. Trust me and my instincts."

"I'd feel a lot better if we got out of here!" Nader replied. "I've seen what their missiles can do, and I don't want to be around if they unload one."

As soon as Cook joined the colonel at 10,000 feet, Wells informed him that headquarters had already been contacted and he was waiting for a reply.

"What do you think, Ed?" a metallic voice asked. "You think I should send a stinger across its bow, while we're waiting for an answer?"

"It's up to you, Colonel. I would, if I had one, but they didn't give me any this trip. We're supposed to be on a recon. They gave you some, though."

"They probably figured you were too young to handle 'em," Wells joked.

"Funny."

"I'm not waiting for permission," the colonel said. "I'm going in! Watch my back!"

"Be careful, we don't know what that thing's capable of," Cook warned.

"Don't worry, if it handles this ATG without any damage, I'll be back real soon and we'll call for backup, or get the hell out of here. If it takes the damn thing out we'll know it's vulnerable, and we can play it by ear with Elmendorf."

"It's one of those UFO's we've been hearing about, isn't it, Colonel?" Cook asked.

"After what you just witnessed, what do you think?" Wells replied, as he peeled off and headed for the object. The instant he fired the missile, the black object darted out of the tree line and moved several hundred feet straight up and stopped. The missile landed on the forest floor and exploded, sending fragments of tree limbs high into the sky. "My God!" he shouted into his oxygen mask. "That damn thing knew I was going to fire, as soon as I pulled the trigger. It's definitely intelligent!"

"Hell, I could have told you that!" Cook shot back. "What do you want to do?"

Wells pulled his F16 up sharply and joined him. After leveling off he said, "Cook! You there?"

"Where else would I be, Colonel?"

"What I meant was did you see that? It knew I was going to fire, before I even pulled the trigger!"

"What do we do now, that's what I want to know?"

"Hell, I don't know!" Wells replied curtly.

"Maybe we should call for backup?" Cook replied nervously.

"Don't think that would work, Ed. As intelligent as that thing appears to be, it would probably be gone before they got here. Let's wait it out…see what happens next. It can't stay there forever. If it does, it's dumber than I think it is."

The speakers in their helmets sounded. "Colonel Wells," Elmendorf's voice blasted their eardrums. "What's your situation? Is the object still there?"

"Yes sir, it's hovering above the treetops, as we speak. We tried to scare it off but it wouldn't budge. It doesn't appear to be afraid of us."

"What do you recommend, Colonel?" Elmendorf asked anxiously. "Has it made any offensive moves?"

"You mean other than wiping out half an Indian Reservation?"

There was a long pause. "Are you trying to be cute, Colonel?" Elmendorf blasted back. "I know it wiped out some houses on that reservation. What the hell do you think we should do about it?

That's what I'm asking. You're there and I'm here. I don't know your situation!" The speaker went dead. After a few seconds the voice returned. "Colonel, can you get a picture of that thing and send it to me?"

"I'll see what I can do," Wells replied. He told Cook to stay put while he went down to get a snapshot. As he peeled off and headed toward the object, it shot into the sky and within an instant was gone.

Wells pulled up sharply and headed in the direction the object had taken, but he could see nothing visible, and there was no image on his long-range radar.

"Cook!" he shouted. "Did you see that thing take off? It was faster than a rocket!"

"Yes, I saw it. I don't have anything on my radar though, it just disappeared!"

"Captain, call Elmendorf," Wells demanded. "Tell him we're on our way back to the base. I've got to make a report on this…whether they believe it or not. Also, tell him to call the police in Grande Ronde and see if they'll get some help out to that reservation. It looks like they sure as hell could use it! Ask him if he can get the government to send in some people. Maybe he could also get the Red Cross in there, see if they need their help. You saw what it looked like down there. The government should at least do something about it…be a little responsible."

"Wow, Colonel," Cook replied, "all of a sudden you've got compassion. I always took you for a mean, heartless mother—"

"Watch it, Captain! You give me any crap and I'll tell 'em you couldn't hit the broad side of an outhouse with that fifty of yours."

"If I remember correctly, Sir, you didn't do so well with that missile, either."

Except for a few muted chuckles, silence prevailed in both cockpits.

They were about to make a turn to return to the base, when Cook's voice broke the silence, "Colonel!" he shouted. "Before we head back, I just got a faint blip on my long-range radar, it seems to be just sitting there about twenty miles from us. I'm pretty sure it's that bogey from the reservation. What do you want to do, go after it or head back?"

"I'll call Elmendorf, see what he wants to do," Wells replied. He switched to channel one and said, "Ranger, this is Ranger Two."

"Yes, Colonel, what is it?" Elmendorf's tired voice returned.

"Sir, we just located that bogey from the Indian reservation. It's about twenty miles from us just sitting there. What do you want to do about it?"

"You're sure it's the one that hit the reservation?"

"Yes sir, we're fairly certain."

There was a long pause, before Elmendorf's voice returned, "See if you can get within range and send a Stinger at the damn thing, see what happens. If anything does happen, we'll handle the consequences later, if there are any."

"Roger, will do!"

NINETEEN

It had taken Borak only a few minutes to reach the pre-determined location where he could create a vortex. He turned on the ion drive and set all controls on automatic. As the worm-hole began to form, the ship started rolling uncontrollably, blocking their view of the stars and sun.

Tumac sat at the bow window watching an array of multi-colored particles speeding by the ship's hull. As he looked across the bridge, everything appeared to be swimming in a vast pool of motion. He knew the captain was strapped into his chair at the helm, but his body appeared to be floating about the bridge. Nothing seemed normal or real; everything was distorted and unrecognizable. What was happening, he wondered? Would the ship make it through the vortex? Do other ships go through the same scenario, when they travel to Earth? His mind suddenly filled with unanswerable questions.

"Captain?" he called out, his voice bouncing off everything it came in contact with. "Captain, can you hear me?" he repeated.

Borak looked over. "Yes, what is it? I'm rather busy here," he answered, his voice echoing throughout the bridge.

"Is this normal? Are we in some sort of danger?"

"No danger," the captain replied, his voice drifting across the open bridge, as if it were floating on a mountain stream. "This is normal. It will all be over in a few minutes. Hang in there, Sir." For a brief moment a distorted smile spread across his broad face, and then drifted aimlessly across the bridge and disappeared through a porthole.

Before Tumac could ask another question, everything had returned to normal. He looked out the porthole and saw stars, and the deep blues and whites of a planet far below with a pale, full moon in the distance.

He hoped he wouldn't have to go through that strange phenomenon again, but he knew he would.

"Well," the captain said with a grin, "that wasn't so bad, was it?"

"Depends on your point of view, I guess," Tumac replied, wiping his brow with his sleeved arm.

"We'll have to stay several thousand miles above Earth, until it gets dark enough to go down," Borak told him.

"How long will that be?"

"It should only be a couple hours. The sun has just now set over the Pacific Ocean. When it gets a little darker, we'll try to get in touch with Washington, D. C., that's where the American government is located." He walked over to Tumac, still strapped into his chair. "Sir, you must understand something, there could be problems when we arrive."

"What do you mean problems? What kind of problems?"

"To my knowledge, this will be the first time in modern history Earth will be contacted officially by aliens, and that would be us."

"Do you really think there will be problems, when we contact them?"

"I have traveled to Earth on many occasions and discovered that for millenniums visitors, from who knows where, have plagued Earth with visitations. Their governments have all been aware of those visitations, but they will not tell their people what they know about them. They deny they even know about them. The information they've acquired over the years has been kept under wraps, leaving their people in the dark and totally confused. They believe if the public were made aware of alien visitations they would panic. I don't believe that, but that's what their governments seem to believe." He pulled a small cigar from his shirt pocket and started to light it.

Tumac gave him a puzzled look. "What is that…in your mouth?"

Borak pulled it out, looked at it and caressed it with his thumb and forefinger lovingly. "It's called a cigar. I picked up the habit on one of my previous trips. I like it very much, it's quite soothing. You light it and enjoy the smoke it produces."

"Strange habit!"

"Yes, it is," Borak replied. After lighting it, he walked to a bow porthole and looked down at Earth.

"You have been to Earth many times?" Tumac asked. "What are the people of the United States like? Do you really believe they will accept me as a representative of our King? And are they an understanding people?"

The captain took a long drag and blew a large blue smoke ring into the air, which was immediately sucked into the ventilation system. "The majority of the people are, but their government is not when it comes to the wishes of its people. They have a form of democracy similar to what we had years ago, before the war."

"I hope it worked out better for them than it did us."

"Some say yes, others are not so sure."

"What do you think, Captain? You seem to know them fairly well."

"Yes, I know them well enough, because I have learned their language, with the help of our teaching devices. I have listened to their archaic communications many times over the years, and have learned to understand them quite well, at least well enough to communicate with them. I have had many conversations with one of their senators, without him knowing who I really was. From him, I learned about their culture."

"Then you may be quite helpful to me," Tumac replied. "I too have learned their language, but only by our artificial means. I'm afraid it may not be good enough to have a diplomatic conversation. Maybe you could speak for me, if I told you what to say."

"First things first, Sir," Borak said. "First, we must make official contact. That's where I believe I can be the greatest help. Like I said, I have been in communications with a person high up in their government. We communicate by what he calls a 'ham' radio. It's a long story, but one day I found a way to acquire one of those machines, so I could better understand their way of thinking. I didn't really know what it was supposed to do. Then, I heard his voice and understood the device well enough to answer. Jokingly, I told him I was from the spaceship USS Enterprise. Of course he laughed it off." He took another long drag on the cigar and continued. "Even so, after a few more contacts,

I believe he actually considered that possibility, especially after I told him about parallel universes and vortexes. Although I'm sure he thought I was joking, he seemed quite interested and wanted to hear more. Every time I came to Earth, we usually communicated. I told him if he left his equipment on I would contact him whenever I was here. He told me he left it on most of the time."

"Can you contact him now?" Tumac asked. "And does he have any real authority in his government?"

"I believe he has a lot of authority. He said he was a senator, a position quite similar to our own senators. If he did leave the device on, like he said he would, it shouldn't be difficult to contact him."

"Would you try now?" Tumac asked. "It may be our best chance to set up a meeting with their president. Assuming this man has the power to do so."

"I believe he does. He said he was the Speaker of the House, whatever that is. It sounded impressive." He went to a console at the far end of the bridge and lifted a rectangular metal box from a drawer. After plugging in several cables, and attaching a long wire to a stanchion, he turned on the device and picked up the mike. He looked over at Tumac and winked. "I hope he's listening, it's almost eleven o'clock in Washington. He should be home by now."

"Let's hope so," Tumac said. Then he added, "Captain, before you make the call, I have a question. If you happen to get in touch with him, what will our next course of action be? How will we meet with their president? With a ship as large as this, do you really think we could land without being detected and harassed by their military? I wouldn't want that to happen."

"I have a plan," Borak answered. "But first we have to make contact with the senator. Please be patient, this may take a while."

Tumac walked across the bridge and stood behind him. "Assuming we do get a meeting," he said, "I would like it to go undetected by the population, if at all possible."

"I understand," Borak replied. "I will make certain the Senator and the President are the only ones that have knowledge of it."

"Good."

Borak had been calling on the senator's frequency for only a few moments, when a voice boomed over the speaker.

"Is this who I think it is?" a cheerful, but distorted voice said. "Is this Captain Kirk of the USS Enterprise?" A faint scoff filtered through the background noise.

"Senator Kent," Borak replied. "It was nice of you to respond so quickly."

"Captain Kirk?" Tumac questioned. "What does that mean?"

"Just a little humor between us," Borak explained, covering the mike with his hand. "Let me get on with my conversation. Senator Kent, it's been a long time. I have just now arrived from my planet, Golan. How are things here on Earth?"

"If I remember correctly," Kent came back, "you told me before your real name was Captain Borak. Is that correct? How have you been?"

"I am fine, Senator. And yes, my real name is Captain Etan Borak." After a brief pause he continued. "I have a problem perhaps you could help me with."

"And what would that be, Captain Borak? I have just led the Senate in the passage of a House Appropriations Bill and I'm in good humor. What can I do for you?"

Borak took a deep breath and let it out slowly. "Sir, I don't believe at our last meeting you were totally convinced that I was from another universe, although we spoke of it on many occasions. I would like to take this opportunity to inform you that what I told you is indeed the truth. I am from Golan, a planet in a parallel universe. My planet is doomed by the convergence of our dying sun and about to be destroyed, as I believe I told you before. I have the Prime Minister of my planet with me and he will confirm what I told you is indeed the truth. He came with me as a representative of our King to speak to your President, if that is at all possible. Do you have the authority to set up a meeting?" The hissing of dead air filled the bridge. "I am not playing games with you, Senator," he continued. "I am not trying to embarrass you with what you might call a flight of fancy. Please, hear me out. Our King Oltar is extremely ill and needs immediate medical attention." He turned off the mike and listened for a response.

Several moments past, then the squelch broke. "Captain, or whoever you are, it has been a blast talking to you, but I have no proof of who you really are...only your word. I would need something more concrete, before even considering a meeting with our President. Do you understand?"

"Yes, I fully understand," Borak replied, "and I can appreciate that. But I have a suggestion, if you are willing to listen."

"I can't seem to get you off the air," Kent replied with a quiet chuckle, "so I guess I'll have to listen. Make it quick though, and no more Captain Kirk of the Starship Enterprise. Okay?"

"Yes sir, no more Captain Kirk. My name is Etan Borak. I am the captain of my own ship, sent here by my King to set up a meeting between your President and his representative, Prime Minister Tumac. Like I told you, my King is very ill and needs medical attention. My people are extremely advanced in technology, but lack the medical skills or knowledge to cure him. I believe your government has that ability.

"My planet is truly in trouble. It is, in fact, about to be destroyed by the expansion of our dying sun. I know how this must sound, but believe me it is the truth. To prove to you I am telling the truth, I request you contact your Area Fifty One at Groom Lake in the state you call Nevada in exactly one hour. I will fly over that location, hover for ten minutes and blink my high-intensity lights ten times. I will then return to my present location and wait for your response. If I am telling the truth, I will be there and you will have all the proof you need. If I do not appear, you will know it has all been a ruse. Is that acceptable?"

There was a longer pause, then he answered, "How do you know about Area Fifty One, it's top secret?" Kent said in a hushed voice. "As a matter of fact, it's not even supposed to exist. But if it does, what makes you think you can enter its air space, without being shot down?"

"I will take my chances, to prove a point."

"Very well, I will contact the Area and let them know you will be there in one hour. But don't play games with me, Mr. Borak. I lose my sense of humor, when it comes to my country's security."

"I understand. Then it's settled, I will be there in one hour. Please, let me know as soon as you get confirmation. Thank you. Out."

"Senator!" Nader shouted. "If I may be so blunt, that was a very stupid move you made on that village. Their military will be looking for us. And don't think they don't have the capability to down us. I have seen their weapons in action."

"Like I said before, you worry too much, Nader," Abron replied. "The people of Earth are stupid idiots. Even if they did have that kind of weaponry, they wouldn't know how to use them on us effectively. We're too fast for anything they could throw at us."

"You think so, Senator?" Nader shouted, looking at his scanner. "Then what's that coming at us?" Abron rushed to his side and looked down at the screen. His face paled, when he saw the vapor trail of a missile headed straight for them, a few seconds away and traveling at super-sonic speed.

Nader rushed to the weapons console and frantically pushed buttons and turned knobs. A powerful beam of plasma shot from the ship headed for the missile. The missile's war-head exploded, sending showers of bright tracers toward them. Due to its close proximity, the ship sustained heavy damage.

After picking his huge body up off the deck, Abron shouted, "Nader! What happened? Did it hit us?"

Nader checked the instruments on his console and looked over. "It wasn't a direct hit, but it did do damage." He glared at Abron and added sarcastically, "That near miss damaged our external ion drive grid, and also the gravity grid. We still have some anti-gravity, but I don't know how much longer. If we take another close hit like that, it will be all over."

"Call that idiot in engineering and see what he can do about those grids!" Abron shouted. "We can't stay here long. Obviously, we're within their missile range. It looks like it was that plane that shot at us before, down at the village. We've got to get out of here, fast!"

Using auxiliary power, Nader nursed the ship into a much higher orbit, where he believed another missile couldn't reach them. He put the ship's controls on automatic and rushed down to engineering. When he arrived, he found Kersey lying on the deck. He knelt beside him and lifted his head. He was still alive, but unconscious. He checked him for injuries and saw a large gash on his forehead.

"Kersey! Kersey!" he bellowed, slapping him in the face. "What happened here?"

Kersey opened his eyes and looked around groggily. After clearing his head, he said, "I don't know. Did something hit the ship? All I remember is hearing a loud explosion, and then everything went black."

"One of their planes shot a missile at us," Nader explained. "It wasn't a direct hit, but it did do damage to our external ion and gravity grids, and who knows what else. You have to fix the problems, immediately. We had enough auxiliary power left to move out of their range, but we still have to get out of here. With the grid damaged we have very little anti-gravity. We're running on auxiliary power now, and can't get much speed out of her. As it stands right now, we can't even make a vortex to get home."

The engineer attempted to stand but fell backwards onto the deck. He tried again and finally stood, but he was still groggy.

"Must have hit my head on something," he said. He put his hand to his forehead and it came back bloody. "I'm getting this all over my uniform, you know!"

Nader found a medical kit on the far bulkhead and searched its contents for a large bandage. Finding one he wrapped it around the engineer's head.

"I see you still have a sense of humor," he said. "Here, hold this while I tape it to your head." When the gash had been covered, he stood up and glared at him. "What a time to get injured!" As he turned to leave, he looked back. "Do you think you can do anything about those grids? You think you can handle them by yourself?"

"Who else is here?" Kersey shot back. "Does Abron think it was my fault we got blasted?" he mumbled. "I could have told him we'd be shot at, if we stayed only twenty miles up. But he wouldn't listen. He's an ass, anyway! I can't keep fixing this drive. It isn't going to hold together much longer, anyway. He didn't give me much of a chance to fix it properly, the first time. I could have told him they'd shoot at us if we hung around. But no, he wouldn't listen. Stupid man!"

Borak's ship came in low over Area 51. A few seconds later it hovered directly over the main buildings, its bright lights flooding the area. Men in white coveralls stood outside the long buildings looking up at the huge, dark object swaying back and forth silently several hundred feet above them. For a few moments, the huge ship dipped slowly front to back, and then stopped and remained perfectly still.

"I guess the senator got through to them, they're not shooting at us," Borak commented. "Either that or they don't know what to make of us."

"Look, Captain!" Tumac shouted. "There's a light pointed directly at us."

"Yes, I see it," Borak replied. "Now, let's see what happens!" He pointed a powerful beam at the light and blinked it ten times.

The light on the ground returned the blinks, and then went out.

"We've done all we can, for now," Borak said. "We'd better get out of here, before they change their minds." He applied full power to the ion drive and the ship shot into the night sky and disappeared. When they had reached the ionosphere, he turned on a long-range scanner and watched the men on the ground slowly return to the buildings as if nothing out of the ordinary had happened. He looked at Tumac. "I guess what I heard about this place is true, they didn't seem overly concerned about us. It's as if they've seen ships like ours before."

"Amazing!" Tumac said, looking at the scanner. "You would think they would be at least a little alarmed by what they saw."

"There have been many stories about that base," Borak told him. "Some are probably true, but others are downright ridiculous." He walked to the Captain's Chair, pulled out another small cigar and lit it. "There's no doubt in my mind they've been trying to reverse engineer ships from crash sites, or ones they've captured. The Earth has been plagued for millenniums with tall tales of strange craft and creatures from other worlds. I did a little research and discovered that many things about their strange visitors were true." He took a long drag and blew a smoke ring. "Unlike us, some of the craft may have come from distant planets. However, it's highly unlikely, due to the impossible distances. Or, they may have come from other universes, through worm-holes even we know nothing about. On the other hand, it could be mass hysteria; like their government insists. But I doubt it. Most people on Earth are sensible and rational...except those who believe they were abducted, taken aboard ships and transported to other worlds."

"Are you certain it isn't our ships they have been seeing all along?" Tumac replied. "After all, we've been coming to Earth for a number of years. I believe at least some of those sightings could have been our ships. Don't you?"

"According to my research Earth has had sightings for thousands of years," Borak stated. "We've only been coming since we discovered vortexes. And that certainly isn't thousands of years."

"Captain Kirk...oh, sorry, I meant Captain Borak," a cheerful voice broke through the squelch of the super-sideband ham-rig.

Borak grabbed the mike. "This is Captain Borak, go ahead."

"Captain, I just got off the phone with Fifty One. They confirmed your presence." There was a slight delay, and then he continued. "I guess I'll have to believe you after all, Captain." There was another pause while he cleared his throat. "Give me a few minutes to get in touch with the White House. If President Simmons is available, I'll see what he thinks about a meeting."

"If he does agree, where would you recommend we meet," Borak asked, "possibly Area Fifty One? That's probably the safest place for us."

"If the President were to go to the Area it would take four to five hours, just to get there. First, let me find out if he will even meet with you. I'll explain everything to him, as you explained it to me. Under the circumstances, I believe he would love to meet your Prime Minister; he never passes up an opportunity for limelight. Stay close to the rig, my friend, I'll make the call."

Borak looked at Tumac and winked. "Well, we're halfway there, Your Honor." Before Kent signed off, he pressed the mike key. "Senator, remember what I told you about keeping the meeting low keyed. Only the President and a few of his staff members should be aware of this. Also, if it doesn't work out, I must be assured that we can return to Golan without interference from your military." He looked at Tumac with a grin and again keyed the transmitter. "Please, first tell your President about King Oltar's health problems. That's the most pressing matter. Then, you can inform him of our world's impending doom."

"Yes, I will. Please stand by. Out."

Meesha stood at the edge of a small creek, a hundred yards from the remains of Quasi's shack, skipping flat rocks across it. What a wonderful place, he thought. It was too bad they didn't have anything like this on the mother-ships. They had small, artificially colored ponds for their enjoyment, but nothing like this. If it hadn't been for the destruction of the village, and the many needs of its people, he could have stayed there all night watching the small minnows darting back and forth below the slow-flowing brook. However, it was time to return and help Quasi and Nakomi with the remains of their home. If only he could speak their language, it would be so much easier. But he couldn't

"Meesha!" A shout interrupted his daydream.

He looked up and saw White Feather standing beside him with a rifle, and a long-bow slung over his shoulder.

"My Father wants me to take you into the forest where you will be safe. The town is sending people to help us, and he doesn't want them to see you." He suddenly realized the boy couldn't understand and motioned for him to put his finger on his forehead.

Meesha closed his eyes and images of walking into the forest appeared. The scene changed to an open truckload of men and women entering the village with shovels, picks, saws and hammers in their hands. He understood and they left for the forest.

They had barely made it to the edge of the tree line, when a large helicopter came in low over the village. It hovered for a few moments, and then gently settled to the ground. Eight men jumped out and started to unload boxes. White Feather suddenly ran back the cabin. He came out several moments later with a WWII battle lantern his father had acquired from the local store in exchange for Indian artifacts. They continued on down the path and into the dense, dark forest.

"Captain Borak?" a voice thundered over the side-band's receiver.

"Yes, this is Borak, go ahead."

"Captain, I have spoken to our President and he is quite interested in meeting with you and your Prime Minister. I explained everything, your King's medical dilemma and the concern for the people of your planet. At first, he was skeptical, but when I asked him to check with Area Fifty One, which he did, I guess your little visit there was the determining factor."

"Will he meet with us at the Site?" Borak questioned.

"He asked why you couldn't come to the White House. It would be more convenient for him. He said it would be difficult for him to make it to the Area in any reasonable amount of time."

Borak jostled the mike in his hand, then replied, "Senator, tell him we will split the difference."

"Meaning?" a slightly garbled voice replied.

"Just what I said, we will meet him some place in between, but not directly at the White House. If you can give me a landing location near your White House, but out of the mainstream of air traffic, and thinly populated, we will meet him there and take him to the Area in my ship. We couldn't stay long at that location or we would be discovered."

There was a moment of silence, then the squelch broke. "Give me a few minutes to contact him," Kent replied. "I will get back to you as soon as possible. He sounded extremely interested in your problems. I just hope he doesn't make it a photo-op, like he sometimes does."

"Photo-op?" Borak questioned. "What does that mean? Is that serious?"

"He is noted as a photo-fetish, a person who loves to have his picture taken."

"I understand," Borak cut in. "Tell him to come with only a minimum of personnel, bodyguard of course, a recording secretary and maybe an advisor. No more than that. Is that acceptable?"

"I will inform him of your request," Kent returned. "Also, he said not to worry about our military, he will tell them it's a covert operation and they are not to interfere. It will be the highest level of security, if that's what you're worried about. Out."

"Nader!" Abron shouted. "How is that engineer coming along? Has he accomplished anything yet?"

The first mate didn't look up from his screen. "He's doing the best he can, under the circumstances," he replied. "He said the damage was compounded by the original problem, which he didn't get a chance to fix properly in the first place."

"Well, tell him he has two hours to fix it! No more! I want to get down to Earth and get my son. And then go after Ekron. Understood?"

"Yes sir," Nader muttered under his breath. He looked down at his screen and saw a green blip suddenly shoot up from the western corner of the United States and race across his screen to a location on the other side of the planet. He would keep his eyes on it, but not tell the senator, at least not yet.

"Kerac," Lulla said, turning to look at him. "I think you should see this, I just picked up a blip on my scanner."

He walked over, stood behind her and looked down at her screen. "What do you have?"

"I have another ship close to us…about two hundred miles away. I know it's not of Earthly origin; they couldn't get this high. It could be another ship from Golan, but I'm not certain."

"Keep your eyes on it," he said, as he walked back to the helm. He turned and added, "It isn't Abron, is it?"

"No, it doesn't have his signature. I'm getting a reading similar to a ship from Golan Two."

"Golan Two? he said with a frown. "What would they be doing here?"

"I don't know, but I'll give you odds on it."

"Try to communicate with it...assuming you're certain it's not Abron."

"I'm certain." She sighted in the directional communicator, set the frequency for a Golan Two ship, and keyed the mike. "Unknown ship, please identify yourself."

After a lengthy pause, a voice returned. "This is Golan Two," it said. "Identify yourself, please."

"Golan Two, this is Lulla Oltar from Golan One. To whom am I speaking?"

Tumac took the mike from Borak and keyed it. "Lulla? This is Prime Minister Tumac. What are you doing up here? I thought you and Kerac were searching for Meesha and Luchak?"

"It's a long story, Sir. I might ask you the same, what are you doing here?"

"That's also a long story. Nevertheless, I will tell you this much I am here at the King's request."

"Are you alone?" she asked. "I mean, who is with you?"

"I have Captain Borak, a navigator, an engineer, and two fully armed military men."

"Wow!" she came back. "What are you going to do, start a war?" She giggled.

"Not unless it's absolutely necessary," he answered dryly. "What is your situation? Why are you still in orbit?"

"We're waiting until it's dark down there on Earth," she said, "then we'll go get Meesha. We also have Luchak and Senator Ekron of Lechi with us."

"Is that your only plan, Lulla, to go get Meesha? Do you have any other?"

"At this moment, we have nothing else planned. Abron is looking for us. Ekron damaged his ship and I'm sure he'll want to retaliate."

"I have a little time on my hands," Tumac declared. "We are waiting for a message from Earth. While we're waiting, I would like to come aboard and discuss something with all of you, if at all possible."

"Of course it is, Sir," she replied. "Tell Captain Borak to bring you over in one of his pods." She hesitated, and then added, "Please make it quick though, we're not sure if Abron knows our exact location. If he does, he may be here at any time."

"I understand," he answered.

A few minutes later a small shuttle pod entered through Kerac's open bay door and immediately secured to the perforated deck by an autotron. The bay was re-pressurized and Tumac and Borak went to the bridge.

"Nice to see you gentlemen," Kerac said, extending his hand. "What's this all about? You said you were sent here at the King's request?"

"Nice to see you too, Kerac," Tumac said, shaking his hand. "Ekron, I assume by your presence you were unable to get the boys, or Abron. As you must know, King Oltar's illness has not improved over the past few months. He gave me permission to come to Earth and make contact with the United States, primarily to set up a meeting with their President; his government may have the necessary medical facilities to cure him. Also, he wanted me to ask about assimilation for our people, when the time comes."

"That's a fairly large order," Kerac said. "I don't know if the Americans are ready for assimilation. Their government has kept their people in the dark about aliens for so many years they may be afraid to deal with us."

"I told King Oltar the least I could do was try," Tumac said. "Captain Borak has made arrangements for us to meet with their President. We are to meet as soon as we hear back from his contact."

"What about Abron?" Kerac asked. "What should we do about him? He's determined to find and detain Meesha until after the meeting at the end of this week. He has already caused havoc on Earth, a place where Meesha is presently staying."

"Then you <u>do</u> know where he is?"

"Yes, we know," Kerac replied. "But I assume Abron also knows. As soon as his ship is repaired, I'm sure he will go down and attempt to get him."

"If you knew where he was, why didn't you get him before?"

"It wasn't quite that simple," Kerac replied. "Meesha is staying with some native Indians, where Abron did some damage to their village. If we had attempted to go down after him, more than likely he would have attacked us. His weaponry is far superior to ours. We wouldn't have been able to get the boy, under those circumstances."

"I see," Tumac said, lowering his eyebrow. "So what do you plan on doing, staying up here out of harm's way?"

"No," Lulla replied. "We've been waiting for Ekron's ship to join us. At his request, his men hid the ship on the other side of Earth, until it was needed. He sent for it a few minutes ago. We figured two ships would be better than one against Abron. Especially since he has more weaponry on board than both of ours put together."

"I see," Tumac repeated. "I suppose you know what's best. Captain Borak and I will have to leave. It shouldn't be long before we get an answer back from his senator friend. It appears you may need a lot of luck to get Meesha." A sullen expression etched his long, gaunt face. "We must go back and wait for the message." They left the bridge and took the pod back to Borak's ship.

"I was certainly surprised to see the Prime Minister," she said. "Things must be getting pretty bad, if our King sent him to negotiate with the Earthlings."

"The trip is mainly to cure the King's illness, Lulla," Kerac interrupted. "I can't blame my brother for wanting to live."

"I didn't mean it disparagingly," she replied. "It's just that to my knowledge it's the first time the Prime Minister has ever set foot on Earth. He may not understand these people well enough to bargain with them." She stared at the ceiling for a few moments deep in thought. "When he gets back, I wonder if a stoic person like him will relay to the people back on Golan the strange and wonderful things he saw here on Earth?" She giggled.

When they arrived back on Borak's ship, Tynon was waiting on the bridge with a message from the senator. They were to land at a secluded spot a few miles from Baltimore, Maryland. He gave Borak the coordinates and asked if he was familiar with Earth's GPS.

Borak scoffed. "Son, I've been coming here for quite a long time now," he told the young engineer. "A coordinate is a coordinate, here on Earth or on Golan. Tynon blushed and returned to engineering.

"Is it a go, Captain?" Tumac asked.

"I believe so," Borak answered. "At least, I have the coordinates of a remote site outside Baltimore. I've flown over that area a few times, and apparently nobody ever noticed me. There shouldn't be a problem."

"Then the President will meet us there?"

"I would assume so; the senator wouldn't have given me the coordinates, if he wasn't going to show. He said they would be there in about an hour. After we arrive, we are to wait for a signal of ten light flashes before landing. I assume they picked that isolated spot for privacy."

Two black, stretch-limos with their lights out drove covertly onto Joshua Brown's newly cut and harvested cornfield. President John Simmons got out of the first limo and stretched his arms over his head to relieve a cramp he had acquired from sitting so long in the back seat of the limo. He went to the second limo and leaned up against it.

"What's going on?" he asked the driver. "Weren't they supposed to be here by now?"

"I don't know, Sir," the driver answered, "I wasn't told anything about what's going on around here. Except that I was supposed to blink my lights ten times when we arrived, and keep doing it at five minute intervals." He glanced at Simmons through the open window. "Sir, aren't we supposed to have twenty or so cars accompanying us, like we always do? What about all your FBI, CIA, and guards, aren't they supposed to be here?"

"We were to come with only a small party," Simmons informed him, "that's the way they wanted it." He walked into the cornfield, stumbling on deep cultivation ruts and short corn stalks, looking up at the starlit sky for signs of the ship. Noticing faint lights off in the distance, he turned and waved to the driver. The high-beams turned on and blinked ten times, then waited for a response.

When Borak saw the ten flashes he returned them, and then silently maneuvered the ship to a spot close to the President's entourage and hovered.

"My God!" Simmons shouted, as he surveyed the entire length of the150-foot craft. He shook his head in disbelief. "So, this is a ship from another universe," he mumbled to himself.

The ship settled down gently on the soft soil of the cornfield, with only a faint whirring sound. When its landing pads touched the ground, it came to a complete stop.

After staring wide-eyed at the massive hull, Senator Kent walked over and stood next to Simmons. They both reached out to touch it, and then quickly drew back when they heard a whooshing sound. A door opened in the side of the vessel and a long ramp slid to the ground. Two men in silver uniforms walked down and approached the President.

"President Simmons, I assume," Borak said with a smile. He pointed to the slightly balding man next to him and chuckled. "And you must be Senator Kent. It's nice to finally meet you. I am Captain Kirk…I mean Captain Borak." He pointed to the tall, white haired man next to him. "Gentlemen, this is Prime Minister Tumac, the President of our Parliament."

President Simmons stared at him for several seconds, and then extended his hand. "You do shake hands, don't you?" he asked with a smile.

"Of course, Mr. President," Tumac answered. "There are really not that many differences between your culture and mine. We are also physically quite similar. There are a few cosmetic exceptions, of course, but nothing major. Contrary to what you may have heard, we are not all little green or gray men." He took Simmon's hand, and with a broad smile added, "At least most of us are not."

"Now, what's this all about?" Simmons asked.

"I would like to tell you right here, Mr. President," Borak said, "but I don't believe that would be advisable. For one thing, we don't have time, we have to leave immediately." He motioned toward the ramp. "If you will join me, we can leave for your Area Fifty One. When we arrive, we will tell you all about our situation." He looked at the President and frowned. "You did say you would come with us, didn't you, Mr. President? At least that's what Senator Kent told me." He glanced at the senator for confirmation, and he nodded.

Before he entered the ship, Simmons went to his limo and opened the door. Moments later he returned with an army colonel and a young lady with a voice recorder and camera. They all walked up the ramp and into the ship. But before Simmons entered, he dashed back to the limo and spoke to the sergeant.

"Sergeant, you are not to mention to anyone what you saw here tonight," he told him. "Is that understood?" The sergeant nodded.

After they were all seated and strapped in, Simmons glanced over at Borak, sitting at what he believed to be the helm. "Maybe you could fill me in on our way there, it would save time."

"We wouldn't have enough time, Mr. President," Borak replied

"With almost two thousand miles to go, I believe we'd have plenty of time," Simmons replied with a smirk.

"The trip will take about ten minutes, Mr. President. When we land we will tell you about our problems."

President Simmons was sitting in front of a porthole looking out the window at the stars. After a few seconds of flight he nonchalantly looked down at Earth. The ship was traveling at such an incredible speed the lights below were nothing but blurs. He tried to spot landmarks, but even they went by so fast he couldn't recognize any of them. "Maybe I could make a deal to get a few of these things," he joked to the colonel seated next to him. "Captain," he called across the bridge. "Let me ask you a question."

Borak turned and looked at him. "Yes, Mr. President, what is it?"

"Captain, how can you travel so fast in our atmosphere without burning up, when our fastest planes cannot? At this speed, it would melt their fuselages?"

Captain Borak sat at the helm waving his hands deftly over several round objects, occasionally he would turn his head to glance at a huge screen with strange symbols and colored lines darting across it.

"Well, Mr. President," he answered. "I don't know if you can understand this, but we have the ability to displace all particles in your atmosphere; molecules, atoms and electrons, making a simulated vacuum around us, the same as in your outer space. Our ship's hull is a huge, positive magnet. That magnetic field sends enough energy into your atmosphere to compress and bend space in front of us and expand it behind. Therefore, we travel on the crest of space waves. It would be like riding a tsunami. The 'crest' alone takes us to our destination; we use very little ion energy. All particles surrounding the ship are displaced, therefore there is no friction. We travel in that 'outer space' environment as if we were in outer space, where there is no friction to detain us. Do you understand?"

"I see," Simmons said nonchalantly, not understanding a word he had said. He looked out the porthole and discovered the ship had arrived at its destination and was hovering over a tarmac in front of a large hangar with several other strange looking craft parked inside. He stared in disbelief, when he saw the ships. To his knowledge his military had no such craft.

"Mr. President?" Borak said, turning to face him. "They motioned for us to go inside. Are you ready, Sir?"

"Yes," Simmons replied, looking at his wristwatch. "Let's make it snappy, I have a very important meeting this afternoon."

Borak stared at him disdainfully. "Mr. President, you didn't seem overly impressed with your ride in my 'flying saucer', or meeting us aliens for the first time in recorded history. Why is that, Sir?"

"Well, I'll tell you, Captain," Simmons answered with a grin, "the ride was incredible, I'll say that much. Even so, I have never been overly impressed or taken back by strange things. For many years, I have believed there were others out there like us, so our meeting today did not shock me. Somehow, I knew it wouldn't be long before we made contact with someone out there. I guess this was meant to be the day."

Simmons and his staff followed Borak down the ramp, stopping in front of a group of men assembled outside the hanger.

A stocky, gray haired man in a general's uniform approached them.

"Mr. President," he said, as he saluted. "I'm General Watson the Base Commander. What can we do for you, Sir?"

Simmons didn't return the salute, and didn't answer. He slid the palms of his hands into his back pockets and glanced at the brightly lit buildings throughout the base.

"So, this is the infamous, or should I say notorious, Area Fifty One, huh?" he muttered. "The secret base everybody is talking about…but knows very little about." He turned and looked at the general. "How long has it been here, General? I knew very little about it, only hearsay, until the senator told me. Why wasn't I informed?"

The general shifted from one foot to the other. "Sir, you were not informed because it's a matter of national security. It's a black project and on a need to know basis."

"Need to know basis, even for the President of the United States?"

"Yes sir, this is a covert operation even the Pentagon knows very little about. At least they won't acknowledge it."

"I see," Simmons replied. "Well, General, let's go inside and see this 'covert' operation of yours…which must have cost the taxpayers a ton of cash."

After introductions all around, they walked through a huge door into a massive hanger, where a large van had been waiting. After they were seated the van left the hangar and sped down a long side street. A few minutes later it pulled up in front of a small, white building. They went inside and were directed to several stylish couches in front of a small conference table, where they sat and stared at each other.

Borak, seated next the president, said, "Mr. President." He turned and looked at Borak. "I am speaking on behalf of Prime Minister Tumac, the official representative of our King. He has come to ask for your help. Our King is extremely ill and desperately needs your country's medical expertise. We have been told of your medical abilities. Our doctors, those who have remained on our mother-ships, are at loss for a cure, or even a diagnosis. Would you allow our King to come here and be checked out by your doctors? And, if they find his illness curable, give them permission to operate…or whatever is necessary?"

Simmons stared at him blankly. "Why doesn't your Prime Minister speak for himself, Mr. Borak? I would rather hear it from the representative of your King."

"Although the Prime Minister is somewhat familiar with your language," Borak answered, "he asked if I would speak for both him and our King. He does not know your language well enough to hold an intellectual conversation, especially one of such grave importance." Tumac glanced at Simmons and nodded.

Simmons eyed Borak cautiously. "If I may be so blunt, what would be in it for us…possibly technology?"

"Possibly," Borak replied, taken back by his brusqueness. "But that's a topic for the future, Mr. President. First things first, if I may also be so direct."

Simmons leaned back in the softness of his chair and scanned the man's rugged features. Should he believe everything he tells him, accept it at face value? Or, should he ask for more details, first? He knew nothing about these men from another universe; who they were or where they really came from. He thought it strange they chose the United States, above all other countries. Why was that? What made the United States the Master of the Planet? He should ask more questions, before committing his country to the aid of someone from another world, especially one as important as a King. Assuming he really was a King.

"Captain," he said. "I am not one easily persuaded into making commitments, when I know relatively nothing about you or your alleged universe. Granted, I have seen your superior technology in your flying machine, but that doesn't tell me everything I need to know about you or your planet, before I entrust myself and my country to your plight. I must know more." He leaned back and gave Borak a long, calculated stare.

"What is it you wish to know, Mr. President?" Borak asked. "I would be more than willing to tell you anything you want to know about us, our planet and our universe."

Simmons looked at him guardedly. "I would be more impressed if you could give me positive proof of your planet's existence, and of its dilemma. And, proof of your King's illness. Senator Kent has told me of your planet's impending doom, but I only have his word, and now yours. Normally, I believe a man's word is his bond, and that he is truthful in what he says. But these are trying times. Wouldn't you agree?"

Tumac looked at Borak, and said in Golanese, "Captain, ask if he would agree to a mind probe. Tell him it wouldn't hurt a bit." He smiled. "Tell him it might be the only way to fully understand our plight. It would definitely explain our quandary. If he was not convinced of our honesty, sincerity and integrity after that, all would be lost anyway. Our trip would have been in vain."

Borak nodded. "Good idea, Sir," he replied, also in Golanese. "Mr. President," he began, "would you trust us enough to allow the Prime Minister to put his finger on your forehead? It would not hurt, and I guarantee it's not a trick. It is our way of communicating when we want privacy in our conversations, or to give or get information otherwise difficult to obtain."

"I don't understand." Simmons answered with a frown.

"It is merely a technique to show you pictures in your head of our world, and anything else you would want to have conveyed to you. Your world would call it a form of tactile communications, meaning sending pictures and information to your subconscious by touch or thought. Like I said, it would not hurt. You would be shown pictures of our world and its impending destruction, and of our King's quest for life." He looked into Simmon's eyes and continued. "Have you ever seen Mr. Spock on Star Trek? Our mind probe is quite similar. It would tell you everything you would want to know about us."

The small room became silent. Simmons lowered his eyes and stared hypnotically at the polished floor. He leaned forward, put his elbows on his knees and dropped his face into his hands. After a few moments, he looked up and said, "You can really show me pictures of your world…in my head? No tricks?"

"Yes, Mr. President. Our planet, our sun, our five mother-ships, everything you would want to know about us. We would leave nothing out, hold nothing back."

Simmons glanced at his secretary seated across the room. "Maria, I want you to get pictures of this for the record." He motioned to the colonel standing next to her. "John, I want you to make sure nothing goes wrong. Do you understand? Keep alert at all times. If you think something isn't right, you know what to do."

"Yes, I know exactly what to do, Mr. President." The colonel lowered his hand and placed it next to his .9 mm.

"Then you agree, Mr. President?" Borak asked.

"Yes, I agree. Nevertheless, you must be warned that if anything goes wrong you are at risk. Is that understood and agreed to? If anything at all goes wrong—"

"Nothing will go wrong, Sir, I promise," Borak replied. Then he added with a quiet snicker, "It's not a lobotomy, Mr. President. Please, lean back and close your eyes."

Tumac got up and sat next to Simmons. When he was certain the President's eyes were closed, he put his finger in the middle of his forehead and closed his own eyes.

Instantly, pictures of Golan, its solar system and the converging sun raced through Simmons' mind. He was first shown the beauties of Golan before the sun's convergence, and then its possible devastation after the sun's plasma flares reached critical mass. He was given a virtual trip through a vortex. Moments later, the five mother-ships of the armada came into view, and he was given a picture-tour through them. The scene changed to King Oltar lying in bed with Tumac standing over him speaking about a meeting with the American President. Several moments later, Tumac dropped his finger and leaned back.

Simmons opened his eyes and looked around the room, with a vacant stare. After his staff realized nothing had gone wrong, they were anxious to know what he had seen. He took a deep breath, exhaled loudly and looked at Tumac, leaning back with his eyes closed. The colonel removed his hand from his pistol and the secretary struggled to reload her camera.

"Well, Sir," Borak said, "did you see our plight? Why we are asking for your help?"

Simmons sighed. "Yes, I saw your problem. If that wasn't some sort of illusionary trick you just played on me."

"I can assure you it was not," Borak replied indignantly. "Do you think we would come all this way, especially with all the problems of our world, and the dangers of the vortex, to play tricks on you?"

"No, I guess you wouldn't," Simmons agreed. "Let's get down to the crux of the matter. Precisely, what are you asking for?"

"You saw the image of our King lying in bed deathly ill," Borak replied. "Your country has medical abilities we do not posses, which could possibly save his life. The question is would you let us bring him here to possibly be cured? He has been our King for many wonderful years, and is a good man. If he passed away, we would not only lose a great man, but it would be difficult to find another with such eminence to take his place. At present there is nobody worthy of the throne, except his son Meesha, who is at this moment hiding somewhere on your planet. Unfortunately, he has to be voted in by our Parliament before he can become prince, and then on to be King. However, the boy has enemies who do not want him to be prince, let alone King. Those enemies are also on Earth, and they would like nothing more than to keep the boy, who by the way is only twelve years old, from becoming prince. They have tried to capture him to hide until after the Parliament's vote, but fortunately they have not yet succeeded. However, if our King was cured of his illness he could return and rule his people, as he has for the past forty of your years. Then, there would be no need for a prince."

Simmons leaned forward and put his elbows back on his knees. After a long moment, he looked up. "I believe it could be arranged to have medical attention for your King. What about your planet, though? What could we possibly do to help your planet avoid the cataclysm it faces? We cannot travel between universes, as you apparently do."

Borak looked at Tumac and said in Golanese, "Your Honor, do you believe this is the right time to ask for assimilation?"

"I believe this may be our only chance."

"Mr. President," Tumac said softly. "You saw the impending destruction of our planet. We have millions of people on our five mother-ships who must be relocated, before the sun's final convergence. We would like to know if it would be possible to bring some of them to your planet to assimilate with your people. Not all, of course, only those who wished to come. The rest would remain on the ships to travel to the nearest habitable planet, which even at near light speed would be a life time. We would be extremely grateful for anything you could do for our people."

Simmons leaned forward. "Grateful? You mean like quid pro quo?"

"I don't understand," Tumac replied.

"It's an old Earth expression, meaning if I scratch your back you scratch mine," Simmons replied with a cynical grin.

Borak thought for a moment, and then turned to Tumac. "Do you understand that?"

"Yes, I believe so," Tumac replied. "He is saying if they do us a favor, we must reciprocate in kind."

"I thought that's what it meant," Borak replied. He turned back to Simmons. "I believe something could be arranged. However, we could not allow your military to have our weapons technology. If we did, we would be obligated to share it with the rest of your world, and I don't believe that would be in your best interest. It would definitely create wars all over your planet. I'm sure you can understand that." He hesitated for a moment, and then continued. "For thousands of years our planet was blessed with agricultural splendor. We could give you assistance in that area. And, possibly aid in manufacturing and metallurgy. How does that sound, Mr. President?"

Simmons thought for a moment. "It sounds reasonable to me—for a start. When would this take place?"

"First things first, Mr. President," Borak replied. "First, we must make arrangements to transport our King to your medical facility. I believe Senator Kent would assist us in that endeavor." He looked over at Kent. "Am I speaking out of turn, Senator? You would help us with that humanitarian venture, wouldn't you?"

"Of course, I wouldn't miss it for the world," Kent replied. "I will keep in constant communications with our President to make certain everything goes along smoothly for your King. If it's all right with the

President, you can make arrangements to bring him here as soon as possible. Just let us know when he comes. We could use this base as a rendezvous point. It's secluded and top secret."

"That's good," Borak replied. "I will keep my ham rig in good working order so we can communicate. Right now, I have to take everyone back to Baltimore, before the sun comes up."

Simmons looked at General Watson, quietly standing by the door. "General, you must have excellent medical facilities right here on the base. What are your limitations, do you have operating facilities?"

"Of course," he answered, "we have the best hospital outside Boston General. As a matter of fact we're quite versed in operating on…aliens." He smiled subtly. "We have done it on numerous occasions. We would be honored to help their King. I'm certain we could find his problem in no time at all, and solve it."

"Good, then it's settled," Simmons replied. "Bring him here, Prime Minister, we will do our best to accommodate him." He added with a wryly smile, "We'll discuss the other matter at a later time."

TWENTY

"Meesha!" White Feather shouted. "Come on, we have to find a place for you to hide in the forest." Meesha had fallen behind and ran to catch up. When he was alongside, White Feather handed him the rifle. "Here, carry this," he demanded. Meesha seemed to understand; he took the rifle and slung it over his shoulder.

They had traveled but a short distance, when White Feather suddenly veered off the trail, thrashed through the dense foliage and raced up a small hill. Halfway up the slope he turned and looked back at the boy fighting his way through the tall shrubbery and snickered mischievously.

"We're going to see Mr. Digger," he yelled at the boy. "He'll protect you."

"Digger? See Digger? See Corky?" Meesha yelled back with a broad grin.

"Yeah, see Digger, see Corky." White Feather chuckled, and recited a line from a first grade reader, "See Spot run—" A few minutes later they arrived at the campsite. "I'm going to surprise the old man," he mumbled to himself, and started up the trail to the shack. Suddenly, he heard a faint growl in the bushes. He pointed the battle lantern at a nearby bush and it illuminated a small bear cub thrashing its way out of the brush. It headed in their direction, stopped for a moment to stare at them, then continued toward Digger's fire pit.

"Bear!" Meesha cried out excitedly. "Cub! Cub bear!" he shouted again.

"Yeah, cub bear," White Feather mimicked. "If it follows us, maybe it'll lure the momma bear out of the woods and we can shoot her. Come on boy, let's hurry before it gets light."

As they approached the remains of Digger's shack, they noticed a faint light through one of the broken windows. White Feather crept up closer to the shack. He looked through the window and saw Digger sitting at the table, his head bobbing as if asleep.

Curled up in his lap with one eye open, Corky cocked his head at the sound outside. He looked up at the old man, then jumped down and started barking.

"What's the matter with you, dog?" Digger said groggily. "Ain't nothing out there Go back to sleep."

Meesha crept up to the door and was about to enter when Corky spotted him. He ran up to him, his tail wagging like a propeller, and put his front paws up on his legs. He barked several more times, and then ran back to Digger.

"Corky! What the hell's gotten into you?" the old man yelled. He glanced at the doorway and saw Meesha standing there. "Meesha! What are you doing here?"

White Feather joined the boy at the door. "Hello, Mr. Digger," he said. "What happened to your house? I don't remember it looking like this."

"Well, hi there little Injun," the old man quipped. "What are you guys doing up here? Come for some of my stew?"

"No sir," White Feather replied. "I came to hide Meesha!" Then he added, "Somebody knocked some of our houses down, now they look like yours."

"What? What happened?"

"One of those spaceships shot a beam of light at the houses, and all of a sudden they fell down. My dad said I was to take him into the forest and stay with him until he came and got us. I didn't tell him I was coming to your house, though."

Digger shook his head. "You mean a spaceship did that to your village? Why? Did you find out why?"

"No, but I guess it had something to do with the boy." He pointed to Meesha.

"Same thing happened to me, as you can see," Digger replied, pointing around the room at the remains. "You boys hungry? I still got a stove, a smoke house and a chicken coop. I could whip somethin' up real quick."

"I hated to bother you, Mr. Digger, but I didn't know where else to go, or what to do with him."

"Well, don't fret none about it. Nothing's going to happen to him up here, I can tell you that!"

"Mr. Digger, a bear cub followed us up here," White Feather said. "It's outside. What should we do with it? Maybe its mother will come for it and you can shoot her."

"It could be the cub that belongs to that momma-bear your father shot," Digger stated. "Even if it ain't, the little critter will attract other bears. But don't worry none, if they come snoopin' around here I'll get your dad some fresh bear meat." He got up and went to the sink. "I can still pump water, so we can eat. And that sofa over there is still in fair shape, you boys can flake out on it. Make yourselves at home, while I go fetch somethin' out of the smokehouse. I'll get some eggs too. It's close to breakfast time anyway. Come on dog let's go to the hen house." He walked out and Corky followed.

A few minutes later he returned and put the items in the sink. He pointed at the door; the cub had followed him into the cabin. "Can't let the little guy starve, he's only about ten pounds. We gotta put some meat on the little critter's bones. One thing though, we better be on the lookout, we don't know if that bear Quasi shot was its mother. I'm afraid we don't have much protection in this old shack. It wouldn't take a helluva lot for any bear to get in here. They can be vicious, if there's a cub involved, especially if it belongs to them."

Meesha walked over and petted the cub. He looked at Digger and held his arms out in front of him.

"So, you want to hold the little critter, do you?" he asked. "Be careful, he can take a chunk out of you with those sharp teeth." He picked the cub up by its nape and put it in the boy's arms.

Meesha's eyes lit up when he petted its soft fur, and giggled when it licked his face. He carried it back to the sofa, sat down and cuddled it.

White Feather joined him. "I ain't never seen a bear take to anybody like he has to him," he told Digger. "They usually shy away from humans, unless they were raised by 'em." He reached over to stroke the cub's neck and it growled and nipped at him. He yanked his hand back and got up from the couch. "Dang! I guess he don't like Injuns."

After Digger finished frying the meat, he put three plates on the dilapidated table. "Come on boys get some vittles," he called out. "We can decide what to do with that little varmint, after we fill our guts." He set a tin plate of cut-up meat and a saucer of milk on the floor in front of the cub. It wasted no time lapping up the milk and devouring the meat. "Guess he was hungry, he sure as hell finished that plate off in record time."

After they had finished eating they heard a loud noise outside. Before they could react a huge sow bear knocked down the remains of the door and charged into the room. She looked at them and snarled, then stood up on her hind legs and flailed her paws out in front of her. For several moments she stood motionless, then roared and gnashed her teeth, saliva dripping from her mouth.

"Boys!" Digger whispered. "Don't make any quick moves! Bears usually won't attack if they're not threatened. However, if this is her cub, that ain't good! Move to the back of the room, slowly."

Meesha picked up the cub and went to the sofa. He stared into the huge sow's eyes, and for several moments she stared back eying him as if he were prey. Without warning, she snarled and lumbered toward him.

Digger picked up a large, cast-iron skillet from the sink and hit her over the head with all his strength. Undaunted, she turned and faced him. With a swing of her massive arm, she sent him flying across the room.

Cautiously, Meesha walked toward her, holding the cub out in front of him. Slowly, he lowered it to the floor. She locked her eyes on him, then without warning dropped down on all fours and waddled out of the door, the cub close behind.

When he was certain she had left, White Feather ran across the room where Digger lay in a pile of rubble. He lifted pieces of wood and broken furniture off him and checked for a pulse.

"Meesha!" he shouted. The boy stood by the door watching her large butt swing back and forth down the barely visible path. "Come here, Digger's injured, help me move some of this stuff off him!" He made frantic gestures with his hands.

Meesha looked over and saw his motions and ran to help.

"Digger good?" he asked.

"Digger good," White Feather mimicked.

"Good! Digger good!"

The old man opened his eyes and focused on the boys. "I'm okay, guys," he said, attempting to get to his feet. "Just a few scrapes and bruises. Boy, what a right-cross that critter's got." They pulled him to his feet and helped him to the table. He sat down, folded his arms across the table and rested his head on them. "That must have been the momma bear, after all." He gave them a feeble grin.

TWENTY-ONE

The return trip had been mostly uneventful. After they entered the hanger bay to Golan One, Borac discharged his passengers, and then waited for the ship to be secured. When everything was tied down, Tumac asked him if he would go with him to speak to the King; his voice would add validation to the agreement they had made with the President. He agreed and they took the elevated tram to the King's quarters. As they approached the door, two armed military men confronted them.

"What's this?" Tumac asked. "Why are you men here? Where are the King's Guards?"

"The King ordered us here, Sir," said the taller of the two.

"The King ordered you here?"

"Yes, Sir," the guard replied. "Last night there was an attempt on his life. It was avoided, but in the future he wanted more protection than his own guards could give him. One assailant was killed in the attempt, the other was chased off in a fierce gun battle…so we were told."

"Did you find out who was behind the attack?"

"No, Sir." He shoved his ion rifle out in front of him and patted it lovingly. "But we will, you can be sure of that. If there's another attempt, they won't get by this baby!"

"You know who I am, don't you?" Tumac asked.

"Yes, Sir, you're Prime Minister Tumac."

"Then you wouldn't mind letting us in to see the King?"

The guard looked at Borak and smiled. "I even know the captain, here. He helped me pass my flight tests at the academy."

"Yes, I remember you…Sergeant Taag, isn't it?" Borak replied. "How are you? Have you made it through the academy yet?"

"This is my last year. I'll graduate with flying colors, thanks to you." He opened the ornate double-doors and ushered them into the King's quarters.

Borak stopped in the small foyer and Tumac went on into the King's bedroom and over to the large canopied bed.

King Oltar was propped up on a huge pillow, and watched him enter.

"Tumac," he said. "I see you made it through the vortex with no problems. I understand you had reservations about it."

"Yes, I did, Your Majesty. There were no problems though, just a little headache."

"And, what did you find out? Were the Americans agreeable to our proposal?"

"Yes…and no, Your Majesty."

"Am I supposed to ask what you mean by that?"

"It means they had no problem with you coming for medical attention…but—"

"Yes? But?"

"They didn't seem overly enthusiastic about assimilating with our people. I don't believe they will allow it, at this time. I couldn't get a clear, mental reading on it, though."

"Like you always said first things first," Oltar answered. "If they accept me as a patient and can cure my illness, we can discuss assimilation later."

"There might be another problem, Your Majesty."

"Yes?"

"Have you ever heard the expression, quid pro quo?"

Oltar frowned and looked up at the ceiling in thought. "Yes, I think it means if they do us a favor we must return it in kind…or something like that."

"Yes. That's what it means in any language. They describe it as…if I scratch your back you scratch mine."

"I see," Oltar replied. "Then what did they want for 'scratching our backs'? I hope it wasn't weaponry. You know what that would mean."

"Yes, I know," Tumac replied. "I told them we would give them advice and assistance in agriculture, manufacturing and mining... things along that line. But I told them weaponry was out of the question. They seemed to understand. However, we could easily put ourselves in a no-bargaining situation. I mean by that, if they cured you and also agreed to assimilation, it could very easily pave the way for them insisting on weaponry." He walked several paces from the bed, turned and said, "Not that they would do that, but we don't know them well enough to disregard that possibility."

"I see. Then are you saying we should be careful about making any agreements with them?"

"No, not really. It would be like a statement I once heard on Earth, 'walk softly and carry a big stick', or something like that."

Oltar laughed, and then grabbed his sides. "That's a good one, Tumac. I believe I understand what you mean...they give us what we want and if everything goes as planned, we reciprocate with the things you suggested...everything but weaponry and advanced technology. But, if things turn ugly and they want more and will not compromise, we can use the 'big stick' rule. Is that how you read it?"

"Precisely."

"All right, go ahead with the first phase," Oltar said. "Make arrangements for me to go for medical attention. If everything goes well with the first phase, we can discuss the next one later."

"I'll get right on it, Your Majesty," Tumac said. "We will be taking you in Captain Borak's ship. He has a contact on Earth, a Senator of the United States Government." He looked at the King and smiled. "I would like to go along, if you don't mind."

"Be happy to have you," Oltar said. "By the way, have they found my son? And what did you find out about Luchak, Abron, and Kerac? Fill me in."

"Your son is with friends he made on Earth and is quite happy and safe, at least for now. Luchak is with Kerac on his ship. At present, they are all safe. Luchak has defied his father by coming over to our side, so to speak. But Abron is on the warpath. Not only is he searching for Ekron and Kerac to possibly destroy them, he is also getting us into a lot of trouble with the people we will have to deal with on Earth. He attacked an Indian village, a tribe of copper-skinned people where Meesha has been staying, and I believe a woman was killed by his actions. He is also trying the patience of the American military, by playing games with them. They don't think it's the least bit funny, as you can imagine."

"Does Captain Borak's ship have the latest weaponry on board?"

"He has some, but I don't believe it's anything like Abron's. That man has the most advanced weaponry available."

"Is Captain Borak with you now?"

"Yes, he's waiting in the foyer."

"Tell him to come in I want to speak with him."

Tumac went to the foyer and found Borak sitting in a chair eying a video screen. "Captain, the King would like to speak to you."

Borak followed him into the bedroom, bowed and said, "You wanted to see me, Your Majesty?"

"Captain, Tumac tells me you have a fine ship, but it is not outfitted with the latest weaponry. Is that true?"

Borak thought for a moment. "Yes, Your Majesty, that's true. But why would I need more weaponry, we're not at war with anyone?" He gave the King a subtle smile.

"If we are going to take your ship to Earth, I want it armed with as much advanced weaponry as possible. Do you understand?"

"Yes, Sir, I understand," Borak replied. "However, I've traveled to Earth on many occasions and have befriended a person from their government who is going to help with your medical arrangements. Therefore, I don't believe there will be any problems."

"I understand," Oltar replied. "Nevertheless, I would prefer to go with as much weaponry as possible. Not for the sake of starting anything with Earth, mind you, but to be prepared for the possibility of a less-than-friendly contact with Senator Abron. If he discovered I was on board, and he has many spies who keep him informed, he would try to stop you from delivering me for medical attention. I'm sure he has already realized that with both me and my son out of the way Parliament would vote for his son. And, he would be his advisor.

With the latest weaponry, at least we would be prepared in case he tried anything. Do you understand?"

"Yes, Your Majesty, I understand. I will go to the armory immediately. It shouldn't take them long to install the latest ion and plasma weapons." He moved closer, lowered his head and whispered, "I already have some very impressive plasma torpedoes, and a slightly less than perfect ion gun. But I guess it would be wise to have the latest."

"Then get to it!" the King replied. "I will send word to the armory you are coming, and that they are to outfit you with the latest weaponry, as soon as possible, preferably this afternoon."

Borak bowed and left the room.

At the King's request, Tumac remained.

"Prime Minister, are you certain you want to accompany me to Earth?" he asked. "Do you really want to go through that vortex ordeal again?" A smile spread across his soft, pallid face. "I understand you didn't care much for it.".

"I'm positive, Your Majesty. I wouldn't have it any other way. We can leave this evening, if that's possible. When we get there, Borak will contact the senator to make arrangements for your delivery to their hospital facility."

"Thank you, Tumac. I'm sure you will keep me informed if a problem of any significance arises." He lifted his head and plumped the huge pillow with his fist. "You may go. I must get some rest, before our little adventure."

TWENTY-TWO

"Nader!" an angry voice shouted. "Do I have to remind you of the time? How is that idiot in engineering coming along?"

"I just called him. He said it would take just a few more minutes."

"Do you know Kerac's location? Is he still on the other side of the planet? As soon as this ship is repaired, I want to go after him and Ekron!"

"Do you think that's wise?" Nader countered. "If we left our present location Earth's radars could pick us up and send another missile at us."

"Don't be an idiot, Nader, you know very well Earth has nothing that can reach us at this altitude," Abron bellowed. "Even if they did, we could destroy it before it got here. You know that!"

"Do you really want to start a war with them," the First Mate shouted back. "You've already got their ire up by destroying that village. You know they'll do everything in their power to find and come after us!"

"Why are you so concerned about the Earthlings?" Abron bellowed. "Even if things did go bad, we could always make a vortex and go home, and they couldn't follow."

"Senator!" Kersey shouted over the ship's speaker. "She's all set to go! She's all fixed and ready to travel."

"About time!" Abron shouted into the intercom. "Give me everything she's got."

"Yessir, you got it!"

Abron pushed the thruster lever and the ship streaked across the upper atmosphere headed for the other side of the planet. As soon as he had reached a pre-determined location, several hundred miles from Kerac's ship, he stopped and obtained orbit.

"I've got Kerac's ship on the screen," Nader said, his eyes glued to the green blip. "What do you want to do, go after him?" He lowered his head to look closer at the screen. Another blip suddenly appeared. "Senator, I believe Ekron's ship has just arrived. He stopped alongside Kerac's."

"Good, we can kill two birds with one…ion blast!" Abron said with a cynical smirk. "First, let's wait and see what they're up to. Maybe they plan on going after the boy. Whatever the case, I'm going to rain all over their little party."

"Kerac!" Lulla called out. "Look at this! I believe Abron found us! He's about two hundred miles from us in orbit, the same one we're in. What do you want to do?"

He went to her screen and looked at the ship's signature. "Yes, it's him all right. Let him make the first move. Don't do anything to give our intentions away."

"Give our intentions away? What <u>are</u> our intentions?

"We'll wait here until it's dark down there, and then go after Meesha. With Ekron's ship as support, and assuming Abron's ship is still slightly damaged, we shouldn't have too much trouble getting the boy. Patience, Lulla, I think I know what I'm doing."

"Patience has never been one of my virtues," she replied, "as you must know."

"Yes, I know."

Ekron's ship had just returned from its hiding place on the other side of Earth and stopped close to Borak's. Ekron boarded his pod, which had been parked in Kerac's hangar, and left for his ship. When he arrived, he called Kerac by coded message to see if anything had changed since they located Abron's ship. He was told things had not changed; they were going to wait until dark and go down after the boy.

TWENTY-THREE

Queen Moina entered the King's bedroom ever so quietly, and for a moment stood over him looking at his emaciated body lying in a fetal position on the over-sized bed. Tears moistened the corners of her eyes, as she sat down gently on the edge of the bed.

"Are you sure you're doing the right thing, Jailo?" she asked, when he opened his eyes. "As much as I want you to get well, I have reservations about you going to Earth. I have heard rumors."

He looked up with a frown. "Rumors? What kind of rumors? What have you heard, Moina?"

"I have heard there are people who do not want you to recover. And they will do almost anything to keep you from doing so."

"Don't worry, Moina," he replied with a weak smile, "my friends will take good care of me. They won't let anything happen to me. I'm certain of it." He pushed his head deeper into the pillow, and for a moment closed his eyes. "Besides, even if Earth takes me in there is no guarantee I will even make it out of the operating room." He reached over and took her hand. "Do not worry dear Moina, I am too tough and mean to succumb to my illness, or any other threats planned against me. You know that."

She got up from the bed and looked into his soft, pale-blue eyes. "I know that, dear. I just thought I'd try to talk you out of going, especially when you don't know what to expect. By the way, your things are all packed and ready when you are."

He scowled. "Please don't tell anybody about my trip, especially your friends on Golan Two. All right?"

"Of course. You know I won't." She smiled, kissed him on the forehead and left.

A few minutes later, Borak and Tumac rolled a gurney into the room. They pushed it over to the bed and helped Oltar onto it. After making him comfortable, they rolled it to the door.

The King raised his head and looked at them. "Gentlemen, don't we have people to do this sort of work?" he said. "It's rather undignified for you two to be doing menial labor like this." He laughed.

The gurney stopped in front of the military men at the door. "Men," Tumac said, "you will remain at this door at all times. Understood? Do not let anybody into that room, and do not tell anyone the King is gone. If word gets out, I'll know where it came from. Do you understand?" Both men nodded. "One more thing, when your relief comes, tell them the King is extremely ill and they are not to let anyone for any reason into that room." He gave each a sharp look, and they left. A hundred feet down the hallway, a door opened and the gurney disappeared.

A military vehicle, large enough to accommodate the two men and the gurney, had been waiting for them. The gurney was rolled into the vehicle and it sped off. A few minutes later it arrived at the hanger bay where Borak's ship was powered-up and waiting.

They securely bound the King to the gurney and rolled it up the ramp into a small stateroom aft of the bridge, where they secured it to a vertical stanchion.

Borak brought the ship up to power and moved it slowly toward the huge hanger bay door. Several minutes later he was instructed by the bay coordinator to remain there until he had received clearance for their departure. As they waited for authorization, minutes seemed to turn into hours, and tensions grew. Earlier that afternoon Tumac had called the hanger deck with orders from the King to let Borak's ship leave as soon as it had arrived. However, the huge outer-door remained closed.

A voice finally broke the silence, "Captain Borak, you are cleared to depart as soon as the outer door is opened and locked."

Borak emitted a sigh of relief and leaned back in the Captain's Chair. He realized there was always the possibility of them being detained by a countermanding order from any number of unknown sources, especially if those sources knew the King was on board. The massive door was finally opened and locked and the ship departed.

The ship raced through Golan's thin upper atmosphere to a predetermined location several thousand miles above the planet and stopped at a designated coordinate where they could make a vortex. He signaled for everyone to buckle up. After making several critical adjustments, he pushed a red button on the console, and within seconds the process of creating a vortex began.

The moment they entered the newly constructed vortex their bodies appeared to fade in and out of existence, growing faint and almost disappearing, and then suddenly reappearing and stretching like bungee cords in every conceivable direction. Their physical features appeared dramatically distorted and floated back and forth across the bridge. The complex process of altering atoms, molecules, and particles in and around the vortex was almost complete.

The subatomic particles in and around the ship were systematically controlled by software instructions from the mainframe, and then sent to the vortex drive. The atomic particles in and around the ship and its crew, had been slowly and methodically altered to allow them entry into the inter-dimensional void between the two universes. The process had changed the atomic structure of all atoms, molecules and particles around the ship; the positive protons at the entrance to the vortex had been attracted by the negative electrons of the ship and its surroundings, and the positive elements of Earth's atmosphere had been attracted by the negative elements of the ship as it departed the vortex. The process had only taken a few moments, and the passengers were totally unaware of the changes that had taken place in themselves and the ship.

The ship shot out of the worm-hole and materialized as a solid object two thousand miles above Earth, where it automatically established an orbit.

Oltar put his hands to his forehead and winced in pain.

"The pain will leave in a few minutes, Your Majesty," Borak told him.

Oltar attempted a smile, but he saw no humor in the process.

"Kerac!" Lulla shouted across the bridge. "Look! I have another ship on my screen. It suddenly appeared out of nowhere!"

He went to her screen and looked at the green blip. After watching it for a few seconds, he straightened up and said, "That ship came out of a vortex, it's still sparkling from the effects." He looked at the screen again. "My SigGen tells me it's Borak."

"What would he be doing here?" she asked. "I thought he went back to Golan." She took a quick reading of its range. "If it is him, he's in orbit about a thousand miles from us." She gave him a puzzled look. "I repeat, what would he be doing here? I'll try to contact him."

"No!" Kerac shouted loud enough to make her flinch. "Don't call him! Abron might hear you."

"Then what should we do?" Lulla insisted. "He must be here for a reason. I want to know what it is."

"Patience, we'll find out soon enough." He returned to the helm. "He must be here for something important. Don't do anything stupid, Lulla. I know you!"

She gave him a rude gesture.

"Senator!" Nader yelled over the intercom. "I have something on the screen I think you should see."

The door to Abron's cabin flew open and he rushed up the passageway to the bridge. "What is it this time?" he growled.

"It looks like another ship from Golan."

Abron stood behind him and looked down at the blip. "Is Golan invading us?" he asked jokingly. "I wonder what it's doing here. Who is it? Do you have a signature?"

Nader flipped several switches. "According to the SigGen, it's Captain Borak from Two."

"Borak? What would he be doing here?"

"I don't know, shall I ask him?"

"Don't be stupid! Keep doing what you're getting paid for…keeping tabs on the boy. That's all I want you to do, for now. Understood?"

"Yes sir, completely!" Nader said, giving him an impudent salute.

While Borak was busy operating the ship's many functions, Tumac un-strapped Oltar from the gurney, helped him to the bridge and found him a seat next to a porthole.

"Well, how did you like your little joy ride, Your Majesty?" he quipped.

"I've had better times," he replied, lowering his six-foot frame into the chair. "What's our next move? When can we make arrangements to meet with their President?"

"That's up to Captain Borak," Tumac said. "He'll have to make contact with the senator first, then we'll know more."

"Prime Minister," Borak called. "Please come here, I have something on the screen I want you to see."

Tumac rushed to Borak's side and looked down at his screen. "Yes, what is it?"

"I have the signatures of three ships on my scanner. One I can readily identify as Kerac's, but the other two…I haven't the faintest."

"Don't you have a SigGen on board?" Tumac replied.

"No sir, they took it to make room for more weaponry. I told them to leave it, but they said I wouldn't need it on Earth, that it was no good for identifying earthbound ships."

Tumac sat down at the console and threw several switches. After pushing a few buttons, a series of numbers lit up on the screen. "There," he said, "that should do it, assuming you have the codebook, of course. Or did they take that too, when they took your equipment?"

"No sir, I have it here someplace," Borak replied sheepishly. He walked across the bridge and rummaged through several drawers of a filing cabinet. "How did you do that?" he asked. "I mean, how did you get the SigGen co-ordinates without the generator?" He found the book and held it up. "Here it is."

"Trade secret," Tumac replied. He gave the co-ordinates of the three ships to Borak, and he spent the next few minutes thumbing through its pages attempting to find the names of the ships coinciding with the coded numbers. After several unsuccessful attempts, Tumac took the book and flipped through its pages. The code names of the ships magically appeared.

"As you can see," Borak said, "I'm lost without the SigGen. Forgive my incompetence."

Ignoring him, Tumac took the codes and matched them to the names of the ships. "All three are roughly two thousand miles from us," he told Borak. "But one is miles lower than the others, closer to Earth. That would be Abron. The other two are Kerac and Ekron." He laid the book aside and leaned back in his chair. "I can't imagine what they're up to, just sitting there looking at each other…and possibly us."

"Probably the same as we're doing, waiting for darkness on Earth," Borak replied.

"You're probably right," Tumac agreed. "While we're waiting, can you contact Senator Kent? If so, will the other ships hear your conversation?"

"I'm ready to make the call now," Borak said. "To answer your question, they won't hear me. Even if they did, they couldn't understand what I'm saying. I have a rather unique communicating device they occasionally use on Earth for their own enjoyment. It's called a side-band-transceiver. No ship from Golan has such equipment."

"Good, see if you can make contact," Tumac said, "the sooner the better."

Borak walked to a console and slid a drawer out containing the antique radio. After connecting several plugs and adjusting it to the right frequency, he picked up the mike and winked at Tumac.

"Senator Kent, Senator Kent, this is Captain Borak. Come in, please," he said softly. After several minutes, he repeated the call, "Senator Kent, if you hear me, please answer. Over."

There was a long pause before the squelch broke on the receiver. "This is Kent. Over," a Mickey Mouse voice came back.

"Senator, this is Captain Borak. Do you have instructions for me? I hope nothing has changed, since our last conversation."

"Nothing has changed, Captain," a high-pitched, garbled voice returned. "I have been instructed to tell you to go directly to the Area. There, you will get further instructions. They'll be waiting for you.

But please wait until it's dark down there. There are those around the area who would like nothing more than to see a real—you know what. And, as you can imagine it would be a madhouse in the town of Rachael, Nevada." He chuckled. "Good luck and give my regards to your King. President Simmons will be available, after he gets word from the Area that everything went smoothly. Land where you did before, the general will be waiting. Over."

"Thank you, Senator. Out."

"You don't believe they would try to put something over on us, do you?" Tumac asked.

"I don't believe so," Borak replied. "I've spoken to the senator on many occasions, and I've always had the feeling he was an honorable man, a person I could trust."

"What about their President?" Tumac asked. "I got bad vibes when we met the other day. For one thing, he didn't react to our visit the way I expected—first physical contact and all. It was as if he knew we were coming, and the reason we were coming."

"Are you getting paranoid, Sir?"

"No, I don't believe so. But I am slightly skeptical, and a little suspicious."

Borak went to a porthole and looked down at the blues and whites of Earth. "It will be several hours before it is dark enough down there. While we're waiting, please make yourself comfortable in my quarters. I'll get us something to eat."

"What about Abron?" Tumac asked. "Do you think he knows we're here?"

"If he doesn't, he's not a very good captain," Borak replied. "If he does, he's probably up to no good, something that wouldn't be to our advantage."

"Senator!" Nader called from the navigation console. "What are we going to do about Borak? Don't you want to find out what he's here for?"

"Don't call him," Abron shot back. "He's just sitting there not bothering us. We'll wait until he makes a move toward Earth, then we'll find out where he's going, and what his plans are."

"That could be too late!"

"What do you mean, too late?"

"According to my sensors he has the latest weaponry on board, which he never had before. What if he's here to take us back to Golan by force?"

"Let him try! My ship can handle anything he has! He wouldn't dare try anything!"

Nader shook his head. "Very well, but we can't stay in orbit much longer, my instruments also tell me Earth's ground radar has locked onto us. We may be at the mercy of their long-range missiles, where we are now."

Abron switched to another scanner and saw the blinking red lock-on light on the radar indicator. After a few computations, he looked over at Nader.

"They're semi-locked-on to us, but we're out of their missile range for now," he mumbled. "However, to play it safe put the ship behind one of their larger orbiting satellites. They have so many floating around up here they wouldn't be able to get a clean shot, without hitting something of their own."

"Clever. But are we just going to sit there?"

Abron gave him a disgruntled look. "Yes, we are. We're going to remain there until someone makes a move, Borak, Ekron, the Earthlings, or Kerac. Is that clear, Nader?"

"Yes sir, it's completely clear!" he replied, and gave him another offensive salute.

TWENTY-FOUR

A dozen large stake-trucks and several vans rolled onto the reservation, a trail of red dust billowing high in the sky behind them. Men standing two-deep along the slat-board railings, loaded down with tools, equipment and building supplies, took up the remainder of the trucks. As soon as they stopped the police chief of Grande Ronde jumped out of a van and began to delegate work.

Social workers from the YWCA unloaded massive amounts of food from a canvas-covered truck, and then rounded up the native women to instruct them on its proper distribution to the village. Within an hour the sound of pounding, cursing, and sawing could be heard throughout the village.

An earlier dispute between the people from town and the tribe, which had gone on for many years, was soon forgotten and coordinated work began. A pact had been reestablished between them and harmony and camaraderie prevailed throughout the village.

Quasi took charge of the Indians, instructing them in the proper use of the hammer and saw; they were hunters and fishermen not builders. Even so, it didn't take them long to semi-perfected the art of building.

Lumbermen from the logging camps in the area soon bonded with the tribe, leaving their animosities behind. Something the tribe had not experienced in many years.

An army helicopter hovered over the village, and then came in for a landing. A number of military men, from a Construction Battalions, trained in various aspects of the building trade disembarked and the helicopter took off. Two earth-movers lumbered into the village and started bulldozing streets between the cabins. Before long, wood-framed skeletons were the landmarks of the village. Brick chimneys were quickly reattached to the four-room cabins by out of work masons, and downed electric wires reconnected by electricians. Before long the village resembled a small town with the addition of a central playground, compliments of the CBs.

As the sun slowly descended in the west, the sounds of diesel trucks were heard off in the distance. Huge vehicles lumbered into the village, a massive funnel of red dust swirling behind them. Four large canvas stake-trucks halted in the center of the village and waited for the dust to clear. When it had finally settled, eight men jumped out and began unloading furnishings: stoves, refrigerators, freezers, couches, beds, tables and chairs, and accessories; lamps, end-tables, silverware, dishes, and pots and pans.

Nakomi climbed to a high knoll that overlooked the newly constructed village and her eyes filled with tears. What could this mean, she wondered? Why was this happening? The white man rarely set foot in their village, unless to get permission to hunt deer, or get fishing rights to their trout streams. The townspeople had never given them anything but grief, when they went into town for supplies. Why was this happening now? She couldn't figure it out. She went to their newly raised cabin and went inside.

Quasi was bent over a new sink in the kitchen flipping a switch up and down, watching a light in the ceiling go on and off.

"Look at these, Nakomi," he said, pointing to a slightly used refrigerator, electric stove and dining table with chairs. "And this!" He ran into one of two bedrooms. "Look, a new bed with all the trimmings. And White Feather has one too." He went back into the living room, sat down in a slightly used couch and jumped up and down to feel its softness. "Everyone in the village has these things," he told her, "not just the houses that were damaged. The people in town brought them."

"Why?" she asked. "Why would they do this? They have always looked down their noses at us. Why would they all of a sudden do this? Answer me that."

He got up from the sofa and joined her at the door. "Are you unhappy with your new house?" he asked. "It's new, something you never had before. Do you hold it against them for doing this, after what they've put us through over the years?"

She put her arms around his waist and snuggled up to him. "Of course I'm happy to have a place to live, but I was happy in our old house, too. This new one can never bring back the happiness we had before. It can never bring back old memories."

He put his arms around her. "Now that the majority of the village is finished, I believe I should go after the boys, see how they're doing on their own." He went to the back of the cabin where Red Wing was grazing and whistled. The pinto perked up his ears. "Come on boy," he shouted, "we're goin' on a little trip." The pinto raced over, reared up on his hind legs and clawed the air.

"Come on, boys," Digger said, getting up from the table. "Let's square this place away, make it somewhat livable, then we'll go after that critter."

Following his instructions, the boys made quick work out of carting broken remnants of furniture outside, propping up the weakened struts holding up the roof, and putting the furniture not too badly damaged back in place. Within an hour the shack had been made more or less livable. They finished by sweeping out the leftover trash, and carting firewood in for the cooking stove.

When they had finished, Digger sat at the table and called them over. They stared at him across the oil-clothed table like he was a professor and they were students waiting for a lecture.

"Boys," he said. "I would like to go after that dang critter myself, but I'm not sure I have enough energy left. I can try, though. What do you think, White Feather, should we go after the sow? You've got your rifle and I got my shotgun." He got up from the table and went to the sink. "Your father could certainly use the meat." He drew a glass of water from the hand-pump, and then turned to face them. "Oh, hell, let's go!"

White Feather jumped up with a broad grin. "Meesha," he said. "I'll take the rifle. I think I can handle it better." Knowing he couldn't understand, he grabbed the rifle off the table and slung it over his shoulder. He looked at Digger and said, "Let's go. I haven't shot a bear in a long time." Before they left the shack, he added, "What will happen to the cub, if we kill its mother?"

"We could bring the cub back here," Digger said. "Meesha seems fascinated by it. Don't let shooting the sow bother you, it happens all the time…a mother bear is either shot or leaves her cubs to go on her own. It's the way of nature. The cub will survive, whether we take it in or leave it on its own."

A few minutes later they arrived at Digger's campsite. There was a slight chill in the air, and it would be several hours before the sun peeked over the mountains to warm them. Most animals were still asleep, and the ones awake were not yet searching for breakfasts. The pungent smell of pinesap invaded their nostrils, as they left the well-worn path and headed into the dense, dark forest.

"Mr. Digger," White Feather called out, walking up behind him. "Why don't you like bear meat? I think it's pretty good, the way my mother fixes it."

"That's the problem I can't cook like your mother. It's always too dang tough and greasy to suit me. I'd rather shoot a nice little fawn." He chuckled, knowing it was illegal. "Hell, I'd rather eat anything but bear meat."

As they made their way through the dew-laden foliage, they swung their flashlights from tree to tree and shrub to shrub, looking for signs of bear. The deeper in they went, the darker the forest got. After trudging several hundred yards through the wet undergrowth, they arrived at a small creek surrounded by patches of watercress and fern. Digger knelt at the edge of the stream, dipped his hands into the icy water and splashed his face.

"This is a good place to wait for the critter," he said, as he picked up a handful of watercress and put it in his mouth. "She'll have to come here for water. If she's still nursin', she'll need lots of food and water to keep her milk flowin'."

After he finished with the watercress he searched the area for a good place to hide where they wouldn't be detected by sight or smell. He found a fir tree with low hanging branches, and handed Meesha his shotgun. After a great deal of effort, he made it up to the first branch. After balancing precariously on the limb, he reached for his gun. Meesha handed it to him and lifted his arms to be hoisted up. White Feather didn't need assistance; he had already shinnied up the tree to its highest branches. Digger shook his head at his gymnastic prowess.

TWENTY-FIVE

"I believe it's dark enough at the Area," Kerac said. "We have to make it quick though, the sun will come up in a few hours. Let's try to sneak in without anyone seeing us, including Abron. If he knew where we were headed, he might think twice about following. I don't believe he would want to get involved with their military, after what they did to his ship."

His ship left orbit, followed closely by Borak. Ekron remained in orbit as a lookout, in case Abron decided to follow.

Within minutes the two ships had arrived at the Area. They hovered a few miles above it and waited for the ten flashes of recognition. After a few moments, they received the signal and descended, floodlights marking the spot where they were to land

After they had landed, curious workers approached the ships, walked around them, touched their hulls and talked amongst themselves.

General Watson crossed the tarmac and stopped in front of the ships. The access ramp on Borak's ship was lowered and the gurney rolled down the incline, stopping in front of him. He gave the King a heel-clicking salute, not knowing what else to do.

"So, this is your King?" he asked of Borak. Then, he looked down at Oltar. "Your Majesty, I was told to take you to our surgeon."

"You may call me Mr. Oltar. I am not a King, here on Earth."

"You speak our language well?" Watson appeared surprised.

"I do speak it but not very well, I might add," Oltar answered softly.

"I meant by that, I didn't expect all aliens to speak our language, especially so fluently." He turned to Borak. "Please, take him into the hangar, there is a vehicle waiting to take him to our hospital complex."

The gurney was pushed across the tarmac and into the hangar, where an emergency vehicle waited. As soon as the gurney was loaded into the van, it rushed down a side street with sirens wailing. A few minutes later it stopped in front of a large, wooden structure with a sign across the front that read "Emergency Ward" in bold letters.

They pushed the gurney into the foyer, where a heavyset, white-haired nurse waited. "I'll take him from here, gentlemen," she said curtly. "The surgeon has been waiting a long time…ever since the President called. He doesn't like to be kept waiting. You gentlemen can rest in that room over there." She pointed to a large glass door across the lobby. She grabbed the handlebars and effortlessly rushed the gurney down a long, polished passageway and into another room.

As she entered the operating room, Doctor Morris, a tall, disheveled, gray-haired man stood in the middle of the room, hands on his hips and a frown on his face. He brushed his long, wild hair out of his eyes and stared down at the King.

"So, this is the alien everybody's been talking about, huh," he said, "a King from a parallel universe?" He rolled his eyes. "Don't look like some others we get in here."

"That's what I was thinking," she replied, as she locked the gurney's wheels. "He doesn't look much different than us, except for those eyes and that eyebrow. They're strange."

"We are not that much different than you," Oltar stated flatly. "Other than what you just mentioned, there are no major differences."

"Oh, you speak our language?" she replied, her face flushing. "I'm sorry if I offended you by my remarks. I didn't know you could understand English."

"Do not apologize, it is not necessary."

Doctor Morris brushed his long, tousled hair out of his eyes once more, and looked down at him. "I'm glad we can communicate. It'll make my job much easier, if I can ask questions about your problem." He lowered the sidebar of the gurney and looked at the nurse. "Helen, would you please give me a hand rolling him onto the diagnostic table."

When Borak saw the King had been taken care of, he told Kerac he would wait for the diagnosis, and for him to go back into orbit; he might be needed in case Abron made threatening moves.

"Senator!" Nader shouted over the intercom. "You'd better come to the bridge. A few minutes ago two of the ships left orbit and landed somewhere in the southwest area of Earth."

Abron rushed out of his cabin and stood behind him. "Then that leaves only one in orbit, right?"

"Yes. That would be Ekron," Nader answered, turning to look at him. "What do you want to do, go after him while he's alone?"

"Don't be foolish," Abron snarled. "Like I said, for now I'm only interested in the boys." He bent over the screen and strained his eyes at the green blips. "I wonder what they're going to do down there, the boys aren't at that location?"

"I don't know," Nader replied. "But something is going on down there that seems rather suspicious to me. I believe we should confront Ekron. They may have left him as a lookout, or a possible decoy. If we confronted him, maybe he'd break down and tell us what's going on down there. Even if he wouldn't, we could always cripple his ship so he couldn't be a thorn in our side later. We have the ability, you know."

"I know we do, Nader!" Abron shot back sharply. "Nevertheless, let's wait and see what happens next. Knowing Ekron, as I do, I know he wouldn't tell us anything." He went to the helm and slumped his large body into the Captain's Chair. He was silent for a few moments, then turned and said, "See if you can get the coordinates on those two ships. I want to know exactly where they went. Maybe we can find out why they landed in the middle of nowhere in the dark."

"Maybe it's because they didn't want to be seen," Nader answered.

"That isn't what I meant, Nader!" Abron shot back.

TWENTY-SIX

Quasi bounced painfully up and down on Red Wing's un-saddled back, on his way to the forest. Although his ribs had been tightly bound, he could feel every step the pony took. He had been in that forest many times, but each trip had seemed more hostile, especially after the wolf packs had staked out their claims on most of the mountains around Grande Ronde.

Red Wing had sensed a strange presence, and didn't appear too happy about it. His eyes bulged and his nostrils flared, as he walked guardedly through the darkness tripping on boulders and then snorting his discontent. On several occasions his lack of night vision had nearly forced him to his knees. Suddenly, he reared up and whinnied.

Quasi grabbed the long hair on his mane to keep from falling off. "Whoa, boy," he said softly, and patted his neck. "What's gotten into you, boy? You think there are wolves out there, don't you? Maybe bears?" The pony reared up again, causing Quasi to slide off his back and land spread-eagle on the hard-packed ground. He attempted to grab the reins, but the pony was too quick and ran up the path. He pulled himself to his feet as the horse disappear into the bushes.

As he stood on the path, not knowing what to do next, he heard snarls in the bushes. Frantically, he reached for his flashlight and swung the beam around the area. Six sets of green eyes stared at him ominously. His mind told him to run, but his instincts told him to stay put and be quiet. He scanned the darkness for a place to take refuge and found a small pine tree a few yards away, which he believed he could climb. As he made his way toward it, the beady eyes followed him. He grabbed the limb closest to the ground and painfully swung up. He looked up and there were no limbs above him large enough to support his weight.

The animals had gathered around the base of the tree attempting to get at him. But he was high enough where they couldn't reach him. Several of the larger animals circled the tree, while the others lay panting on the soft grass looking up at him. Two large males raised their heads and howled, followed by short yaps from the others. They had found their prey and they were not going to give it up.

He broke off a small, dead limb close to his roost and swiped at a set of paws clawing at the trunk several feet below him. The animal yelped, dropped to the ground for a few seconds, and then put its paws back on the trunk, its beady eyes glowing menacingly in the beam of his flashlight.

"Get out of here, you critters!" he yelled at the top of his lungs. "Shoo, go away!" The animals jumped up and ran a few feet, but when they saw there was no danger they returned. He let out the loudest war whoop he could muster, and once again the animals jumped to their feet. However, they didn't run away, they remained at their stations looking up hungrily.

"Listen!" Digger whispered. "Did you hear that? That sounded like the big Injun. What the hell would he be doing out here? It sounds like he's only a couple hundred yards from us. I thought I heard wolves howlin' too, a few minutes ago. Maybe he's in trouble. You think we should investigate? I don't know if he has a gun or not. Does he, boy?" He glanced up at White Feather, sitting on the highest branch. "Well, does he have a rifle?"

"No. I've got the only gun we own," the boy whispered. "That was his yell though. I've sure heard that before!"

"I think we should investigate," Digger said. "See if he's in trouble. It doesn't look like the momma bear's goin' to show, anyway. We've been here for a spell now and she ain't showed, so I guess she ain't goin' to." He untangled himself from the crotch of the limb, dropped to the ground, and then raised his arms to help Meesha down. Halfway to the ground the boy fell into his outstretched arms and they both toppled over backwards. Digger looked up at White Feather and told him to come down.

It took him only a few seconds to climb down from the highest branch and drop to the ground. As soon as he landed, he switched on his battle-lantern and they headed in the direction of the war cry.

They had traveled only a few dozen yards, when they heard more snarls, howls and yelps. The wolves had been focusing on their prey and didn't hear or smell them coming.

"Doggies…doggies," Meesha whispered excitedly.

"Doggies?" Digger questioned in a whisper. "What the hell does that mean?"

"He calls them doggies," White Feather volunteered with a snicker. "That's one of the few words he knows."

As soon as they had moved away from the tall willows that surrounded the creek, they spotted Quasi's dilemma. He was sitting on the lower branch of a young fir tree swatting at the wolves with a short stick.

Digger raised his shotgun and fired No. 8 buckshot at a wolf clawing at the trunk. The force of the pellets sent the animal flying into the bushes. The remaining wolves jumped to their feet and ran into the underbrush, yelping and howling. When he was certain they had all left, he stomped his way through the ferns and foliage to the tree that housed the big Indian.

"Well now, Injun, what do we have here?" he said with a broad grin. "Climb a tree, did we? What's the matter you afraid of those overgrown puppies?"

Quasi swung down from the tree. "Thanks. I didn't think anybody would hear me."

"How could we miss it? It sounded like you were on the war path."

"Damn near was!"

"So, Injun, what are you doin' out here without a gun? That's kinda dumb, ain't it?"

Quasi shook his head. "I don't claim to be the smartest Indian, you know," he said, eying him. "I was lookin' for the boys. I might ask you the same, old man, what are you guys doing out here?"

"We came lookin' for the momma bear that attacked us in my shack," Digger replied. "She had a cub with her. I figured she might be dangerous so I wanted to shoot her before she ate somebody. You know how they are when they got youngsters. Besides, I know how you like bear meat."

"Thanks old man, I appreciate the thought."

Digger's face turned grave. "I understand from what your kid told me your village was almost wiped out by one of those alien ships. Is that right?"

"Yes, it was."

"What are you gonna do about it?"

"Don't rightly know," Quasi replied. "But the people from town came to help us rebuild, along with some military men from Portland. They rebuilt our houses, and even furnished them better than they were. It only took 'em a day to do most of the work. What's left we can do ourselves. Nice bunch of people."

"I thought you were havin' problems with the people from town?"

"We were," Quasi answered. "That's why I don't understand it. Why would they all of a sudden come and help us, when for years they never gave us the time of day?"

Digger thought for a moment. "Maybe it was because you never gave <u>them</u> the time of day. Did you ever think of that?"

Quasi glared at him and walked away, deep in thought. What <u>could</u> have gone wrong in their relationship with the townspeople? Maybe it was his people's fault the town had abandoned them. He didn't rightly know. However, he remembered the many times his tribe had not been invited to the town hall meetings, or other community events. Even if they had, he figured it would have been purely out of pity because they were impoverished. Or, maybe they came to help because they felt guilty about what had happened in the past: Many years ago, an incident had occurred between a young Indian girl and a white boy, both in the fourth grade. The boy had accidentally inflicted a knife wound on his face while cutting a rope, and he told his parents a little Indian girl had wanted him to take her to a school dance and he refused. She got angry and attacked him with a knife.

One night she was abducted from the reservation by some of the townspeople, given a 'kangaroo court' and driven to a reform school fifty miles away, where she was confined for two years. Later, the truth came out, but it was too late the damage had already been done. After that incident, the rapport between the townspeople and the tribe had deteriorated to the point where they could no longer put up with each other. Years later, the townspeople admitted their mistake and apologized, but the tribe would not forgive or forget.

That incident had only fortified his belief that it was the white man's fault they were impoverished and dropped from the town's social calendar. On top of that, the Department of Indian Affairs looked down their noses at them, by never living up to their obligations to the tribe. On many occasions, the Department had set aside the tribe's requests for assistance, considering it secondary to their primary function of handing out welfare checks. He was certain the agency believed that as long as they received their checks on time nothing else would matter. But they were wrong. His people wanted to live like white men and be accepted by them. However, they couldn't do it on their own. Maybe things had changed. He thought. Perhaps the townspeople were trying to forget the past and accept the future. Why else would they come to their aid?

"I'll go after Red Wing," he told Digger. "He got away from me." He looked at White Feather. "Come on son. Let Meesha know we're going."

"I'll take the boy," Digger said. "He'll be safe with me." He took Meesha by the hand, headed him in the direction of the shack and nudged him gently along. "Come on, boy, you're comin' with me. Maybe we can get that critter on our way back to the shack." Meesha smiled and gave him an understanding nod.

TWENTY-SEVEN

Decked out in his finest white lab coat, which he never took off even at meal times, and a stethoscope hanging around his neck, Doctor Everett Morris walked over to Oltar's bed, put his hands behind his back and stared down at him.

"Well, Mr. Oltar," he said with a forced smile, "the MRI tells me you have a tumor in your pancreas. The good news is there are no traces of cancer. However, it's a good thing we spotted it in time. If we hadn't, I wouldn't have put my life savings on your chances."

"What is a pancreas?" Oltar asked, staring wide-eyed at him.

"The pancreas is a gland in the digestive tract that produces several important hormones, including insulin, glucagons and somatostatin, which contains digestive enzymes that pass into the small intestine to help your body digest food. Those enzymes break down the carbohydrates, proteins and fats so you can digest food properly. It looks to me like you've been having trouble with your stomach for some time. Correct?"

Oltar thought for a moment. "Yes, as a matter of fact I have been having trouble with cramps, and a lot of stomach pressure including gas, which is very embarrassing at times. Tell me, is it operable?"

"Of course. I've set you up for immediate surgery."

"Then you will have to operate? There is no other option?"

"If you want to live, I'll have to operate."

"Whatever you say, doctor. How long will it take and what about recovery time?"

"Don't be impatient, Mr. Oltar, it's only a small incision in your lower stomach. Assuming there's no surprises when we get in there, you should be up and around in no time. I find it surprising that your body is quite similar to ours. That being the case, we shouldn't run into any complications."

"You say I'll be up and around in no time? Meaning?"

"It will take a couple hours for the local anesthesia to wear off, and a couple days to recuperate, at the very most. That's assuming everything goes without a hitch."

"Do you have reservations? If so, tell me now."

"None whatsoever, I've done this operation many times and haven't lost a patient yet." He smiled, exposing a set of white, but uneven teeth.

"Then get on with it," Oltar said, lowering his head back to the pillow. "Tell my men outside what is happening so they won't worry. Also, that I want to talk to them, before they plan their next course of action."

"Plan their next course of action?" Morris questioned, raising his eyebrows. "What does that mean? It sounds dramatic?"

Oltar smiled. "We are trying to keep my visit here on Earth a secret from some unsavory characters who would love to know I'm here. If they found out, they would more than likely try to…get me out of the way, shall we say. They know that without me around there would be no one to 'tend the store', as you Earthlings say. They would then be free to install their own government; a sinister one at best. The Parliament has not yet voted for my son to take my place should anything happen to me." He turned his head and looked resolutely at Morris. "If I make it back to Golan in one piece, after this operation, a few heads will roll." He smiled wryly

Captain Borak was informed of the King's request and went to the operating room. "You wanted to see me, Your Majesty?" He stood beside the bed with a grave look on his face. "What's the diagnosis? Did they find your problem?"

Oltar looked up with a smile. "Yes, I have a tumor in my pancreas… whatever that is. They are going to operate in a few minutes."

"Should I wait for you, or go back with the others? How long did they say it would be before we could move you?"

"I didn't find out, exactly," Oltar answered. "Go back into orbit and wait for word from me. Tell my brother what is happening, but be careful you don't inadvertently let Abron know I am here—which I'm sure you won't."

"If his men on Golan Two haven't already found a way to inform him, I'm certain he doesn't know, Your Majesty."

"It would be impossible for them to get word to him from Golan Two," Oltar replied. "They cannot communicate through the vortex. I'm certain he doesn't know I'm here, and what I plan on doing once I'm completely cured and back in fighting form."

"We assume he don't know, Your Majesty," Borak countered. "He's quite devious."

"You don't have to tell me about him, Captain," Oltar replied. "However, I want him to continue believing I'm still on my deathbed on Golan One, and that I may soon die. I want to see his face when I walk into the chamber on my own, sit down beside Tumac and pass judgment on him and his cohorts."

"I'll go back and join the others," Borak said. "I'll try to find out from the doctor, when I can pick you up. I'll ask him to get in touch with Senator Kent, when you're ready to be discharged. He can contact me by our 'special' radio. If Abron leaves us alone long enough, I'll be waiting for his call. If he doesn't call, I will try to contact him." He turned and left.

Oltar watched him disappear through the door. He exhaled a long sigh, and then said, loudly, "All right, doctor, let's get on with it!"

"What's going on here?" Nader muttered to himself, looking down at his scanner. He grabbed the mike and yelled into it, "Senator! I think you'd better come up here, again!"

"What is it this time?" Abron barked harshly.

"Senator, all three ships are back in orbit. I can't figure this one out. Ekron's ship was there all by itself then Kerac came back, and now Borak has joined them."

"I'll be right there, don't do anything stupid!" Abron shouted into the intercom. "Wait until I get there, then we'll decide what to do."

TWENTY-EIGHT

After they had returned to the shack, Meesha sat down at the table and motioned for Digger to sit beside him. He hesitated for a moment, and then joined him. Meesha put his finger on the old man's forehead, and pictures of a schoolyard filled with children appeared. The scene then changed to a small, white cottage with young girls hop-scotching on the sidewalk in front of it. A woman came to the door, spoke to the girls for a few moments, and they all returned to the schoolyard. An elderly, unshaven man hobbled to the door and joined her.

Digger reared back and Meesha dropped his finger. "That's Charley and Grace Bertell," he said, surprised. "I guess you're telling me you want to go back there, huh? Don't think that would be a good idea. What if those bad guys came and found you there? They'd raise all kinds of hell with those folks. I don't think you'd want that."

Meesha shrugged his shoulders and put his finger back on his brow. A picture of a bear with a cub alongside appeared. The scene changed to the two of them wading through thick underbrush with Digger holding a shotgun. He dropped his finger and looked at him questioningly.

When Digger realized what the boy had tried to convey, he smiled. "So, you want to go after that bear cub too, huh? And then go to Charley's? If that's what you want, I guess we'd better get some grub in us before we leave. I still don't understand why you're so damn attached to that cub."

Meesha appeared to understand and put his finger back on the old man's forehead. He sent an image of the female bear lying dead on the ground with the cub snuggled up to her. The next image was him picking up the cub and cuddling it in his arms.

“That’s what I thought. You really want that cub, don’t you? But let me tell you something about bear cubs, boy, they ain’t so cute when they grow up. You can’t treat ‘em like cats or dogs, they’re still wild critters.” He realized his words were drifting in the wind, but he believed the boy understood. He walked to the sink and cracked half a dozen eggs into a bowl. “Let’s eat first, buddy, we can go after that critter on our way to Charley’s. If that’s what you really want.”

TWENTY-NINE

"Colonel!" a young lieutenant shouted over the din of computers and printers at NORAD. "I think you should see this."

Colonel Steel rushed over and stood behind him. "What is it lieutenant?"

"Sir, I have four blips on my screen. Three are a couple thousand miles above Earth in high orbit. The other one I'm not sure of, but it appears to be hiding in our satellite field. With all the junk up there I can't be certain it's a valid contact, but the image is much larger than most of the junk up there. I checked the maps for known satellites and they're all accounted for except that one."

"When did you first spot the contacts?"

"I've had them on my screen for some time now. I didn't want to tell you earlier, they kept going in and out of orbit. Now, they all appear to be just sitting there. What do you think we should do, sir?"

"Keep an eye on them. Let me know if any leave orbit. Get their exact coordinates, I want to be able to do something about them, if there's a problem."

"Yes sir, I've already recorded them."

"Thank you, lieutenant," Steel said on his way back to his desk. "I hope we never have to use those coordinates, but they're nice to have, just in case." He sat down at his console, and after a few strokes on a keyboard the screen lit up with the NORAD icon.

It took Kerac and Ekron only minutes to board Borak's ship. As soon as they arrived in their pods and secured them in the hangar bay, they went to the bridge and found the captain sitting at a console staring into a long-range scanner looking at little green blips.

"Captain," Kerac said, walking up behind him. "What do you have on the screen that's so interesting?"

Borak turned and looked at him. He pointed at the screen. "I think I finally found Abron's ship. It appears to be hiding in the satellite field, not far from Earth's Skylab. I guess he figured nobody would look for him there."

Ekron joined them at the console. "What was important enough that you wanted us to come aboard, Borak? Does it have something to do with Abron?" He glanced around the bridge. "And where is Tumac?"

"I thought I should inform you about the King's progress," Borak replied, "rather than broadcasting it all over outer space, where Abron might be listening." Then he added, "Tumac isn't feeling well, he's in the aft stateroom. Vortex sickness, I guess."

"What do you know about the King's condition? Is he all right?" Kerac asked.

"He's undergoing surgery on his pancreas, at this very moment," Borak told him. "It shouldn't take long for the operation, but the recovery time is about two days. I wanted to find out what you think we should do in the meantime. Should we stay in orbit and take our chances with Abron? Or, go back to Golan and return for the King in several days?"

Kerac thought for a moment. "If we went back to Golan, how would we know when he was ready to be picked up? You know ee can't communicate through the vortex."

"I thought of that," Borak said. "The doctor said it would be a couple days, before he releases him…follow-ups, check-ups and such. But, he also said we could pick him up earlier, if we were very careful with him. He said we should call first, if we're going to get him earlier. Or, we could come back in several days."

"I think we should stay in orbit and take our chances with Abron," Ekron stated. "We have three armed ships and he has one, although his is heavily armed and quite formidable. Even so, if we joined forces I'm sure we could disable him so he couldn't be a menace to anyone, including Earth. Before we do anything, I believe we should let the

Prime Minister decide, he's the reigning power around here. The King would trust him to do the right thing, and so would I. After all, he was voted in as Prime Minister for a reason—he's smarter than us." He grinned.

Tumac heard them talking and walked onto the bridge. "Did I hear my name?"

"Did you hear our suggestions, Sir?" Kerac asked

"Yes, the cabin isn't that far away. I heard it all. I believe Ekron has the right idea. I think we should go after him. If something isn't done right away, he will definitely be a menace to us, and possibly Earth. I believe his intentions are to get Earth riled up. We all know what he's capable of, given the opportunity."

"I believe that's the only option we have," Ekron said. "Which of us has enough fire-power to disable him? Could you do it, Borak? You have the newest weaponry."

"When we left Golan the King insisted I have the latest stuff," Borak replied. "I have the newest ion gun, and the most advanced laser. I believe I could knock out his weaponry so he couldn't use it on us. However, it would have to be a well planned covert operation."

"It might be a gamble," Ekron said. "He is not the average man. You may not be aware of this, but during the war, long before he was a senator, he was an extremely experienced fighter pilot. He had many skills and kills. Of course that was many years ago, long before our countries signed the non-proliferation treaty. So I guess I don't have to tell you if things went awry, you would be putting you and your crew at risk."

"I was aware of his military exploits," Tumac said. "That's one reason I recommended him for Senator of Keeti. If I had known then what I know now, I doubt if he would be senator of anything."

"You sound bitter, Sir," Kerac said. "What do you think changed him into what he is today, the war between our countries?"

"Who's to say?" Tumac replied, with a shake of his head. "Any man could change for the worse, after being subjected to the horrors he went through during the war. Before the war, our planet had close to two billion people, now there are only about twenty-five million, and most of them are on our mother-ships. The ones who remained on the planet will soon be lost forever. Those souls, regardless of their beliefs, cannot be saved by any deity…or us. We gave them ample opportunity to come aboard, but they rejected us believing some divine intervention would rescue them." He lowered his head and stared at the deck.

"All right," Kerac said, "then it's settled. Let's get our heads together and plan this thing out, hopefully without a hitch. We don't want anyone getting hurt or killed, and that goes for Abron. My brother would have our heads, if anybody got killed."

THIRTY

As Meesha and Digger walked down the barren path toward the rock-lined fireplace, they could hear night-prone birds warbling their concertos in the treetops, and farther down caught glimpses of small animals scurrying about the forest floor searching for anything edible. It was pre-dawn and the sun had not yet peeked over the horizon.

It was going to be another beautiful day, Digger thought. He pulled out a plug of tobacco and took a small bite. Several minutes later he spit a long stream of the dark, red juice into the shrubbery alongside the path.

"Come on, boy," he yelled. Meesha had been moving slowly and cautiously down the same path the bear had confronted him on earlier. "Hurry up, boy. There ain't no bears around here, we gotta go deep into the forest to find 'em."

Still cautious, Meesha scanned both sides of the path for signs of danger. Seeing none he quickly caught up with the old man.

They had only traveled a few hundred feet past the fire pit, when Digger veered off the path and headed for a row of small fir trees at the edge of the forest.

Meesha hesitated for a moment, but when he saw him plowing through the thick underbrush and disappear, he quickened his pace and followed. Minutes later, they approached a small meadow with a blue, pristine beaver pond in the middle.

Meesha stopped and stared at the pond. The sight took him back to a similar, but artificial, pond on Golan where he and Loree would sit for hours and talk. At the time, they were both ten years old and quite fond of each other. They would go to the artificially colored pond and plan their future: get married, live in one of the beautiful houses on the outskirts of Alphia, the capital of Golan One, have children and live happily ever after. However, Loree was a commoner, and his father would never have allowed them to get married.

"Meesha!" a soft but firm voice called out. "Why are you standing there? We have to climb onto the blind. Come on, we don't have much time, the critter could be here for water soon and we have to be prepared."

The blind was a small wooden platform eight feet off the ground, nailed haphazardly to the lower branches of a medium-size fir tree. When Meesha saw its flimsy construction he shook his head and giggled.

Digger clasped his hands together and motioned for him to put his foot in them. He hoisted the boy to the closest railing on the blind, and then grabbed one of the boards and hoisted himself up onto the platform.

"Now, that wasn't so bad, was it?" he asked. "I come here when I need camp meat, which of course is a fawn. Tender meat those baby deer." He chuckled, knowing the boy couldn't understand. "The Injun don't know about this place. At least I don't think he does. Good place to shoot critters, though." He eyed the boy, wondering if he really could understand, or if he was just faking it. He guessed it didn't really matter it was somebody to talk to, even if he didn't get an answer.

Soon after they had made themselves comfortable on the platform, they heard rustling in the bushes, not far from the blind. A large, black sow bear lumbered out of the forest and approached the pond. Digger put his finger up to his lips for silence. She sniffed the air, looked around and grunted. A cub scurried out of the bushes, stopped at the edge of the pond and began to drink the cool water. The huge sow raised her head and sniffed the air again.

Digger picked up his shotgun and silently pumped a shell into the chamber. Although he had been extremely careful, he believed she could sense something was wrong. She moved away from the pond, waddled over next to their tree and scratched her butt against it.

Meesha stared wide-eyed at the huge creature scraping her behind against the tree trunk and giggled. The animal looked up and when she saw them she instantly stood up on her hind legs and roared, her red, beady eyes staring at them.

Although the blind was nearly ten feet off the ground, by standing on her hind legs the huge animal could easily reach the lower planks. Snarling, she pulled down on the boards and Digger slid to the edge of the blind. He knew he was going to fall, so he tossed the shotgun to Meesha. She gave the board another powerful tug and Digger fell to the ground on his back.

She dropped on all fours and straddled his prone body, snarling and gnashing her teeth, saliva dripping onto his neck and chest. He lay motionless, staring up into her eyes. She stopped growling and lowered her long, drooling snout next to his face and sniffed it. He didn't know if she was playing with him. or was going to eat him.

When he figured she was about to take a bite out of his face, he spit a long stream of tobacco juice into her eyes. She let out a loud roar, backed off and headed for the pond. When she got there, she rubbed her eyes frantically against the tall grass standing beside it. Not getting any relief from the pain, she plunged into the water and shook her head violently.

"Meesha!" he yelled. "Toss my gun down!" He made the motion of firing a weapon. The boy understood and threw him the shotgun. He clicked the safety off and sighted in on the sow. He stood there for several moments sighting down its barrel, and then glanced at the small cub still lapping water at the edge of the pond. He lowered the weapon. He knew he should have shot her for his Indian friends, but he couldn't. How could he kill her when she was still nursing? He watched as she attempted to wash the pain out of her eyes. He could sympathize with her agony; he knew what it was like to have tobacco juice in the eyes.

After she regained some of her vision she snorted a few times and rushed into the nearby bushes. The cub glanced up from the pond, and then scampered after her.

Digger looked up at the boy sitting on the edge of the damaged blind. "Come on boy, let's go," he yelled. "I guess I don't have a stomach for it, after all." He held up his arms and the boy dropped into them.

Abron had hidden his ship behind a huge, dead Russian satellite a few miles from Earth's Skylab, believing he wouldn't be detected there. He figured he would be safe, as long as he remained next to it. He believed the Earthlings didn't have the ability to detect him that close to the satellite. He figured he would stay there until one of the ships made a move, and then make his.

"Nader!" he shouted. "What's happening?"

"What do you mean what's happening?" the First Mate yelled back.

"Have any of those ships changed locations? Are they still in orbit?"

"None of them have moved an inch, since Borak came back and joined them."

Abron rushed onto the bridge, stood behind him and looked down at the blips on his screen. "What about the boy? Do you have anything to tell me about him?"

"I got his brainwave reading a few minutes ago, but that's all. They were extremely strong, like he was in trouble, then they disappeared."

"Did you get his location?"

"His waves appeared to be close to that Indian reservation you wiped out!"

"Don't get cute, Nader, I did that for a reason, and you know it."

"I'm sorry but I don't know it. I'm still trying to figure it out."

Abron didn't answer he slumped into the Captain's Chair and glared at him. "You know very well we have to demonstrate our strengths to these weaklings," he said with a scoff. "If we don't, they could very easily get the upper hand. It's quite obvious they have us outnumbered, but our weaponry makes up for it. As all good fighting men know, you must have the upper hand before you can dominate an enemy."

"Dominate an enemy?" Nader replied, raising his voice. He got up, walked behind the senator's swivel chair and spun it around. Staring defiantly into his eyes, he said, "Did I hear you correctly? Did you say, dominate? Dominate the people of Earth? You must be joking!" He had tried to be civil to the man, but he was finding it extremely difficult. The senator had finally revealed his true feelings about Earth. He obviously considered its inhabitants second-rate and inferior. He realized he was obligated to give the man his due respect as a senator, and for now he would. But how long could he hide his true feelings? "What about your son? I thought you wanted him more than the boy. Don't you want to go after him? I thought you wanted to take him back to Golan before Meesha was returned."

Abron spun around to face the helm and stared vacantly out the porthole. "Things have not changed," he replied. "However, it has become increasingly difficult to get my son away from Kerac. Therefore, I must go after Meesha. When I get him I will exchange him for my son." He was silent for a moment, and then added, "My son has defied me in the worst way, by not wanting to return to Golan. However, if I have Meesha, Kerac will be forced to make a deal. I'm sure Parliament will wait on the vote, until I return with Luchak. If Meesha were not there, and I'm trying my best to insure he won't be, they would be forced to vote for my son, the only other viable candidate." He turned, and with a glare added, "But you know all this. Get on with your surveillance! Find Meesha!"

"Yes sir, right away."

THIRTY-ONE

After they returned to the shack, Meesha sat down in the sofa, leaned back and closed his eyes. Why had his father sent him to Earth? He couldn't figure it out. He could not understand his reasoning. He could have left him on Golan with his beautiful Loree, the one who made his heart twitter and his knees buckle whenever she gives him that certain smile and touched his hand? They had so much fun together, walking beside the artificial tree-lined pond, and looking through the portholes at the stars in the universe wondering what was out there. Why couldn't they have left him on the ship and hid him someplace, if their intentions were only to keep him out of harm's way until the senators were ready to cast their votes. It was hard to believe he had enemies on Golan, at least any that would do him harm. He believed his father was getting paranoid in his old age; he seemed to be worrying more about the vote than the welfare of Golan.

He didn't want to be Prince or King of Golan. He had tried to make that perfectly clear to everyone. He just wanted to live his life as a little boy and not worry about anything. Later in life, if his father gave permission, he would marry Loree. It all sounded so simple. Why was everyone trying to make it difficult?

"Meesha!" Digger's voice invaded his reveries.

He looked up, startled by the voice.

"I guess you'd like to go back to Grace's house, now that we can't get that cub. Is that right?" Realizing he couldn't understand, he went over and put the boy's finger on his forehead.

Pictures of the little white cottage appeared in Meesha's mind's-eye. He saw Grace and Charley sitting on the porch, her knitting and him reading the Oregonian. The next scene he and Digger were walking up to the porch. His eyes widened and he smiled.

They left the shack, and an hour later arrived at the cottage. Meesha raced through the gate, ran up the steps of the porch and stood in front of the door.

Digger lumbered up the path and joined him. He knocked on the glass door, and then stood back and looked at the boy's beaming face.

The door opened and Grace stood in front of them.

"Land's sake alive, it's Meesha!" she cried out, her face glowing. She opened her arms and he rushed into them. She embraced him, and then looked over at Digger. "Aren't you the one they call Digger?" she asked. "Don't you live up on the mountain?"

"Yes ma'am, that's me."

"Well for goodness sake, come on in," she said. "We were just about to sit down to eat. Would you join us? Got lots of pasta on the stove… just made it."

"I'd like that," he replied. "I'm gettin' kinda tired of my stew. But that's about all I can make worth a dang."

"Well, if it ain't Digger," Charley said, getting up from the sofa. "I'll be damned; ain't seen you in a coon's age. Where you been keepin' yourself?"

"Hi, Charley, I ain't been down in the valley much. Have to keep my eyes on my gold stash, you know. Those varmints from town are always tryin' to find it. Besides, the boy said he wanted to come see you, so here we are."

Charley smiled at Meesha. "Nice to see you boy, I kinda missed you." He looked at Digger skeptically. "He <u>said</u> he wanted to come see us? He <u>told</u> you that?"

"Well, he didn't exactly tell me. He showed me pictures of your house and you and Grace, so I figured he wanted to come. You know how he shows us pictures."

Meesha attempted to put his finger on Charley's forehead, but he pulled it away. "Whoa, boy, let's eat first," he said. "You can show me pictures later. Okay?"

Meesha dropped his hand, walked into the small kitchen and stood beside the table. An aroma he had never smelled before filled the room. He appeared puzzled.

She noticed his confusion and smiled. "This is ziti, son, it's Italian pasta with Marinara sauce. I think you'll like it. Sit down I'll be there shortly with a plateful."

"Ziti?" he mimicked.

"Yes, ziti, you'll like it. I promise."

Grace put a plate in front of him and he grabbed his fork. She served him a large portion and he devoured it in a matter of minutes. After he had finished the plate he looked up wide-eyed, as if asking for more.

"Land's sake alive, you certainly have a healthy appetite," she said.

When they finished eating, they went into the living room and sat in their favorite spots; Charley on his sofa, Gracie in her Belcher and Meesha on the windowsill.

Digger had found a comfortable spot on the love seat, and leaned back and closed his eyes. After a few minutes, he said, "I guess you heard about the Indian reservation."

When Charley heard Digger's voice, he opened his half-closed eyes, turned the TV down and looked over. "You mean about the flyin' saucer?"

"Yes. I guess it did a job on some of their houses."

"I heard some of the townspeople came to their rescue," Charley said.

"Yep, them and a bunch of military men, I guess," Digger replied. "Them Injuns will survive, always have always will. They're a hearty bunch, them Injuns."

"Yep, they're a hearty bunch all right." Charley echoed. With that, he turned the volume up on an old episode of "I Love Lucy".

Digger got up from the love seat and stretched his tall, bent frame. "Thanks for the wonderful meal, Gracie, but I think I better get back to my shack…poachers you know, gotta keep 'em at bay. Never know when they'll try to steal my gold."

She laid her knitting needles aside and got up from the chair. "Oh, you have to leave so soon? We haven't seen you in such a long time, it's a shame you can't stay."

"Thanks, Gracie, but I think I better go." He looked over at Meesha and smiled. "You got the boy there, he's in good hands." He turned and waved to Charley, who was totally engrossed in Lucy, then turned and winked at the boy. As he walked through the gate, he looked up at the almost transparent moon climbing over the eastern horizon. He turned and waved to Meesha in the window, and then headed up the path. "Nice night for huntin'," he muttered.

The only sound in the small room was the shrill laughter of Lucy, and the ticking of the cuckoo clock on the wall.

Meesha turned and looked at them. Charley's head lay deep in the pillow, his eyes half-closed, opening only for a scene he had seen a hundred times. Grace sat in the rocking chair knitting, occasionally looking up at the antics of Lucy, and then back to the afghan shawl she had been manufacturing.

He looked around the room and saw a wood cabinet, which he had never noticed before. It was about three feet tall and highly polished. Its gleaming beauty appeared out of place in the sparsely furnished room. He climbed down from his perch and walked over. It had a domed lid that he was barely strong enough to lift. After much effort he managed to get it open and locked into place. Standing on his tip toes, he looked inside and saw a large metal disc with thousands of tiny rectangular squares punched out of it. On the outside of the box there was a small metal handle, similar to a toy he remembered from his childhood. He turned it several times, and then reached inside and pushed a lever. Instantly, the disc started turning. Several seconds later a loud, metallic sound filled the room. Startled, he jumped back.

Charley's eyes popped open and he lifted his head to look around the room. When he spotted Meesha by the music box, he said, "Dang, boy, what are you tryin' to do give me a heart attack?"

Grace looked up from her knitting. When she realized what was making the sound, she got up and went to the box. She reached down and attempted to push the lever to turn it off, but it was stuck and wouldn't budge. She smiled, grabbed his hands and began to dance with him to the tune of "The Blue Danube". He was completely confused, but after several minutes he started swaying to its tempo. They both laughed and giggled, as they spun around the room. Suddenly, the music stopped.

Charley lowered his head back to the pillow and grunted.

THIRTY-TWO

Tumac walked across the bridge where Borak sat beside the ham rig with his eyes closed.

"Captain," he said softly. "I believe it's dark enough down there to pick up the King."

Startled, Borak opened his eyes and jerked his head around. He stared at him for several seconds, and then looked through the forward porthole. Except for the extreme west coast, the entire United States was ablaze with millions of tiny specks of light. He searched the barren wasteland around Area Fifty One and found it also to be dark, except for a few isolated specks of light.

"Yes, I guess it's about time," he replied. "I'll tell the engineer to bring all systems on line." He sat down at the helm, and then looked over at Tumac. "If you will be my navigator, Your Honor, we can go. I believe I could find the Area on my own, but I'm not positive."

"Don't you think you better inform Senator Kent we're going there?" Tumac said. "I definitely don't want to go down unannounced."

"Yes, I guess I should," Borak said. "Thanks for reminding me." He left the helm and sat down at the ham rig. After the unit had warmed up, he picked up the mike. "Senator Kent, are you there?" he called. There was no immediate response and he repeated the call, "Senator, if you are there, please answer."

The eerie sound of a side-band transmitter loading broke the silence and a Mickey Mouse voice came through the speaker. "Is that you, Captain Borak?"

"Yes, it is. We have a request."

"Please, make it quick," Kent said, "my family is about to leave for a restaurant and play. I don't get many opportunities, you know." There was a slight hesitation, and then he added, "What can I do for you?"

"We are about to go to the Area to get our King," Borak said. "The doctor said if we picked him up earlier than the recommended two day recovery time, we should call first to inform them we're coming. I wouldn't want to invade that air space unannounced."

"Excellent idea, I'll call them now. If you don't hear back from me in a few minutes, go on down. It will mean I've contacted them and informed them you're coming. If for some reason they don't give their approval, I will call you back immediately. Do you understand?"

"Yes, I understand," Borak answered. "If I don't hear from you, I'll leave for the Area in about half an hour." Before he turned the rig off, he clicked the mike once more. "By the way, you and your family have a great time on your evening out."

"Thank you, we will. Good luck with your King."

"Senator!" Nader shouted over the intercom. "You had better come up here. I have some activity on the scanner. I believe it's Borak."

Abron swung his feet down from his berthing cot onto the cold, metallic deck and rushed the short distance to the bridge. Nader was bent over a console looking down at a blip on the screen.

"What is it, Nader?" he said gruffly.

"I'm not certain, but I believe Borak is bringing his ship back on line. At least that's what my instruments tell me."

"What do you think? Is he getting ready to leave orbit?"

"I believe so. He hasn't left yet, but it looks like he's about to."

"Keep your eyes on him. If he leaves I want to know where he goes."

"I'll keep you informed, sir."

"Captain, are we on line yet?" Tumac asked.

Borak glanced down at the massive array of flickering lights on his console. "Everything appears to be ready, Sir. We can leave orbit at any time."

"Good," Tumac replied. "I have set the coordinates for the Area, and downloaded them into the bridge console. Follow them and I think you will be all right."

"You <u>think</u> I'll be all right?" Borak replied with a grin. What does that mean, you <u>think</u> I'll be all right?"

"I'm just adding a little levity to our situation," Tumac said with a grin.

"Oh, that's funny," Borak replied, as he engaged the ion drive. "Here we go, for better or worse!"

"Colonel!" Lieutenant Beaver shouted across the control room. "I think you better see this!"

Colonel Steel rushed over and stood behind the young lieutenant. "What is it, Chuck?"

"Sir, one of the blips I've been monitoring just left orbit. It looks like it's going down to Earth."

"Where?" Steel's eyes widened. "Can you get a fix on it, possibly its trajectory?"

"It'll take a couple seconds."

The colonel bent over the young man's shoulder to get a better look at the screen. "Well, do you have a fix on it, yet?" he asked impatiently.

"I believe so. It looks like it's headed for Nevada, around Area Fifty One."

The colonel thought for a moment. "Area Fifty One? That's impossible, nothing is allowed in there. It's a restricted area. I can't even fly our planes over it." He stared intently at the screen. "Are you sure about that location?"

"If it doesn't change course, that's where it's headed."

The colonel rushed across the room to his console. "I've got to contact headquarters. Keep your eyes glued to that monitor, Chuck!"

"Yes sir!"

The Area appeared shut down for the evening. Only the dim, ghostly glow of a few security lights lit the peripheral of the compound. However, the larger buildings and hangars were illuminated by extremely bright flood-lights. The only other lighting on the base was two strings of landing lights alongside the five-mile-long runway, which had suddenly been activated.

A command car with its lights out rolled onto the tarmac and stopped. General Watson got out and looked into the night sky. He pulled out a pack of cigarettes, lit one and blew a long stream of blue smoke into the night air. After a few minutes, he returned to the car and knocked on the driver's window.

"Sergeant," he shouted through the glass.

The window rolled down and a Master Sergeant stuck his head out. "Yes sir?"

"When is that damn thing supposed to be here? I don't have all night!"

"It's already here, look over your head," the sergeant replied with a comical grin.

Watson looked up, sucked in a deep breath and his eyes widened. A huge, black object was hovering directly over him.

"My God!" he shouted. "When did that thing get here? I was looking up there not two seconds ago and didn't see a thing."

"It just seemed to appear out of nowhere," the sergeant said.

The ship settled on the tarmac gently several hundred feet from the vehicle and powered down. Its outside lights came on illuminating the parking area with a powerful incandescent glow. A ramp slid down from its under-belly and two men came down and approached the general. Several moments later, two fully armed military men marched down the ramp and stood beside them.

"General Watson," Borak said, extending his hand.

The general shook his hand. "Captain Borak?" he answered, squinting in the bright lights. "Did you come to get your King?"

"Yes, we did." He hesitated for a moment, and then added, "Senator Kent did call to let you know we were coming, didn't he?"

"Yes, he did. I was stunned to find that Doctor Morris would let him go so soon." Watson answered. He glanced into the night sky. "How did you do that, Captain?"

"Do what?"

"How did you creep in here without us seeing or hearing you?"

Borak smiled. "Trade secret."

"Come, I'll take you to your leader," Watson said with a wry smile. "According to the doctor, he's out from under the effects of anesthesia. But he'll be unsteady for a spell."

Borak pointed. "You do remember Prime Minister Tumac, don't you?"

Watson gave the tall, white-haired man a fleeting glance, and extended his hand. "Of course, it's nice to see you, Sir."

They entered the command car and headed for the hospital complex. When they arrived they found the gurney outside waiting, the nurse standing beside it.

"Your Majesty!" Borak said, looking down at his distraught face. "Your Majesty!" he repeated.

King Oltar slowly opened his eyes and focused on them. "Captain Borak? Tumac?" he mumbled groggily.

"We're here to take you back to Golan."

Oltar thought for a moment. "Don't tell me we have to go back through that vortex!"

"Yes, Your Majesty. But it won't be so bad this time."

"Good. I hope not."

An ambulance drove up and stopped. They rolled the gurney into the van, strapped the King in and headed back to the ship with all sirens wailing.

"Senator!" Nader shouted. "Borak's ship just landed on Earth, somewhere in Nevada. What do you want to do?"

Abron rushed over and stood behind him. After scanning the screen he went to the helm and sat down in the Captain's Chair.

"Are you sure of his location, without a doubt?" he asked the First Mate.

"Yes, he landed at a place called Area Fifty One," Nader replied. "From what I've heard about it, it's a highly restricted area. Nothing is allowed to enter or even fly over, unless they have authorization. It's a highly sensitive area."

"Good!" Abron shouted. "Let's go after him!"

Nader turned and stared at him. "Go after him? You've got to be kidding! That's a good way to start a war! Or get us shot down!"

"If they want to start something, let them," Abron said obstinately. "We can handle anything they have." He turned around and faced the helm. "Bring the ship up to readiness! All weapons on standby!"

Nader went over, stood behind him and glared down the back of his neck "Sir, I can't do that!"

"What? What did you say?"

"We came here to get your son, and possibly Meesha, nothing else. I won't be a party to a war with Earth. And, I'm certain there would be one, if we provoked them by going into their restricted air space."

"Nader!" the senator screamed. "You are relieved as my First Officer! Go to your quarters and stay there! I can handle this by myself!" He stopped long enough to make an adjustment on a control, and then turned and glared at him. "My last command to you is to tell that no good engineer to bring everything on this ship up to full power."

"Do it yourself, Senator!" Nader shouted back. He turned to leave the bridge, but before he left, he added, "I am completely fed up with your hostility toward the people of Earth!" He stormed off the bridge, leaving the senator alone turning knobs and throwing switches on his console. As he entered his quarters, he heard a call over the intercom, "Kersey! Bring this ship up to full power and activate all weapons. We're going to Earth to torment them!"

"Colonel Steel!" Lieutenant Beaver yelled across the control room.

Steel jerked his head up and looked over. "Yes, what is it this time?"

"Colonel, that blip landed in Nevada, Area Fifty One to be exact."

Steel rushed across the room and stared at his screen. "Is it still there?"

"Yes sir, it landed about half and hour ago. It went down there so fast I could barely keep a fix on it."

"It couldn't have landed there, that's a restricted zone!" Steel replied. "Are you sure it's there?"

"I lost contact when it landed," Beaver answered, "but I didn't see it leave so it must still be there."

"Keep your eyes on the screen," Steel commanded. "Let me know if it leaves." He thought for a moment, and then added, "I wish to hell we could get something down there to investigate, but even we can't penetrate that area without authorization. Are the other two blips still on your screen?"

"Yes, two of them, a couple thousand miles up. And the one closest to the Space Lab is still there."

"Keep tabs on them and keep me informed, I'm going to call headquarters to see if they want us to do anything."

"Yes sir."

Borak had been in the process of bringing his ship on line, when Abron's voice suddenly boomed over a speaker. "Borak! What are you up to? What's going on down there?" The voice hesitated for a moment, then added, "I know you're in that restricted area, but I'm still coming after you. You and Ekron are going to pay for what you did to my ship, one way or the other!"

"Abron, you're crazy, you can't come down here!" Borak shot back. "This is a restricted and highly sensitive area. You'd be shot out of the sky! Stay where you are! We'll talk later when we're back in orbit."

"They better not try to shoot me down!" the metallic voice came back. "It would be their undoing. By the way, what are <u>you</u> doing there if it's so sensitive?"

"I have friends in high places," Borak replied.

Lieutenant Beaver re-ran the blip on his screen several times, and then called across the room.

"Colonel! Colonel Steel! You'd better come and look at this. I just lost another one of the blips. It was there a moment ago, and then it just disappeared."

Colonel Steel walked over and stared down at his screen. "Where did it go?"

"I haven't the faintest. The last I saw of it, it was in the junk field, but now it's gone. It just disappeared off the screen!"

"Can't you bring the contact back and run it in slow-mo?"

"Maybe, give me a minute," Beaver replied. He threw several switches and pushed a button, then turned and looked at him. "Yes, here it is. Good idea, sir. As you can see, it moved toward Earth at such a fantastic speed I thought it had disappeared. But it was just too fast for my scanner."

"All right, Chuck, keep your eyes on it. See if you can find out where it went. Can you do that?"

Beaver slowed the image down even more and found what the colonel was looking for. "It went where the other ship landed, Area Fifty One."

"Keep your eyes on it," Steel demanded, "don't lose it! I have to call this into headquarters." He rushed across the room to his console.

Before Borak could get his ship ready for take-off, Abron had made his way into Area 51 and positioned his ship directly of top of him and hovered.

General Watson was informed of the situation and immediately activated the Base Defense System. However, after looking closer at the situation, he discovered the ship was too close to Borak's to make any offensive moves against it.

Military personnel had been ordered to the scene and were strategically located around the two ships, guns drawn and waiting for orders.

General Watson rushed across the tarmac to get a closer look at the hovering craft. When he saw the complexity of the situation, he grabbed the arm of a nearby soldier.

"Sergeant!" he shouted. "Go to the hangar and tell Captain Allison I want him here, right away!" The sergeant raced across the tarmac and disappeared into the hangar.

Abron lowered his ship to within a few inches of Borak's hull, and then settled on top of it. When the two ships made metal to metal contact, he gave Kersey the order to cut the anti-gravity and ion propulsion engines, and allow the weight of his ship to pin Borak's ship to the tarmac.

Borak picked up his communicator. “Okay, Abron, now what are you going to do, sit here until they shoot you off me?”

“They wouldn’t be that foolish,” Abron replied. “They know from past experiences we could annihilate them, if they tried! Besides,” he added with a sinister chuckle, “they might hit you instead. Did you ever think of that?”

“Then what do you propose we do?”

“I haven’t decided yet,” Abron shot back. There was a pause, and then he added, “You know what I want, I want my son. You know very well King Oltar is on his death-bed of Golan, and Meesha cannot be found to take back for the vote, so that leaves only my son, and you know very well they would vote for him if the boy was not available.”

“First things first, Abron,” Borak said calmly. “I don’t have your son, and you know it. Kerac has him on board, and he’s not about to give him up. Besides, he doesn’t want to go back to Golan, especially with you.”

General Watson noticed the ramp to Borak’s ship had been left in the down position and motioned for several of his men to accompany him up the incline and into the ship. When they got to the bridge Watson put his finger to his lips for silence.

Borak put down his communicator and stared at him. “What is it, General?” he said in a whisper. “Why are you here? What do you think you can do?”

The general scanned the room, and then said, “I don’t know, but I believe between the three of us we should be able to come up with something.” He glanced over at Tumac, sitting on the other side of the bridge looking at a screen.

“Four of us,” Tumac said. “You forgot our King. Although he’s still recovering, he could come up with something we could use.”

Borak went to the bow porthole and looked up at the keel of the massive ship sitting on top of him.

“General,” he said, “if I could get that ship off me for a few seconds, what could you do about it, knowing your regular bullets have no effect on our ships? Do you have anything that could cripple him without totally destroying him?”

Watson joined him at the window and stared up at the keel. "Let me talk to my aide, Captain Allison. He should be outside by now waiting for orders." He pulled a cell phone from his pocket and punched in several numbers.

Within seconds a voice returned, "Captain Allison here."

"Allison, do we still have that weapon we recovered from that crash site in the desert?"

"You mean the one we've been trying to get to work?"

"Yes, that's the one. But I thought you had it working."

"We do, to a point, but we haven't yet fired it." There was a brief pause, before he continued. "We're pretty sure it'll work, though. Nothing appears to be damaged and it's completely intact. However, we haven't even attempted to fire it, not knowing what it will do."

"General," Borak interrupted. "You mean you have one of our weapons? How did you get it?"

"I don't know if it's one of yours," Watson replied. "We retrieved it from a crash site in the desert, several years ago. The men have been reverse-engineering it, but so far I guess they haven't had much luck with it. Do you think you could help us with that?"

"Yes, I'm certain we could, if we had the time," Borak replied. "But I don't know how much longer he's going to stay on top of us, or what his plans are. Besides, you couldn't use it on him while he's still on top. If that were the case, you could use one of your own ground-to-ground missiles."

"I was thinking," Watson said, "we could use it when he leaves and goes back into orbit. We have nothing ourselves that could even damage him at that great a distance, but I'll bet that weapon could. Assuming you can get it working."

"It's a long shot," Borak told him. "We don't even know when he's returning to orbit. We have no idea what his plans are. He might decide to disable or destroy us before he leaves here. There's not much we could do about it, either. His ship is very powerful." Then he added, "How big is the weapon, and can you get it here, without being seen?"

"The gun itself isn't large, one man can handle it." Watson said. "But we had to improvise a power supply, just to activate it to the point we've already reached. That unit itself is much larger than the gun."

"Can your men get them here without being seen by the other ship?" Borak asked.

"I believe so," he replied. "Let me call Allison and find out." He went to the far corner of the bridge and spoke into his cell. After a few moments he returned. "Captain Allison said he would have no trouble getting it here, but he would definitely need help with its activation and operation."

"I'm sure we can help, if in fact it is one of ours," Borak said. "Even if it isn't, we'll get it to work. It can't be too much different than one of our ion guns."

"Ion gun?" repeated the general.

"I'll explain later," Borak said. "Right now I have to come up with some way to get him off my back."

Tumac had been listening to their conversation and walked over to Borak.

"I have an idea…a plan," he said.

"Yes, what is it? We're open to any suggestions."

Tumac settled down in a nearby chair and took in a deep breath. "What is your ship capable of, as far as anti-gravity is concerned?"

"What do you mean, what is it capable of?"

"Would it have enough power to lift both ships off the ground?"

Borak thought for a moment, and then picked up the intercom. After several moments he turned back to Tumac. "The engineer tells me we have plenty of power. Especially since Abron has turned off both his anti-gravity and ion propulsion drives. Like us, he's dead-in-the-water, so to speak. He said weight has nothing to do with anti-gravity, it would be as if both ships were light as feathers."

"Terrific!" Tumac replied. "My idea is to use our ship's anti-gravity to lift both ships into the atmosphere at the same time, and as quickly as possible, close to where his ship was before, and then veer off leaving him stranded in a temporary orbit. He would naturally try to reactivate his anti-gravity and ion drive, but it would take a few minutes to bring them both on-line. Before he could get them up to full power, the men on the ground would have a clear shot with that ion gun. What do you think?"

At that moment, King Oltar walked hesitantly onto the bridge and found a chair.

"Your Majesty, what are you doing out of bed?" Tumac asked. "You're not supposed to be up and around yet. You'll pull your stitches, or something." He smiled. "You've been listening to our conversation, haven't you?"

Oltar shifted in his seat. "I couldn't help but overhear you," he replied. "I thought I should find out exactly what you're planning on doing." He paused for a moment, and then added, "Captain, I have a question."

"Yes, Your Majesty?"

"What if he gets his ship re-activated, before we get ours a safe distance away so they can fire the cannon? That would make us quite vulnerable, don't you think?" He thought for a moment, and then added, "What if the men can't get the ion weapon to work in time—or at all? What then? You cannot take a practice shot; it would give the plan away."

Tumac went to the porthole and glanced up at the huge ship's hull. He turned to Oltar, and said, "As soon as we veered away, we would be completely armed and ready…just in case."

"How long would it take him to activate his systems?" Oltar asked.

"It would take him a few minutes to bring everything up to full power," Borak told him. "By that time we should have his ship high enough where we could fire the weapon safely. If we could damage his external gravity cells he wouldn't have anti-gravity and would have to either crash-land, or remain in orbit. Without hovering capabilities, he wouldn't be able to land for repairs. After that, we could play it by ear."

"If we could damage his cells?" Oltar mimicked, looking at him skeptically. "Play it by ear, you say? If the plan didn't work, think of our predicament. Not that I'm reluctant to die, but if I do the whole future of Golan might be put at risk."

“General, we have the weapon outside,” Captain Allison blasted through his cell. “What do you want us to do with it?”

Watson thought for a moment. “Can you get it on board without being seen by the other ship?”

“Yes, I believe so.”

Several moments later the ramp rattled and Captain Allison and three men came aboard; one carrying the gun the other two lugging a large power supply. They carried the units onto the bridge, laid the gun on a nearby desk and put the large power supply in the middle of the bridge.

“You men hang around for a few minutes,” Watson said. “We’ll try to get this thing to work. If we do, you can carry it outside and station it at a strategic location.”

“Tynon!” Borak bellowed over the ship’s intercom. “Come up here, I have a job for you.”

Several minutes later a disheveled, beady-eyed engineer in dirty coveralls ducked his head through a small hatch and reluctantly came onto the bridge.

“Yes,” he said brusquely. “What is it? Make it snappy! I have a lot of work to do.”

Displeased by his brash remarks, Borak stared him down. He pointed to the weapon on the desk. “Look at that thing and tell me if it’s one of ours. In any case, see if you can get to work.”

Tynon carefully inspected its external mechanisms, and then delicately ran his fingers over its entire length.

“Looks like one of ours,” he said. “It’s an older model though…quite outdated. It must have come from one of our downed observation ships, a long time ago.”

“We lost an observation ship?” the King asked, raising his eyebrow.

“Yes, we lost two, when they were still experimenting with the vortex,” Borak informed him. He looked at Oltar and added, “As a matter of fact, Abron’s brother was on one of the ships when it crashed. He was taken captive and later died.”

"I guess that explains why he has such ill regards for Earth," Oltar replied. Then he continued. "You mean those small observation craft had weapons, even then?"

"Of course, Your Majesty," Tynon said with a grin. "Do you think they'd send them through unarmed, without knowing what was on the other side?"

"Do you think you can get it to work?" Watson interrupted.

"Looks like it would work right now," Tynon replied smugly. "All you have to do is throw this little red switch to the right, and then push this button." He turned the switch and pushed the button and a faint whirring sound came from the unit.

"Wait! Stop!" Tumac yelled. "We don't want to fire it in here!"

"Don't worry," the engineer replied, shaking his head. "It won't fire until it's locked onto a target. Then, you still have to pull back on this thing here." He pointed to a small, half-concealed lever.

"What about that power supply the men brought?" Borak asked, pointing to the heavy device in the middle of the bridge.

"Power supply?" The engineer laughed. "You don't need a power supply it has its own built into the unit. All you have to do is turn the switch, push the button and pull back on the lever…after you have a target locked-on in the telescopic sight, of course."

"Do you think it will still work, after all these years?" Tumac asked with a frown. "If it's as old as you say, it may not work."

"Not to worry," Tynon replied. "I've never seen one of these things not work, in my entire life. It's fool-proof. Any idiot can fire it. It will automatically lock onto a target, once you have it in the range finder… here." He pointed to a long, black cylinder on the top of the weapon.

Watson looked at Allison. "Did you get all that? Do you think your men can handle it?"

"Well, the man said any idiot can fire it," Allison replied with a grin. "I guess that includes us." He motioned for his men to carry the weapon and the power supply back down the ramp. "I'll be waiting for orders, General."

Before Allison left the bridge, Watson pulled him aside to explain what their intentions were. His face lit up

"Don't get too enthusiastic, Captain," Watson told him, "I don't want you locking that thing onto the wrong target!"

Allison laughed, as he followed his men down the ramp.

Colonel Steel had been sitting in front of his computer screen half asleep, when two musical tones rang out. He jerked his head up and shook it to return to reality. Characters were starting to print across his screen: "This is General Elmendorf at Headquarters. Colonel," it began, "we evaluated your situation and have come to the conclusion that you must not, under any circumstances, make contact with the suspect UFOs. However, keep us informed at all times as to their whereabouts. We are contacting the White House to see what, if anything, they want us to do about them. Until we know where they came from and what their intentions are, you must not engage them. I will keep you informed."

"Tynon!" Borak said. "Is there any way you can get everything up and running; ion drive, anti-gravity generator to full power and above all weaponry, without Abron knowing what's going on?"

"Maybe," Tynon said. "He might hear or detect a little something, when I bring her up to full power…but not too much. I'll give it my best shot!" He gave him a perfunctory salute and rushed back down to engineering.

"Borak! What do you take me for, a fool?" Abron's gruff voice came over the communicator. "I know you're bringing your ship on-line! What do you intend to do, with me sitting on top of you? I'm not leaving until you contact Kerac and tell him to bring me my son. You know you can't slide out from under me, unless I let you. Your ship is completely under my control, so relax and make the call."

"Tynon!" Borak shouted in the intercom. "How are you doing down there?" "Do we have full power yet? I don't have control of the helm. We've got to have full power, immediately!"

"It's coming, It's coming!" came an irate response. "Give me a second!"

"We don't have a second! He knows you're bringing the ship online!"

There was a momentary lull, than Tynon shouted through the speaker. "Okay, go for it! You've got all she's got."

"What about anti-gravity? Do you have that up to full power?" Borak replied.

"Like I said, go for it!"

Borak threw several switches and turned a few knobs and within seconds both ships lifted a few inches off the ground. When they had cleared the tarmac, he applied full power to the anti-gravity generator and instantly both ships shot into the upper-atmosphere, high above Area 51.

"Kersey!" Abron yelled over the intercom. "Get us back on line, immediately! Get anti-gravity up and running and bring the ion engines up to full power! That idiot did something I didn't expect! We're easy targets up here, without power!"

"It'll take a few minutes to bring us up to full power," a metallic voice replied. "I'm not a miracle worker!"

When both ships had reached the satellite zone, several hundred miles above Earth, Borak slid out from under Abron's ship, leaving it in orbit without power. He called General Watson on the cell phone he had been given.

"Okay, General, do your stuff!" he yelled. "Be sure to tell your man I'm the one farthest to the left."

General Watson had been standing off to one side looking through a pair of long-range binoculars, when he gave the order to fire. Seconds turned into moments and nothing happened.

"What's the matter, Allison?" the general screamed at his aide. "Why isn't your man firing?"

The sergeant pulled back on the firing lever several times, but nothing happened.

"Did you turn the red lever and push the button like you were told?" Allison shouted at the young soldier.

"Yes, but nothing's happening! I can't get the damn thing to fire!"

Allison rushed over and repeated the cocking procedure. "Try it now!"

Using the long-range telescopic sight, the corporal locked onto the target and pulled back on the trigger. Instantly, a green shaft of plasma shot through the darkness and headed for the target.

The sergeant was thrown backwards by the weapon's powerful recoil and landed butt first on the warm sand.

"Wow!" he muttered. "That thing's got one helluva kick!"

When the ion beam hit Abron's ship it tore the levitation grid from its under-belly and damaged the external rods on the ion drive. The impact threw Abron and his crew around the cabin like balls in a pinball machine.

Kersey was thrown across the engineering room landing face down under a work bench. He attempted to get up, but one of his leg had been severely twisted by the fall. He tried to pull himself over to the intercom, but his back had also been sprained and he couldn't drag himself over to it. His vision grew dim and he passed out.

After Abron had regained his footing, he grabbed the intercom and shouted, "Kersey! What's going on down there? We need power, immediately! That was an ion blast we just took! It wasn't Borak, he's somewhere up here. Where did the Earthlings get a gun like that?" Not getting a response, he scanned the bridge for damage. Borak now had the advantage, and he knew it! His ship had been damaged to a point where he possibly couldn't make a vortex to get home. His thoughts turned back on Kersey. He ducked his head under the small hatch and raced down to engineering.

When he arrived he found Kersey lying on the floor in a pool of blood. He ran over and felt his pulse, it was weak but he was alive. He took him by the collar and dragged him to a small workbench.

"Kersey!" he shouted in his face. "Don't do this to me; you've got work to do. We're dead in the water. You've got to fix this ship." He looked around the room for a medical kit. Finding one, he pulled out a strip of cloth and wrapped it around his bleeding head. He slapped him several times and shook his shoulders. "Kersey, snap out of it, you've got work to do!" The engineer opened his eyes and looked at him groggily.

"What was that?" Kerac yelled. "Lulla, come here! Look at this!"

"What is it? What do you have?" She left her console and rushed over

He pointed to the scanner. "See that? Abron's ship is back in that junk field. My instruments tell me it's no longer operational. It has no power. It's dead!"

"That can't be," Lulla said with a frown. "What could have happened?"

"I don't know, but I believe I saw Borak's ship on the screen a few seconds ago!"

"I thought he was on Earth getting our King," she replied.

"He was. But I'm sure it was his ship I saw."

"What do you want to do?"

"I don't know. Maybe we should get in touch with Borak, find out what happened."

"Sounds reasonable, but are you sure Abron's ship is dead? I wouldn't want to go down there if he's faking it by playing dead."

"See for yourself, there's absolutely no energy level coming from it."

"I'll try to contact Borak," she said, returning to her console.

At that moment the ship's communicator sounded. "Kerac!" a slightly garbled voice came over the speaker. "This is Borak. How are you guys doing up there? We have King Oltar with us, and Abron's ship has been disabled. What do you want to do, now?"

Kerac thought for a moment, "Borak, are you sure he's no longer a threat?"

"At the moment, he isn't," Borak replied. "However, I imagine it won't be long before he's up and running. The Earth hit him with an ion gun and damaged his anti-gravity cell and ion propulsion grid. I don't know how long they'll be out. We'd better think of something, before he gets back on line."

"Where did Earth get an ion gun?" Kerac asked.

"It's a long story I'll fill you in later." For a moment, the speaker went dead, and then Borak's voice returned. "Get in touch with Ekron and tell him what happened. Let me know what you guys decide to do about this new situation. Okay?"

"Okay," Kerac replied. "But I believe Ekron is listening to us now."

"Hi, guys," Ekron's voice broke through the static of the speaker. "That was a brilliant idea you had, Borak. I was aware of everything that went on down there. However, under the circumstances, I couldn't do a thing to help. Give my regards to King Oltar, when you take him back to Golan. Let him know that we're all behind him."

"Will do," Kerac replied. The speaker went dead.

THIRTY-THREE

Meesha sat on his favorite windowsill staring at the security light in the school yard. After walking all the way from Digger's shack, and then dancing to the tune of that strange music box, he was exhausted. He hadn't had that much physical exercise since he helped cart the bear meat back to the village.

He closed his eyes and images of his beloved Loree appeared. She sat beside the artificial pond in the fake forest looking out over the simulated blue water. Pictures of his father lying on his death-bed flashed before his eyes, and then men sitting around a long table appeared—he hoped they were not there to vote for him. Why couldn't everybody leave him alone? Why couldn't they let him enjoy his new-found world, his new way of life? He liked the people of Earth. Everyone on Golan was much too serious and extremely unhappy. Although he could sympathize with their dilemma, the fate of their planet, he could not understand their way of thinking or their way of life, which was based both on technology or science and rarely on fun, like here on Earth.

Grace had just put her knitting away for the evening. She got up, went over and put her hand on his shoulder.

"Meesha, dear," she said. "I think it's time for bed." She gave him a concerned look and pointed to the bedroom. He understood and jumped down from the sill. He followed her into the bedroom, jumped up onto the goose-down bed and within minutes was sound asleep.

As a full moon crept slowly over the treetops on the eastern skyline, a dark figure moved silently toward the cottage. It hesitated for a moment at the gate, and then crept behind the house, where Meesha's bedroom window was partially open. For a few moments the shadowy figure stared through the window, and then slid it half way up.

Although he was half asleep, Meesha could sense a presence. He opened his eyes and looked at the window.

"White Feather," he said, after recognizing him. He threw the covers aside and sat on the edge of the bed.

"My father and I are going bear hunting," the boy whispered. "We want you to come along." Remembering the boy couldn't understand, he motioned for him to come closer. He took his finger and put it on his own forehead. Instantly, images of them walking into the woods appeared. Then, a picture of a huge female bear, with a small cub trotting alongside, came into view. Quasi stood motionless pointing a gun at her. When he believed the boy understood, he pushed his finger away.

Meesha made a sour face and shook his head negatively. He didn't want anything to happen to the bear, or the cub. Except for the bear he had shot to keep Quasi from being mauled and possibly killed, he had never witnessed the killing of any creature. He had become fond of Earth's wildlife, especially bears. They were so big, strong and strange looking. Again, he shook his head.

White Feather could not understand his reluctance; he knew how he wanted to hold a cub in his arms. He put the boy's finger back on his forehead, and showed him images of the village; men busy skinning and cutting up bear meat, and the women gathering it up and distributing it to the village. He tried to tell the boy they were storing food for the winter. However, because of his reluctance, he realized he wasn't going with them. With a disgusted shake of his head, he switched on his battle-lantern, turned and quickly disappeared into the night.

Meesha remained at the window staring into the darkness, images of the small cub flashing through his mind. Would they harm the little cub? He didn't know. But he didn't want that to happen. What could he do? If the cub was with the mother bear when they went after her, it could be harmed. He wanted to chase after him and tell him not to harm the cub, but he had already disappeared into the darkness.

"Kersey," Abron shouted in the intercom. "How are you coming with those repairs?"

Several moments later Kersey replied, “Senator, you know I’ve been injured, or don’t you remember…or care?”

“I know you were, but we have to have power, immediately! Don’t you understand? We could be in deep trouble without power or weaponry.”

“You have weaponry,” his voice replied indignantly. “That wasn’t damaged.”

There was a long pause, before Abron answered. “Kersey, it’s imperative we have power to the ion drive and anti-gravity grids. Without them we can’t do anything. You should know we can’t operate our weaponry without power from the ion drive! We might have to stay in this junk field forever!”

“I’m doing the best I can, under the circumstances,” the engineer shouted back. “But I don’t know if I have the strength to repair the ship by myself.”

“Do what you can! Do you think you can at least get us enough power to make a vortex to get home?”

“Senator!” Nader shouted from his confinement. “What just happened, I was knocked clear across the room?”

“Nader!” Abron shouted back. “I almost forgot about you! Go down to engineering and give Kersey a hand, he’s been injured and certainly could use one. We’ve lost all power to anti-gravity, and the external ion grids are damaged. We’re helpless, unless you and Kersey can find a way to get us up and running. Right now, we’re stationary in a low orbit! Do you understand?”

After a long pause, Nader answered, “Don’t you remember, you relieved me of my duties?”

“Nader, we have a desperate situation here, and it includes you!”

“All right,” Nader replied calmly, “I’ll do what I can. But only if you promise not to go after the Earthlings.”

“I just want to get us home,” Abron replied. “Can you understand that? Just get me enough power to engage our ion drive so we can make a vortex. That’s all!”

“Abron!” a voice came over his communicator. “This is Kerac. What’s your situation?”

"What do you mean what's my situation?" he replied angrily. "You know very well what my situation is! You could have at least left me enough power to get home!"

"I had nothing to do with that, and you know it! That shot came from Earth."

"Where did they get an ion gun? Did you give them one?" Abron yelled back.

"It's a long story, but if you'd like to come aboard we can discuss it," Kerac said. "We'd be happy to have you. Besides, you don't have many options left. Either you come on board or stay in that junk field the rest of your life—or at least until you can find a way to repair your ship, which is unlikely. My long-range scanner tells me your anti-gravity cell has been severely damaged, and your ion drive matrix is almost wiped out."

"Don't worry about it, Kerac," Abron shouted back, "we'll repair them! And when we do, you'll answer to me!"

"Good luck, Senator! We'll be standing by, in case you change your mind."

Both communicators went dead.

"Nader!" Abron shouted into the intercom. "How's it coming down there? Can you fix the problem or not?"

"Or not!" was Nader's scathing response. "We don't have spare parts for the gravity cells, and the ion matrix is virtually useless. Even if we could fix a portion of the matrix, without anti-gravity we couldn't leave orbit, Earth's gravity would pull us down like a rock. We'd either have to stay in orbit or remain in flight forever, just to overcome gravity. And, you know very well we can't land without anti-gravity assistance!"

"Then what do you propose we do?" Abron interrupted him. "Should we take Kerac up on an offer he made us to go aboard his ship? It's either that or we'll have to remain here and rot!"

"If we did go aboard, at least we'd be able to get home," Nader replied. "Right now we can't do anything—we can't leave orbit and we can't make a vortex." There was a long pause, and then he added, "If I were you, I'd take him up on the offer. After that, we could improvise.

Between the three of us I'm sure we could take over his ship, if it became necessary."

"Do you really believe he hasn't thought of that?" Abron shouted back. "The instant we got on board, we'd be taken into custody and confined. Then what?"

"Like I said, improvise."

Abron leaned back in the Captain's Chair and stared blankly through the bow porthole. "You might be right," he mumbled. "There's only him, his engineer and Lulla. There shouldn't be too much trouble taking over his ship."

"You've forgotten one thing," Nader stated.

"What?"

"Your son is also on that ship, and he's a big boy now. Or hadn't you noticed?"

"He wouldn't dare defy me!"

"Well, you might have to find out. We can't stay here much longer. Earth knows we're here and you can bet they have their long-range missiles locked onto us—and possibly that ion gun."

"You worry too much," Abron grumbled. "Let's worry about our own predicament first, and then we'll worry about the Earthlings and their missiles." He picked up the communicator. "Kerac, are you there?"

"Yes, I'm here," he replied. "Have you considered my offer?"

"Yes," Abron answered. "But only because our life support is beginning to fail! We have only a few hours of oxygen left, and the heating system is almost gone. And, to top it off, I don't know how much longer I'll have auxiliary power to this communicator."

"You have your observation pods," Kerac stated. "You could stay in them for quite a long time, before they ran out of oxygen and power."

"Are you telling us to stay here? I thought you said we cold come aboard."

"I did. Give me a little time to set things up, and then I'll bring you on board. First, I have to make some necessary arrangements. In the mean time, turn off your communicator, get in your pods, open your outer bay door before you lose ship's power completely, and wait for my call. In about an hour I'll be in the junk field alongside and you can bring your pods aboard. Is that clear?"

"Yes, perfectly," Abron said indignantly. There was a slight hesitation, and then he added, "Regardless of your feelings toward me, Kerac, think of my two men. They had nothing to do with this situation."

"Unlike you, I'm a man of my word!" Kerac replied. "Do as I say and everything will be fine."

There was a click, as Abron's communicator went dead.

"I know they're in dire straights," Lulla said, "but do you think it's wise to bring them on board? There's only the three of us, and of course Luchak, who I've never been too certain about. Do you think his father will try to get him back in his graces, when he comes aboard?"

"I won't give him the opportunity," he replied. "Besides, I honestly believe the boy is on our side. He's changed quite a bit over the past day or so…for the better, I might add."

"Hope you're right," she answered. "I don't feel like fighting with those men when they get here, especially not knowing if the boy is truly on our side."

"Don't worry, I have a plan." He picked up the communicator, switched channels, and keyed it. "Borak, are you there?"

"Yes. What's up?"

"Could you bring your ship alongside and transport your two armed guards over to my ship?"

"Yes, I could, but why? Why do you need armed guards?"

"I guess you weren't listening to my conversation with Abron."

"No. What's going on?"

"He's lost all power and has very little life support left," Kerac replied. "At least that's what he told me. I told him he and his men could come aboard my ship. However, before that happens I would like your armed guards to be present, just to be on the safe side. Abron has two men with him. I don't want to sound paranoid, but I'd feel much safer if your men were here."

"Can Abron hear our conversation?" Borak asked.

"I don't believe so. He said he was about to lose his communicator and couldn't talk much longer until he got into his pod. If he's not lying, he can't hear us on this channel."

"I certainly hope not," Borak replied. "I don't trust the guy!"

"Neither do I," Kerac agreed. "That's why I want you to send your two men over. King Oltar will be perfectly safe without them."

"All right, I'll send them over, as soon as you're alongside," Borak said. "However, I have one other question, what are we going to do with his ship, if it's not repairable? We can't leave it in the junk field. If the Earthlings found a way to get it down they would have a field-day with its technology. Don't you agree?"

Kerac thought for a moment. "I believe the only solution would be to take it into outer space and blow it up beyond recognition. By the way, where are you now?"

"Well, let's see," Borak replied. "Abron's ship is about two hundred miles above Earth in the junk field, and I'm about two thousand miles above him, where Earth can't get at me. At least I don't think they can."

"What makes you think they can't," Kerac said with a chuckle. "The people down there aren't as stupid as you may think they are. They've come a long way in the past hundred years. You say you're about two thousand miles above Earth?"

"Yes."

"Okay, give me your coordinates and I'll see you shortly," Kerac replied. "I'll open my bay door when I get there."

A few minutes later his ship stopped alongside Borak's and the transfer took place. Ten minutes later, he was headed back to Abron's disabled ship.

Meesha lay back on the soft goose-down bed, his eyes wide open. He glanced at a clock on the night stand, it was ten-thirty. It was hard for him to believe that White Feather and his father went hunting at that hour. Where would they go? Would they go where they had killed the bears before, or a place he had not been shown?

He pushed the heavy blanket aside and sat on the edge of the bed. Maybe he should go find him, after all. They could harm the cub, if they found the mother bear. But where were they? Could he find them in the dark? He suddenly remembered a flashlight he had seen on the dresser. He jumped down and ran across the room. Finding the light, he pointed it at the window and flooded it with a brilliant beam.

He threw on a shirt and pants, stuffed the flashlight in his pocket and rushed back to the window. He climbing onto the sill, and then jumped onto the soft dirt and took off running in the direction he had seen White Feather take. He wasn't sure he could catch up to him before he made it to the forest, but he was going to try.

A few hundred feet down the path, he stopped and looked back at the little, white cottage. Was he doing the right thing? He wondered. He knew Grace would be concerned if he was not there when she woke. Nonetheless, he was determined to find White Feather, if for no other reason than to protect the cub.

"All right, Abron, I'm alongside," Kerac's voice thundered into the pod's speaker. "You and your men can come aboard. But don't try anything foolish, I have two fully armed military men on board, and they have instructions."

"What is this, you don't trust me?" he replied indignantly. "You have to receive me at gun point?"

"Only a precaution," Kerac answered. "Would you trust me, if I had wiped out a small village, just for the sport of it?"

"It wasn't for the sport of it, Kerac. I wanted to show them we have the power to annihilate them."

"The power to annihilate them?" Kerac shouted back. "That was an odd way to show it, wiping out an innocent village and possibly killing an Indian woman."

"I didn't kill anybody. There was just a little damage done to a few houses…shacks, I might add. That's all!"

"That isn't what we were told. And don't you think the destruction of those houses doesn't matter to those people?" Kerac replied. "By now Earth's military is probably after all of us, because of that little stunt!"

There was a long pause, then Abron replied, "All right, it's water under the bridge now. We're in our pods. Bring us on board so we can get home."

"You'll have to wait for a bit on going home," Kerac said. "There is some unfinished business we have to attend to, before going home."

"What do you mean unfinished business?"

"It will be explained, in due time."

The outer-bay door opened and two observation pods entered the hanger bay and settled on the perforated deck. The door closed and the bay refilled with oxygen. Several minutes later, a door from the main cabin opened and two armed guards came into the bay. They stood beside the pods waiting for the men to exit.

Abron opened his hatch first. After a few choice words, he freed himself from the small seat and stood beside the pod. He turned and noticed that the door on the other pod had not opened.

The door finally flung open and Nader stuck his head out gasping for air. "I almost suffocated in there!" he shouted, taking in several deep breaths. "This pod's nearly out of oxygen. Good thing we got here when we did or we'd be dead!" He looked at Kersey, slumped over in the seat next to him, his head and shoulders drooped across the instrument panel. He called to the guards, "You men, help me with this man he's been injured!" One guard walked forward and the other remained at attention with his weapon poised.

Kersey was pulled out of his seat and the guard carried him through the hanger bay, up the passageway and into a small berthing compartment aft of the bridge. After laying him on a cot, the guard took his position at the door, while the other escorted the senator and Nader to the bridge where Kerac and Lulla were waiting.

"Well, if it isn't Senator Abron and his First Mate," Kerac said. "I see you've been quite busy irritating Earth."

Abron threw him a disgruntled look.

"So, you weren't able to repair your ship?" Lulla asked with a grin. "After thinking about it, we decided the best thing would be to take it thousands of miles into space and blow it up."

"Blow it up?" Abron exploded. "What do you mean, blow it up? That's a perfectly good ship…and it's mine! I don't want it blown up! We can come back with the necessary parts and repair it, later. It's not that badly damaged."

Kerac glared at him. "Senator, you know perfectly well if we left that ship there for any length of time their military would find a way to get it down, and they'd have a ball with its technology."

"I suppose you're right," Abron agreed. He walked across the bridge, the guard close behind him. "I never thought of that." He sat down in front of a forward porthole and looked at the multitude of stars. "So, what's your next move?"

Lulla got up from her console and stood behind him. "We'll be leaving for Golan in a few hours," she said. "Right now we're waiting for the outcome of their President's meeting with King Oltar." She suddenly realized her verbal slip-up and quickly sat down at her console. "Oops!" she mumbled under her breath.

"Oops is right!" Kerac mimicked.

"President…King Oltar?" Abron questioned with a raised eyebrow. "Is there something I'm not being told, Lulla? What's this about King Oltar? Is he here on Earth?"

Lulla hunched her shoulders, lowered her head and pounded vigorously on her keyboard.

Kerac motioned to one of the guard. "Sergeant, take these two men where you have the injured man. Lock them in the room and stand guard."

The guard grabbed Abron's arm and tried to pull him toward the door.

"Wait!" Abron yelled, jerking his arm free. "I want to see my son. I know he's here."

"He doesn't want to see you," Kerac replied. He motioned the guard to proceed.

"Damn it, Kerac!" Abron erupted. "Don't treat me like a commoner, I'm still a senator. You'll pay for this lack of respect, when we get back to Golan!"

Kerac swung around to face him. "You better get all the glory you can now, because you may not be a senator for long."

"What exactly is that supposed to mean?"

"It means when we get back to Golan, King Oltar is filing charges against you. And, he's also relieving you of your senatorial seat in Parliament."

"He can't do that, I was voted in by the people of Golan. The King has nothing to do with it." The guard grabbed his arm and pulled him toward the hatch. Again, he yanked free and yelled at Kerac "If I am to believe the King is here, where is he?"

Kerac swung his chair around to face the helm. "He's not here, he's with Borak."

"What is he doing here, anyway?" Abron insisted. The guard re-gripped his arm and forced him toward the passageway. He yanked his arm free again, and shouted, "He's on his death bed on Golan! Don't play games with me!"

Before the guard could get him through the hatch, Kerac motioned for him to bring him back. He looked at Lulla and sighed. "We may as well tell him everything. He can't do anything about it, now that he's in custody. Go for it, Lulla! But wait until I get our ship back to its original coordinates. As much as I respect the Earthlings, I believe they might do whatever is in their best interests…like shooting us out of the sky."

"Good point!" she said. "By the way, don't you think it would be wise to tie their hands, while they're on the bridge?"

The guard pushed Abron to a metal chair and told him to stand still while he tied his hands behind his back. After he was secured, he was shoved roughly onto the chair. The guard bent down, looked into his eyes and whispered, "I never did like you, Senator!" He went to Nader, secured his hands and directed him to another chair.

"Okay, Lulla, what do you want to tell me about the King?" Abron asked, repositioning his butt on the hard seat.

"He <u>was</u> on his death-bed," Lulla stated, "but Captain Borak found a way to get him to Earth for medical treatment. As you must know, our doctors were not capable of taking care of his illness. However, we discovered Earth was. While we were trying to find Meesha, to keep him away from you, Borak brought him here for an operation."

"So what if they do cure him?" Abron interrupted. "What difference will that make?"

"They have already cured him," she replied. "We're taking him back to Golan to continue as our King."

"I don't believe any of this!" Abron erupted. "If he came to Earth and was cured, why would we have to vote for a prince? I don't understand."

Kerac turned to face him. "Meesha was already here, before we found out Earth could cure him. The boy wouldn't have been safe on Golan, while waiting for the vote."

"What makes you think he wouldn't have been safe?" Abron asked.

"We had heard of threats made against both him and the King," she said.

"By whom?"

"Senators from your own Parliament, that's whom."

"If you give me names, I'll take care of it."

"Our sources told us you were also involved."

"Don't believe everything you hear, Lulla. Is the King all right now?"

"He's recuperating on Borak's ship."

He turned and scowled. "What about my son, Lulla? You said he didn't want to see me, or return to Golan? Is that correct?"

"That's what he told us, and I believe him."

"Can I at least see him, talk to him?"

"No!" Kerac shot back. "He said he didn't want to see you." He looked at the guard. "Take them to the cabin and lock them up until I tell you otherwise."

The guard took Abron by his armpits, hoisted him out of the chair, pushed him roughly toward the hatch and motioned for Nader to follow. He walked them down the short passageway and into the cabin where Kersey lay on a cot. He shoved them into the room, slammed the door and locked it.

"Don't try anything funny, Senator," Kerac's voice came over a speaker in the passageway. "The sergeant has orders to stun you, if you don't behave." He looked at Lulla and grinned.

"I think we should concentrate on getting Meesha, now that things have changed in our favor," she told him.

"You're right," he agreed. "I'll contact Borak and tell him to get in touch with Senator Kent. He said the President wanted to see our King before he went back to Golan. To make arrangements for the quid pro quo, I guess." He shrugged. "Then, we can go after Meesha. By the way, were you able to pick up his brain waves? It would be foolish to go after him, not knowing exactly where he is."

"I haven't had his waves in some time," she answered. "Maybe he's asleep. But I know approximately where he is. I believe he's at Grace's house. He really likes her."

Kerac swung the ship around and quickly returned to the junk field.

Noticing his maneuver, she turned and faced him. "What are you doing?" she asked. "Aren't we going where Earth's missiles can't reach us?"

"I have a plan," he answered. A wily grin spread across his face.

"White Feather! White Feather!" Meesha's shrill voice pierced the darkness. "White Feather!" he yelled several more times. He stopped to listen for a response. Hearing none, he waved his flashlight from side to side and up and down, hoping they might see it. He heard a crunching sound behind him. Startled, he swung around and Quasi was standing there looking down at him. Frightened, he jumped back and almost fell.

White Feather stood beside Quasi pointing the battle-lantern in Meesha's face. "I see you finally made up your mind," he said. He walked away, then turned and said with a snicker, "Come on, boy, let's go shoot some bears."

They moved slowly through the tall, wet bushes, until they had reached their favorite hunting ground. Meesha scanned the area and noticed the tree he had fired the gun from earlier. He walked over and looked up into its branches.

"Yep, that's the tree," Quasi told him, and pointed. "I still got the scars to remember it by." He turned to White Feather. "Son, I think you better help him climb the tree. He doesn't have a gun and I don't want him getting hurt."

"Yes, Father," he answered. "Come on kid, let's climb that tree." He motioned toward the tree. Meesha understood and began to climb. With White Feather's help, he was hoisted to a large limb, and then he effortlessly swung up next to him.

Quasi took refuge behind an old, rotting log and loaded his rifle. "Okay, boys, be very quiet," he whispered. "A bear could be here any time, they like this spot. It has a few berries left over from summer. I don't want any distractions. Understood?"

White Feather nodded. He grabbed Meesha's hand and put his finger on his brow to explain what they were going to do. Before he could send any images, a crashing sound came from the edge of the forest. He took the boy's finger away and stared into the darkness.

"Shush!" Quasi whispered. "I think one is coming this way. Get prepared boys, sounds like a big one…lots of meat for our coffers."

Meesha's eyes grew large. He shoved his back up against the tree trunk as far as it would go. Not knowing what he should do if the bear comes, he attempted to put his finger on White Feather's brow.

"What are you doing?" the boy whispered irritably. He pushed his hand away and stared intently at the tree line across the small clearing, looking for any activity.

Meesha attempted to put his finger on the boy's brow again, and again it was pushed aside.

After a third attempt, White Feather let him have his way. He closed his eyes and images of a huge bear with a small cub alongside came into view. Then an image of the mother bear lying dead with her cub snuggled up to her appeared. He knew what the boy was trying to tell him, but what could he do, they had to have meat for winter?

A huge sow bear lumbered out of the underbrush, crushing fallen limbs as she walked. Quasi raised his rifle and took aim, but before firing, he heard more bushes rustling at the edge of the forest. He lowered the rifle and squinted to see where the sound was coming from.

White Feather had heard the commotion and turned on his battle-lantern. He swung it in all directions looking for the source of the sound.

"White Feather!" Quasi whispered hoarsely. "Turn that thing off, immediately! Do you want to scare it away?" Instantly, the light went out.

For a few moments the forest was silent, and then the sounds of breaking limbs and rustling bushes returned. An enormous male bear emerged from the edge of the forest, stopped for a few seconds to sniff the air, and then stood up on his hind legs and scanned the area. Smelling the female's presence, he dropped down on all fours and walked heavily toward her. A few yards from her, he stood up again and roared. He flailed his massive paws out in front of him, to display his power, and then continued toward her. Instinctively, she guarded her cub with her huge body, nudging the youngster to one side with her snout. She stood up on her hind legs and snarled at the oncoming male. They stood face to face growling and swiping the air viciously with their long, sharp claws, occasionally taking patches of hair out of each other's hides.

As the fight progressed Meesha's eyes grew even larger. He had never seen such ferocity. Was this what Digger had tried to tell him, when he planted those images of a cub growing into a huge, wild animal? If so, he believed he understood.

"Kerac!" Lulla shouted. "I believe I have his waves. He appears to be in trouble, his waves are almost off the scale!"

"Get his exact coordinates. We'll go down and see what kind of trouble he's in, this time."

The ferocious battle between the two enormous beasts had finally taken its toll on the sow. The male had sensed it and came in for the kill. With a powerful swipe of his enormous paw he made contact with her head and she dropped to the ground and lay still. The cub backed into the bushes and stuck its head back out. The huge male shook his body like a dog coming out of the water, attempting to get relief from his own injuries. As he approached the sow's body to sniff it, he heard a faint whimper under the mangled bushes. The cub was shivering and whimpering under the twisted vines. He let out a deafening roar and the cub backed farther into the bushes. He made a lunge for it, but the cub was too quick and scurried even deeper into the heavy shrubbery.

Meesha could take no more, he jumped down from the tree and raced toward the huge bear, flailing his arms and yelling in a strange language.

Startled, the bear backed off. However, after seeing there was no danger, he turned and with a loud growl thrashed his way toward the boy.

Quasi leveled his rifle, and was about to pull the trigger, when White Feather called out, "Father! Father! Don't shoot, you could hit the boy!"

He lowered the weapon and looked at his son. "The boy will be killed, if I don't!"

At that moment a huge, dark object came in low over the clearing and hovered over all of them. Within seconds the entire area was flooded by a pulsating, high-intensity light. The bear stopped in his pursuit, stood on his hind legs and raised his head upward. A green, pencil-thin shaft shot down from the object and hit him squarely on his chest. He let out a ferocious roar and toppled over.

White Feather jumped down from the tree and ran to Meesha's side. "You stupid kid!" he screamed in his face. "That bear would have eaten you for breakfast! Don't you know that?"

"Lulla, friend," Meesha said. He pointed to the dark object overhead.

A voice suddenly echoed in his head, "Meesha, are you all right? We came to pick you up. Your father is here and wants to see you. He is now cured of his illness."

"Lulla, I do not wish to see him," he sent back his thoughts. "He will insist that I go back to Golan. I like it here and want to stay."

"But you can't," the voice returned. "Your place is with your people on Golan."

"If my father is cured of his illness," he sent back, "they will no longer need me. They only needed me if my father were to die. If he is alive, they will not need a prince. Is this not true?"

There was a long pause. "We will set the ship down and discuss the matter," Kerac's slightly agitated voice returned. "Please, do not leave until we talk."

"I will stay here, Uncle."

"White Feather," Quasi shouted. "Look at all the meat we have, our people will be happy. I have to return to the village and get help with the butchering and skinning. We will celebrate tonight!"

Meesha swung his flashlight all around the underbrush in search of the cub. He found it hidden under some thick shrubbery and slowly approached it. When he reached for it, it growled and swiped at him, and then backed farther into the brush. He reached in and pulled the frightened, wiggling cub out and cradled it in his arms. It clawed and nipped at him for a few moments, and then relaxed in his arms.

Quasi looked at the boy. "Meesha!" he said sternly. "You can't keep that animal. It ain't a dog or a cat. That's a wild bear. It would grow up and eat you. Besides, we need more of those little critters around here, they grow up to be big…good for our coffers."

Meesha stared at him blankly. Why was he so angry, he thought, it was only a baby bear? It couldn't harm him.

White Feather walked up to Meesha, took his finger and put it on his brow. Instantly, images of a bear not yet fully grown appeared, baring its teeth and growling. The next image was a fully grown bear snarling and gnashing its teeth, saliva running from its mouth.

Meesha understood and lowered the cub to the ground. Instantly, it made a dash for the bushes and disappeared.

Where they were standing was a fairly large area, surrounded by a stand of second-growth timber, close to a small brook that emptied into a larger beaver pond. The ship's exterior lights dimmed to a soft glow, as it hovered over a clearing a few hundred feet from them. It extended its landing pads, moved silently over the clearing and gently settled to the ground. A hatch opened and two dark figures emerged.

As they approached the hunters, their flashlights beams swayed back and forth like ghostly metronomes.

Kerac stopped in front of Quasi and extended his hand. "Good evening, we meet again," he said. He pointed to Lulla. "And this is Lulla, my wife. I don't believe you have met her. We have come to take Meesha back to Golan. I trust there will be no problems."

"There could be," Quasi said with a frown. "The boy doesn't want to go back."

Kerac looked sternly at the boy, and said in Golanese, "Son, do you remember my promise, that if your father agreed I would bring you back?"

"Yes, I remember," he answered, squinting in the darkness. "But I do not believe my father would let me return."

"Your father is no longer ill," Kerac said, "thanks to a doctor here on Earth. He will resume his duties as King, which means they will no longer need a prince. You would not be needed, unless your father died…which could be a very long time. By then you would be old enough to make up your own mind about being King. No one could force you. At this time, you are only needed on Golan to prove to Parliament that Lulla and I brought you back, like we were ordered to do."

Meesha lowered his head and stared thoughtfully at the ground, and then replied in Golanese, "Uncle, I will go with you, if you truly meant what you said about bringing me back. I like it here very much. I have made friends and want to stay with Grace and Charlie."

"What about them, would <u>they</u> want you to stay? You do understand that you're slightly different than the other kids here, don't you?"

"Of course. But they seem to like me the way I am."

Kerac put his hand on his shoulder. "What about your mother, Moina? She would miss you."

He smiled. "My mother has never missed me. She has always been too busy with her friends on Golan Two to miss me."

Kerac turned to Quasi and explained in English what Meesha had told him about wanting to stay on Earth with Grace and Charlie.

Quasi looked at the boy. "Well, if they don't want him, I'll damn sure take him. He could stay with me and my family. The two boys seem to get along pretty well, and Nakomi would adjust."

"Thank you Mr. Quasi, it can be resolved later." He looked at Meesha. "Are you coming with us, then?" he asked. "We will see your father, and if he agrees I will bring you back. I promise."

"Uncle," Meesha answered. "If I was given permission to stay on Earth, would I be allowed to bring a friend?"

"A friend? Who do you have in mind?"

"Loree."

Kerac smiled. "You mean the commoner your father doesn't want you to get serious about?"

Meesha lowered his head and stared at the ground. "Yes, but he does not understand her. She is not like the others on Golan."

"We'll see. I will speak to your father about it." He took the boy by the arm and turned him toward the ship. "By the way," he said to Quasi, "I believe Meesha said he left Grace's house without telling them where he was going. Would you please explain to them what has happened, here? When they wake, I'm certain they will be concerned."

"Of course," Quasi answered. "I'll tell them." He added with a smile, "By the way, that was not your ship that wiped out our village, was it?"

Kerac looked at him and frowned. "No, it wasn't. It was someone we now have in custody. He is well guarded and will be punished for what he did to your village."

Quasi watched the ship lift off, silently hover for a few seconds above the tree line, and then dart into the night sky, a thin shaft of light trailing behind it.

Kerac's voice came over Borak's communicator, "Borak, what is your present location?"

Borak picked up the mike. "At present I am waiting for the American President to arrive. I am at the same location as before, Mr. Brown's cornfield."

"What are your plans after he arrives?"

"At the request of Senator Kent, I am taking both the President and our King to Area Fifty One, where they will be safe while they talk," Borak answered. "After that, unless you have objections, I will take the King and the Prime Minister back to Golan. The King is anxious to return."

"How is he doing, physically?" Kerac asked.

"He's surprisingly strong, and recovering nicely," Borak replied. "I'm certain when he gets back a few heads will roll, as he so adeptly put it." He hesitated for a moment, and then added, "By the way, what are we going to do about Abron's ship? We can't leave it where it is. And we can't blow it up at that location either, too many communication satellites in that area. They could be damaged."

"Yes, I know," Kerac returned. "I'm contacting Ekron to see if he will take care of the matter."

"Meaning?"

"I would rather not say, at this time," Kerac answered. "But keep me informed of the quid pro quo, if you can. I'm anxious to find out what the King will have to give them in return for that operation."

"We have already discussed that, and you might be surprised," Borak replied.

"By the way," Kerac came back, "after they have finished with their talks, do not leave for Golan immediately. Wait for me at the Area. I will join you there. I have Meesha with me and he wishes to speak to his father. Also, I will give you Abron and his crew to take back with you. I imagine the King will be pleased with that…he will have his prisoner on hand for a hearing. However, I don't believe the senator will be very happy about it." He switched channels. "Ekron, are you there?"

A few seconds later, a disgruntled voice came over the speaker, "Where did you think I would be, Kerac? I've been sitting up here, two thousand miles above Earth, waiting for someone to let me know what's happening."

"All right, Ekron, hold your temper," Kerac replied. "I'll fill you in on what has happened over the past few hours. First, we picked up Meesha and he and Luchak are now on board. Secondly, as you must know, Abron's ship was damaged by that blast from Earth and is beyond repair. After the King meets with their President, I will take Meesha to see his father at the Area. Also, we have Abron and his crew confined to quarters on board—it's a long story."

"What about our King?" Ekron interrupted. "Is he recovering well? When is he to meet with their President?"

"Be patient my friend and I'll tell you," Kerac came back, agitation in his voice. "As you must know the King is on Borak's ship. They are waiting for the President to arrive at Mr. Brown's cornfield. When he gets there, he will take them to the Area. After they have finished with their little get together, he will take King Oltar back to Golan, where he plans to press charges against Abron for the damages to that Indian Village, and possibly the death of an Indian squaw…among other things."

"What are we going to do about his ship?" Ekron asked. "We can't leave it in that junk field, Earth might find a way to get it down, and that wouldn't be good!"

"Yes, I know, that's mainly why I called," Kerac replied. "I would like for you to go down and piggy-back it a couple thousand miles farther into outer space and put it in high altitude orbit. At present, the Earthlings do not have anything sophisticated enough to retrieve it at that distance. And, it could be some time before they do. Furthermore," he hesitated, knowing what he was about to say might upset him, "I would like for you to set a remotely-activated charge on it. If things don't go well at the meeting, we can always destroy the ship before we leave for Golan."

"Before I do that, let me get this straight," Ekron replied. "You have Meesha and you're taking him to meet his father at the Area. Then, Borak will take the King home, after he meets with the President? You have Abron confined on your ship and he will go before Parliament when they return. That I've got to see, him being condemned by his own senators." He guffawed and continued. "If King Oltar is well, and he's going home after the meeting, why did you go after Meesha? The Parliament will not need him. Besides, I thought he insisted on staying here."

"Are you quite finished?" Kerac replied.

"Not quite! I would like to know what he had to give them for his operation."

"We won't know that until after the meeting."

"Hope he don't give any trade secrets away," Ekron said.

"Our king is not stupid," Kerac replied. "I'll keep you informed, if we make any changes in our plans."

"When and how do you want me to set the charges?" Kerac asked.

"Set it with a remote detonator that can be activated, if necessary, when we leave for Golan. After you set the charge, wait for word from me. Our plans could change. We will only blow up the ship if absolutely necessary. I would have to get permission from the King before doing anything that extreme, anyway. You can come home after we've all left for Golan. "

"Gee, thanks, you're all heart, Kerac!" Ekron said. The speaker went dead

THIRTY-FOUR

Several hours had passed, before Simmon's entourage arrived at Mr. Brown's corn field. After the usual protocol, they all loaded onboard Borak's ship, and it departed for Area 51, a journey of about fifteen minutes.

When they arrived at the Area, General Watson was waiting on the tarmac. They were escorted into a large hangar, across the highly-polished floors, and into the main administration building. They walked into a huge, gaudy room adorned with flags from all nations. A dozen civilians in black suits and red power-ties, and several high-ranking military officers, sat at a long conference table talking in low tones.

After a lengthy conversation with several colonels, General Watson directed President Simmons and King Oltar to chairs across from each other. He stood at attention at the far end of the long conference table and brought the meeting to order.

"Mr. President, King Oltar and gentlemen," he began. Please accept my appreciation for selecting our base for this historic occasion. We are honored to have such venerable gentlemen seated at our table." He looked at King Oltar. "Your Majesty, you have our best wishes for a speedy recovery from your surgery. I have been informed by our surgeon that you came out of the operation with flying colors." He forced a smile. The men at the table turned, looked at Oltar and gently clapped.

King Oltar nodded and slowly stood. In hesitant English, he said, "General, I would like to commend your surgeon for his expertise. I am doing fine. However, it will be some time before I run a race." The table erupted in nervous laughter. "Before we continue, let me say I sincerely appreciate for everything your President has done for me."

He smiled at Simmons and extended his hand across the table. They shook, and Oltar sat down.

President Simmons stood, cleared his throat and took a sip of purified water.

"King Oltar," he said, looking into his eyes. "I wish I could say that you and I have something in common, but truthfully I don't know anything about you, other than what your Prime Minister has shown me in that…mind probe." He smiled, and continued. "Be that as it may, I'm certain we both had our worlds' interests at heart, when the quid pro quo was brought up, the other day."

The King smiled weakly, and then shifted his frail body in the contoured chair.

Simmons gave him a sympathetic nod and continued. "For those not familiar with what this meeting is all about, let me explain." He took another short sip of water. "King Oltar, as you must know by now, is from a planet from a universe parallel to ours. I realize that must be difficult for you to fathom, but as far as I can tell it's the truth. His planet will soon be destroyed by its dying sun." He looked down the table at the skeptical frowns. "Gentlemen, don't look so astonished, some day it will be us. His world has developed the technology to travel into our universe through what he calls a vortex—what Captain Kirk of Star Trek might call a worm-hole." He glanced down the table at non-responsive faces. "He has come before us with a request for asylum for his people, here in the United States. He is in command of five huge ships with millions of people on board. At present, they do not have the technology to bring the larger ships through the vortex, only the smaller ones similar to the one parked outside can come through. Several days ago, an exchange of thoughts or ideas was briefly discussed with their Prime Minister; if I gave their people asylum, they would give us some of their technology, which we could certainly use." He sat down and pointed to Oltar, indicating he should speak.

Oltar shoved his chair aside and stood. "Gentlemen," he said, looking down the long table. "You must understand one thing; I cannot give you military assistance, only technology to improve your lifestyle.

I cannot give you anything that would help conquer your enemies. If I did, I would be obligated to give them the same. Your world would then be no better off than mine a number of years ago. I cannot be responsible for your downfall at the hands of technology you could not possibly comprehend. Do you understand what I am saying?" He stared down the table at the confused faces, and then sat.

President Simmons scanned a folder in front of him, and then glanced over at Oltar. "Of course we understand, Your Majesty," he replied, but with a frown. "I had assumed you would give us something of more substance than agriculture and manufacturing…possibly technology that might otherwise take us years to accomplish. The other day I thought your Prime Minister meant you would give us at least <u>some</u> of your sophisticated technologies."

Without standing, Oltar bent over and looked down the table at the solemn faces. "Gentlemen, I cannot be responsible for improving your war machine, or anything to help it along. You have enough to worry about, as it is. If I gave you…let's say the ability to defy gravity, or travel at almost the speed of light, for a short time you would be elated. However, when that technology became widespread, as it surely would, you would then be angry because the rest of the world had it too."

Simmons leaned back in his chair. "Then what <u>are</u> you proposing, sir? Before, if I understood you correctly, you said if we gave your people asylum you would return the favor with something of similar value. That's the way quid pro quo works."

Oltar leaned back, his face pale and fatigued. He took a sip of water and closed his eyes for several seconds. After a long moment, he replied, "Mr. President, at this time, and considering my world's present predicament, I do not know if my five ships will <u>ever</u> enter your universe. Therefore, for me to propose something with a considerable technological value would be rather presumptuous. It is true. I must give you something in return for what you have already done for me, personally, but other than that we will have to wait and see what happens with my ships. Will they make a vortex large enough, or will they not?"

"King Oltar," Simmons replied, his face drawn and pale, "we have gone this far, what do you propose our next step should be?"

Oltar thought for a moment, and then turned to Tumac seated next to him. In Golanese, he asked, "What do you think, Prime Minister? What should we give them in return for what they have already done for me?"

Tumac glanced down the conference table at the wide-eyed men attempting to understand the unrecognizable words they were hearing.

"Gentlemen," Tumac said, leaning over the table. "Please excuse me while I speak with my King." He continued in Golanese, "Your Majesty, before we landed I received a call from Kerac. He told me what they intended to do with Abron's damaged ship. They have taken it into outer-space and plan on destroying it with an explosive device, as soon as we leave for Golan—if it becomes necessary. However, they said they would not act on it until you gave the word. My suggestion is you let the Earthlings have the ship. It is damaged to the point where it cannot be repaired by us, at this time. Let them have it. Tell them when they have the technology to retrieve it from outer space, they can then utilize its secrets. It could take years, at the rate of their technological growth. Tell them it's in orbit and will remain there until they have the means to retrieve it."

Oltar stood, looked down the long table, and then over at Simmons. "Mr. President, gentlemen," he began, "the head of my Parliament, Prime Minister Tumac, has suggested something that could be of interest to you." He took another sip of water and continued. "He has suggested we give you one of our small space crafts, similar to the one parked outside. It is now in orbit several thousand miles above Earth. Regrettably, it has been damaged. However, it still has many features you would find most interesting and useful. Your only problem would be retrieving it. If you now have that technology, the ship is yours for the taking. If you do not, you could retrieve it when you did, it would be there waiting. If you should decide against this proposal, the ship will be destroyed, blown up. If it remained in orbit for any length of time, it could very easily become a hazard. Eventually, its orbit would decay, and it would plunge to Earth and be destroyed, along with whatever it might hit." He took another sip of water and sat down.

General Watson leaned over and whispered into Simmon's ear.

Moments later, the President looked over at Oltar.

"Your Majesty," he said. "General Watson has just informed me we already have several of your ships, or someone else's, in our hangars. His men are presently in the process of reverse-engineering them. I don't believe we could use another one." He shook his head and added, "Could your ship be that much different than those? I think not."

"Have you had much luck reverse-engineering them?" Tumac interrupted, an uneasy smile stretching across his face "From what I have seen, here on your base, it appears you have not mastered their technology. I did not notice any of those ships flying around your base."

Simmons looked at him disdainfully, irritated by his comment. "According to the general," he said brusquely, "it has been difficult to understand their advanced technologies, due to the inscriptions and strange symbols on their ships, and in their manuals. Even so, he is confident they will overcome the problem."

"Gentlemen," Oltar interrupted. "I will make you a solemn promise, here and now. If you can successfully retrieve that ship, I will send a team of technicians to help you understand its many secrets. There is enough advanced technology on that one craft alone to satisfy your needs for many years. However, if you do not accept our proposal, and do not want our assistance, you may never develop anything meaningful for many years."

The men at thc table huddled together in small groups and talked among themselves. After a few minutes, their faces indicated they were happy with the proposal.

Simmons looked at the ceiling in thought. What if he did accept the deal? He would get everything he had ever hoped for, a ship, its technology, and assistance with its inner-most secrets. If it worked out, he would be the envy of the world—and possibly the master of it.

"If that were to happen," Oltar replied. "I would still honor my agreement. I would have several volunteer technicians brought here, before we left for a new home. However, you would be obligated to give them asylum, with all the amenities, as they could no longer return to Golan." He hesitated for a moment, and then added, "That ship in orbit would be payment for what you have already done for me. If we did somehow manage to get our mother-ships into your universe, I assure you much more technology would follow."

Simmons lifted his head and again stared at the tasteless ceiling. Several moments later he lowered his eyes and looked over at Oltar.

"If I may ask one more question, Your Majesty," he said, looking into his aging, cat-like eyes. "Why would we have to wait for our technology to evolve to go after that ship? Why couldn't you bring it down for us? You obviously have the ability; you put it there."

"Mr. President, in the first place, we do not have the time required to retrieve it. I have pressing matters back on Golan, which must be resolved immediately, before the imminent destruction of my world. Now that I am cured of my illness, thanks to your wonderful surgeon, Doctor Morris, I must return to my world right away, it needs me. There are many things that must be done before we begin our journey to either Earth, or another solar system. Furthermore, our proposal would give you the time needed to evolve to the point where you could retrieve the ship on your own. And, by that time you would be much more likely to comprehend its secrets."

"Your Majesty," Simmons replied, "if you and your Prime Minister will leave us for a few minutes we will discuss your proposal. It shouldn't take long. I will inform you when we are finished. Thank you."

The King and Tumac were escorted from the room to a spacious lobby across from the conference room and made comfortable in huge, over-stuffed sofas.

After being seated, Tumac leaned over and whispered in Golanese, "Your Majesty, do you really believe we did the right thing by giving them one of our ships?"

A triumphant smile stretched across Oltar's haggard face. "I have thought long and hard about it. W happens, I will take full responsibility for any consequences, when we return and inform Parliament what I have done. You know very well we will never get our mother-ships to

Earth before the final days of our planet. I have accepted that fact, and you should too."

"In other words, that ship may be our only gift to them. Is that what you are saying, Your Majesty?"

Oltar looked at him with a crooked grin. "You could say that, Prime Minister." He lowered his voice and continued. "If they could retrieve that ship right now, they would certainly deserve it; they have already spent too many years developing inefficient war machines, rockets, atom bombs and such. Do not let it bother you, Prime Minister. We will no longer be around to be held responsible for what might happen to Earth in the future, when they finally conquer that ship's technologies."

The pneumatic door swung open and Borak hurried into the lobby. He spotted the King and rushed across the room, slipping and sliding on the heavily waxed floor. He took a deep breath and said, loudly, "Your Majesty. I have just received word from Kerac. He requests that you get permission for him to land at the Area. He has your son on board, and he wishes to speak to you. He also has Abron and his crew on his ship, confined and guarded. Your son said it was very important." He sucked in another mouthful of air, exhaled loudly and slumped down in a nearby sofa.

"I'll see what I can do, captain," Oltar said, glancing over his shoulder. "I see no reason for them not to allow his ship to land. Relax, you are too tense." He leaned back and closed his eyes. "I believe I know what my son wants. He must have found out I am not going to die and wants to stay here. If that is the case, he already knows he will no longer be needed for the vote." He looked at Borak and smiled.

"Something like that, I guess," Borak said between breaths. "Then what should I tell Kerac, that you will see your son?"

Oltar lowered his head and stared at the floor in thought. "Tell him I will try to get him permission to land. Other than that, tell him nothing. As for Abron, I don't want to see him until we get home. Is that clear?"

"Yes, Your Majesty, I'll see to it," Borak replied. He struggled out of the deep sofa and rushed across the polished floor. Before reaching the door, he turned and yelled, "Did everything go well at the meeting, Your Majesty? What did you have to give to them?"

"The meeting is still in progress," Oltar replied. "I offered them a proposal, but I don't know if they will accept it. When I find out I will let everybody know. Tell Kerac I will get him permission to land, right away."

"Yes, Your Majesty," Borak replied, as he disappeared through the double doors.

"Lulla!" Kerac called. "I just received word from Borak that the King is getting us permission to land at the Area. Make the necessary preparations."

"I'm on it!" she replied.

"Also, tell one of the guards to bring Abron up here I want to talk to him." He hesitated for a moment, and then added, "But only Abron, not the others. And tell him to make sure he's well bound and guarded."

A few minutes later Abron came onto the bridge, his hands tied behind his back.

"Sir," the sergeant said, "do you want me to stay?"

"No, I guess that won't be necessary," Kerac told him. "I see you've taken care of the matter." He pointed to the bonds. "You can rejoin your partner to guard the others."

"What is this, Kerac?" Abron shouted. "Why are you treating me like this? I am still a senator."

"I know you are," Kerac replied. "I believe you told me that on several occasions. I wanted you to be here to watch Ekron strap your ship with high explosives. We may not have to use them. It will all depend on the King's conversation with the President."

"What are you saying?" Abron said, baffled by his statement "What does the King or the President have to do with my ship?" He stared at Kerac, and then added, "And where is my son? I want to talk to him."

"Your son is in my quarters," Kerac replied coldly, "and he still doesn't want to see you. By the way, I thought you would like to know that when we return to Golan, the King is bringing you up on charges for what you did to that Indian village, and the murder of that woman—and a few other things. How does that make you feel?"

Abron glared at him. Then, without warning he rushed his 250-pound body toward him, his hands still tied behind his back. However, due to a quick side-step, the charge was avoided and Abron hit the helm console head-on.

Lulla witnessed his quick move, and reached into her console drawer and pulled out a stun-gun.

"Okay, Senator, that's enough!" she shouted, pointing the gun at him. "Sit down and don't try that again, or you'll definitely be sorry."

He spun around and glared at her, his face flushed. "Don't threaten me! I eat little girls like you for breakfast!" He stared at the gun for several seconds, and then sat down heavily in a nearby chair.

"Well, Senator, eat all you can now because I haven't had my breakfast either, and I'm famished!" Her defiant eyes scanned his angry face.

His hands had been tied behind his back with plastic straps, which dug into his wrists. Even so, after a few unnoticed yanks of his powerful arms, he could pull the bindings free. He kept his unbound arms hidden behind him, as he watched her every move. She laid the stun-gun on her console and gave him a threatening look.

Noticing that the gun was momentarily unguarded he stood up and stretched his body, as if to relieve pain. "Can't you loosen this binding a little, Lulla?" he asked. "It cuts into my wrists. They're bleeding!"

She looked at him with a frown. "Okay, come over here. I'll loosen it a bit, but don't try anything funny."

He went to her workstation and turned so she could get at the bindings. As she swiveled her chair around, he grabbed her arm and flung her across the bridge. Before she could react, he had picked up the stun-gun and pointed it at her.

"Okay, little lady, go over to that chair and sit!" He pointed across the room. "I don't want any trouble from you! Do you understand?"

Before Kerac realized what had happened, Abron pointed the gun at him and fired. He reacted instantly to the sheer force of the gun's charge and dropped to the deck, arms and legs flailing spasmodically.

Abron spun around and pointed the gun at Lulla, but before he could pull the trigger, Luchak had rushed out of a nearby hatch and tackled him, knocking the gun out of his hand. Abron threw his arms up in self-defense, but it was too late the boy had knocked him across the bridge and up against the helm controls. The operating controls became jammed by his body, and the ship tilted at a severe angle. The gun slid back across the deck, stopping at Luchak's feet.

Lulla had previously turned off the ship's internal gravity to save energy while in orbit, but by doing so the ship had to use the gravitational influence of their orbit around Earth to maintain equilibrium. Consequently, when the ship veered, it was necessary to hold onto a console frame or anything secured to the ship's hull to keep from sliding across the bridge. When Abron fell free of the controls, the ship slowly returned to its original attitude.

Abron looked up from his horizontal position and saw his son standing over him with the stun-gun pointed at his face.

"Luchak!" he roared. "What are you doing? This is your father, stop pointing that thing at me! Give me the gun! I am taking over this ship!"

"No, Father, you're not," Luchak said calmly. "Lulla, get one of the guards, I think we might need him."

She raced down the passageway and motioned for one of the guards, who had just finished picking himself up off the deck. The larger of the two rushed to the bridge, his weapon drawn and pointed at Abron. After binding the senator's hands, he shoved him roughly into a nearby chair.

"What are we going to do, Luchak?" she asked.

The boy slid the gun into his pocket, and said, "We'll check on Kerac first, see if he's all right. If he is, we'll let him take it from here."

She rushed over and slapped him in the face. "Kerac!" she shrieked. "Kerac, are you all right?"

He opened his eyes slowly, and focused on her. After rubbing the back of his neck, he stretched his arms and legs to regain feeling in them.

"That hurt!" he announced. He looked across the bridge and saw the sergeant standing over Abron, his weapon drawn. "What happened, Lulla?"

"The senator got a little frisky, and we had to subdue him," she replied. "I'll tell you about it later. Right now, we have to decide…do we go down to the Area, or not? We still haven't received permission to land."

Still rubbing the back of his neck, Kerac slowly got to his feet. "I guess we'd better contact the Area. It's quite obvious we have to get rid of Abron, as soon as possible." He looked at the guard and pointed his finger at the senator. "Take him back and confine him with the others." He glanced over at Luchak, the gun sticking halfway out of his pocket. "What happened, Luchak? You must really be on our side to have that weapon in your possession. If that's the case, what do you think is going to happen to you when you, and your father returns to Golan?"

Luchak smiled. "Like Meesha, I don't want to go back either," he replied. "If he's allowed to stay, why shouldn't I be allowed, under the circumstances?"

"That will be up to the King," Kerac told him, still rubbing his neck. "If he says you can stay, I will have no objections. But I have a question, where would you live? You don't know anybody here on Earth, except that big Indian and the old man up on the mountain. If Meesha is allowed to remain he will probably stay with Grace and Charlie. Even so, I don't believe they could handle the both of you."

"I would ask the Indian, or maybe the old mountain man," Luchak said. "I liked both very much. They could easily take my father's place. If that didn't work out, I'm sure I could find someplace to live, especially with my special abilities."

"Your special abilities?" Kerac mocked. "If the King were to let you stay on Earth, he would not allow you to use your 'special' abilities. He would see to that. You would have to promise you wouldn't use them." He sat down at the helm and turned to face him. "As far as the Indian is concerned, what would happen if he found out your father was the one responsible for destroying his village and killing that woman?" He turned back to the helm. “We’ll discuss this later, when we land at the Area.”

Luchak walked over and sheepishly handed him the stun-gun. “It’s a deal. Nevertheless, please put in a good word for me, when you see the King.”

THIRTY-FIVE

Kerac finally received authorization to land, and it took him only a few minutes to approach the Area, hover over it for a moment, and then gently settle to the tarmac.

After the anti-gravity generator and ion drives were shut secured, a ramp was lowered and Abron, Nader, and Kersey walked down the incline, followed closely by the armed guards.

Borak and Tumac had been waiting at the edge of the tarmac, and when Abron got closer Tumac stepped out in front of him, blocking his way.

"Senator," he said in a soft but firm voice, "what has gotten into you? Before the war, you were a man I could respect, a man of honor and dignity. Now look at you. Did the war really change you that much? Is this some sort of grudge you have against Earth…and Golan?"

"Golan has given me everything I ever wanted or could hope for," Abron replied. He hesitated for a moment, lowered his head and stared at the tar-lines in the tarmac. "It's the people of Earth I despise. They treated my brother, my best friend, like an animal, and then let him die. I merely wanted to even the score."

"What do you mean, even the score?" Tumac replied. "What could the Earthlings have possibly done to change you into what you are now, a renegade, a mad man?"

Abron raised his head and looked callously at him. "Many years ago, when Golan first started experimenting with the vortex, I lost my brother in one of the observation ships that crashed shortly after it had arrived here. The ship was recovered by this very site. I found out later that he had survived the crash but died shortly after, due to their meddling with his body and mind. I told myself I wouldn't rest until they had paid for it. They paid somewhat at the Indian village, but not enough."

"Your brother's inadvertent death does not justify killing an innocent woman, senator," Tumac said.

"Maybe not, but it makes me feel better," Abron replied arrogantly.

Tumac shook his head and stepped aside. He looked at the two guards. "Take him away. Put him and his crew in Borak's ship. Lock them up in one of the cabins and stand guard."

As Abron walked away, he turned and shouted, "My crew had nothing to do with my actions, everything rests on my shoulders! Do you understand?"

"Yes, I figured as much," Tumac replied. "That will be taken into consideration, when you stand in front of Parliament on charges of murder…and other things."

Borak went to his ship and lowered the ramp, then returned to Tumac, who had been waiting for Kerac and the others to join them.

"Don't you think we had better get back to the lobby?" Borak said. "I imagine they're finished with the conference by now. I'd like to know what the King ended up giving their President." He laughed. "Hopefully he gave them our planet. At the least, they could see what Earth will look like in a few million years."

"Yes, that would solve some of our problems, wouldn't it?" Tumac joked.

General Watson's brown limo raced across the tarmac and screeched to a halt in front of the two ships. The general got out and directed the small entourage to his vehicle.

"If you'll come with me, gentlemen," he said, "we'll go see your King."

The vehicle sped across the runway and stopped in front of the main building housing the conference room. They went into the spacious lobby and walked across the gleaming floor, where King Oltar sat in an over-stuffed sofa talking to a general.

Oltar looked up. "Well, this is quite an entourage we have here," he said lightheartedly. "I didn't expect to see all of you." He glanced at them briefly, and then spotted his son. "Meesha, my son, come here and sit beside me. I understand you have something important to ask me?"

Meesha looked closely at his father's haggard face. "Father, how are you feeling, after your operation?" he asked.

"I am fine. But I'm sure you have something more important to ask me than that. What is on your mind? I am really not the ogre you have always believed me to be. I will listen to you with an open mind. How does that sound?" He shifted in his seat and turned to face the boy. "But before you say anything, let <u>me</u> tell you what I believe you want to ask me. You want to stay here on Earth. You and Luchak both want to remain. And, you want my permission and blessings. Is that correct?"

"Yes Father," he answered. "Luchak and I would like to stay on Earth. We would have a much better life here than on a spaceship headed for nowhere, and would take both our lifetimes to arrive."

Oltar leaned back and stared up at the ceiling. "Hmm," he murmured softly, "you may have a point. I never thought of it that way. However, you are correct. It would take both your lifetimes to reach the nearest solar system. Even then we might not find a suitable planet." He looked at Luchak, standing next to Kerac. "Please come here."

He walked over and stood in front of the King. "Yes, Your Majesty?"

"Is that also your feelings?" Oltar asked. "Do you really want to stay here on Earth, even with the knowledge you are slightly different than these people? It's quite possible you wouldn't fit into their life-styles."

"Yes, Your Majesty, I would like to stay," he replied. "We both understand the possible consequences. And, whatever they are we believe we can overcome them."

"Hmm, very well, Meesha and Luchak may remain on Earth, while we wander the far reaches of the galaxy in search of a home." He chuckled at his theatrical reply. "However, you both must have a place to stay on Earth. You cannot roam the planet aimlessly. You must have a place to call your home."

"We both have a place, Father." Meesha said. "I will stay with Grace and Charlie, and Luchak can stay with Quasi, the big Indian, or with Digger and Corky up on the mountain."

The King glanced over at Kerac. "Do you know these people, Brother?"

"Yes, I know them. They are fine people. You would like them."

"Then it's settled. I will explain this to your mother, if and when she returns from Golan Two," he replied with a cynical grin. "She will be disappointed, but she will get over it. What about your family, Luchak, will they object?"

"Your Majesty, my father is Senator Abron of Keeti. Under the circumstances, I doubt that he is in a position to object. My mother died several years ago."

"Then it's settled," Oltar said. "But first, you must return to the mother-ships to get prepared for your lives here on Earth."

Meesha frowned. "What do you mean, Father…get prepared for life on Earth?"

"Our surgeons will make you look exactly like the people of Earth."

Meesha lowered his head and said meekly, "Father, would it be possible for Loree to come with me? I know how you have felt about her, being a commoner and all, but this would be an unknown world for her, a fresh start. Because of the war, she has no parents. She is staying with an aunt she doesn't like very much. She would be with me. I could teach her everything I know about Earth. Please, Father!"

"We can discuss this later, Son," he said with a frown. He looked at the small group and motioned at them to come closer. "The meeting is over and the President and I have come to a satisfactory agreement—understanding, if you will," he whispered. "I have given him Abron's ship, in return for what he has already done for me. Furthermore, I told him if we can bring our mother-ships to Earth, there will be more technology to follow." He scanned the lobby for curious ears. Finding none, he added, "However, it is highly unlikely we will ever get our mother-ships to Earth. It would be a long-shot, unless they have solved the vortex problem during our absence."

"What about the technicians you promised us?" Tumac asked. "You told their President you would send them to help with the ship's technology, should they recover it."

"I told him I would send men to help, before we left our universe. I also told him we didn't have time to bring the ship to Earth; we had important matters at home that had to be resolved. I am certain they will not recover it, by the time we leave on our trip through the cosmos. Even so, I am still going to send several technicians to help them, in case they do. I am certain those men will enjoy it here on Earth. However, we could certainly use their expertise on the long journey to nowhere."

"Then we should commit ourselves to a life in space?" Kerac asked. "Is that what you're saying, Your Majesty? You don't believe our scientists will come up with a solution to the vortex problem in time, do you?"

"Yes, to two of your questions, and no to the vortex problem."

"Then the twenty years and millions of man-hours spent building the mother-ships, let alone the crushing cost, could all be in vain," Kerac stated.

"No, of course it was not in vain," Oltar replied. "Remember, without those ships our lives would soon be over. At the very least, we can live in relative comfort and happiness, while traveling into the unknown. We may or may not find life on a distant planet, but at least we will have a home in space. That will be much better than what we would have if we remained. Don't you agree?"

Watson approached the small group his heels clicking loudly on the tile floor.

"King Oltar," he said with a smile. "If you and your men are ready to depart I will escort you to your ships. Hopefully, we will see you again. We're looking forward to your advanced technology. That is, of course, if you can get your mother-ships to Earth." A broad smile stretched across his pudgy face.

"Thank you for your hospitality, General," Oltar said. "We are ready to leave."

Borak's ship had been left unattended, except for two guards on the bridge, and his engineer, who rarely came topside. Suddenly, a muffled sound caught the guard's attentions, and they rushed down the passageway to investigate. When they arrived, they found the cabin door smashed in and its occupants missing. On their way back to the bridge to call Borak, they were confronted by Abron and his men, with stun-guns they had taken from a shattered gun locker.

"Well, what do we have here?" Abron said with a deep, commanding voice. "It must be the King's Guards. Fine guards you guys are! Kersey, take their guns and tie their hands behind their backs."

"We shouldn't take them with us. They would only be a hindrance," Kersey replied.

"I'm not taking them," Abron answered, "I'm leaving them here. Even so, I don't want them to call for help, before we can get airborne. After they're tied, take them down the ramp and bind them to whatever you find, and stuff their mouths so they can't yell for help."

"What are you going to do?" Nader asked. "I told you before I don't want any part of your little vendetta. If your plans are to take over this ship, leave me out of it. I don't want any part of it."

Abron gave him a disgusted look and pointed his stun-gun at him. "Kersey, tie Nader's hands too, I'm going to honor his wishes. We'll leave him here with the guards. We don't need him, anyway. I'm sure he'd find some way to screw up my plans."

On their way back to the ships, everyone in the limo was quietly indulged in their subliminal thoughts. Suddenly, Luchak yelled out, "Look, up in the sky! That looks like Borak's ship!"

"That <u>was</u> my ship!" Borak shouted. "What's going on here? Those guards can't fly that thing!" He quickly jumped back into the limo, followed by the others. "Driver, get us to that parking area, and step on it!"

The driver stomped down on the accelerator and within seconds, the limo skidded to a stop beside Kerac's ship.

"That has to be Abron!" Borak screamed, as he watched his ship disappear. "He has my ship! How did he get it?"

Luchak heard rustling behind a nearby bush and went to investigate. "Captain Borak!" he shouted, as he parted the branches. "I believe I found your answer."

Borak rushed to his side and saw the two guards and Nader bound securely to a small tree, hands tied behind their backs and their mouths covered with tape. He pulled out a utility knife and cut them free.

"What happened here, Nader?" he shouted. "Was that Abron, who took my ship?"

Nader brushed dirt and leaves from his jump-suit, and then said, "Yes that was Abron."

"Well, Nader, what happened?" Borak yelled in his face. "Weren't you and the others supposed to be confined and guarded?"

Nader stretched his long, muscular arms over his 6' 4" frame to relieve the pain from being tied. "Abron got free of his bindings and smashed the cabin door," he replied. "He untied Kersey and me and we all headed for the bridge. He put his fist through the gun locker on his way up and handed us stun-guns. When he told us he was going to take over the ship, I said I wouldn't be a part of it. He was incensed and took my gun and tied me and the guards to that tree. That's all I know."

"What's he up to, Nader?" Kerac insisted. "Is he going back to Golan?"

"I don't know, he wouldn't tell me. Only that he was taking over the ship."

"Are you sure that's all he said?"

"That's all I heard."

"Do you have any idea what he's going to do?" Kerac asked, an angry frown forming on his face. "You must know him better than anyone. What do you think?"

"Knowing how he hates the people of Earth he'll probably do something stupid," Nader told him. "More than likely he'll go after their military. He told me before he wanted to prove that our weapons were superior. I think we had better find him, before he does something both our worlds will regret!"

"All right," Kerac shouted, "everybody into my ship. We're going after that maniac! We'll make plans, after we get airborne." He looked at General Watson. "General, you had better inform your military and the President what's going on here. I suggest you put your base on high alert. As soon as I find out what he's up to, I'll have Captain Borak contact Senator Kent. There isn't a 'ham rig' in my ship, but I'm sure he'll find a way to contact him."

General Watson returned to the limo and ordered his driver to take him to the administration building. When he arrived, he headed for the conference room where Simmons had been enjoying a light snack. He stopped at a large punch bowl and waved to draw his attention.

Simmons noticed his frantic gestures and joined him at the bowl.

"Yes, what is it, General?" he asked, as he munched on shrimp cocktail.

"You won't believe this, Mr. President," Watson said, and filled a cup half-full of spiked lemonade, "Captain Borak's ship was just stolen by one of their prisoners, a Senator Abron I believe they said."

"How did that happen?"

"They were all confined, but somehow they got loose and swiped the ship."

"This could be a serious problem, General? What are you going to do?"

"I'm putting our forces on high alert. I'd scramble fighters, if I thought they could catch them…but from what I've seen of those ships, they couldn't!"

"Don't do anything too extreme, I still have that agreement with King Oltar."

"I'll do everything in my power to avoid unnecessary carnage, if we find the ship," the general replied with a smug grin. "I just hope he doesn't do anything stupid where I'll have to shoot him out of the sky. I'll keep you informed, Sir."

"Kersey!" Abron shouted. "Now that we're airborne go down to engineering and wait for orders. I may have to do some fancy flying, and I want you to be ready with all she's got."

Kersey rushed through the small hatch to engineering. When he got there, he saw Tynon sitting at a desk reading a book.

"Hey you!" he shouted. "What are you doing? Engineers don't read books on duty!"

Startled by the gruff voice, the young man jumped to attention. After eying him up and down, he said, "Who are you?"

"I'm Kersey, the best engineer in the fleet. Who are you? What's your name?"

Flustered, the young man hesitated before answering. "Tynon," he replied, and sat back down at the desk. "What are you doing here? I'm Captain Borak's engineer!"

"Not any longer. Senator Abron took over the ship, and I'm here to keep it running for him."

"Then what am I supposed to do, sit here on my ass and read?" Tynon replied derisively.

"I don't really care what you do," Kersey answered, "just keep out of my way, unless you want to be bound and gagged. Understood?"

Tynon threw him a confused look. "Are you sure you can handle this ship? It has the latest ion drive and weaponry. Few ships in the fleet have that."

"Yes, I know. That's why the senator took possession of the ship," Kersey came back. "We had the same things on ours, before it was crippled."

"Crippled?"

"Yes. Didn't you hear about our ship being disabled by an ion blast?"

"I heard something about a ship in orbit around Earth, and that it might remain there forever. Is that true, sir?"

"Why do you want to know? What else did you hear? And don't call me sir, my name is Kersey. Call me that."

"I heard nothing else, sir…I mean Kersey. I just stay down here out of the way, until the captain needs me."

"Good man. Either stay out of my way or help me with this thing. Neither of us has anything to do with what's going on upstairs. Right?" He went to the ion generator and inspected it visually. He ran his hand over its smooth exterior, and then looked over at Tynon. "He really does have the latest stuff here, doesn't he? Even our ship didn't have most of these improvements."

"The ship, more or less, runs itself," Tynon replied. "That's why I'm reading. It doesn't need me very often. I didn't even know the ship was taken over!" He thought for a moment. "I guess I can help, if you really need me. The pay's the same, no matter who I work for. Right?"

Kersey walked over and held his hand out. "Okay, it's a deal, buddy. Between the two of us, we'll make this thing do hand-stands. In the meantime, I'm going up to the bridge to find out what's going on up there." He threw him a long stare, and then added, "Are you going to keep our agreement, while I'm on the bridge? I do have your word on it, don't I?"

Tynon scanned his face. "Yes, you have my word."

"Senator," Kersey said, as he walked onto the bridge. "What are we going to do now?"

Abron turned and looked at him. "What do you think we're going to do? I didn't steal this ship just to take a joy-ride."

"Then what?" Kersey asked. "I believe I'm entitled to know what your intentions are, under the circumstances."

Abron threw a switch on the console panel and turned to face him. "Sit down at the weapons console," he ordered. "Bring the ion gun on-line and give her as much power as she'll take. I'm going to demonstrate to those weaklings on that obscure little planet that we're a force to be reckoned with."

"Why, do you always have to prove something?" Kersey replied cautiously. "Why don't we just make a vortex and go home?"

Abron mumbled something under his breath, and then lowered his head and looked through the long-range telescopic sight of the gun. "Is it on-line and powered up with all she's got?"

"Yes. It's ready any time you are."

Before Kersey could say anything more the ship was jolted by the recoil of the ion gun. He stood behind the senator and looked down at his screen. A green shaft of light seared the atmosphere, as it headed for Earth.

"What the hell are you doing?" he shouted, checking the coordinates. "That beam is headed for Area Fifty One!"

"Yes, I know. Beautiful, isn't it? Now they'll see my power, and they can't do a thing about it."

“What did you hit down there?” Kersey asked, still confused by his actions.

“Not to worry. I tore up a little of their long runway a half-mile from any structures, and that was just a warning shot over their bow! However, they won’t be able to launch any aircraft for some time.”

An airman rushed into General Watson’s office. “General! General!” he shouted. “I think you better see this! We’ve just been attacked!”

The general stared at the young man’s pallid face. “What do you mean attacked?”

“A green shaft of light came out of nowhere and wiped out a portion of a runway! We all saw it. It came out of nowhere and hit our longest runway!”

“A green shaft of light?”

“Yes sir, a huge, green shaft of light came out of the sky and hit our runway. It put a hole in it large enough to hide a tank.”

“Did you see where it came from, what direction?”

“Yes sir, it came from the same direction the ship that was stolen took.”

“Tell Captain Allison I want to see him, immediately!”

A few minutes later Allison came into the room “General, did you hear☒”

“Yes! Of course I heard. Get two F16s in the air, immediately!”

“I can’t, sir.”

“What do you mean you can’t?” Watson exploded.

“I didn’t mean I can’t I meant they couldn’t take off,” Allison replied. The long runway is severely damaged, right in the middle. They wouldn’t have enough runway to get airborne. We’re sending crews out there now to see what they can do about it. However, it doesn’t look good. Even if they could repair it, it would take hours, if not days.”

“Captain, we have other runways, don’t we?”

“Yes, but none are long enough to launch those fighters.”

“What do we have that can take off on the other runways?”

"We have nothing left. Everything was confiscated by the Air Force and sent overseas for active duty."

"Then we have nothing left to defend our base?" Watson cried out. "Is that what you're saying?"

"That's right, General," Allison replied. "There is nothing left in the hangar but a couple of surveillance Piper Cubs…and a couple unfinished UFOs"

"What in God's name is wrong with our government?" Watson mumbled under his breath. "The most sophisticated developmental base in the world and they can't leave us with anything to protect it. We can't even fly the president back to Washington. His plane couldn't land, it'd need at least a couple miles of runway. He'll be our guest for awhile."

"That's right, Sir," Allison agreed, shaking his head. "And we have no way of getting in touch with that Kerac fellow to ask if he would take him back in his ship."

"See what can be done about that runway, Allison," the general demanded. "I've got to inform the President, and he isn't going to be happy about it."

"Kerac!" Lulla shouted. "Come and look at this!"

He rushed over and looked down at her screen. "What is it? What do you have?"

He switched on his scanner. Using her co-ordinates, he took the ship to within several hundred miles of Abron's motionless vessel and stopped. He used a long-range imager to get a better view of the vessel, and then magnified it to where he could see Abron sitting in the bow porthole. "Wonder what he's up to?" he mumbled. "He's just sitting there."

"Got something," Lulla called out. "A pod just came out of his old ship. He opened his bay door, and it went inside." She looked at Kerac in disbelief. "Why do you suppose somebody went back inside his old ship?"

"I don't know, let's find out." He swung the ship around and closed the distance to within a few miles. "I think I'll call him."

"Be careful, you know how tricky he is," she lectured.

"Abron!" he shouted into his communicator. "What are you up to? My sensors tell me you don't have your weapons powered up. What's going on? Aren't you worried I might come after you?"

"Come ahead, Kerac," Abron replied. "But first, point your life-scanning sensor at my old ship."

Lulla brought the scanner on line. "Kerac!" she shouted. "There's a life-form on that ship! He left somebody there! Without life support, he'll die!"

"You're crazy, Abron!" Kerac shouted into the mike "Who did you leave on that ship, Kersey? You told me there was little or no life support left on your old ship. He'll die!"

"I lied!" Abron replied. "No, it isn't Kersey. I left Tynon, Borak's engineer." There was a pause, and then he added, "He's my ace-in-the-hole, Kerac. I had Kersey redesign your explosive device. It now has a detonator with a remote control. You have two hours before it all goes boom! Oh, by the way, I almost forgot, if you attempt to come after me or harm my 'new' ship in any way, I have the red button in my grubby little hand. I have the remote frequency, too. I could very easily put a damper on the King's so-called quid pro quo." A faint chuckle came through the speaker, and his ship darted away.

Nader had heard the conversation over the ship's intercom and insisted on being escorted to the bridge. "Kerac," he said when he arrived with the guard. "Let me use one of your pods. I'm familiar with the timer, he more than likely installed. I could get there, get the kid, disable it and be back in an hour."

"Oh, by the way," Abron's voice came back over the speaker. "I forgot to mention that the bay door on my old ship doesn't seem to be functioning very well. It must have been damaged by my pod when it left the ship. What an unfortunate incident…but that's life." The speaker went dead.

"That—" Lulla started to say, then put her hand over her mouth. "What are we going to do now, Kerac?"

Borak had heard the conversation and went to the bridge. "Lulla, did I hear him correctly? Did he say Tynon was on that ship?"

"Yes," she answered. "Apparently he has oxygen, at least for now, but we can't get on the ship because of a damaged outer bay door. At least, that's what he told us. Do you have any suggestions?"

Borak thought for a moment, then said, "There could be a way through the ion generator's exhaust grid. It could be our only chance." He frowned and added, "But it's too small for any of us to crawl through, and we wouldn't have time to cut a larger hole. That's the toughest metal known. Unfortunately, that's the only other way I know to get on board."

Lulla swung her chair around. "What about Meesha, he's the smallest one here?"

"Yes," Borak replied. "He could easily get through the vent and into the ship, but then what? He knows nothing about timers or explosive devices. What could he do? Even if he got on board Tynon couldn't make it back through the vent, it's too small for him."

Hearing their conversation from his cabin, King Oltar made his way to the bridge.

"What's going on?" he asked. "Did I hear correctly? Did Abron leave a man on his old ship?"

"Yes, Your Majesty, he left Tynon, Borak's engineer," Kerac replied. "Abron said we had only two hours to deactivate that explosive device we installed. And to top it all off, he modified it."

"Hmm," the King mumbled. "Did I also hear you say Meesha was the only one small enough to get on board?"

"Yes, Your Majesty, he's the only one," Borak replied. "But unfortunately, he knows nothing about explosive devices. And we have less than two hours before the charge is set to go off, unless Abron is tricking us into believing that. Even so, we won't know unless we get somebody on board."

"Hmm," Oltar mumbled again. "Bring Meesha to me. Let me talk to him."

"I am here, Father. I heard everything," Meesha said, as he walked onto the bridge.

"Son, are you willing to do what they suggested, to save a man's life?"

"Nader, did you say you were familiar with that device?" Oltar asked.

"Yes, Your Majesty, everything."

"If you told Meesha how to disarm it, do you think he could do it?"

"Your Majesty—" Nader started to say.

"Please, use the power of your mind," Oltar interrupted. "Everyone on Golan has that ability, and I doubt if you are an exception."

"Of course," Lulla said. "Why didn't I think of that? Meesha is a good subject too; we have communicated with our minds on many occasions."

Nader pulled the boy aside, took his finger and put it on his own brow. Then, he placed his finger on the boy's forehead and they both closed their eyes. Five minutes later they opened their eyes, and Meesha slumped into a nearby chair, his face pale and his lips quivering.

"Did you get through, Nader?" Oltar asked. "Are you confident he can do it? If he doesn't succeed, the ship may go up in a ball of fire… with us in its wake."

"Yes, I am confident," Nader replied. "I gave him the information, he would need to disarm it, and he sent it back exactly as it was given him. I am confident he can do it, Your Majesty."

"Are you all right with this, Son?" the King asked. "Do you truly believe you can do this?"

"Yes, Father, I am certain."

"Good," Kerac said. "He will need a space suit, a breathing apparatus, tools, a communicator, and a metal-cutter. Lulla, take care of that quickly, please."

She took Meesha by the arm and ushered him down a short passageway to the utility room. A few minutes later they returned, him in a space suit with all the trappings, and her with a satisfied look.

"All right, Meesha, listen up!" Nader said through the face-piece of the suit. "When you get the pod alongside, open the utility door and use your jet-pack to take a tether-line to the ship. After you get to the ion grid, tie the line securely to anything available, so you and Tynon can get back to the pod. Without that line, you could be in a lot of trouble. You might not make it back to the pod. Take the cutting tool from your utility pouch and cut through the remainder of the grid to enter the vent shaft. Once inside, crawl down the vent until you find an inspection panel. There, you will use the cutting tool to break through the panel. The opening will let you into the hangar bay. Replace the panel the best you can to retain whatever oxygen is left in the bay. If you cannot replace it, make your way to the hatch that leads to the bridge. Go through it quickly and shut it behind you to keep oxygen in the living quarters.

"If our sensors are correct, Tynon is somewhere on the bridge. Unless Abron has moved the explosive device and detonator, they both should be under the helm console. I told you how to disconnect the timer, but I want you to leave the remote detonator attached. You have to reset the activation codes so only we can detonate it remotely." He looked into the boy's eyes. "Are you sure you understand everything I just told you?"

Meesha looked at him with a self-satisfied grin. "Yes, I remember everything. And I still have the pictures in my mind." He turned and walked toward the hangar bay.

"Meesha!" Lulla shouted. "I just thought of something, you don't know how to pilot a pod!"

"Not to worry, Lulla," Luchak intervened. "I'll be the designated driver. There isn't much I don't know about a pod. I've certainly had enough experience in one." He gave her a meaningful grin.

"Well, don't just stand there, go with him, quickly!" Kerac ordered. "Time is running short! I'll open the outer door, when you two are in the pod. Remember, you don't have a space suit, Luchak. All the oxygen <u>you</u> have is in your breathing mask. So close the bay door after he leaves the pod. And remember to keep your oxygen mask on at all times."

Luchak rushed down the passageway into the hangar. When he got there, he climbed into the pod and brought it up to power. Moments later Meesha forced himself and his oversized suit into the small seat beside him.

"Are you ready to go on our little adventure?" Luchak said with a grin. Meesha's only reply was a nervous grunt.

The bay door opened, and the small craft floated into the darkness of space. When the pod drifted completely free of the ship, Luchak turned on the maneuvering jets and headed for the derelict ship, several miles away. A few minutes later it stopped twenty-feet from the damaged ion grid.

"Okay, Meesha, your turn," Luchak said. "Go get that engineer!"

"I just thought of something," Meesha's voice came over Luchak's helmet speaker. "What if there isn't a space suit on that ship? I can't bring him back without one."

"All ships have space suits," Luchak replied. "Don't worry, you can get one at the utility room. I'm sure they're still there. I can't imagine Abron taking them. You worry too much, kid. Go do your stuff and get back here as soon as you can."

Meesha opened the outer door of the pod and attached the tether line. With the aid of the jet-pack, he floated toward the abandoned ship. When he arrived, he discovered the ion vent had been damaged to the point where it was almost torn free from the underbelly of the ship. However, the opening was big enough to squeeze through without using the cutting tool. He wanted to contact Luchak to tell him of his success, but Kerac had told him not to communicate with the pod, Abron might be listening. He crawled through the vent and climbed down the duct to the inspection panel. It took several minutes to cut through the panel, but it finally tore free and dropped inside the bay.

Due to the cut-out panel, the oxygen remaining in the bay was evacuated. He replaced the panel quickly and spot-welded it in place. He then pushed a button beside the door to replenish the bay with what little oxygen was left in the ship. When the bay had been refilled, he took off his helmet and headed up the passageway to the bridge. When he got there, he discovered Tynon strapped to a metal support beam in the middle of the room. He severed his bonds with his cutting tool and set him free.

Tynon stood up and stretched. "It's about time somebody came to get me!" he roared. "Who are you?"

"Never mind who I am," Meesha replied brusquely. "Let's get out of here while we still can! However, before we go, I have to disarm this bomb."

"How did you get in here?" Tynon asked.

"I came in through the ion vent. It's small, but I think we can still get back out through it. At least, I hope so! Everything will be okay, as long as you can fit through it."

Tynon thought for a moment, then said, "Fit through the ion vent? You must be joking. That vent is less than eighteen inches wide. I'm not that small, especially with a space suit."

"Don't worry, you'll make it! I have a cutting tool."

With Tynon's help, Meesha found the explosive device hidden under the helm console. He spent the next few minutes tracing wires, flipping switches, and resetting activation codes. When he was confident that everything had been taken care of, he turned and gave Tynon a thumbs-up.

"I hope that'll do it," he said. "I've followed my instructions to the letter."

"You hope that will do it?" Tynon came back with a comical grin. "I hope you're right, too!"

"Do you know where Abron kept his space suits?" Meesha asked.

"Yes, I know where they're supposed to be, in the utility locker. Assuming he didn't take them when he left."

Meesha glanced at the watch on his wrist. "Well, you better go get one, fast! We only have a few minutes before we find out if I did a good job or not."

Tynon raced down the passageway to the utility room. "Oh, you're funny," he shouted. "I'll return in a couple of minutes."

"I'll be in the hangar bay. Make it quick!" Meesha yelled to him.

Five minutes later Tynon wobbled unsteadily into the hangar bay in an over-sized space suit. "Okay, let's get out of here, kid!"

When they got to the welded panel in the hanger bay, Tynon inspected it from every angle. "Like I said, I can't fit through that thing the hole is not big enough. I'd get this suit hung up on it, or punctured it trying to get through."

"This is our only way out," Meesha told him. "You have to make it through, or we'll both be stranded. I don't have time to enlarge the opening with the cutter."

Tynon pointed across the hangar bay. "Look, they left a pod. This ship had three on board, two for observations and one for defensive purposes, in case they ran into trouble."

"What good would a pod do?" Meesha countered. "It can't fit through that hole. And the bay door has been damaged. We can't get out that way!"

"Listen to me! The one they left has an ion canon mounted in its bow. We could possibly blast our way through the hangar bay door."

"Possibly?" Meesha said, lifting his eyebrow.

"Don't worry, I've seen these guns in action, and they're pretty powerful," Tynon assured him. "Trust me, I know what I'm doing, kid." He turned and motioned for him to follow. "Put on your helmet, kid. When we knock out the door the only air will be in that pod, or your helmet."

"You're sure this will work?" Meesha asked, as he opened the small door of the pod and crawled into the passenger seat.

"What do we have to lose, kid? It'll work. I promise." He looked at Meesha and grinned. "If it doesn't, we'll be in a lot more trouble."

As soon as they were strapped in, Tynon brought the pod up to full power and pointed its bow at the hangar door. He looked over at Meesha. "Are you ready, kid?" he asked. Meesha closed his eyes and mumbled something inaudible.

Tynon pulled the trigger, and the blast ripped the hangar door off its hinges and sent it sailing toward Luchak's pod, missing it by inches.

"Wh…what the—where did that come from?" Luchak stammered. The pod slowly emerged from the large hole in the side of the ship and headed toward him.

When he realized what had happened, he motioned through the bow porthole for them to follow him back to Kerac's ship. When they got alongside, the bay door opened and both pods entered and were secured by robotic arms. The outside door closed, and the bay was refilled with oxygen. As soon as it was safe Meesha and Tynon stepped out and took off their suits. A few moments later, Luchak left his rescue pod and joined them.

Tynon held out his hand. "Hi, there," he said. "You must be Luchak."

Luchak ignored his hand and motioned for them to follow him to the bridge. "Of course I am, and you must be Tynon," he yelled back, sarcastically. "No one else would be stupid enough to volunteer for that little stunt."

The young engineer hurried through the hatch and caught up with him. "What do you mean volunteered? What stunt? They tied me up and left me there."

"Why would they do that?" Luchak said, turning to face him. "Something strange is going on here, Tynon. My father is a low-life, but even he wouldn't stoop that low. He wouldn't let you die for a no-good reason."

"Are you accusing me of something, Luchak?" Tynon replied angrily. "Are you saying the senator and I set this whole scenario up? Why would we do that?"

"Call it what you will," Luchak said, "but something isn't right here." He stared at him for several moments, and then added, "Knowing my father, he would do something like that only to divert attention long enough to do something he had already planned. Something he didn't want us to know about, or be able to do anything about."

"Which would be?" Tynon asked, annoyed by his inference.

"I don't know, but I'm going to find out! I'm working on it!"

When they arrived on the bridge, they were greeted like warriors back from a successful raid.

Several moments later a lull interrupted the celebration, and Luchak pulled Kerac aside. "Sir," he said. "I believe we should talk. Something is going on here I can't figure out."

Kerac frowned. "What do you mean? What can't you figure out?"

"I don't know," Luchak replied. "But I think we had better leave the area immediately! I have a bad feeling about that ship."

"I don't understand," Kerac said. "Did Meesha find something on that ship that makes you think we're in some sort of danger?"

"Yes, and that bothers me."

"Explain!"

Luchak glanced across the room and held his stare on Tynon. "Sir, I believe that rescue mission was a farce. For one thing, Meesha said it seemed much to easy to disconnect the device from the timer and reset the remote codes. There's something else, why would my father leave the only pod with an ion gun, if he didn't believed we would use it to escape?"

"You're beginning to sound a little paranoid," Kerac said. "Why would he leave Tynon tied up on the ship, and then tell us about it, if he didn't think we would come to his rescue. He's a bad man, but I can't believe he would leave the boy there to die."

"I believe it was to give him enough time to do something he had already planned," Luchak replied. "Something he probably had on his mind all along. And, knowing him it would be dramatic. How long did it take us to rescue him, several hours?"

"Then you believe this little rescue was just a ploy to give him time to do more of his dirty-work on Earth?"

"Yes, I do," Luchak affirmed, glancing over at Tynon. "I also believe that young man was involved. I think he volunteered for it, to give my father the time he needed."

"Then you don't trust him? Is that what you're saying?"

"Yes sir, that's exactly what I'm saying. Of course, I have no proof, but I believe he was working <u>with</u> my father. Why, I have no idea, except for what I just told you."

"In case you're right I'll move my ship out of harm's way, to be on the safe side," Kerac told him." He looked at Tynon and added, "We'll keep our eyes on him. Let me know if you see or hear anything to support your suspicions."

The ship darted into the upper limits of the atmosphere and stopped several thousand miles above Earth. After obtaining orbit, Kerac asked the King to join him in his stateroom.

"What is it, Brother?" Oltar asked, following him into the cabin "You seem reticent, is something going on I should know about?"

Kerac walked to the other side of the room and opened a cabinet door. "Would you care for a stiff shot of Earth's brandy? I sure could use one."

"Are you going to tell me what's on your mind?"

Kerac returned with two snifters and handed him one. "Luchak has a reason to believe Abron is about to do something stupid here on Earth, and I believe him. As a matter of fact, it could be something that involves your agreement with the President. You must know by now Abron hates you, almost as much as you hate him. I believe he would do anything to harm you, or at least screw up your deal with their President."

"Such as?" Oltar asked.

"I don't know, but I think I should contact Ekron. He's waiting for a call. He's been here ever since we went down to pick you up."

"That's a good idea," Oltar answered. "Contact him and see if he knows where Abron is, and what he's up to."

Kerac finished his brandy in one gulp and set the glass aside. "One thing more, you do realize he would do anything in his power to keep you from returning to Golan. Now that Luchak is no longer on his side, there is nothing left for him on Golan except to try to be voted in as King. If you were not there to dispute it, he could easily take over Parliament and vote you out. He controls most of the senators, as you must know."

"Then we can't let that happen," Oltar replied. "Do what you must. You have my permission, as long as I'm still King."

The door to the cabin flung open and Lulla rushed into the room. "Kerac!" she shouted, and then looked over at the King. "Your Majesty, my sensor has just picked up a blast from an ion gun. There was a tremendous explosion, and Abron's ship was destroyed! What do you want to do, now?"

"Could you tell where it came from?"

"Yes, it came from an area about five hundred miles west of our present location…same altitude."

"Contact Ekron and ask if he picked it up."

She rushed out the room and slammed the door behind her. When she got to the bridge, she picked up the communicator.

"Ekron!" she called. There was no answer and she called again, "Ekron, if you hear me, please answer. It'svery important!"

"Well, it's about time somebody contacted me," came a disgruntled voice. "Where have you guys been? I've been waiting patiently for someone to call. What's going on? Did you get the King? Is he all right?"

"Cut the small-talk, Ekron, this is important," she yelled into the mike. "Did your sensors pick up an ion blast a few minutes ago?"

"As a matter of fact, they did," he answered. "What's going on? I haven't been told a thing, you know."

"Could you tell precisely where it came from?"

"Yes, I have the coordinates, if you want them."

"Hang on to them, we may need them. I'll get back to you."

"Did you contact Ekron?" Kerac asked, as he returned to the helm.

"Yes. He has the coordinates the beam originated from. What do you want to do? You know perfectly well it was Abron."

"That's quite obvious, Lulla. Get me the coordinates and we'll go after that maniac! Whether he realizes it or not, he just wiped out the King's quid pro quo. I don't know what will happen, now that the King has no bargaining tool."

"Wait!" she shouted. "Why don't we take the King back to Golan, before we go after Abron? He is needed there. Not only is he on board, but two senators and several citizens of Golan are also with us. It would be illogical to believe you could capture or defeat him on your own. If you remember, he has Borak's ship, which I might add is equipped with the latest and most sophisticated weaponry. Do you really want to put all of us at risk, just to go after that lunatic? Why don't we go home and regroup? We can drop everyone off, and you and I can return and help Ekron go after him."

"Wow!" he said, looking at her admiringly. "Those are the most logical things you've said in weeks." He looked at Oltar and winked. "What do you think, Brother? Should we go back to Golan and regroup? Now that Abron's ship is destroyed, you have nothing to bargain with. Maybe we should go back, anyway. When they find out what happened to their prize, their military will undoubtedly be on the alert. The President isn't going to be too happy about his loss."

Oltar lowered his head and stared at the deck. "I believe Lulla is right, maybe we should go back while we still can. I don't want the Earthlings getting any angrier with us than they probably already are. Like you said, I have nothing left to give them." He was silent for several moments, and then added, "I will have Captain Borak contact Senator Kent to explain the situation. When he tells President Simmons, I hope he understands it was not me who had the ship blown up."

"Kerac," Lulla shouted across the bridge. "I have Ekron on the line, what do you want to tell him?"

"Tell him we're going back to Golan and drop off the King, and that he is to wait for my return before going after Abron."

"I will contact him on channel two?" she said. "Abron might be listening on one."

"What?" Ekron shouted into her headpiece. "You want me to bide my time up here, while you go back to Golan? I think I should go after that maniac right now, before he does more damage!"

Kerac yanked the mike out of her hand. "Ekron, don't do anything foolish," he yelled. "You know you can't handle him by yourself. Wait for us to return, and we'll go after him together. Between the two of us we should be able to take care of him."

There was a long pause, before Ekron replied. "All right," he answered with a sigh, "if that's what you want." The communicator went dead for a moment, and then his voice returned. "By the way, Abron just left orbit and went down to Earth, in case you're interested. The coordinates tell me he's headed for Oregon. I'll follow him, just to keep tabs on him."

"Stay where you are, Ekron!" Kerac shouted. "We'll return in a few hours…maybe a day. It won't take long to drop off my passengers, and then Lulla and I will help you contain him."

"Okay, as you wish," Ekron replied with a sigh.

THIRTY-SIX

The trip back to Golan was relatively uneventful, except for the usual strange occurrences encountered while passing through the vortex. After arriving, they hovered by Golan One's bay door and waited for it to open. However, after fifteen minutes, there was no indication that it would open.

Kerac shouted into his communicator, "Golan One! This is Kerac! By orders of the King, open the bay door!"

"Be whose orders?" and irate voice shouted.

"King Oltar's orders! He's on board and would like that bay door opened!"

"What are you trying to pull?" the voice said calmly. "He's in his quarters and does not wish to be disturbed."

King Oltar grabbed the mike. "Listen closely, this <u>is</u> King Oltar. Open this door, immediately!"

The voice returned, "I don't know who you are, but the King is in his quarters!" Then it added, "What mother-ship did you say you were from? I have no record of any ship due to arrive on Golan One."

Borak took the mike and spoke into it softly, "Who is this, please?"

There was a brief pause, and then the voice answered, "This is Sergeant Taag. Who is this?"

"Is this <u>the</u> Sergeant Taag from the Academy?" Borak questioned, raising his voice. "This is Captain Borak. What are you doing there, sergeant, I thought you were at the Academy on Two? It's about time for finals, isn't it?"

"Captain Borak?" the sergeant replied excitedly. "It's nice to hear you, Sir. Now that I know who you are, I'll open the bay door. You can't be too careful who you let in these days. We've had problems with one of the mother-ships. It'll take a few minutes. Glad you're back, Sir."

"Thank you, sergeant. It's nice to be back."

While they waited for the door to open, King Oltar took advantage of the lull. "Everybody," he called out, "please gather around. I have some things I want each of you to do, after we get into the hangar." They formed a tight group in the middle of the bridge. "Tumac, I would like you to set up a special meeting of Parliament, immediately. Contact the news media and tell them I will be making an impromptu address to all five ships in two hours.

"Kerac, you and Lulla take Meesha and Luchak to the Information and Rehabilitation Center. Go to personnel and see if they can select two volunteer technicians, the one we promised their president, and take them with you. Have IRC download all information and statistics they have on Earth and its people into their minds. Tell them the transfer must be completed by this afternoon. After IRC is finished with that process, take them to the plastron-surgeon and have their facial features altered. That also must be done by early evening, at the latest."

"Captain Borak," Oltar said, turning to face him. "I've saved the best for you. Go to Golan Two and see Lord Taag. Tell him what Senator Abron has been up to on Earth. I'm sure he will be pleased to hear it."

"Lord Taag?" Borak questioned, surprised by the name.

"Yes. I guess you didn't know Sergeant Taag is his son. He's only here on One to stand guard duty, and to finish his schooling for the Aviation Academy."

"No sir, I didn't know."

"Tell him we will bring Senator Abron back, as soon as we have him in custody."

"What about me, Your Majesty?" Nader asked. "What should I do while we're waiting for the others?"

Oltar pointed to Tynon. "Take this young man to the Military Interrogation Center," he said softy. "I want to find out how much he really knew about the destruction of Abron's ship, and if he knew what the senator was about to do on Earth. MIC will find out. You can be certain of that."

THIRTY-SEVEN

"Kersey!" Abron shouted into the intercom. "Is everything up to power? Are weapons still on line?"

"Everything is up and running. What are your plans?"

"Come up here and I'll tell you!"

Several minutes later Kersey barged through the hatch and stood behind him. "What are we going to do invade Earth all by ourselves?" He laughed.

"Don't get cute. I just turned on my long-range infrared and pointed it in the direction of that Indian reservation in Oregon. It told me there's a fire in that village. I don't know what it is, but I'm going down to find out. Maybe it's one of their new houses going up in flames. What a shame!" He chuckled to himself.

"You're going down there just to look at a fire?"

"I want to know what's going on down there with that fire. Maybe I can help put it out." He laughed cynically.

After setting in the coordinates, it took only a few minutes to arrive at the village and hover below a nearby tree line. Abron turned on a video scanner and zoomed in on the village, a half-mile away. There appeared to be a raging fire at the very top of four poles, which contained an object the size of a human body. He watched in disbelief, as the fire rapidly consumed the object.

"Kersey, look at this!" he said. "I wonder what's going on down there."

"I saw something like that on their television," the engineer replied, staring intently at the strange scene. "Sometimes, when an Indian dies his body is lifted onto poles, set on fire and burned until there's nothing left but bones and ashes. It's a bizarre ritual. I never thought I'd ever see one…in person."

"I'm going to move in closer and get a better look," Abron said. "I want to see this with my own eyes up close and not through a scanner."

"I wouldn't do that, sir," Kersey replied, "leave them to their grief. That's probably the Indian squaw you killed when you attacked the village. I don't believe we would be welcomed at the funeral."

Ignoring his comment, Abron slowly and methodically maneuvered the vessel from the tree line to a spot several hundred yards from the pyre and hovered a few feet above ground, and then tilted the ship to get a better view through the bow porthole.

"Look!" someone shouted and pointed. "Over there! It's back!"

Walking Bear looked up and shook his fist at the ship. "You devil!" he shouted. "You're the demon who killed my Velma!" He ran into his cabin, took his hunting rifle down from the fireplace and returned. When he saw Abron's image in the porthole, he fired at it until his gun was empty. Seeing his actions, the others raced into their houses, got their rifles and started firing.

Walking Bear saw that the .30 Caliber rifle was doing nothing, and returned to his cabin to get his .50 Caliber Sharp buffalo gun. He fired at the porthole, and it shattered.

The broken porthole caused a momentary evacuation of the internal atmosphere in the ship and sent both Abron and Kersey flying across the bridge. Kersey had been thrown up against the far bulkhead and momentarily knocked unconscious. After several moments, he opened his eyes and noticed the senator lying motionless in a pool of blood.

Without control of the ship, it slowly nosed toward earth. When Kersey noticed its precarious attitude, he rushed to the helm, grabbed the maneuvering stick and pulled back on it. He pushed another lever and took it out of hover control. By applying power to the anti-gravity grid, the ship leveled off. As soon as it was relatively stable, he applied full power and the ship darted into the lower atmosphere.

Realizing he couldn't travel into outer space with a broken porthole, he stopped a few miles above Earth where he still had a small amount of oxygen. When he was certain the ship was in low, a power-on orbit he checked on Abron, who had been thrown across the bridge and landed face down in the debris of the shattered porthole.

"Senator, are you all right?" he shouted. He turned him over and discovered a large puncture wound below his left shoulder. "Oh, no!" he mumbled, his face turning white. "He's been shot!" He knelt beside him to check his pulse and found it to be extremely weak. He appeared to have lost a lot of blood. "Senator!" he shouted, again. He slapped his face but got no response. "Now, what am I going to do?" he mumbled, cradling his head in his arms. "Senator, if you hear me open your eyes!"

Abron blinked several times, and then slowly opened his eyes. He looked up and focused on him. "What hit me?" he asked, his face displaying pain.

"It looks like you've been shot, sir. What should I do? I'm no doctor."

"Don't worry about it," he replied, coughing sporadically." He attempted to say something more, but blood in his throat prevented it.

"Sir, let me take you to your quarters where you'll be comfortable."

Abron coughed again, and then said through a mouthful of blood, "Don't bother, a pillow won't cure this." He pointed to his chest. "Before I leave you, what is your situation? Will this ship make it home?"

Kersey attempted to find the right words, but he couldn't think of anything meaningful to say. "Sir, we can't get home in this ship. The porthole has been knocked out, and we have no replacement on board. Without oxygen, we can't go into outer space. We couldn't make a vortex, let alone go through one." As he bowed his head in despair, his eyes filled with tears. "I don't know what to do, sir, I'm no helmsman."

"Try to contact the other ships," Abron muttered through more spasmodic coughs. "I'm sure they will take you home." He closed his eyes for a moment, and then added, "Even if you are with the mad man from Golan." With a slight smile, he turned his head to the side, closed his eyes and exhaled a long, last breath.

"Senator! Senator!" he shouted into his bloody face. "Please, don't die. I don't know what to do. Please, don't die!"

"Abron!" a voice came over a speaker on the bridge. "This is Ekron, what's going on down there? Why are you still in Earth's atmosphere?

You should be hiding somewhere in outer space with your tail between your legs!"

Kersey laid Abron's head back on the deck and ran to the communicator. "Ekron!" he shouted. "Please come and get me, I don't know what to do!"

"Who is this? This isn't Abron!"

"No, this is Kersey. Senator Abron is dead. He was shot by an Earthling."

There was silence for several moments, and then Ekron replied, "Shot by an Earthling? Are you sure? What happened?"

"He was shot through the bow porthole."

"What are you talking about? Those portholes can withstand meteor showers! How can their bullets break one?"

The young man's hands trembled, as he held the mike to his lips. "I'm not sure what happened. We were close to that Indian village, the one he attacked before, and they started shooting at us. Before we could do anything a bullet shattered the porthole and hit the senator. He's dead! What should I do, I don't know anything about driving this ship? I only knew enough to get us where there was still a little oxygen...about two miles up!"

"Listen to me, Kersey," Ekron said calmly. "I'm coming after you, get in one of your pods and wait. When I get there, I'll open my bay door and let you bring the pod inside."

"Sir, I don't know how to operate a pod."

"I thought you were an engineer!"

"I can fix them, but I can't fly them."

"Hang on kid, I'll send my engineer over in one of ours. Get the senator's body down to the hangar bay. I want to return it to Golan. He may have been an absolute mad man, but he still deserves a descent burial." Then he added, "You better keep the ship's power on so it will stay at that same altitude. We don't want it to fall to Earth."

It took only minutes for Ekron to maneuver his ship alongside. Kersey looked through the bay porthole and saw his bay door open. Suddenly, he realized he didn't know how to open his own outer-bay door. He raced across the hangar to the communicator on the far bulkhead.

"Ekron!" he shouted. "How do I open my bay door?"

A voice crackled through the speaker. "There are two push-buttons, a red and a yellow one beside the door?"

"Okay, then what?"

"The red one closes it, and the yellow one opens it. Is that clear enough?"

"Thank you," an apologetic voice returned. "I'm really not as stupid as you probably think."

"I should hope not."

Kersey ran back to the bridge, grabbed Abron by the legs and dragged his huge body down the passageway to the hangar bay.

Keral, Ekron's First Mate, maneuvered a pod to within a few feet of the ship and called him on the communicator. "Okay, Kersey, it's time to open your bay door. Hang onto something stationary; there could be a rush of air when the bay door opens. However, by being in Earth's lower atmosphere, there still should be enough oxygen outside where it won't be too bad. However, put on an oxygen mask, just in case."

A few moments later the bay door opened, and Keral brought his pod into the ship and settled gently onto the perforated deck.

"Okay, let's load the senator into the pod and get the hell out of here!" he commanded. "We're in Earth's radar range. We've got to get our ship into the upper atmosphere, as soon as possible!"

"What about the senator's ship?" Kersey asked. "We can't leave it here."

"Why not?" Keral answered. "We can come back for it later. It'll be safe. The Earthlings don't have the technology to steal it." Then he added, "We'll let Ekron decide what to do with it."

After struggling with the huge body to get it on board the small pod, they left the hangar and headed for Ekron's ship. Halfway there, Keral pushed a button on the pod's control panel, and the deserted ship's bay door closed."

"I didn't know you could do that from your pod," Kersey said. "This pod's not from that ship."

"Trade secret," Keral replied. "I could have opened your bay door for you too, but I wanted to test you. Not everybody knows that little trick, but being an engineer you should." Kersey's face flushed.

When they were alongside Ekron's ship, Keral opened the bay door remotely and took the pod inside. They secured it and walked up the narrow passageway to the bridge.

When they arrived, Ekron was seated at the helm. He glanced at Kersey briefly, and then turned back to the helm. He brought the ship around, made a quick dip and positioned it directly under the derelict ship. The anti-gravity engine whined and the ion drive whistled loudly, as both ships shot into outer space. They stopped several thousand miles above Earth and secured an orbit.

"Well, Kersey," Ekron said, turning to look at him. "I guess you've had quite an eventful day, haven't you?"

"Yes, I guess you could say that," the young engineer replied. "I'm just thankful you were around to rescue me. Thank you."

Ekron looked deep into the young man's eyes. "Okay, tell me everything that happened down there. Don't leave anything out. Understand? It could be important."

Kersey found a chair and sat. He exhaled loudly, and then began, "I guess Abron wanted to return to that Indian village to finish what he had started. You must know by now he wiped out a portion of that village before, and I guess that wasn't enough for him, he wanted to finish the job. I don't know exactly what was on his mind, but I believe it had something to do with wanting to get even for his brother's death, and also for them not turning Meesha over to him…or something like that." He paused long enough to catch his breath, and then continued. "We were hovering only a few hundred feet from a pyre, a burial fire the Indians use to cremate their dead, probably that woman he killed earlier, when they started shooting at us. Fortunately, most of their bullets bounced off our hull. However, suddenly I heard this explosion and this missile, or whatever it was, smashed through the porthole and hit the senator in the chest. He fell across the helm controls, and the ship started to drift toward earth. After working with him for so many years, I knew enough about the controls to keep us from crashing, and to get us out of there. That's the reason you found me in Earth's atmosphere. I knew I couldn't go any higher, with the porthole missing. That's the whole story."

Ekron leaned back and stared at him. "Then you believe he was going to do something more to that village, like completely wiping it out?"

"Yes sir, I got that impression. For some reason, he disliked them. Why, I don't know, he wouldn't tell me. He kept me down in engineering most of the time, so I rarely knew what was happening on the bridge."

Ekron turned to his controls. "I guess there's nothing left for us here so we'll go back to Golan," he mumbled. "By now, everyone else is there."

"You mean King Oltar is back on Golan, too?" Kersey asked. "If that's the case, I guess he'll have a much easier job, now that the senator isn't around."

"Now that we have another derelict ship orbiting Earth," Ekron stated, "we'll go back and tell the Prime Minister the quid pro quo is still intact. I'm sure the President will be happy to hear that. I heard he was concerned when he heard about the destruction of the other ship." He turned the ship around and headed back toward the derelict. "I have to get Borak's ham rig out of that ship, before we leave. Then, I have to figure out how to use it so I can contact Senator Kent and tell him about this new development."

"Sir," Kersey interrupted. "You don't have to get that equipment to call him."

"What do you mean?"

"I have one of Earth's cell phones," Kersey replied. "It fell out of the senator's uniform, when I was dragging him to the hangar bay. I haven't the faintest idea what he was doing with it, but I have it here." He dug into his pocket and pulled out an object the size of a deck of cards. "All you have to do is enter the senator's phone number and push this little red button. When he answers you talk, that's all."

"Am I supposed to know his phone number?" Ekron asked. "How can I get it?"

"I believe if you punch the number zero, someone will ask who you want to talk to," Kersey replied. "Tell them you want Senator Kent in Washington, D.C."

Keral attempted to reach for the cell, but Kersey slapped his hand away.

"Okay, Kersey," Ekron replied, "do me the honor, get his number."

After several fruitless attempts, Kersey begrudgingly handed the cell over to Keral. "Here, smart ass, get his number," he said with a sneer.

Keral took the phone, went to the other side of the bridge, punched in a few numbers and spoke into it. A voice came over the speaker, and he handed it to Ekron. "Here you are, sir. The senator is on the line."

Ekron looked at him skeptically and took the phone. "Senator?" he asked softly. "Is this Senator Kent?"

"Yes," Kent replied. "Who is this?"

"This is Senator Ekron. Your Captain Borak is back on Golan. He had to leave early…pressing matters. I'm taking his place, so to speak."

"What's on your mind, Senator Ekron? What can I do for you?"

Ekron paced back and forth across the bridge, as he spoke into the device "I have something that could be of interest to your President." He hesitated for a moment, and then continued. "I assume President Simmons knows that the ship we originally gave him was blown up, doesn't he?"

"Of course, I told him, as soon as I was informed. What do we do now?"

"As luck would have it, we have another ship in outer space, just sitting there waiting for you to retrieve it."

"Good. I'll pass this information on." There was a long pause, and then he added, "What about the men your King promised as technical advisors?"

"That of course is up to him, I have no authority in such matters. I am leaving for Golan immediately, and I will pass that information on to him. I'm sure he will do the right thing…he always does."

"Then all your ships and men have returned to Golan?"

"Yes, I am the last to leave," Ekron replied. "I must go back and find out the status of my planet…how much longer before we're forced to leave. And, to see how our scientists are coming along with the development of larger vortexes to accommodate our mother-ships. That will determine when we leave for a new home, either in space or here on Earth."

"Well, no matter what the outcome," Kent replied, I wish you and your people the best. By the way, say goodbye to my friend Captain Kirk." He snickered.

"Yes, I will," Ekron replied. "We will try to return at least once more before leaving our solar system, if for no other reason than bringing you those technicians you were promised. My honest feelings are that we will never make a vortex large enough to let our mother-ships pass through."

"Well, I say again, good luck," Kent said. "Have a nice trip to the stars." The line went dead.

"Let's go home, men," Ekron said.

THIRTY-EIGHT

Tumac sat at the end of the long table, waiting patiently for the senators to be seated. After a few moments, he banged his mallet on the table and stood.

"Gentlemen," he began. "Our scientists tell me we have only weeks, if not days, to make final preparations for our journey. As you must know, they have been unable to develop vortexes large enough to accommodate our mother-ships for passage to Earth. Therefore, it will be impossible to assimilate with their people.

"It is with the deepest regret that I inform you of Senator Abron's deplorable actions while on Earth. He has committed the ultimate crimes…killing a human, and attacking Earth with no provocation. I have invited Lord Taag from the nation of Keeti to this meeting to hear the charges brought against him. The senator is not present, so he will be charged in absentia." He looked at Lord Taag. "Do you wish to say anything in his behalf, Your Lordship?" Taag raised his hand and waved him off.

Before Tumac could read the specifics of the charges, an intern rushed into the chamber and stood behind him. After a few moments, he tapped the Prime Minister on the shoulder and whispered in his ear. Tumac's face turned grave, and he stared wide-eyed at the young man. After gathering his composure, he said, "Are you sure, Daka?"

The intern nodded.

Tumac lowered his tall, frail frame into the chair and glanced down the long table at the confused faces. "Gentlemen, I have rather disturbing news to share with you. I have just been informed that Ekron has arrived back from Earth with Senator Abron's body. It appears that he was killed while attacking a small village on Earth. I do not know the details, but as soon as I have them, I will let you know."

Daka turned to leave, but before he got to the door Tumac called to him, "Daka, please inform King Oltar that all members of Parliament are present. He wished to speak to them, and all of Golan." The expressions on the senators' faces turned anxious, when they heard their King was about to speak.

Senator Kelt, from the Nation of Kolby, stood to address Tumac. "Your Honor," he yelled over the din of the confused voices.

"Yes, Senator Kolby, you are recognized."

"Did I hear you correctly? King Oltar is well enough to address Parliament?"

Tumac smiled. "Yes, he should be here at any moment. He will explain everything." He slammed the mallet down on the table. "Gentlemen, we have food and refreshments in the outer room, please indulge yourselves while waiting for your King." The members wasted no time retreating to the concession room.

"Hold still, Meesha," Doctor Korb commanded irritably, while attempting to implant the simulated spherical irises in his eyes. "This will not hurt, unless you fight it. It will only take a few more minutes to complete this operation, and then we will modify your eyebrow and teeth. After that, they will hook you up to the subliminal implant machine and send images of Earth into your subconscious memory bank, along with the necessary vocabulary to hold on a conversation with the people of Earth. After that, you will have the knowledge of most Earthlings, and the ability to communicate effectively." He stepped back several paces to admire his work, then added, "How does that sound?"

"All of this will make me look exactly like the people of Earth?" Meesha asked.

"Yes, of course. We have done this procedure many times on children who have gone there and remained, mostly from those parents who are no longer with us. However, understand one thing—you will not be human. You will only look and act like one."

Meesha raised his head and stared at him skeptically. "You mean other children my age have gone to Earth and remained?"

"Not only children, but some adults, too."

Meesha smiled and said, "Good, at least I won't be alone."

"You probably wouldn't be able to pick any one of them out of a crowd," Korb said with a smile. "They look exactly like Earthling. That's the way they wanted it."

Kelok, a uniformed man with a pock-marked face and a large pot-belly walked into the interrogation room and sat across from Tynon. He glanced at the young man, then lowered his head and thumbed through some sheets of paper in front of him.

"You are Tynon?" he asked.

"Yes sir."

Kelok got up, went to a water cooler and drew a cup of ice water. He brought it back and set in front of Tynon. "What happened on that ship?"

Tynon picked up the cup and took a sip. He raised his head and stared at the huge man across the table, still sifting through sheets of paper. He held his stare for several seconds, then lowered his eyes and ran a finger around the rim of his cup.

"Sir, I told Senator Kerac everything. Why do I have to go over it again?"

"Because I want you to go over it again, that's why!" The man's beady eyes narrowed, as he leaned across the table. "I want to know everything that happened on that ship, and what happened prior to your rescue. Understand?"

Tynon took another sip and set the cup down, almost tipping it over. He stared at the man uneasily, and then said, "Sir, like I told Senator Kerac, Senator Abron tied me up and forced me to stay on that ship."

"But why? That's what I want to know." He glared at him. "Why would he leave you on that ship, knowing you could be killed? He must have had a reason. Did he leave you there as a decoy? Did he set it up so somebody would be forced to come after you? I don't understand what he could possibly gain by doing such a thing." He got up and walked behind Tynon. He stood there for a moment looking at his neck, and then bent down and whispered in his ear, "He didn't force you to stay on that ship, did he? He asked you to stay, and you agreed, didn't you? Weren't you trying to gain his confidence, admiration, maybe his respect by doing that? What did he offer you for your complicity?"

"Nothing!" Tynon shot back. "I guess he figured somebody would come and rescue me."

"Did he tell you that?" Korb fired back.

"No. Not in so many words."

"Then why do you think he put you there in the first place, if he thought somebody would come to your rescue? Was it to set up an ambush for the rescue ship?"

Tynon's forehead began to sweat, and he looked for something to wipe it on.

Kelok pulled out a slightly used handkerchief and handed it to him.

"Well, I'm waiting," he said. "Are you going to tell me why Senator Abron would do such a thing?"

Tynon wiped his forehead, exhaled a big sigh, and leaned back in his chair. "Sir, I don't know why you're asking me these questions you should be asking Senator Abron. Only he knows and only he can tell you."

The door to the interrogation room flung open, and a corporal rushed in and approached the sergeant. He bent over and whispered something to him. Kelok stared at him for a moment, and then turned and looked at Tynon.

"I'm afraid asking Senator Abron anything will be out of the question," he said. "I was just informed that he's dead."

Tynon's eyes widened, and his face flushed. "What?" he shouted. "What do you mean he's dead?" He stared into the man's eyes. "What happened?"

"I was told that somebody just returned with his body. That's all I know."

"Then are you quite through with my third-degree?" Tynon asked, glaring at him. "I had nothing to do with his death, and you know it."

"I know you didn't, but my King insisted I find out what happened on Abron's ship."

"If he's dead, this interrogation means nothing. Doesn't it?"

"Probably not, but I have this tradition of obeying my King," the sergeant said, and stood. "But I suppose I have all the information I need, under the circumstances. You can go. I'll tell the King that he put you on that ship against your will so somebody would have to come after you, to give him time to do the rest of his dirty work on Earth. That should clear you with the King." Before walking out the door, he turned and looked back at the young man. "But tell me, just to satisfy my own curiosity, and off the record, did you volunteer to be tied up on that ship, or did he force you into it? And, was the senator planning to attack the rescue ships, when it came for you?"

Tynon looked at him with a crooked grin. "Would it make any difference, now that the interrogation is over?"

"Like I said, to satisfy my own curiosity. That's all."

"He did tie me up and put me there to give him time to do whatever it was he wanted to do," Tynon confessed. "He let Kerac know I was there. He knew either he, or someone else, would come to my rescue. He also promised me a Senatorial Internship, if I went along with it. He told me he was going to wait until Kerac came to my rescue, and then possibly cripple him, so he couldn't go home. But before that, he was going down to that Indian reservation and raise some hell, and that he would return for me later. Fortunately, he didn't have time to do anything to Kerac's ship, he was too busy with that other plan, I guess."

"I thought as much," Kelok said, and headed for the door. "But he had his chance when Kerac came to your rescue, didn't he? He had not yet gone to the reservation. Why didn't he do something then?"

"I don't know. Maybe he was too concerned about going down to that village, to do anything at that time."

"So you think that's why he left you on that ship? To give him time to go after that village?"

"I guess so. I don't know why he would set it up the way he had, if that wasn't his plan."

"By the way," Kelok added, "weren't you the least bit worried? If Kerac hadn't come to your rescue, and things hadn't worked out the way they had, don't you think he would have blown you up anyway, just to negate his promise to you?" He stared into the boy's flushed face, and added, "You know he was the one who blew up that ship you were on, don't you? And it wasn't long after you were rescued!"

Tynon's face turned ashen, as he watched the sergeant leave the room.

"Will the senators please return to the table and be seated," a speaker in the refreshment room blasted. "King Oltar will be here momentarily. He would like to speak to you, and to all ships of Golan."

Oltar walked tentatively through the door and sat at the head of the conference table. The senators took their time returning from the concession room, unaware he had arrived. Tumac watched with irritation, as they casually walked to their seats. When satisfied all members had been seated, he pounded the mallet on the table.

"Gentlemen," he said loudly. "King Oltar wishes to address you, and all the ships of Golan. He has just returned from Earth, where he went through a surgical procedure to cure his medical problem. Once again, he is in full command and control of Golan. He is ready to continue his duties as your King." He held out his hand. "Nice to have you back, Your Majesty."

Oltar took his hand and nodded. "Do we have communications with all ships in the fleet, Tumac?"

"Yes, Your Majesty, they know you're back and are waiting to hear from you."

Oltar looked down the long table and gave each face a lengthy stare, then cleared his throat, straightened his aging body and stood.

"Prime Minister Tumac, senators, and citizens of Golan," he began. "I am certain every citizen of the kingdom has been made aware of my illness. It debilitated me to the point where it affected my duties as your King, and I must apologize for that." He took a sip of water and continued. "I have just now returned from where I sincerely hoped would be our new home, Earth. I went there to take advantage of their medical expertise, with the hope they could cure me. They did in deed restore me back to health, but it came at a price—some of our technology in exchange. In addition, I made them a promise that if we could get our mother-ships into their world and assimilate with them, we would give them even more. Unfortunately, I have been informed by our top scientists that it would be impossible to get our ships through a vortex before our plant's demise. Therefore, assimilation with Earth will not be possible.

"By now, all of you must know of our ability to travel to another universe…a parallel universe. However, we soon discovered our small observation ships were the only vessels that could travel into that universe; our mother-ships were much too large, and a vortex could not be made big enough to accommodate them. Consequently, unless we find a suitable planet in our own galaxy, by the time our beloved planet is destroyed, we will be destined to live the rest of our lives, and the lives of our children, on our five ships.

"One thing more—" He took another sip of water, glanced at Tumac, winked and continued. "While on Earth, I observed their many forms of governments: democracies, monarchies, socialism, and several others not worth mentioning. It did not take long to realize that democracy would be the best suitable form of government for us to pursue. Therefore, I am calling a special session of Parliament to vote for the establishment of this new order of government. We have an amendment already which will allow us to revert to another form of government should our monarchy fail…and it has. If this modification is passed by Parliament, we will no longer have a King but a President, no longer Senators of the Parliament but congressmen and senators, controlled by a Congressional House of Representatives and a Senate. The President and the governing bodies of the House and Senate will be voted in by all the citizens of Golan. In the future, our new system will be known as a government of the people, by the people, and for the people. That is what Earth calls democracy. It is a just and honorable way of life.

"My friends, we have but a short time left, before we are forced to leave our beloved planet and search for another that will support life. We have been bountiful on Golan, and our Kingdom has flourished… to a point. However, our future must now be voted on by our citizens, not the sometimes devious decisions of a Parliament." He looked down the table at the solemn faces. "Thank you, citizens of Golan. Bless each and every one of you. And may we soon find a new home."

A few hours later, King Oltar returned to his residence and found his wife, Moina, and Meesha sitting at the long dining table. Her huge purse sat at her side, and was leaning up against a table leg, ready for her daily departure to Golan Two. He went to the table and sat beside Meesha.

"Well, Moina, I see you're ready to visit your friends on Two," he said cynically. "And you, Son, have you talked to your mother about your plans? Are you ready for your little adventure?"

"Mother, you do understand, don't you?" Meesha asked, concern in his voice. She gave him a distant look, picked up her purse and set it on the table, ready for a quicker departure.

"Yes, I understand," she replied indifferently. "I only wish you would change your mind. It's really not as bad here as you make it out to be."

He laughed impudently. "How would you know, Mother, you are always with your friends on Two."

She looked at him coldly. "Don't talk to your mother like that. I have always been here to enjoy you and your friends."

"He's right, Moina. You were never around when he needed you," Oltar interjected. "I truly believe he will be much better off with his friends on Earth. I have made the necessary arrangements, and he is to leave for Earth immediately."

She stood up and snatched her purse from the table. "Well, whatever," she said, an ugly frown forming on her face. "I guess I don't have anything to say in this matter, so let him go." And then she added, "He doesn't look like my son any longer anyway, with those funny eyebrows, and those round eyes." She bent over, kissed him on the top of his head fleetingly, and then turned to leave. When she got to the door, she said, "Meesha, dear, I'll miss you." She walked out the door and slammed it.

Oltar shook his head. "She will miss you about as much as she misses me."

"I see Carlina has packed my things, Father. I am ready to go."

"We will never see each other again, Son," Oltar said, deep furrows lining his aging brow. "You know that, don't you? There is no turning back, once you're on Earth. I will miss you, Son. Make lots of friends and live a good life. Remember, you are not to use your mental powers on Earth. It would only bring you grief, if the wrong people found out about it. Do you understand?"

"Yes, Father, I understand." He wiped his moist eyes on a napkin. "I will miss you too, Father. I love you very much. Nevertheless, I know I will have a better life on Earth than if I stayed here." He stood up, then sat back down and looked into his father's eyes. "What about Loree? You said you would consider her coming with me."

"Son, I'm sorry, but I don't believe that would be wise. She seems perfectly happy here. Besides, she would have no place to stay on Earth. You have your Charlie and Grace and your Indian friends, but she would have no one, and no place to live."

"She could live with me…with Grace and Charley."

"From what your uncle told me, they were old people. I don't believe they could handle both of you. Besides, how would it look for them to have two children in their home with no logical explanation of how or why they were there?" He reached over and put his hand gently on the boy's shoulder. "Son, I wish I could say yes, but I don't believe it would be wise to allow her to go with you. I hope you understand, if not now sometime in the future."

Carlina came into the room with tears running down her cheeks. She looked at Meesha compassionately and set a duffle-style bag on the floor next to him.

"Meesha, my sweet little boy, I will miss you," she said. She bent over and kissed him on the cheek. She pulled a tissue from her pocket, dabbed the moisture from the corners of her eyes, turned and walked quickly out of the room.

"See, you are missed already," Oltar said with a grin. He got up from the table, went to the other side of the room and spoke into a communicator. "Kerac, are you there?" he asked. "Your nephew is ready to leave."

"Is Kerac taking me, Father?" Meesha asked excitedly.

"Yes, he and Lulla will take you back. They know your friends, Charlie and Grace. Besides, he made you a promise that would bring you back to Earth. Remember?"

"Thanks you, Father, I like Kerac and Lulla very much. I am only sorry that after they leave I will never see them again." He stood up and wrapped his arms around his father's neck. "I love you very much, Father. I pray you find a home for you and mother, and Golan."

"I hope your prayer works, Son," Oltar said with a weak smile, "we will need all the prayers we can get." He stood up from the table, took Meesha by his shoulders and pushed him gently toward the door. "Now get out of here, before I break down. You don't want to see a King cry, do you?"

THIRTY-NINE

Although it was only September, a northerly wind had already made its way down the mountains and into the valley, leaving a premature chill behind. The days had drawn shorter, and the remnants of summer slowly turned the valley into a sweater-bearing life-style. It would not be long before the winds of winter had brought the cold, steady rain, and never-ending snow.

The only program on local TV, of any interest to Charley, was the I Love Lucy show. He could barely wait for the episode to begin. Lying on his favorite sofa, his eyes half closed, he tried his best to stay awake for the beginning of the first re-run of the season. The installment finally flashed onto the screen, and he laughed hysterically at each absurd scene. A seemingly endless commercial raced across the screen and he closed his eyes until the next scenario, which he had seen a hundred times before.

Grace was not the least bit interested in Lucy's tomfoolery and continued knitting. Every few minutes she lifted her head and looked over at Charley, especially when his comical snorts became exceptionally loud. The cuckoo clock burped out a few raspy notes, and she looked up and cringed. "I've got to get that thing fixed," she mumbled to herself."

The clock barely finished ten guttural tones, when three faint knocks came at the door. Startled, she dropped her knitting and focused on the doorway.

"Wonder who that could be at this hour," she mumbled. "Kinda late for guests." She got up and cautiously walked to the door. When she opened it, a small boy was standing in the doorway looking up at her. She put her glasses on and squinted. All of a sudden, a broad smile spread across her chubby face. "For Heaven's sake, it's Meesha…I think!" She lowered her head and stared intently at the boy. "It is Meesha, isn't it? You look different. What happened to your eyes… and your hair and eyebrow?"

Charlie heard the commotion, got up from the sofa and painstakingly joined her at the door. When he saw the boy, a smile broke through his three-day growth of salt-and-pepper whiskers.

"Well, I'll be danged, if it isn't the little twerp," he said, and held out his hand. "How you doin', boy?" Meesha grabbed his hand and shook it vigorously. "What are you doing here? I thought you went back to that planet of yours."

Kerac and Lulla had been standing off to one side, and finally walked into the light of the doorway.

"Hello, Gracie," she said with a broad grin. "It's nice to see you again."

"Lulla!" Grace said, startled by her sudden appearance. "What are you doing here?" She held out her arms to embrace her. "Land's sake, I thought you went home."

"I came back for that cup of coffee you promised," she said with a smile.

"Please, come into the kitchen while I make it," Grace said. "Tell me all about yourself. What have you been doing?"

Without acknowledging Kerac, Charley returned to the sofa, and Meesha joined him.

Lulla followed her into the kitchen and watched as she poured water into the percolator.

"Gracie, I have a favor to ask," she said bluntly.

Grace turned and looked at her. "Yes, dear, what is it?"

Lulla pulled a chair out from under the table. "Gracie, remember what I told you about our planet coming to an end, that our sun was going to destroy it?"

"Yes, of course."

"Well, it's going to happen very soon, in a matter of days or weeks."

"Yes, you told me that before. Is that what you came to tell me?"

"No, not exactly," she replied nervously. "I don't know how to say this delicately, so I will come right out with it. I wanted to ask if you would take Meesha into your home…raise him as your own son." She lowered her head and looked down at the worn oilcloth. "I know both of you are elderly, and Charlie is not in the best of health, but you have an extra bedroom where he could stay." She shifted her body uneasily, not knowing how she should continue. "What I'm trying to say is that Meesha wants to remain here on Earth, when our ships leave to look for a new home. He would like to be your adopted son, so to speak."

Grace sat down across from her, reached over and grasped her hands. She looked into her eyes and said, "Sweetheart, do you know how long it's been since we've had a child his age in our house? It's been many years. It's not that we wouldn't love to have him, but I don't believe we couldn't give him a proper home. One like he's been accustomed to." She was silent for several moments, and then added, "What about school? He's only twelve years old and must go to school…it's a law here. He can't even speak our language. What about the children and the teachers? What would they think? What would they do?"

Lulla smiled. "Gracie, he can speak your language now. Our scientists made that possible. He not only knows your language but everything about your world. School would be quite simple for him."

"How is that possible?" Grace asked, raising her eyebrows. "A few days ago he couldn't speak he had to show us pictures to tell us anything."

"I know," Lulla replied. "But things have changed since then. He no longer has to use his special powers to communicate. He now has full knowledge of your world and your people. And, as you saw, he looks like other children his age." She rose from the table and pulled Grace out of her chair. "Come, I'll show you."

Charley was sitting on the sofa next to the boy, when they walked into the living room. Kerac remained at the door, apparently guarding it from some unknown danger.

"Gracie!" Charley shouted. "Come listen to the boy talk. I asked him to show me some pictures, but he said he couldn't he wasn't allowed to anymore. Gracie, he can talk as good as we can."

"Well, that isn't saying much," Grace replied with a giggle. She sat next to the boy and looked into his eyes. "Have you told Charley what you would like to do?"

Meesha glanced at Lulla for approval.

"It's all right, honey," Lulla said, "you can tell him. I have already told Gracie."

He looked into Charley's eyes, and said, "I don't want to go with my people when they search for another planet. I want to stay here with you and Grace. I love you both very much. I could be your adopted son, or relative, or something." He gave him a nervous smile. "You know from my brief stay with you, I don't eat much, and I don't snore when I sleep." Another faint, eager smile spread across his pixie face.

Charley dug his hand deep into the crease of the sofa to find the remote to turn off the TV. He stared blankly at the boy for several moments, and then looked over at Grace. She gave him a slight shrug. "Son, we would love to have you, but I'll be perfectly honest; I'm not sure we could support anybody else in our house, with our meager income and all. To put it bluntly," he added, "we don't have very much money. We can barely feed ourselves and pay our bills." His face flushed from having to confess his innermost secret, but he wanted to be honest with the boy.

Lulla went to Kerac and whispered in Golanese, "Do you still have that Earth money?"

"Yes, as a matter of fact, I do," he replied. "And I believe I know what you want to do with it, don't I?"

"It certainly isn't going to do us any good, when we leave Earth," she answered. She looked at him coyly, and then added, "You never did tell me where you got it."

"Yes, I know."

"Where is it, on the ship?"

"Yes. If you want it, I'll go get it."

"How much is there?"

"I don't really know, but it's a lot."

"Did you get it honestly?"

"Of course," he answered indignantly. "A few years ago, on one of my trips, I brought the diamonds I received from the accounting office for part of my salary. When I arrived, I happened to meet a rather shady character who gave me paper money in exchange for them. I had no idea how much the diamonds were worth, but he was rather impressed and quite generous with his paper money. I thought I could use it later when we assimilated, but you know how that went."

Lulla sat on the sofa next to Grace. She looked into her eyes and said, "I have something to tell you, and I don't want you to get upset."

"Yes, dear, what is it?" she reached over and took her hand. "I could never get upset with you."

Lulla blushed and said, "Gracie…and Charley…I don't want you to think we are being condescending, but you do not have to worry about money. Over the years Kerac has accumulated a quite a bit of your paper money. It will do us no good where we are going. We would never be able to spend it. We would like you to have it." She stared at Grace, and then added, "Please don't take this the wrong way. It is not intended to be a bribe. But if you take him, we would like for you and Meesha to have a good life."

"We can't take your money. It wouldn't be right," Charley broke into the conversation. "If we took him in, it would be for love, not money."

"But money would help, would it not, sir?" Kerac spoke for the first time. "Do you want us to throw it out the window of our spaceship?" He smiled, and then his face turned solemn. "We have absolutely no use for your money. The monetary system on Golan is diamonds. Whether you take the boy or not, we would still like for you to have the money. I am certain you could use it for something…maybe a new car." He looked at Grace and smiled. "One more thing, your Indian friend said he would take the boy, if you didn't want him."

"It's not a matter of wanting or not wanting him," Charley said, giving Kerac an annoyed look. "You know very well we would take him at the blink of an eye, if we thought we could raise him properly. However, at our advanced ages—"

"Please Gracie," Lulla pleaded, "would you and Charley at least talk it over? In the meantime, Kerac will go to the ship and get the money.

Whether you take Meesha or not, we are still giving you the money. And that's final!"

Grace helped Charley up from the sofa. "Come on, honey, the least we can do is talk it over."

Charley followed her into the kitchen. Several moments later, she returned with a cup of steaming coffee and set it in front of Lulla.

"What do you think, Meesha?" Lulla asked, as she put several lumps of sugar into the cup. "I know how much you want to stay with them, but consider their dilemma. They are very old and poor, and I'm sure they no longer know much about twelve-year-old boys."

"They will not be poor when Kerac gives them the money," he replied.

"Money cannot solve the problems they could be faced with."

Meesha got up and walked across the room to the music box in the corner. He opened the lid, cranked the handle several times and pushed the switch. Instantly, the tune of The Blue Danube filled the room. Lulla appeared curious about the box and joined him. He took her hand and pulled her slowly around the room to the tinny beat of the music. She caught on quickly and began to sway to its tempo. He stepped on her toe and they both laughed.

The kitchen door swung open and Grace and Charley came into the room. They watched with amusement, as the two of them swayed clumsily around the room. Suddenly, the music stopped.

Lulla looked at Grace and smiled. "Did you come to a decision, Gracie?" she asked, as she sat down breathless from the strenuous activity.

Charley sat back down in the sofa and looked over at Lulla. With a sullen face, he said, "Yes, we have. We'd love to have the little twerp. However," he looked sternly at Meesha, "you must promise us something; that you'll live here without complaining, especially when times get rough. We'll tell everybody a little white lie that you're our nephew from out of state, and you'll be livin' with us for quite a spell. The only part that'll be a lie is the part about you being our nephew. And you'll have to go to school. We don't know right now how we'll work that out, but somehow we will."

As the cuckoo on the wall burped eleven annoying notes, a knock came at the door. Before Grace could make a move toward it, Kerac had walked into the living room. He went to the coffee table, laid a leather briefcase on its polished surface. He leaned over and opened it. The briefcase was completely filled with bound twenty-dollar bills. Charley gasped when he saw them.

"I have no idea how much is in there," Kerac confessed. "I never bothered counting it. Even so, I'm sure there is enough to pay for Meesha's keep for some time to come." Realizing his verbal blunder, he quickly added, "I'm sorry, I wasn't thinking. Have you come to a decision?"

"It's all right, Kerac," Lulla said. "They have agreed to take him. He will be their nephew from out of state." She looked at Grace and smiled weakly.

Charley leaned over and eyed the twenty-dollar bills. He thumbed through one of the packets, and then looked at Kerac.

"For God's sake mister, what are we going to do with all that money?" he asked. "We can't deposit it. They'd ask too many questions, and I wouldn't have an answer."

"We could deposit a little at a time," Grace volunteered. "Tell them it's back pay from your retirement…or something. When we buy anything, we'll get it in another town. That way, there won't be any questions asked. Don't worry dear, we'll figure it out. Maybe we can keep it under our mattress." She giggled at the thought. Charley glared at her.

"Kerac," Lulla said. "I believe we should be going. It's late. What about Luchak? He said he was going over to see a Mr. Digger. I wonder how he's handling the matter. And what about the two men you're supposed to drop off at the Area?"

"You're right. It is late," he answered. "Look at the boy he's half asleep, his eyes are drooping." They all turned and looked at Meesha. His eyes were half closed. "We have to get back to the ship and find out if Luchak has been accepted by the old man."

"Meesha!" Lulla called out. "Open your eyes and get your suitcase off the porch."

He stared at her sleepily, and then got up and went to the porch to get the little suitcase containing his belongings. After carrying it into the small bedroom, he returned and threw his arms around Lulla.

"I will miss you, Lulla," he said. "I will never forget you or Uncle Kerac." He held out his hand. "Uncle, take good care of my father, he will need you."

"Yes, I will," he replied. "And you take good care of your new family. If you love them as much as they seem to love you, everything will work out." He reached down and shook Charley's hand, then went over and kissed Grace on her forehead. "Please, take good care of my little nephew." He turned and walked out the door.

"Gracie, thank you for the coffee," Lulla said. "I loved it." With tears in her eyes, she walked to the door. "I don't know what to say, Gracie, I only wish we had met under different circumstances."

Grace got up from the sofa and rushed into the kitchen. As she went through the swinging doors, she yelled back, "Lulla, just a minute, I have something for you." Several minutes later, she came out holding a plastic bag. "Here, this is for you."

"What is it?"

"It's coffee. You said you loved it, and you don't have it back home. It's something to remember me by."

Lulla took the bag and gave her a hug. "Thank you. I could never forget you, anyway, Gracie." Before she left the porch, Meesha ran over and threw his arms around her. She hugged him and kissed him on the forehead. "Go to bed, it's late," she scolded.

They spent the better part of a half hour trudging back through the tangled bushes to their ship. When they arrived, they went to the bridge and found their engineer at the helm reading a Playboy magazine he had picked up on an earlier trip. He looked up with a start and quickly hid it behind his back.

"Hi," he said with an uneasy grin. "What's up?"

"Never mind the 'what's up,'" Lulla ordered. "Did Luchak come back from Mr. Digger's house, or is he still there?"

"He left some time ago and hasn't returned, so I guess he's still there." The young engineer picked up the magazine, rolled it up and covertly stuffed it in a drawer. "Do you want me to go look for him?"

Kerac motioned for him to get out of the Captain's Chair. The young man jumped down and moved to another console.

"No, that won't be necessary," he said. "I'm going after him." As he walked down the passageway to the outer hatch, he yelled for Lulla to keep the ship hidden with no lights on, and remain completely silent. That he would be back within the hour."

He trudged through the thick underbrush for half an hour, before finding the shack. As he approached it, he was confronted by a hairy little creature chewing on his pants leg. "Corky," he said softly, shaking his leg free. The dog looked up and started barking.

The door flung open and the silhouette of a figure holding a shotgun filled the doorway. "Corky!" he shouted. "Stop that damn barkin', you'll wake up the chickens." As he walked toward the dog, he noticed a dark figure standing in the shadows. "Who's there?" He yelled. "Come on out if you know what's good for you. I got a shotgun here, and I ain't afraid to use it!"

"Mr. Digger," Kerac said, moving cautiously toward him. "How are you, sir?"

Digger squinted at the figure for several seconds before recognizing him. He lowered the gun and held out his hand. "Well, I'll be danged, if it isn't another one of those aliens! What brings you here? Kerac, isn't it?"

"Yes," Kerac replied. "I came to see if Luchak was still here."

"Yep, he's here, all right. He's inside chowin' down on some of my stew. Come on in and have some."

Kerac walked inside, and the first thing he saw was Luchak bent over a large bowl of steaming stew, scooping spoonfuls of the dark-brown substance into his smiling mouth. He walked over and sat across the table from him.

Luchak looked over with a smug grin. "Hi, Kerac, how are things going? Did you drop off Meesha?"

"Yes we did, and I see you've also found a home," Kerac said. "Am I to assume you're going to stay?"

Digger sat down beside Luchak and put his arm around his shoulder. "Yep, he's gonna stay," he said. "We've gone all through it, and since he's eighteen years old and don't have to go to any school, we're all set. We can hunt, and he can help with chores. Even Corky likes him." He looked down at the dog curled up at Luchak's feet. "And if he's a good boy, he can pan some of my gold, help us out a bit." He looked at Kerac. "Don't worry, he's explained everything, and I want him to stay."

"Are you certain this is the right thing for you, Luchak?" Kerac asked. "You do realize you can never return to Golan. You will live out the rest of your life on Earth. Either here or some other place, it really doesn't matter you will be earthbound forever. Does that bother you in the least?"

"No, it doesn't," he replied. "Digger can be the father I never had. You knew my father, would you have wanted to spend the rest of your life with somebody like him? I don't think so. I hate to say that I'm happy he's gone, but in many ways I'm thankful. Now, I have somebody who will take his place, or at least be a good friend…somebody who will treat me as an equal." He put his hand on Digger's shoulder and squeezed. "That's right, isn't it, sir?"

"Don't call me sir," Digger said. "You know my name." He got up from the table and went to the stove. "How about a bowl of my famous stew, Kerac, I just made it?"

Without answering, Kerac extended his hand across the table. "Good luck, Luchak, I believe you've made a wise decision. Don't do anything to jeopardize your welcome." He looked at Digger. "I appreciate the offer, but I really must be going. I have to drop off some men at Area Fifty One on my way back to Golan."

"Do you really think they will ever retrieve that ship from outer space?" Luchak asked.

"No! Not a chance! At least not for many years," Kerac said definitively, as he walked out the door.

FORTY

"Colonel Steel!" a sergeant at a radar console called across the room. "There it is again! It just shot up from somewhere in Oregon at a fantastic speed, and then darted back down to Earth and apparently landed."

The colonel rushed over to his monitor. "Where did it land?"

"I'm almost certain it landed at Area Fifty One," the sergeant said. "What the hell's going on down there? We've had a hell of a lot of activity there in the past several days."

"Just keep your eyes on it," Steel commanded. "I was told by headquarters something big was going on down there, something only the President and a few of his advisors know about."

The early morning was dark and overcast, as Kerac settled his ship gently on the tarmac at Area 51. Kerac and the two engineers walked down the ramp and General Watson and Captain Allison were there to meet them.

Kerac shook the general's hand, and then nodded at the two aging men standing beside him. "We brought the two engineers you were promised. I'm in a hurry so if you take them off my hands I'll be on my way. Let me remind you, our King told your President these men were to be treated as if they were your own engineers. They know they can never return to their homes, so we expect you to supply them with whatever needs they might have. You are instructed by President Simmons to treat them like your own family."

"Are they allowed to help with the recovery of that ship?" Watson asked.

"They cannot help with any attempts to bring that ship down prematurely. They have the ability, they are fully qualified engineers.

But even they couldn't retrieve it with your outmoded technology. And only when you are capable of bringing it down on your own will they reveal any of its secrets."

General Watson instructed Captain Allison to escort them to their living quarters, and then said, "You say you have to leave immediately? I was hoping you would stick around long enough to give me more background on your planet, and those mother-ships. They sound extremely interesting." Then he added, "By the way, I hope those men speak our language. It would be rather difficult, if they didn't."

"I wish I had the time to explain more about our universe," Kerac replied, "but we have to return at once, our sun is very close to a total convergence with our planet. We must move our mother-ships out of our solar system very soon or they will be swallowed up by the sun's flares, along with our planet. And yes, the men speak your language… and a dozen others. Our scientists saw to that!"

"I understand," the general replied. He shook his hand and turned to leave. Before climbing into the station wagon he turned and said, "I guess we won't be seeing too many more UFOs around here…at least not from Golan." He laughed loudly, and the vehicle sped across the tarmac and disappeared.

Kerac walked up the steep ramp, and then slid it back into the side of the ship. He closed the hatch, then went to the bridge and sat at the helm. He brought the ship up to power, lifted it slowly off the tarmac and hovered for a few moments. When certain everything was clear for departure, he applied full power and the ship shot straight up, many miles above the Area and stopped. He remained there long enough to key in the coordinates where he could make a vortex, and then applied full power to the ion thrusters. He was going home for the last time.

FORTY-ONE

It was early morning in Grande Ronde, but the sun had not yet peeked over the horizon. Meesha lay half-asleep on the huge feather bed, and his nostrils picked up the scent of bacon. He opened his eyes and looked around the room. For a brief moment, he forgot where he was. After a few moments, he regained his senses and pushed the covers aside. He jumped out of bed and threw on a pair of Levis, donated by one of Charley's grandchildren, and rushed into the kitchen.

Grace stood over the stove turning bacon and breaking eggs into a large, black skillet. He walked up behind her and put his hand on her shoulder. She squealed and jumped back, almost knocking the oil-filled skillet off the stove. He stood wide-eyed looking at her. After she regained her composure, she smiled.

"Heavens-to-Betsy, child, you almost gave me a heart-attack," she blurted out.

When Charley heard the commotion in the kitchen, he got out of bed and joined them. "kind of early for breakfast isn't it?" he said. "The dang crows ain't even up yet." He went to the table and sat next to Meesha. "Well if it isn't my new nephew." He laughed quietly. "What are you doing up so early, isn't any school today?"

"I was hungry," Meesha replied with a smile. "Besides, I wanted to get an early start…maybe go over and see my friend White Feather, if that is all right with you."

Grace brought the skillet to the table and ladled several eggs and strips of bacon onto their plates.

"What do you think, Gracie?" Charley asked. "Do you think it'd be all right if he went over to that reservation? He dang sure knows where it is."

She turned off the stove, poured a cup of coffee and joined them at the table. “I guess it’ll be all right. He and White Feather seem to be pretty good friends.” She looked over at the boy and added, “As long as you make it back at a reasonable hour, young man. I want to take you into town and buy you some school clothes. You only have that pair of jeans and a shirt the grand kids left. I don’t think you should wear any of those clothes you brought. They’re a little strange lookin’ for around here. Don’t you think?”

Charley wolfed down the last of his bacon and laid the silverware across his plate. “Go ahead, boy, give my regards to that big Indian.”

It didn’t take long for Meesha to finish his breakfast and head for the door.

“Whoa, young fellow,” Charley yelled after him. “It’s only five-thirty. Don’t you think you should wait at least until the roosters crow?” Meesha gave him a curious look. “It’s still kind of dark out there. How you gonna find your way in the dark?”

“I know my way,” Meesha replied. “I have been there several times. I want to catch him before he goes hunting for bears.”

“Huntin’ bears?” Charley said with a scoff. “It isn’t huntin’ season. If he gets caught, he’ll end up in jail.”

Meesha looked at him curiously. “I will tell him about jail, but in order to tell him I must get there before he leaves.”

Charley thought for a moment. “You got me there, son. Go ahead, but be back in time to go to the store with Gracie. Okay?”

“Yes sir, I will,” he replied, as he rushed out the door and into the semi-darkness.

Fifteen minutes later he arrived at the perimeter of the reservation. Quasi’s house sat beside a small stream at the edge of a clearing, a few hundred yards from the forest. He stopped and inspected the house for lights or activity. Seeing none, he moved in closer to look through a bedroom window. Quasi and Nakomi were both huddled together on a large bed, and he was snoring loudly. He moved to the next window and pushed it slightly open. White Feather sat on the edge of the bed buttoning a buckskin shirt.

“White Feather,” he whispered.

Startled, the boy looked over at the window. "Who's there?"

"It's me, Meesha."

"Meesha?" he questioned. "What the devil you doing here, I thought you went back home or to your planet, or whatever?" He went to the window and squinted at him. "What happened? You don't look the same...your eyes and things. And you can talk."

"I will tell you all about it, later," Meesha replied. "I have decided to stay with Charley and Grace. The others have all gone back to Golan."

"You mean you're gonna stay here all by yourself?" White Feather asked, a puzzled look on his face. "What about your parents, don't you want to be with them?" He frowned, and then added, "And what's this talking bit? You never did that before, you always showed me pictures."

"On my planet they do something to your brain so you can talk like Earthlings. They also gave me the knowledge of your world. To answer your other question, my parents understood my desire to stay. And I'm not by myself. Luchak is here too. You know the one whose father destroyed some of your village and killed that woman?"

"How could I forget?"

"Justice has been done," Meesha assured him. "The man whose wife he killed also killed him, out of revenge."

"My father will be happy to know that," White Feather said. He hesitated long enough to button a pair of buckskin pants, and then returned to the window. "But why are you here so early? It's only about six o'clock, and no one is up, not even my father."

"I wanted to catch you before you went hunting," Meesha said. "Charley told me to tell your father he could go to jail for hunting bears; it's not the season for them."

"Don't worry, we never get caught," he replied. "The Game Warden is afraid to come onto the reservation." He climbed through the window and jumped onto the hard-packed ground. "As a matter of fact, we're going as soon as my father gets up."

"Can I come with you?"

White Feather thought for a moment. "I will ask father." Then he added, "What about Charley, did he say you could go?"

Meesha gave him a crooked grin. "He said I had to be back at a reasonable hour. That's all he said."

A bedroom door opened and Quasi trudged through the living room and headed for the kitchen clad only in his underwear, scratching himself all the way. A few seconds later the sounds of running water and rattling pots and pans came from the kitchen. Several minutes past, and Nakomi joined him.

"I guess my mother and father are up, now," he said with a chuckle. "Let's join them. We can ask father if it's okay for you to come."

They went around to the front door and then into the kitchen. "Good morning, Mother, Father. Guess who came to visit us?"

Quasi put the lid on the coffee pot and turned to face them. He gave Meesha a fleeting glance, and with a grin said, "What's this, a new boy in town?"

"Father, it's Meesha, don't you recognize him?"

Quasi turned around, and with a grin looked at the boy closer. "That's not the boy I remember." He turned back around and put the pot on the stove. "The boy I remember had eyes like a cat, and a funny-looking haircut." He chuckled.

"Father, it is Meesha," White Feather insisted. "The people of his world gave him a new face. And he can now talk, without showing pictures. He's staying with Charley and Grace Bertell. He didn't go back to his spaceship. They let him stay here on Earth. Isn't that cool?"

"You don't say."

"Good morning, sir," Meesha said, slightly embarrassed by White Feather's commentary. "How are you today? I know you don't recognize me, but I assure you it is me, Meesha. My world made me look like this. Now, I look like Earthlings."

Quasi slid a chair out from under the table. "Sit down, boy, let me look at you." After a close inspection, he grinned mischievously and said, "Well, I'll be danged, it is him. They did one hell of a job on your face, son. Nakomi, come look at the boy. He sure doesn't look like the little fellow you almost clouted with that stick."

She threw the boy a casual glance, and then turned back to the stove. Moments later she returned to the table with a homemade corn muffin and set it in front of him. Without a word, she went back to the stove and continued breaking eggs for breakfast.

Quasi got up from the table, poured a cup of coffee and handed it to the boy. "What brings you this early? The chickens ain't even up yet." He laughed quietly.

Meesha took a sip and squirmed nervously in his chair. "I asked my father if I could remain on Earth, while they went looking for a new planet to live on." He took another sip of coffee and then bit into the muffin. He turned and looked at Nakomi. "Ma'am, this is the best muffin I ever ate." She gave him a shallow smile. "I am staying with Charley and Grace," he continued. "I will go to school there." He took another bite and glanced over at Quasi. "Sir, White Feather told me you were going hunting this morning."

The big Indian looked at his son. "Yes, that's right. We're leaving shortly. We were told there was another large bear down by that beaver pond."

"Sir, may I go with you?" Meesha asked, and his face flushed.

"He only wants that little cub, Dad," White Feather volunteered with a snigger.

Ignoring him, Quasi said, "What about Charley? Do you think he'd agree to you goin' on a bear hunt?" He looked at the boy sternly. "Do you think he would let you go?"

Meesha looked into his dark eyes. "I don't know, sir. All I know is that on Golan, I had always wanted to do the things that I've already done here on Earth. But we didn't have animals there…except the ones we ate, which were frozen most of the time. I love it here in the forest, especially when I'm with you and White Feather. You are great hunters and friends, which I never had on Golan."

Nakomi set a cup of coffee in front of Quasi. He took a loud sip and looked at the boy. "Son, do you think you're going to be happy stayin' with Charley and Grace?"

He looked into the big Indian's eyes and frowned. "I believe so, but I'm not certain. I only know that I love Grace very much. She is unlike my mother, who was never home. I believe I will be happy there."

Quasi noticed a slight sadness on his face. "Do you remember what I said a few days ago…about if you're not happy there?"

"Yes, but I thought you were not being serious."

"I am always serious when I say things like that." He turned and looked at Nakomi. "Sweetheart, would you come into the bedroom for a moment?"

She turned off the stove and followed him. When they were in the bedroom, she said, "You don't have to tell me, I already know what you have in mind. You want the boy to stay with us, don't you?"

"You're quick," he said with a grin. "I can tell by his expression he would rather be here than at a house with no kids, and very little life left in it."

"That's a terrible thing to say."

"Well, it's true," he countered. "He'd only last a short time there, and then he'd want to go somewhere else. He might as well come here now, rather than later." He pulled her up close. "Besides, the boys get along quite well, together. He could go to our school with White Feather, here on the reservation. He'd fit in, as smart as he appears to be. He could stay in our son's bedroom. We could get another small bed, there's room for it."

"Are you quite finished?" she said, pulling away from his embrace. "What if it didn't work out, did you ever think of that? I'm sure Grace would have reservations about taking him back if it didn't, after giving him up."

"You worry too much, sweetheart. I have no doubt it would work out." He looked into her eyes. "One thing though, you would have to forget what happened to our houses. You know very well it wasn't his fault."

"If that's what you really want, I'll go along with it," she agreed. "But I'm not going to be his mother, just a friend. That's where I put my foot down."

"You won't have to," he said with a broad grin. "I'll be his mother and father. How does that sound?"

"I'm warning you," she came back, "don't expect too much from me. We have enough problems as it is, with your son."

"You mean <u>our</u> son, don't you?"

She giggled and swatted him on the shoulder.

"I'll go over and explain things to Charley and Grace," he told her. "I'm sure they'll understand. Besides, it'll take a load off their minds. They haven't had a kid in that house in years. It wouldn't be long before he got bored to death."

They went back into the kitchen and sat at the table. Quasi cleared his throat and looked across the table. "Boys," he said, "I have a little errand to run. Why don't you take Red Wing and meet Digger by the pond, he told me he wanted to go with us?"

"You mean Mr. Digger is going, too?" Meesha interrupted. "I hope Luchak will be with him. I'll get to see him." He looked at Quasi, "That is if you let me come."

"Luchak?" Quasi replied, surprised "Oh, yes, he's the son of the man who almost destroyed our village and killed Velma, isn't he?"

"His father was a very bad man," Meesha countered. "But his son is a good friend, and I believe he is going to stay with Mr. Digger."

"You say he's the son of the man who killed Velma?" Nakomi asked a frown forming on her face.

"Yes," Meesha replied. "But her husband killed the man in retaliation for killing his wife. Luchak is nothing like his father. He is a good friend. You will like him."

"I doubt that!"

"Remember what you said in the bedroom, Nakomi," Quasi mumbled, as he got up from the table and headed for the door. "Do you think Charley's up yet, Meesha?"

"Yes, he was when I left. Are you going to see him?"

"Yes. I will join you boys at the pond. Don't shoot too many bears while I'm gone. Okay?" He walked out the door, a triumphant grin on his long, weathered face.

"Why is he going to see them, Nakomi?" Meesha asked.

She sat down beside him. "He's going to see them about you," she told him. "He wants you to stay with us. He must get their approval, first."

"And you, do you want me to stay?"

"I'll give it a shot, if you're willing," she said with a weak smile. "Besides, I always need firewood for the fireplace, and I can't rely on him." She pointed to White Feather.

He looked at Meesha and grinned.

A soft knock came at the door. Grace got up from the table and looked out the kitchen window.

"For Heaven's sake, it's Quasi," she said, loud enough for Charley to hear above the sound of the TV. "What could he be here for, at this hour?" She opened the door and ushered the big man into the foyer.

"Hello, Gracie," he said. "I know it's early, but Meesha said you were up and around so I thought I'd pay you a little visit."

"Nice to see you, what can we do for you?"

"I know it's early, but I figured it was a good time to come over and talk to you and Charley."

"Well, come into the kitchen and have a cup of coffee."

Charley heard them talking, and joined them. "Hi there, Quasi, what's on your mind?" he said. "It must be something important, to visit at this hour."

She poured them coffee, and sat next to Quasi. "Now, what brings?" she asked. "It isn't often we see you or your family."

Quasi fingered the rim of his cup nervously, and then looked over. "It's about Meesha."

Grace's eyes widened, and she sucked in a quick breath. "What? Has something happened to him? Did he have an accident or something?"

"No, ma'am, it's nothing like that."

"Then what?"

"I would like for him to come live at our house," he blurted out quickly. "He and my son get along very well, and here he would have no one to hang around with."

"Did he say he didn't like it here?" she asked, lowering her head with puckered lips. "Did he say he didn't like us?"

"No, ma'am, it's nothing like that. He loves you both very much. However, I thought it would be best if he had somebody his own age to hang around with…go to school with…go hunting with. Things like that."

Charley took a long, noisy swig of coffee and looked into the big Indian's dark eyes. "I understand," he said. "When we agreed to take him in, I figured it wouldn't be long before he would get bored anyway, hangin' around us old folks with nothing to do but sit on that damn French window and watch the kids go by." He laughed. "Don't worry if you think it's the best thing for him…I have no objections to him livin' with you folks. I don't know about Gracie, but I'm all for him havin' the best time of his life. I remember when I was a young pup and had to go visit my grandpa. All I did was sit in that dim-lit livin' room, listening to that damn grandfather clock standin' in the corner of the room chiming every fifteen minutes. They had no radio or TV, or anything." He took another noisy sip and leaned back in his chair. "What about you, Gracie? What do you think?"

"You know I love the little guy, and I'd hate to see him go somewhere else," she answered. "But if you think it would be best for him—" She dropped her head and stared at her cup, and then looked over at Quasi. "Does he know you're here? Why didn't he come with you?"

"Yes, he knows," Quasi answered. "I told Nakomi to tell him I wanted to talk to you folks without him bein' around…too many emotions and things could get in the way. Don't take this wrong, Gracie, I know how you feel about the little guy, but think of him. You know he would never say anything about being bored or unhappy, but I'm sure you would pick up on it, if he was. But it would be too late, then. Things could easily cloud your feelings toward each other, and then everyone would be unhappy. You know it's true, don't you?"

She raised her head and looked at him "I never thought of it that way, but I guess you're right. I want him to be happy, and if he'll be happier there, so be it." She got up from the table and walked into the bedroom.

Charley winked at Quasi. "Don't think you're hurtin' our feelings by coming here and layin' this on us. She'll get over it. We know he'd be much happier at your house. To be perfectly honest, we're too damn old to have a little guy like him runnin' around the house, anyway."

He glanced at the bedroom door to make sure she hadn't come out, and then added, "The only reason we took him in was because he had no other place else to go. His uncle came knockin' at the door last night and asked if the boy could live with us, he didn't want to go back home. What were we supposed to do?"

Grace came into the kitchen with two pieces of luggage and laid them on the table. "Here," she said, sniffing back her tears, "these are his things. I was going to buy him some school clothes, but I guess I won't have to."

"He had two suitcases?" Quasi asked puzzled.

She sniffed and blew her nose. "Well, this large duffle bag is his things." She pointed. "And this smaller one is for Nakomi."

"Nakomi?"

"Yes, it's something I believe she can use. It will help."

"Thank you. I'll make sure she gets it." He picked up the suitcases and headed for the door. Before leaving, he turned and said, "I'll make certain Meesha knows what we talked about. And, I'll also make sure he comes to visit you regularly."

"Thanks, we'd appreciate that," Charley said. He went to the door and held out his hand. Quasi shook it and left.

When Quasi returned, he saw everyone but Nakomi standing in the living room.

"What's this, a family reunion?" he asked with a grin.

"We didn't want to go huntin' without you," Digger said."

"Well then, let's go," said Quasi. He handed Meesha the duffle bag and told him to put it in his new bedroom. "Where's Nakomi? I have something for her."

"She's in the kitchen washing dishes," White Feather said.

Meesha looked at him questioningly. "I guess you spoke to Gracie and Charley, then?"

"Yes. It's all right, son. You're livin' with us now."

The boy's eyes lit up, and he smiled broadly. White Feather went over and put his arm around his shoulder and squeezed it.

Quasi went into the kitchen and laid the small briefcase on the table. "Here, this is something Gracie told me to give to you. Don't know what it is, but she said you could certainly use it." He joined the hunters outside and grabbed the pony's reins. It was going to be a beautiful day for hunting, he thought.

They were barely out of sight, when Nakomi opened the suitcase. When she saw what was inside her eyes widened, and she sucked in a deep breath. Neatly stacked beneath a quickly scribbled note were packets of bound twenty-dollar bills. She read the note: "Dear Nakomi, we were given this by Meesha's Uncle Kerac. He said he had no use for it. He couldn't spend it where he was going. We have no use for it either, with Charley's retirement checks and our social securities. I thought you could use it to help defray the cost of taking care of Meesha. Don't take this the wrong way, it's not a handout it's a donation for a good cause. Best wishes, Gracie." She laid her arms on the table, dropped her head onto them and wept.

EPILOGUE

Each day the red hot fingers of plasma, belching from the dying sun, inched closer to the planet's surface making it nearly unlivable. The ones who had remained on the planet had spent most of their time searching for shelters from the devastating heat. The time had long passed when they could be taken on board the mother-ships.

Although everyone on the ships was sympathetic to their plights, nothing could be done to relieve their suffering and pain. Too many people had remained to be transported to the mother-ships by small craft or pods, and even if larger ships had been available they could not have landed on the planet's extremely hot surface. Those on the mother-ships could hear faint moans and cries for help on their communicators, but it was not long before even those diminished and disappeared.

The planet had quickly approached a serious melt-down, and within a short period of time, it would become a boiling inferno. The mother-ships had no choice but to leave the solar system within days, or be incinerated with the planet. It was impossible to predict, which devastating surge would be the final death-knell that would completely destroy Golan.

—The End—

CPSIA information can be obtained at www.ICGtesting.com
Printed in the USA
BVOW040956250313

316155BV00004B/180/P

9 781630 004439